THE MEPHIBOSHETH STEPSURE LETTERS

The Centre for Editing Early Canadian Texts (CEECT) is engaged in the preparation of scholarly editions of selected works of early English-Canadian prose. *The Mephibosheth Stepsure Letters* is the seventh text in the Centre for Editing Early Canadian Texts Series.

GENERAL EDITOR

Mary Jane Edwards

EDITORIAL BOARD

Mary Jane Edwards (Chair)
Michael Gnarowski
Robert G. Laird
Robert L. McDougall
J. Jeremy Palin
John A. Stewart
D. Roland Thomas
S. F. Wise

ADVISORS TO THE PROJECT

Fred Cogswell (University of New Brunswick); E. A. Collard (Ottawa); Gordon R. Elliott (Simon Fraser University); Francess G. Halpenny (University of Toronto); Carl F. Klinck (University of Western Ontario); Douglas G. Lochhead (Mount Allison University); R. D. Mathews (Carleton University); W. F. E. Morley (Queen's University); Gordon R. Moyles (University of Alberta); W. H. New (University of British Columbia); J. M. Robson (Victoria College, Toronto); Gordon H. Roper (Trent University); Malcolm Ross (Dalhousie University); Clara Thomas (York University).

Portrait of Thomas McCulloch done in pastel by Daniel Macnee, 1845

The Mephibosheth Stepsure Letters

Thomas McCulloch

Edited by
Gwendolyn Davies

Carleton University Press
Ottawa, Canada
1990

ISBN 0-88629-042-2 (casebound)
     0-88629-044-9 (paperback)

Printed and bound in Canada by The Alger Press Limited, Oshawa, Ontario. The paper in this edition is 50 lb. Finch Opaque Vellum (pH 7.8-8).

Canadian Cataloguing in Publication Data
  McCulloch, Thomas, 1776-1843
    The Mephibosheth Stepsure letters

  (Centre for Editing Early Canadian Texts Series ;
    CEECT 7)
  Originally published under title, Letters of
    Mephibosheth Stepsure
  ISBN 0-88629-042-2 (casebound)
  ISBN 0-88629-044-9 (paperback)

  I. Davies, Gwendolyn   II. Title.   III. Title:
  Letters of Mephibosheth Stepsure.   IV. Series.

  PS8425.C4L48 1990   C813'.3   C90-090270-1
  PR9199.2.M4L48 1990

Distributed by: Oxford University Press Canada
                70 Wynford Drive
                Don Mills, Ontario
                Canada   M3C 1J9
                (416) 441-2941

Cover design: Robert Chitty

ACKNOWLEDGEMENT

Carleton University Press and the Centre for Editing Early Canadian Texts gratefully acknowledge the support of Carleton University, the Social Sciences and Humanities Research Council of Canada, and The Henry White Kinnear Foundation in the preparation and publication of this edition of *The Mephibosheth Stepsure Letters*.

The illustration on the cover of the paperback edition is "Pictou from the S.S.W." by J.E. Woolford, 1817, courtesy of the Nova Scotia Museum, Halifax, Canada.

Contents

Abbreviations

ALS	Autograph letter signed
CEECT	Centre for Editing Early Canadian Texts
DCB	*Dictionary of Canadian Biography*
DNB	*Dictionary of National Biography*
IB	*Interpreter's Bible*
MP	McCulloch Papers
NBSAM	Mount Allison University Library, Sackville, New Brunswick
NLS	National Library of Scotland, Edinburgh
NSHD	Dalhousie University Library, Halifax, Nova Scotia
NSWA	Acadia University Library, Wolfville, Nova Scotia
OOCC	Carleton University Library, Ottawa, Ontario
PANS	Public Archives of Nova Scotia, Halifax, Nova Scotia

Foreword

The Centre for Editing Early Canadian Texts (CEECT) at Carleton University was established to prepare for publication scholarly editions of major works of early English-Canadian prose that are now either out of print or available only in corrupt reprints. Six of these editions, Frances Brooke's *The History of Emily Montague*, Catharine Parr Traill's *Canadian Crusoes*, James De Mille's *A Strange Manuscript Found in a Copper Cylinder*, John Richardson's *Wacousta*, Susanna Moodie's *Roughing It in the Bush*, and Rosanna Leprohon's *Antoinette De Mirecourt* have been published. Another five, thanks to continuing funding from Carleton University and from the Social Sciences and Humanities Research Council of Canada, are being prepared. *The Mephibosheth Stepsure Letters*, the linked letters that earned for their author Thomas McCulloch the reputation of being "the founder of genuine Canadian humour," is the seventh volume in the CEECT series.

In the preparation of these editions, advice and guidance have been sought from a broad range of international scholarship, and contemporary principles and procedures for the scholarly editing of literary texts have been followed. These principles and procedures have been adapted to suit the special circumstances of Canadian literary scholarship and the particular needs of each of the works in the CEECT series.

The text of each scholarly edition in this series has been critically established after the history of the composition and first publication of the work has been researched and its versions analysed and compared. The critical text is clear, with only authorial notes, if any, appearing in the body of the book. Each of these editions also has an editor's introduction with a separate section on the text, and, as concluding apparatus, explanatory notes, a description of the copy-text (or copy-texts) and, when relevant, of other authoritative versions, a list of other versions of the work, a record of emendations made to the copy-text (or copy-texts), a list of line-end hyphenated compounds in the copy-text (or copy-texts) as they are resolved in the CEECT edition, and a list of line-end hyphenated compounds in the CEECT edition as they should be resolved in quotations from it. An historical collation is included when more than one version has authority, and, as necessary, appendices containing material directly relevant to the text.

In the preparation of all these CEECT editions for publication, identical procedures, in so far as the particular history of each work allowed, have been followed. An attempt has been made to find and analyse every unpublished version of the work known to exist. At least five copies of each published version that was a possible choice for copy-text have been examined, as have at least three copies of each of the other published versions that the author might have revised. Every published version of the work has been subjected to as thorough a bibliographical study as possible. All the known information about the printing and publication of each work has been gathered, and the printed versions of each have been subjected to collations of various kinds. Specialists from the University's Computing Services have developed programs to help in the proofreading and comparison of texts, to perform word-searches, and to compile and store much of the information for the concluding apparatus. The edited text, printed from a magnetic tape prepared at Carleton, has been proofread against its copy-text (or copy-texts) at all appropriate stages.

Editor's Preface

On 1 January 1935 the *Halifax Daily Star* paid tribute to Thomas McCulloch's Stepsure letters with an essay by D. C. Harvey and drawings by Robert Chambers. The re-emergence of Mephibosheth Stepsure one hundred and fourteen years after he entered the pages of the Halifax *Acadian Recorder* in 1821, seventy-three years after the publication of the *Letters Of Mephibosheth Stepsure* in 1862, and fifty-three years after the reprinting of four letters in the New Glasgow *Eastern Chronicle* in 1882 is a tribute to the durability of McCulloch's pawky little persona, the slyness of his humour, and the liveliness of his message. It is appropriate, therefore, that *The Mephibosheth Stepsure Letters* should now be published in a scholarly edition in the Centre for Editing Early Canadian Texts series.

McCulloch's surviving manuscripts and most of his correspondence are to be found in the McCulloch Papers at the Public Archives of Nova Scotia. Here, in September 1988, Dr. Mary Jane Edwards, Principal Investigator of CEECT, and I were given generous use of the Board Room to proofread our text of the letters against their manuscript copy-texts. Throughout the project I was greatly assisted by the staff of the Archives, especially Darlene Brine, Barry Cahill, Wendy Duff, Allan Dunlop, Greer Kaiser, and John MacLeod. Mr. Dunlop kindly alerted me to McCulloch material not in the McCulloch Papers; I am particularly indebted to him for telling me of the four Stepsure letters reprinted in the *Evening Chronicle*.

Early in my research I examined the papers of William Blackwood and Sons in the National Library of Scotland but did not find any McCulloch material. After I returned to Canada, I consulted Dr. Fred Cogswell, Professor Emeritus at the University of New Brunswick, about remarks that he had made in the *Literary History Of Canada* on Blackwood's rejection of the Stepsure letters, and he kindly gave me a typescript of a letter about McCulloch and "the Stepsures" that he had copied in Scotland a number of years before. With this evidence Dr. Iain G. Brown, Assistant Keeper at the National Library, was able to locate the letter that Dr. Cogswell had seen as well as another relevant one, both written by William Blackwood to the Reverend Doctor James Mitchell, in the Blackwoods Letter-books then being indexed (1985) at the National Library. On a visit to Scotland in 1987, I was able both to verify the text of the letters and to get a sense of the publishing climate in Scotland in the 1820s when Blackwood rejected for publication "The Chronicles of our Town," McCulloch's holograph manuscript of eighteen Stepsure letters.

In addition to the people that I have already mentioned, I should like to thank several others for their assistance. Susan Buggey, Director, Architectural History, Canadian Parks Service, shared her extensive knowledge of Thomas McCulloch with me during our preparation of the entry on him published in the *Dictionary of Canadian Biography* in 1988. Mrs. Carolyn Earle, Archivist, Maritime Conference Archives, sent me McCulloch material from this repository. At Dalhousie University Karen Smith and Julia Landry of Special Collections and John Ettlinger of the School of Library Science generously gave of their time and expertise in helping me to prepare the bibliographical description of *Colonial Gleanings*. Professor Philip Girard of the Dalhousie Law School kindly sent me pertinent details about the cropping of ears and other legal matters in nineteenth-century Nova Scotia. Dr. Kenneth MacKinnon of the Department of English at Saint Mary's University shared his extensive knowledge of the Stepsure letters and of nineteenth-century Scottish-Maritime society. Dr. Marie Elwood and Scott Robson of the Nova Scotia Museum were particularly helpful in advising me on illustrations for this edition and in facilitating the preparation of photographs for it. Miss Beryl MacFadden, secretary for the Department of English at Mount Allison University, typed the explanatory notes and assisted my research with her considerable knowledge of Biblical sources. Joy Cavazzi, secretary for the Department of English at Acadia University, entered early drafts of the introduction on a word processor.

I am grateful to the librarians at Acadia University and Mount Allison University for lending CEECT their copies of *Letters Of Mephibosheth Stepsure* for microfilming, and to the Public Archives of Nova Scotia for photocopying the manuscript of "The Chronicles of our Town" and that of "William." CEECT is also indebted to the National Archives of Canada for allowing the project to use their Central Microfilming Unit (now defunct) in Ottawa. The Maritime Conference Archives, the Mount Allison University Archives, the National Library of Scotland, and the Public Archives of Nova Scotia kindly gave permission to quote from documents in their collections. The Atlantic School of Theology allowed CEECT to publish in this edition a reproduction of McCulloch's portrait; the Nova Scotia Museum provided the prints of Nova Scotia; and the Public Archives of Nova Scotia photographed a page from the manuscript of each of "The Chronicles of our Town" and "William." My thanks go to all three. Of great assistance to me in 1984-85 was a Leave Fellowship from the Social Sciences and Humanities Research Council of Canada that allowed me to conduct research complementary to my subsequent work on Thomas McCulloch and his Stepsure letters. A grant from the Bell Research Fund at Mount Allison University helped make feasible my trip to Scotland in 1987. I have also benefitted greatly from the generous support of the CEECT project by Carleton University and the Social Sciences and Humanities Research Council of Canada.

For their meticulous help during the preparation of *The Mephibosheth Stepsure Letters*, I should like to express my appreciation to past and present members of the CEECT staff. Heather Avery, Joseph Black, Andrew Kerr-Wilson, Victor Mallet, Marion Phillips, John Thurston, Deborah Wills, and Daniel Wilson all assisted me in my editing and research; Robert Chamberlain and Nadia Shewchenko looked after the many computing tasks involved in the preparation of this edition; Mary

Comfort typed drafts of the introduction and entered the
different versions of the letters on the computer; Michelle Kelly,
Toomas Sepp, and Batoul Zanganeh among them entered a
second copy of each of the different versions. Most of all, to the
Principal Investigator and General Editor of CEECT, Dr. Mary
Jane Edwards, I am particularly indebted, not only for her
constructive advice and editorial expertise but also for the many
stimulating hours that we spent together working on a text that
we both enjoyed.

Finally, I should like to thank Dr. Douglas Lochhead, my
former colleague at Mount Allison University, who was prepar-
ing this edition of *The Mephibosheth Stepsure Letters* when ill health
forced him to postpone his involvement as an editor with the
CEECT project. For the many good conversations we have had
on Maritime literature, for his generous sharing of his knowl-
edge, and for his constant encouragement, I am deeply grateful.

Gwendolyn Davies
Acadia University
May 1990

Editor's Introduction

On 22 December 1821 the first of twenty-five linked letters appeared in the *Acadian Recorder* of Halifax. Purportedly written by a lame farmer called Mephibosheth Stepsure, his neighbour Alexander (Saunders) Scantocreesh, and an unnamed stranger visiting their township, the letters were in fact the work of the Reverend Doctor Thomas McCulloch (1776-1843) of Pictou, Nova Scotia. Even as they revealed McCulloch's austere Presbyterian background, the letters satirized the manners and mores of Stepsure's fellow Nova Scotians and, through the portrait of Stepsure as an "industrious apprentice,"[1] advocated traditional rural, domestic, and religious values. In spite of the severity of their message, by their conclusion on 29 March 1823 the letters had "set the hale kintra laughin' "[2] and, according to Northrop Frye, had earned for McCulloch the distinction of being "the founder of genuine Canadian humour."[3]

Born in Fereneze, near Paisley, Scotland, McCulloch "was descended from the McCullochs, (or Maccullochs . . .) of Galloway, and claimed kinship"[4] with the seventeenth-century Covenanters who had been persecuted for their opposition to the Scottish episcopacy.[5] His father was a master block-printer, one of that body of skilled artisans who flourished when the textile trade in Paisley was at its most prosperous. Educated in parish schools, McCulloch entered the University of Glasgow at the height of the Scottish Enlightenment. The scientific and philosophical ferment of the period had a profound influence on his intellectual development and in the early stages of his studies directed him toward medicine. By the time that he had graduated from the University of Glasgow in 1792, however, he had decided to enter the theological hall at Whitburn to study with the well-known clergyman and professor Archibald Bruce.[6] Here he trained for the Secession Church, the branch of Presbyterianism that separated from the Church of Scotland in 1743.[7] His first call was to the bonnet-making town of Stewarton, where he was ordained in June 1799. On 27 July of the same year he married Isabella Walker, the daughter of a Secessionist clergyman from nearby Pollokshaws. Four years later McCulloch resigned the Stewarton charge because of "inadequate support,"[8] and, after a short period of "supplying vacancies,"[9] he answered the call of the Secession Church for missionaries to North America. Appointed to Prince Edward Island, he left for the Maritimes in August 1803.

Ice was already coating the vessel on 3 November 1803 when the McCullochs and their three young children sailed into the harbour of Pictou en route to Prince Edward Island. The prospect of crossing the Northumberland Strait in an open boat discouraged the family from proceeding until spring, and they therefore decided to winter in Pictou. Tradition has it that two influential Pictonians formed "a high opinion of the owner"[10] when they detected a pair of terrestrial and celestial globes in his luggage. McCulloch's ministrations throughout the winter convinced the community of the desirability of keeping him in Pictou. By June 1804 McCulloch had accepted a call from the congregation of what is now First Presbyterian Church in Pictou and had joined the Reverend Doctor James MacGregor of East River in ministering to Secessionist Presbyterians in a wide area surrounding Pictou Harbour.

McCulloch soon found himself at the centre of religious, political, and educational controversy in Nova Scotia. As a result of a decision taken in 1803, the province's only institution of higher learning, King's College at Windsor, had excluded non-Anglicans from attaining a degree by insisting that all students who wished to graduate swear to the thirty-nine Articles of the Church of England. McCulloch was appalled by this decision that in effect denied the majority of Nova Scotians access to a university in the province. He therefore formulated a program of learning for these dissenters that included a plan to train an indigenous clergy, for, like his colleague James MacGregor,

McCulloch believed that the Presbyterian church in Nova Scotia could not rely on ministers educated and selected in Scotland. In 1806 he began to implement his design by establishing a school in his house; by 1816 he had succeeded in winning support for the construction and operation of Pictou Academy. As the province's first non-Anglican institution of higher learning, Pictou Academy posed a threat to the hegemony of King's College, challenged the conservative predilections of the province's Tory elite, and worried Halifax merchants concerned about the growing political and economic strength of Pictou. Although these forces prevented it from attaining the degree-granting status that it sought, Pictou Academy nonetheless acquired an enviable reputation when its first three graduates travelled to the University of Glasgow and successfully passed the MA examinations there. With its library, museum of natural history, and rigorous scientific and liberal arts curriculum, the Academy reflected the restless intellect and spirit of inquiry of its founder.

During his principalship from 1816 to 1834 McCulloch was involved in every dimension of the Academy's life. He lobbied for its annual grant from the Nova Scotia House of Assembly and the Executive Council, he travelled to Scotland in 1825 to raise money for its support, and he opposed the forces of the Church of Scotland in Pictou that undermined Secessionist authority in its administration. He taught classes in Greek, Hebrew, Logic, Moral Philosophy, and Natural Philosophy and, according to Jotham Blanchard, his former student, was even called into service to make repairs to "half-worn apparatus . . . which none but himself could make."[11] In an attempt to heighten the profile of the Academy, he also, after 1820, lectured on chemistry in various parts of the Maritimes. As he was to say of administrators of American colleges, "A president . . . must be a jack of all trades and drudge in his office like a shopkeepers apprentice."[12]

Typical of his eclecticism and his keen interest in science was his attempt to develop collections of natural history that would assist in the scientific teaching of the Academy and enhance its scholarly reputation outside Nova Scotia. After putting together an insect collection for the University of Glasgow in 1821, McCulloch described himself in a letter to his close friend in Scotland, the Reverend Doctor John Mitchell, as out night and day enjoying "abundantly the comforts of American swamps and musquitoes things much more delectable to hear of than to experience and after coming home from the woods stung in every accessible part and as itchy as any poor Scotchman could be I have frequently spent whole nights making havoc among the moths which in this country are very numerous and beautiful."[13] The discomfort that he experienced in acquiring such collections was somewhat offset by the recognition that they brought him. He received an honorary degree from the University of Glasgow in 1822, and in 1823 he was accepted into the Wernerian Natural History Society of Edinburgh and the Antiquarian Society for Newcastle-on-Tyne. He also enjoyed a rewarding collaboration with John James Audubon, who visited Pictou in 1833 to admire the Academy's own collection of "birds and beasts."[14]

By the time that the Stepsure letters began to appear in 1821, McCulloch was well known to Nova Scotians as a churchman, an educator, a natural scientist, and a scholar whose achievements had been recognized in 1820 by an honorary degree from Union College, Schenectady, New York. *The Nature and Uses of A Liberal Education Illustrated* (1819) and *A Lecture Delivered at the Opening of the First Theological Class in the Pictou Academical Institution* (1821) had also brought him to public attention. As well, theological works such as *Popery Condemned by Scripture and the Fathers* (1808), *The Prosperity of the Church in Troublous Times* (1814), and *Words of Peace* (1817) had not only confirmed McCulloch's reputation as a church scholar but had also revealed the unrelenting religious conviction that informed his battle for educational and social rights for the province's dissenters. On 24 November 1821 McCulloch outlined his "progress" in a letter to John Mitchell:

> Our seminary is as usual making a little progress ...   In the space of four years we have created the most elegant building of its size in the province provided a considerable philosophical apparatus and laid the founda-

tion of a library   We enjoy also the approbation of the
public in the House of Assembly we have no opposers and
in the other branch we have the majority   Still we are
poor and depressed because the province is poor   Our
Antagonists are supported by the interest of the Church at
home and hitherto we poor Scotch presbyterians have had
nobody to help us.[15]

These concerns were to be expressed publicly, and more
explicitly, only a month later in the first of the Stepsure letters.

Nova Scotia in 1821 was a significantly different province from
the one to which McCulloch had immigrated in 1803. He had
arrived in Pictou when it "consisted . . . of sixteen or eighteen
buildings, including barns, a blacksmith shop and the jail, closely
environed by the woods. There was no church, but a place was
fitted up in a shed of Captain Lowden's, on Windmill Hill, where
service was held in summer, but in winter time it was in private
houses, most frequently in . . . McGeorge's tavern."[16] The town
and the province had developed rapidly since that time, a growth
hastened by the impact of the Napoleonic Wars and the War of
1812. The wartime demand for timber had brought "ships,
sailors, money, and spirituous liquors" to Pictou, noted James
MacGregor in 1809, and "in a manner caused us to lay aside
farming, our most innocent, and in the long run our most
profitable earthly employment, and give up ourselves to the
felling, squaring, hauling, rafting, and selling of timber to the
ships, and the squandering of money."[17] The impact on the
province as a whole was equally disruptive, as John Young, a
Scottish-born merchant who had immigrated to Nova Scotia in
1814, observed in 1822, "During the long wars which grew out of
the French revolution, money here, arising from the expendi-
ture of the British government, and from the sale of the rich
cargoes and ships which were daily brought in by our cruizers,
was not only in brisk circulation, but in great abundance." The
result was that "The rewards of the most moderate labour were
so ample, that they begot habits of indolence and luxury. . . . Our
own landholders looked on with stupid indifference. . . . Satis-

fied with the enormous prices they obtained for beef and hay, and trusting that the springs of wealth which flowed so copiously would be perennial, they discerned not the dark cloud at a distance, which was gathering round to overcast their horizon." With the cessation of hostilities in 1815 the "springs" of Nova Scotia's economy ceased to flow, and, "in about two years after the ratification of the treaty of Paris, an universal gloom had settled over the province."[18]

The gloom was exacerbated by several occurrences. An increasing number of immigrants, escaping depressed conditions in Great Britain, came to Nova Scotia and took up land in spite of their having little previous experience as farmers.[19] As well, there were two natural disasters of an unusual and unpredictable nature. In 1815 when farmers were beginning to prepare the fields for potatoes and grain, armies of mice invaded the countryside in what came to be known in folk memory as "the year of the mice." Waves of rodents tumbled into sugar troughs, devoured seed potatoes, cut down acres of ripening grain, and lined the rigging of moored ships. At Cape George near Pictou hordes of mice died along the shore in the autumn. Of such magnitude was the phenomenon that mice formed "a ridge like seaweed along the edge of the sea, and codfish were caught off the coast with carcases in their maws."[20] The shortage of food that followed was not relieved in 1816 when "the year of the mice" was succeeded by "the year without a Summer."[21] By June 1816 the woods were still frozen, greatcoats were worn for ploughing, and flour was scarce.

Nowhere was this malaise in the province better articulated than in the letters of Agricola by John Young. Beginning in the *Acadian Recorder* on 25 July 1818, they continued to appear until 1823. In 1822 the first thirty-eight were published in Halifax as *The Letters Of Agricola On The Principles Of Vegetation And Tillage.* Arguing in the introduction that in general "The keeper of a tavern or a tippling-house, the retailer of rum, sugar and tea, the travelling chapman, the constable of the district" have been perceived as being "more important . . . than the farmer who cultivated his own lands," Young called for a change in public attitudes to farming. Rural daughters would not be caught in a turnip field, and sons "made little other use of the horses than to ride to church or market; and instead of being accustomed to ploughing, drilling, reaping, composting, and such like operations, they became country schoolmasters, crowded to the Capital as clerks and shopboys, commenced petty dealers and many of them turned smugglers." If the people in authority could "be united in one plan and animated by one spirit to confer honour on rural pursuits, and give them some share of countenance and support," he noted, then "the agricultural order would at once be lifted from disgrace, and placed on its just level in society."[22] The letters were favourably received by many people, including Lord Dalhousie, the lieutenant governor of Nova Scotia from 1816 to 1819, who shared Young's view that "the country is capable of great improvement."[23] Consequently, Young's efforts resulted in the establishment of the Central Board (or Provincial Agricultural Society) and local societies throughout the province. His letters also led to many discussions of farming in newspapers and helped create the climate for McCulloch's letters on the need for agricultural and other reforms.

The first letter signed "MEPHIBOSHETH STEPSURE" appeared in the *Acadian Recorder* on 22 December 1821. Seven more letters were published from 5 January to 9 February 1822. The pattern of submission was irregular, for on 26 January the *Acadian Recorder* acknowledged the receipt of four letters. Two of these, one from Stepsure and one from a stranger passing through the township, appeared on 2 February 1822. By the time that the *Acadian Recorder* had published these eight letters, their success had been sufficiently established to enable McCulloch to inform Simon Bradstreet Robie, the solicitor general of Nova Scotia, in a letter written on 9 February 1822, "By the by do you recollect a promise which you once made me to be fulfilled upon condition of my writing a novel   I have some notion that you may be called to perform   I design Mephibosheth to reach at least the twentieth letter and I have some thoughts of then adding notes and illustrations and sending the whole home as a sample of the way in which we get on in the western world."[24]

Between 23 February and 11 May 1822 nine more letters from Stepsure appeared in the *Acadian Recorder*. The newspaper's column "TO CORRESPONDENTS" traced the receipt of the letters and their publication. On 16 February 1822 the editors apologized "to Mephibosheth Stepsure for defering the insertion of his 8th letter till our next."[25] On 2 March they acknowledged that they had "the 9th number of Mephibosheth Stepsure,"[26] and on 6 April they announced that the arrival of the February mail had postponed publication of various items. "The same cause must plead our excuse with Mephibosheth Stepsure:—his 13th letter is in type."[27] By 11 May 1822 the editors were again addressing the public. "In this letter published to-day," they noted, "our correspondent Stepsure takes leave of the public for some time, and discontinues that series of essays, which have been read by all men with so much interest."[28] As Mephibosheth himself wrote in the same issue, "I have now arrived at the end of the first book of the chronicles of our town; and, for a number of reasons, winter must return, before I enter upon the second."[29]

That Nova Scotians did not forget the "chronicles" over the summer is indicated in a letter from David McDonald of East River published in the *Acadian Recorder* on 2 November 1822. Sounding suspiciously in accord with McCulloch's overall design, McDonald demanded, "why y'ere no prenting the queer stories o' the lame body Mephibosheth, that gied a' your freends sae mickle diversion the last winter." Recalling the impact of "them droll letters" on his own "puir settlement," he described the way in which "I was sairly pestered wi' folks coming last winter, and asking the len' o' the Recorder frae me." Finally, noted McDonald, he invited the neighbourhood to his home on post evenings so that he could read Stepsure aloud "for ilka ane's edification. Godsake mon ye ne'er saw sic a gathering o' them there was;—no a frolic in a' the kintra wand tak them awa frae comen to hear the puir body's life read. Heigh man! hoo they used to skirl at the tit bits . . . the rafters o' the house fairly shook wi' the clamer and din."[30] The editors of the *Acadian Recorder* promoted further interest in the Stepsure letters by prefacing McDonald's letter with a note in which they promised to answer his queries "in a short time . . . in a manner both more agreeable to ourselves, and much more satisfactory to the public."[31]

The appearance of a letter by Alexander Scantocreesh, Stepsure's neighbour, in the *Acadian Recorder* on 28 December 1822 heightened the anticipation of more letters by suggesting that Stepsure himself needed only a little more coaxing to take up the pen once again. Arguing that "ye maun gie him some heartnin' afore he sen' you ony mae letters," Scantocreesh admitted that he had done his best "ower the gaet, perswadin' him to gie us anither screed o' his letters."[32] The "screed" appeared from 4 January until 29 March 1823. It contained seven letters in all, one written by Scantocreesh to his friend Willy Whooshlicat in Scotland and six written by Stepsure. One of Stepsure's letters acted as a link to the first book; three chronicled his trip to Halifax and recorded the story that he was told there about William, a young Scots immigrant; and two were his response to the attack on him by a mysterious critic named Censor.

Six letters from "CENSOR" were published in the *Acadian Recorder* between 21 December 1822 and 25 January 1823. They attacked a range of topics from the low-necked dresses worn by women at the theatre to the writings of John Young, the *Free Press*, and James Irving, a Truro schoolmaster, whose essays on English poetry had been appearing in the *Acadian Recorder* since 1820.[33] Sustained by his philosophy that "a society that grows up without the benefit of a public censor, is sure to shoot out into a thousand extravagances and follies," Censor titillated his audience with speculations that he was, among others, "Mephibo' the old fox" in disguise.[34] His identity, however, has never been satisfactorily resolved.

On 28 December 1822 Censor began his letter "*On Mephibosheth Stepsure*" by praising the conception, design, and thrust of the letters. Admirable as he found these characteristics, he nonetheless condemned Stepsure for the indecorousness of

his scatalogical images, "the sameness of his characters," and the
infelicity of his language. "On the whole," Censor concluded,
"these letters are praiseworthy in the design, and are calculated
to do good by applying a wholesome corrective to our manners:
but the execution betrays neither a chaste imagination, nor much
power of language. As moral portraits they may find a place
on the chimney piece of the cottage, but they will ever be re-
fused admittance into the drawing-room of polite life."[35] In "*On
I——g.*," his letter on James Irving published in the *Acadian
Recorder* on 4 January 1823, Censor commented again that Step-
sure was "constantly wading in a dung-pit, bespattered with dirt
and all the marks of vulgarity."[36]

Committed as the editors of the *Acadian Recorder* were to
encouraging "an open, liberal discussion of public questions,"
they felt sufficiently chagrined by Censor's attacks to urge in an
editorial published on 18 January 1823 that Censor should turn
his "reforming rage" to "other and less obnoxious themes."[37]
Controversy over the letters continued in the press, however,
with "AN OBSERVER" noting in a letter published in the *Aca-
dian Recorder* on 1 February 1823 that Stepsure "though lame
seems very able to take his own part."[38] The accuracy of this
observation was soon substantiated. On 8 February 1823 Step-
sure's first letter on Censor was published in the *Acadian Recorder*;
his second on the same subject appeared there on 29 March
1823.

On 11 February 1823 the *Free Press* entered the Censor contro-
versy by noting in its column "To Correspondents" that "*Selec-
tions from the letter of Mephibosheth*" had "also come to hand" and
would "be attended to in due course. *Meph.* seems to know his
man; and we doubt not will teach him before he finishes,—what
it is to meddle with edgetools."[39] On 4 March 1823 the *Free Press*
further fuelled the controversy by announcing that it had
received an "*Extract of a letter from Pictou, dated Feby. 27, 1823*" in
which it was indicated that Censor was a "gentleman of high legal
rank, who is at present enjoying the hospitality of his friends in
Halifax."[40] A week later, on 11 March 1823, the *Free Press*

published this extract, in which the writer affirmed, "I have seen a Letter from a Law Student in Halifax, to a person in this place, in which he declares, most positively," that Censor's "Communications . . . were written by a certain Chief Justice who arrived at Halifax in December last."[41] This extract was followed by a note, dated 10 March 1823, from the same author. Signed "S.," it stated:

> I have too much confidence in the honor of my Correspondent to doubt, for a moment, the correctness of the statement contained in the extract of a letter from Pictou, which I sent you last week.—There are several Gentlemen now in Town who are perfectly satisfied of the truth of it, and who have often expressed their indignation, at the shameful and unwarrantable liberty which has been taken with a certain legal character.[42]

Edmund Ward, the feisty editor of the *Free Press*, added his own commentary to these items on Censor. Arguing that it was "preposterous," "absurd," and "ridiculous" to suppose that a newly-arrived chief justice, "a gentleman who from his childhood, has been accustomed to the intercourse of polished life," should attack Stepsure's letters, "vilify the female part of the community," and criticize the *Free Press*, Ward went on to explore two unpleasant consequences of the speculations: "the name of one of the writers" for the *Acadian Recorder* "has been divulged to the world," and "a gross calumny has been uttered against a person, whose situation in life and claims upon our hospitality, should have exempted him from such aspersion."[43]

Culminating this discussion and redirecting attention to Stepsure was the letter of "A REAL F.———.," dated "Pictou, March 14, 1823" and published in the *Acadian Recorder* on 22 March 1823. Until Censor had "so roughly handled" Mephibosheth, the residents of Pictou had always suspected Stepsure of being Censor, but after Censor had attacked Stepsure, the townspeople had sided with the latter in ascribing the Censor letters to Agricola. However, suggested "A REAL F.———.," the extract of the letter

from Pictou and the note signed "S." published in the *Free Press*
on 11 March 1823 were in fact by none other than Stepsure:

> The secret as I take it, and as it is believed here, is neither
> more or less than this. The extract, the note, and the
> remark before and after is a contrivance of our misguarded
> townsman, I fear, to vent his wrath on somebody for the
> affront offered to his writings, but we are wondering much
> what new information he has got to make him change his
> man. He seems on a new scent and resolved to take penny
> worths on more than one.[44]

The suggestion that Mephibosheth was now implicating in the
controversy an eminent legal gentleman visiting Halifax
provoked an immediate response in the next, and last, Stepsure
letter published in the *Acadian Recorder* on 29 March 1823.
Digressing from his discussion of Censor to answer "A REAL
F.——.," Stepsure argued:

> In the mean time, I would just say to your correspondent of
> last week, that dating his communication from Pictou, and
> ascribing to me the notices contained in the Free Press, are a
> sort of bait which even gulls can detect. Mr. Ward, I believe,
> has already traced them to their source; which renders it
> the less necessary for me to add that my writings never
> extended a line beyond my letters in the Recorder.[45]

With this disclaimer the Censor controversy apparently died.

Despite the diversion of the Censor controversy, the impor-
tance of the Stepsure letters lay in their ability to provoke Nova
Scotians to laughter and self-analysis. The agent of both the
humour and the satire was, to quote David McDonald, "the lame
body Mephibosheth," whose "queer stories" made listeners not
only "skirl at the tit bits" but also recognize their social and moral
frailties.[46] A penniless orphan who had been born with deformed
feet, Mephibosheth Stepsure began life in "our town" (CEECT,
p. 7) with more deprivation than was common to a literary
protagonist, particularly one designed to function as a satiric

norm. In spite of his handicaps, Stepsure worked hard and eventually flourished. Whereas his neighbours squandered their land in pursuit of various schemes that were supposed to allow them to get rich quickly and to rise effortlessly in society, Stepsure stayed home, tilled his fields, and saved his money. "I was neither a great man nor a great man's son," he declares as a credo at the end of Letter 10, "I was lame Meph, whose highest ambition was to be a plain decent farmer" (CEECT, p. 106). Although McCulloch allowed Stepsure's personal limitations to emerge in an ironic light during the course of the twenty-five letters, he never treated ironically either Stepsure's dedication to the land or his economic independence. "The man who redeems a farm from the forest, labours it with ordinary judgment, and manages with economy the fruits of his toil, is rewarded with the necessaries of life and a reasonable share of its comforts,"[47] McCulloch wrote in 1826, and in Mephibosheth Stepsure, his cousin Harrow, and Alexander Scantocreesh, McCulloch created dramatized illustrations of this observation.

To reiterate Stepsure's views that "nature designed" Nova Scotians "to be a farming people" and "that every man who gives the ground fair play, will be able to live very comfortably" (CEECT, p. 29), McCulloch turned the letters into a series of morality tales. In Letter 1 Solomon Gosling mortgages Goose-Hill Farm to pursue the lure of mercantilism, shipbuilding, and greater recognition in society. After prospering for a while, he experiences financial disaster when he becomes overly dependent on credit and overly reliant on the province's artificial war economy. His creditors close in, his clients do not pay their debts, and he is left to face the sheriff and imprisonment. "This event has not added much to the respectability of the Goslings," Stepsure notes drily, "nor is it calculated to brighten their prospects" (CEECT, p. 12). In Letter 2 Jack Scorem spends so much time and money building a stylish white clapboard house with green corners and window facings that he fails to provide a barn for his cow or to harvest more than a few potatoes. Dependent on commercial staples and convivial society, Jack turns to cutting timber as a way of obtaining immediate cash. As with Gosling, debt and disgrace follow.

When characters in the letters actually leave rural life to live in the city, they face even more temptations. The dangers of drinking, gambling, and socializing are nowhere more dramatically illustrated than in the story of William that is narrated to Stepsure by an old gentleman whom he meets in Halifax. Blessed with the promise of youth and opportunity, William forsakes both Scotland and his Christian heritage to waste his financial opportunities in Halifax and to indulge in a life of dissipation and extravagance. The circumstances of William's subsequent death underline the seriousness of McCulloch's message for both new immigrants and native Nova Scotians. Placed as it is as the last of the morality tales in the letters, the story of William serves as a final and dour warning to all who forsake the paths of righteousness advocated and illustrated by Stepsure and Scantocreesh.

This warning note was also sounded by the editors of the *Acadian Recorder* on 11 May 1822 when they observed that the propensity of Nova Scotians "for expense is quite disproportioned to their incomes; and if five pounds is within their reach, in place of being hoarded up as capital, it is expended in some article of luxury.—Saunders Scantocreesh is too rare a character in Nova Scotia."[48] An admirer of the seventeenth-century Covenanters who were martyred for their religious convictions, Scantocreesh particularly reinforces McCulloch's theme that a virtuous man or woman must lead a sober and godly life, preferably in a severe, Presbyterian way. Saunders' stern admonitions that he would make the evangelical Mrs. Sham "eat her own tongue to the root" (CEECT, p. 170) and that he would send Howl and Yelpit "to the house of correction; where, if they did not learn some sense, they would at least get the laziness squeezed out of them" (CEECT, p. 170) reflect McCulloch's scorn for the various evangelical sects that had sprung up in Nova Scotia. Saunders' images of Nova Scotia as "the lan' o' cabteevity" (CEECT, p. 215) and of his neighbours as the Israelites who forsook their true God to follow the pagan "Egyptians" (CEECT,

p. 167) underline the seriousness of McCulloch's chastisement of his fellow Nova Scotians for wandering from the ways of religion and virtue and jeopardizing both their society and their souls.

If the social and moral message of McCulloch's letters was timely, so too was their relationship to the literary climate in the province. Satirical sketches and letters had been appearing in Halifax newspapers throughout the post-Napoleonic period on subjects as diverse as fashionable etiquette and agricultural reform. The best-known, previous to the Stepsures, were the letters of Agricola, although in 1818 McCulloch had himself adopted the pseudonym *"Investigator"* to discuss educational issues in letters to the *Acadian Recorder*.[49] All these newspaper pieces contributed to what D. C. Harvey called "the intellectual awakening" of Nova Scotia, when the "minds of the young Nova Scotians were quickened both by economic rivalry and by the literature of knowledge that was written about their province and its industries." According to Harvey, *"Mephibosheth Stepsure* and the *Letters of Agricola* appeared in the *Acadian Recorder . . .* just in time to take part in the intellectual awakening."[50]

If the letters emanated from McCulloch's familiarity with the literary climate of Nova Scotia, they also emerged from his knowledge of trends in Scottish literature in the late eighteenth and early nineteenth centuries. In spite of the distance separating Scotland and Nova Scotia, the province's readers received works published in Edinburgh and Glasgow shortly after they were issued, especially if the worst of the winter season had passed. The popularity of Sir Walter Scott in the Maritimes provides an illustration. A poem from *The Monastery*, his novel published in Edinburgh in March 1820, appeared, for example, in the Halifax *Free Press* on 20 June 1820; the same issue reprinted a review of this "ROMANCE BY THE AUTHOR OF WAVERLEY" extracted from the *Literary Gazette*.[51] Works by Scott belonging to private individuals were often advertised for sale in the Halifax newspapers; on 21 December 1821, for instance, the Halifax *Weekly Chronicle* announced that "THE following new and very popular Works, belonging to a Gentleman

of this Town, may be had at the Chronicle Office, at less than
Sterling Cost: *The MONASTERY*, 3 vols. by the author of Waver-
ley, &c. *IVANHOE*, 3 vols., ditto."[52]

Nova Scotia's large Scottish population encouraged the literary
connections between the old country and the new, and, as a
result, newspaper editors in Halifax were acutely conscious of the
taste in their constituency for all things Caledonian. Poems in the
Burns tradition were frequently published, and essays such as
James Irving's *"On the Southern Peasantry of Scotland"* were not
uncommon.[53] John Gibson Lockhart's *Peter's Letters to His
Kinsfolk*, ironic portraits of life in Edinburgh and Glasgow that
were published in Edinburgh by Blackwood in 1819, were famil-
iar enough to Nova Scotians to allow the *Acadian Recorder* to
serialize an imitation entitled "Paul's Letters To His Kinsfolk"
from 18 August to 29 December 1821.[54] Employing the same
narrative and epistolary form as its model, these "Letters," which
partly overlapped in the *Acadian Recorder* with those by Stepsure,
helped inculcate a taste for literary letters with a clearly defined
narrative voice.

Nova Scotian readers of John Galt's novels would have been
exposed to a similar approach to contemporary prose. In both his
epistolary novel *The Ayrshire Legatees*, serialized in *Blackwood's
Magazine* between June 1820 and February 1821, and *Annals Of
The Parish*, published in April 1821, Galt employed a non-dra-
matic structure and a pattern of self-revealing narration. His
example may well have appealed to McCulloch, who shared with
Galt not only a background in western Scotland in the late
eighteenth century but also an interest in depicting an agri-
cultural society undergoing changes wrought by war, emigration,
and other far-reaching developments. In *Annals Of The Parish Or
The Chronicle Of Dalmailing* Micah Balwhidder, an elderly clergy-
man, denies that he is "writing for a vain world, but only to testify
to posterity anent the great changes that have happened in my
day and generation."[55] Likewise, in his "chronicles of our town"
(CEECT, p. 75), Mephibosheth Stepsure claims that "the world is
wonderfully changed since I was an apprentice. This province in

particular, is fast growing in importance" (CEECT, p. 87). Stepsure notes, however, "in our town it has been a time of general distress" (CEECT, p. 28). Shipbuilders have collapsed, mortgagees have foreclosed, malcontents have proposed emigration to Botany Bay or the Ohio, and rum dealers have grown rich on the despair of others. In addressing the times Scantocreesh, the stranger, Parson Drone, and Squire Worthy all reinforce Stepsure's descriptions of Nova Scotia. To enlighten those who are "as ignorant as his stots" (CEECT, p. 94), Scantocreesh affirms the value of libraries modelled after the Scottish system. To explore the reasons for the economic ills of the province, the stranger debates the advantages of free trade versus those of preferential trade with Great Britain. To curtail the breakdown of the family, Parson Drone preaches the virtues of domesticity. And, to ward off poverty, Squire Worthy warns, "Debt hangs about the neck of an honest man like a millstone" (CEECT, p. 98).

Convinced like Benjamin Franklin that time is money, Mephibosheth Stepsure is a conservative yet progressive man. He respects the value of reading, illustrates in his own story the vulnerability of the orphaned and the indigent, and exposes the failure of unscientific "old farming" (CEECT, p. 89) to address the problems of contemporary agriculture. With a hoe in one hand and the Bible in the other, he has recognized that "I must learn to take care of myself. . . . I who had nobody to do any thing for me, must learn to be my own helper" (CEECT, p. 88). Although a folk idiom might be close to his lips, he is very much a man of the future when, at the close of Letter 17, he determines "to make the ensuing summer the busiest of my life" and, in an obvious allusion to John Young and the Provincial Agricultural Society, notes, "The exertions of you Halifax gentlemen to promote the agriculture of the province, have suggested to me a great many improvements which my present system of farming needs" (CEECT, p. 185).

Because of the wide circulation of the *Acadian Recorder* in Nova Scotia, Mephibosheth's message had an immediate impact in the province. In 1872, for example, the Reverend D. McCurdy

xxxiv EDITOR'S INTRODUCTION

recalled that in "the winter of '22 or '23," when he attended "the Grammar School" in Truro, James Irving, his schoolmaster, included among his nicknames for students "Shad," "an abbreviation of Shadrach Howl in Stepsure's Letters published by Dr. McCulloch (incog.) about that time."[56] Elsewhere the references were more public. In its issues of 6 May and 15 May 1822 the *Halifax Journal* included a review of "PARSON DRONE'S SERMONS," a work that was supposed to have been published in Antigonish in 1821;[57] the review itself was extracted from the fictitious *Ramshag Review*, "printed by *Timothy Typestick & Co.*"[58] On 11 May 1822 "ODD FELLOW" responded to an earlier attack on Stepsure by publishing a comic poem in the *Acadian Recorder*:

> He *puffs* at Mephibosheth so,
>   About his stepping *sure*, man!
> But *Meph*, if *Puff* begins to blow,
>   Will *Puff*, of *puffing cure*, man![59]

Equally playful with the semantics of the Stepsure letters was "T. S.," Thomas Soley, of Truro, whose poetic *"List of Publicans and Sinners throughout the township of Mephibosheth Stepsure,"* which included "Solomon Gosling, Hob, the Bumpkin, / The bund'ling girls of Peter Pumpkin,"[60] was published in the *Acadian Recorder* on 13 July 1822. In spite of his list, Soley lacked the social consciousness of "X.," who, in the *Halifax Journal* of 20 January 1823, noted the role of Stepsure in "contriving / Improvements in our Country living."[61]

Throughout the 1820s the Stepsure letters continued to have a pervasive influence. Their social dimension was projected in a series of thirteen "Stepsure In Town" poems that ran in the *Acadian Recorder* from 1 January 1825 to 17 June 1826.[62] The satirical nature of Mephibosheth's social comment was described as the *"caustic* of Stepsure" by "AN IMPARTIAL OBSERVER," whose letter to the *Acadian Recorder* was published on 18 February 1826.[63] "The Club" group of the *Novascotian*, Joseph Howe's Halifax newspaper, also remembered the satirical side of McCulloch in its sketch of 15 May 1828. "Troth, Sir," says Donald

McGregor as he recalls McCulloch, "he can be unco severe when he pleases; and when he gets a foe on the braid o' his back, the lard protec him." The foe, continues McGregor, "is first pinned to the yearth wi' an argeement, and then hacked and tattood like a New Sealander, wi' a' sorts o' rideeculous comparisons; so that though ye may pity the puir deil, ye canna keep yere coontenance."[64]

The reference in "The Club" papers indicates that it was well known by 1828 that McCulloch was the author of the Stepsure letters and that Pictou was the model for Mephibosheth's town. Just when this information entered the public domain is difficult to estimate, but it must have been general knowledge by 1823. The fact that David McDonald's letter of 2 November 1822 came from East River, home of McCulloch's intimate friend James MacGregor, might have been enough to direct attention to the district of Pictou and its most controversial citizen. So too would the letters of "S." and "A REAL F.——." that were written from Pictou at the height of the Censor controversy in March 1823. Identifying Stepsure as a resident of Pictou, "A REAL F.——." confided to the reader, "You must know that the affairs of our town are as much talked of among ourselves as in the province, by reason of the chronicles of our lame Mephibosheth; and every thing connected with them has much interest here."[65] With the letter of "A REAL F.——." the Stepsure letters lost the anonymity of place that had made their satire immediately pertinent to every town in Nova Scotia. Just how effective this anonymity had been was later confirmed by the observations of a Nova Scotian quoted in the *Life Of Thomas McCulloch*:

> "We looked with great anxiety for the arrival of the "Recorder," and on its receipt used to assemble in the shop of Mr.—— to hear "Stepsure" read, and pick out the characters, and comment on their foibles, quite sure that they and the writer were among ourselves. Great was often the anger expressed, and threats uttered against the author if they could discover him."[66]

The specific identification of Mephibosheth's town with Pictou just a week before the publication of the last Stepsure letter in the *Acadian Recorder* might well have reinforced McCulloch's decision to end the series, particularly at a time when he had fulfilled his design of writing at least twenty letters and had brought the story of William to a successful conclusion. As early as the previous July McCulloch had begun to execute his original intention of collecting the letters and sending "the whole home"[67] for publication. Writing on 17 July 1822 to George Young, a former student at Pictou Academy, he indicated that he had been spending time on the seventeen letters that had already been published in the *Acadian Recorder*. Calling them "the Stepsures," McCulloch announced that "Since they were concluded I have corrected and copied them and may by and by send them home along with some others as a sketch of American manners   Till I began to copy them I had not the least conception that they were so inaccurately printed."[68] McCulloch entitled his new manuscript "The Chronicles of our Town . . . Or a Peep at America: In a series of letters originally addressed to the Editors of the Acadian Recorder, Halifax, Nova Scotia, for the express purpose of showing our people what they never looked at before."[69] He also added an introductory letter written in Scots dialect by Alexander Scantocreesh to Willy Whooshlicat, his boyhood companion in Scotland. Later published in the *Acadian Recorder* on 11 January 1823 as part of the second series of Stepsures, this letter allowed McCulloch to fill in the background of "The Chronicles" and prepare a Scottish audience for their Nova Scotian context.

McCulloch's chance to send his manuscript "home" came in November 1822 when a Pictou friend left for Scotland. In a covering letter written to John Mitchell in Glasgow, to whom "The Chronicles of our Town" was to be delivered, McCulloch indicated that he was forwarding "a series of letters which I published last winter" to "afford your brother and you to both of whom I am so deeply indebted a little amusement." Although they contained "a little caricature," the Mitchells could "depend upon them as an exact representation of American man-

ners   No writing [in] these provinces ever occasioned so much
talk   Almost every one who read them was angry in his turn
and by and by laughed at his neighbour   One of our Judges
told me that he believed our Governor had them by heart."
Because the printed copies "were so thumbed that such a thing
could not be got," McCulloch had "copied them and added an
introductory letter thinking that perhaps some bookseller who
deals in light wares might some time or other consent to publish
them as a sketch of American manners." No doubt conscious of
his fund-raising activities for Pictou Academy and of his on-
going efforts to have the Secessionist church consolidate its
position in Nova Scotia, he urged that the anonymity that he had
tried to maintain in Nova Scotia be preserved in Scotland. "In the
Secession," he concluded, "perhaps a publication of this kind
known to be mine would not promote my views."[70]

Little evidence survives to indicate what happened to the
manuscript of "The Chronicles of our Town" after McCulloch
sent it to Scotland in 1822. Certainly it was never published. In a
letter to John Mitchell dated 31 May 1824 McCulloch, answering
a letter that he had received from his friend "A few days" before,
advised, "With the manuscripts do as you please   I feel not
about them the least concern   They were designed chiefly for
your own perusal."[71] Although it is impossible to identify these
"manuscripts" with absolute certainty, they probably included
"The Chronicles of our Town." It seems likely, in fact, that
Mitchell still had this manuscript when McCulloch visited Scot-
land in 1825-26.

In the meantime, McCulloch spent the winter of 1822-23
completing the second series of the Stepsure letters. At some
point after the last of this series had appeared in the *Acadian
Recorder* in March 1823, McCulloch extracted the story of
William and began to prepare a manuscript of it for submission
to the *Edinburgh Christian Instructor*. A note to the editor on the
first page of the manuscript, written in McCulloch's hand, reads,
"Sir, By inserting the following little narative in your valuable
paper, you will afford useful information to parents who feel

inclined to send their children abroad. It is part of a series of sketches originally published in this province, and generally admitted to be an exact representation of North American manners."[72] The note to the editor was crossed out, however, and the story does not seem to have ever been submitted to the periodical.

Instead, McCulloch had apparently decided to try to have "William" published, with another of his stories, in book form. An unpublished preface entitled "Colonial Gleanings: William & Melville" announces that "The following little stories were written for the purpose of bringing into view some topics which are too seldom considered. The first," it continues, "was originally published in one of the newspapers of Nova Scotia; and, having been there recognised as an exact delineation of character, it is now submitted to the British public, for the information of those parents and children who found their hopes of happiness upon the acquisition of wealth in foreign lands." The preface then concludes with the justification for writing such a moral tale as "William":

> To those who judge that religion ought not to be blended with fiction, it may be observed, that, for parables, there is the best of precedent. When properly employed, they conciliate to piety and virtue, one of the strongest principles of the mind; and human excellence is not acquired by the eradication or the neglect of original powers, but by rendering the operation of each, subservient to the improvement of the whole.[73]

After McCulloch arrived in Scotland in 1825, he took "Colonial Gleanings" to the publishing firm of William Oliphant of Edinburgh, which bought the manuscript for "thirty guineas."[74] During its preparation for publication McCulloch worked closely with at least two Oliphant editors. Each read "William" and suggested minor revisions, which were written on the manuscript. McCulloch obviously reviewed these revisions carefully: he accepted some, rejected others, and revised still others. He continued to hone the style of his story even as Oliphant typeset the manuscript late in 1825. Finally, a letter written by Oliphant to McCulloch on 1 January 1826, while McCulloch was staying in Edinburgh, informed him that the publisher was sending "a first proof of the last instalment" of "William and Melville" and that the engraver had worked at the plate for the illustration "till one o'clock this morning,—and again resumed his labour at five. So soon as the plate is finished, we shall get a few hundred impressions thrown off, and the work will be published early next week."[75] *Colonial Gleanings. William, And Melville* was published anonymously in January 1826. It included an abbreviated and revised form of McCulloch's draft preface.

Within a month of the publication of *Colonial Gleanings* the *Edinburgh Theological Magazine* had reviewed it and had identified its author as "the Rev. Doctor McCulloch of Pictou, in Nova Scotia," because, "though his extreme modesty seeks the shade, he cannot be concealed." Claiming that the volume "does great credit to his talents, his piety, and his taste," the reviewer went on to praise the two emigration tales as illustrations of "the superior understanding and amiable disposition of its very estimable author."[76] Interest in *Colonial Gleanings* led to the publication of extracts from "Melville" in the *Novascotian*. A note that appeared with the first segment of the story on 21 September 1826 explained that the "little volume . . . contains two tales—the first under the title of William is already known to our readers, from having appeared in the well-known letters of Mephibosheth Stepsure."[77]

Although "The Chronicles of our Town" remained unpublished when McCulloch returned to Nova Scotia from Scotland in December 1826, he continued his creative writing. By 16 January 1828 McCulloch was deeply involved in composing "Auld Eppie's Tales," an historical novel set in the southwest of Scotland, with specific reference to Scottish history and the Covenanting tradition. Writing in late June 1828 to James Mitchell, John Mitchell's son, McCulloch urged him to take the first volume of "Auld Eppie" to a bookseller to ascertain its potential. He also indicated that because of William Blackwood's kindness to him when he had been in Edinburgh, "it is my duty to give him the preference."[78] Shortly after, on 5 July 1828, McCulloch mentioned to James Mitchell that he had "not heard from Blackwood."[79] Since the remark makes little sense in the context of the manuscript of "Auld Eppie's Tales," particularly when McCulloch was still in the process of forwarding portions of that novel to Scotland, the comment suggests that Blackwood was considering "The Chronicles of our Town" during the summer of 1828 and that McCulloch was awaiting the publisher's verdict on this manuscript even as he prepared another.

By 29 December 1828 McCulloch had sent the entire manuscript of "Auld Eppie's Tales" to Scotland and was anxiously writing to James Mitchell to discover its fate. Desirous of making some money from the novel to assist his son Thomas in business, McCulloch urged Mitchell "to lose no time" in submitting the work to a publisher. Worried that John Mitchell might "perhaps feel delicate in submitting to a bookseller" such "a species of writing," McCulloch suggested that the novel might well pass "through some other respectable hands," for "A booksellers opinion is influenced by the character of the man who looks him in the face   I mentioned Blackwood formerly because he had been kind to me   Perhaps another may do equally well   An extensive publisher however is the mark   As my book is only part of a plan I cannot part with the manuscript without a more tempting offer than any bookseller will make." If "a liberal publisher" were found, however, "it is not probable that I will change him afterward." Throughout the discussion McCulloch indicated that "Auld Eppie's Tales," if "they catch the public taste," was the first in a planned series of novels. "If I could write anything which would procure additional regard for Scotch worthies and their general principles," he added in a veiled allusion to Sir Walter Scott's portrayal of the Covenanters in *Tales of My Landlord* (1816 ff.), "it would be well spent labour."[80]

Unknown to McCulloch, however, on 15 December 1828 Blackwood had responded to John Mitchell. In his letter he rejected not only "Auld Eppie's Tales" but also "The Chronicles of our Town." His tone was abject as he tried to explain his tardiness in responding, "I have used you very ill, and I have no apology to offer for my having so long delayed writing you, except the difficulty I have felt and still feel in explaining to you the impressions which your friend Dr McCulloch's MS.S. have made upon me." Blackwood had "perused" "The Chronicles of our Town" many times and had been "struck from the first with the power displayed in these Letters, which are full of the most picturesque sketches of life and manners, and are written in a style of rich humour" that he had "seldom seen surpassed." It was "this very richness," however, that he felt "would startle readers in this country, for the humour is often so broad, or what many people could call coarse, that it would prevent the work from having a general circulation." As well, there were "several topics of a merely local kind, which though suited to the Class to whom the Letters were addressed, would not at all interest readers on this side of the water." If "Dr McCulloch would be inclined to go over the series, and write out letters addressed to some one in this country," suggested Blackwood, "I think he could give a most lively and graphic picture of the state of manners, modes of living thinking etc which would interest every one. In this way he could make use of almost all his previous materials."

In proposing that McCulloch revise "The Chronicles of our Town," Blackwood also suggested that the work be serialized in *Blackwood's Magazine* "at the rate of ten guineas p[er] sheet." Each "letter or chapter might be made from 8 to 14 pages so as to be a proper length to be published in successive issues" of the periodical. "It would be quite unnecessary," he added, "to make any allusion to the Letters having appeared in any of the Canadian Papers." He had intended to make revisions in the manuscript of "The Chronicles" "for Dr McCulloch's consideration," but he had "found that no one could do this but the author himself." This was "one of the causes of" his having "delayed writing" for so long. In the same letter Blackwood explained that he was rejecting "Auld Eppie's Tales" because it was "liable to the same objection of a tendency to coarseness in the humour" as the "Chronicles" and because, "Penetrating as it were into Scott's field, a work of this kind requires to be done with exquisite skill." Blackwood concluded his letter:

> I fear I have not sufficiently explained my ideas, and I despair of being able to do so unless I had the pleasure of half an hour's conversation with Dr McCulloch himself, which I suppose there is no chance of my having by his coming to this country. From what I have said however you will see how very highly I estimate your friend's talents, and I assure you nothing would give me greater pleasure than having it in my power to shew him how sincere I am in my wish to see justice done to him.[81]

McCulloch's response to the news of Blackwood's rejection was decisive. "My novels I see will not do," he wrote to James Mitchell on 18 May 1829, "there is too much dirt in them this must arise from the nature of the beast." Adding that he had heard from Jotham Blanchard, who was then visiting Scotland, that Blackwood would pay him ten guineas a sheet for contributions to his magazine, McCulloch retorted:

> Now dirty as Bl[ackwood] thinks my novels I judge them purity itself compared with his magazine and it would be a subject of serious consideration with me whether I ought to write for a publication whose tendency is so irreligious   I am sorry that you submitted what I sent you to any other bookseller   When it is returned which I anticipate have the goodness to seal it up mark it as belonging to me and let it lie among your papers.

As for Blackwood's concern that "Auld Eppie's Tales" penetrated into Scott's territory, McCulloch replied, "I never intended to be an imitator of Sir Walter   I have neither his knowledge nor talents   But on the other hand I conceived that the kind of information and humour which I possess would have enabled me to vindicate where he has misrepresented and also to render contemptible and ludicrous what he has laboured to dignify."[82]

Time did not diminish McCulloch's sense of injury about the fate of his manuscripts. "Blackwood never wrote to me," he noted to James Mitchell in a letter dated 4 September 1829, "of course I never addressed him   I do not know that I could write for his Magazine it is not the most moral of books." Still rankling over the rejection of "Auld Eppie's Tales" as well as "The Chronicles," he continued, "As for the Lollards I wished him to get the offer of it on account of the kindness which he showed me." The rejection had deterred him from proceeding with "another equally humorous" novel, he added, for "on receiving Mr Blanchard's letter in the spring I laid it aside and have not looked at it since."[83] McCulloch was obviously still brooding about the matter on 3 December 1829 when he wrote James Mitchell again:

> With respect to Blackwood permit me now to say a few words   On account of the donation of books which I received from him I wished him the profit if profit there would be   He thinks me a needy hanger on upon book-sellers but things are not yet so bad with me as that   Pray have the goodness to send for the manuscripts without waiting for his ultimatum seal them up with my name upon them and lay them past   I do not care twopence about their publication   About writing for his magazine I have only to say that I regard it as a very bad book and except in the expectation of helping to render its texture more moral I could not do it   I think I could give him for a few years a series of essays that would be generally read but not being yet a hungry author ten guineas a sheet is no tempta-tion   At present I have too many irons in the fire to engage in any literary undertaking   Still I have not altogether relinquished my plan . . .   Pray send for the manuscripts by the first opportunity.[84]

That Blackwood was conscious of McCulloch's unhappiness and genuinely wanted to placate him is suggested by a second letter that the Scottish publisher wrote to John Mitchell on 31 December 1829. "I would give anything that I had an hour's conversation with Dr McCulloch," Blackwood began, "as I could then so much more satisfactorily explain my sentiments to him than I can in a letter." His explanations in his second letter were consistent with those in his first although his analysis now tended to focus more specifically on the shifts in standards of decorum that were causing him anxiety with respect to McCulloch's work. "The humour and satire have all the pungency & originality of Swift, with I am sorry to say too much of his broad & coarse colouring. Taste in these things has now a days got even more refined, and what was fit for the tea table in the days of Queen Anne would hardly be tolerated now in the servant's hall." Nonetheless, Blackwood still felt that

> your friend's pictures of life are so vivid, and so ingeniously sketched, that if he were to allow a selection to be made by a judicious hand, I could publish portions of these Letters in my Magazine. To publish the whole as a Book would never answer in this country, for though men of sense would enjoy them highly, and make allowances for the state of society which they describe, still the mob of ladies & gentlemen would cry shame, and the book would at once be ____.[85]

Blackwood's timorousness about "the mob of ladies & gentlemen" crying "shame" seems surprising from the man who had already published such satires as the "Chaldee Manuscript" (1817) and *Peter's Letters to His Kinsfolk* (1819). Both the times and William Blackwood had changed, however. While the information would probably have been of little comfort to McCulloch, even a well-established author like John Galt had encountered an unusual degree of fastidiousness on the part of Blackwood as he and his manuscript readers responded to the increasing gentility of the age. Francis Jeffrey had used the word "Vulgarity" several times in discussing Galt's work in the *Edinburgh Review* in October 1823, and when Galt submitted *The Last of The Lairds* to Blackwood in 1825, the publisher and his reader had removed all references that were mildly blasphemous or sexual.[86] It is not surprising, therefore, that Stepsure's references to breaking wind and emptying chamber pots from windows might strike Blackwood as indecorous and that passages such as that which describes the "dissatisfaction" of Job's wife "when some mischievous boy slipped a hornet's nest into Job's trousers" might give the publisher concern (CEECT, pp. 127-28). Elemental as this humour was, however, it was consistent with Mephibosheth's plain-spoken persona and his revelations of the practicalities of life in pioneer Nova Scotia. Years later, on 15 May 1828, it was this humour that the *Novascotian*'s "Club" series recalled as having "set the hale kintra laughin' for months" at Stepsure's "odd stories about gable ends and cabbage."[87]

In spite of his difficulties with Blackwood in 1828-29, McCulloch did not totally abandon the idea of publishing "The Chronicles of our Town" and "Auld Eppie's Tales" in Great Britain. In 1831 Jotham Blanchard, who was visiting Britain on Pictou Academy business, took both manuscripts to London to try to have them published. He had no success with either. In a letter written from Glasgow on 30 September 1831 he reported that he had spoken about "Meph." to "one magazine but no one cd give so much as Blackwood offered." He added that he would "bring" the manuscripts "out or rather try & get them away from here for the[y] half fill my portmanteau."[88]

It is not clear what happened to the manuscripts of "The Chronicles of our Town" and "Auld Eppie's Tales" after 1831. No evidence has been found to suggest that Blanchard brought them back to Nova Scotia. In fact, in a letter dated 29 December 1833 McCulloch wrote to James Mitchell, "In your last letter you mention that my manuscripts are still in Blackwoods possession   You would oblige me exceedingly by sending them out in the spring . . .   I wish to reconsider"[89] them. Since McCulloch had given every indication in his correspondence that he would never again submit material to Blackwood, these manuscripts were probably "The Chronicles of our Town" and "Auld Eppie's

Tales." Why Blackwood still had them in his possession, especially after Blanchard's publishing foray in London, is, however, a puzzle.

In the meantime, McCulloch had not been idle. A letter on Parson Drone from Timothy Ticklemup that was published in the *Acadian Recorder* on 6 April 1833 was almost certainly by McCulloch,[90] and by the end of the year he had completed three new tales, one of them in memory of his colleague and friend James MacGregor. In his letter of 29 December 1833 McCulloch urged Mitchell to take this "little story written expressly for the purpose of commemorating the worth of that good man Dr MacGregor" to William Oliphant in Edinburgh. He commented, "When I parted with Mr Oliphant I told him that my next story instead of thirty guineas would cost him fifty   This is the price which I have now mentioned to him." In the same letter McCulloch also requested that Mitchell ask Oliphant how much he would pay "for a story upon the Days of the Covenant of about 400 pages   I have been looking at Archbishop Sharp and our afflicted fathers   Mr Oliphant can now estimate the price of my pen and he may be assured that for my own sake what I send him will be carefully weighed."[91] The novel does not seem to have been completed, however, and on 18 July 1834, at the age of fifty-eight, McCulloch wrote to John Mitchell that "I wish no more publishing applications   I have not talents bearing pace with the judgment of the public . . .   Necessity does not now force me to write."[92]

McCulloch made only one further reference to the Stepsure letters in his correspondence to the Mitchells. In a letter dated 6 November 1834, in which he outlined the social and agricultural problems of Nova Scotia, McCulloch noted that "My Stepsures were a facsimile so striking that they at first excited the indignation of individuals every where."[93] Of the fate of the manuscript of "The Chronicles of our Town" there was no mention. Since it seems likely that Blanchard did not bring it back with him from Glasgow, McCulloch may have collected it himself from the Mitchells when he visited Scotland in 1842. It is also conceivable that the Mitchells sent it to Nova Scotia in the 1830s or 1840s or that McCulloch's son retrieved it years later when he spent time in Scotland. All that is documented with respect to the manuscript is that it was in the possession of the family some time before 1936 when Miss Isabella McCulloch, granddaughter of the author, presented it to the Public Archives of Nova Scotia.

Since McCulloch's death in 1843 parts of the Stepsure letters have been republished on three different occasions. In June 1862 Hugh William Blackadar, who then owned the *Acadian Recorder*, published as *Letters Of Mephibosheth Stepsure* sixteen of the seventeen letters that had appeared in the newspaper between December 1821 and May 1822; the stranger's letter was excluded. An editorial written for the *Acadian Recorder* of 21 June 1862 explained the reasons for printing this new edition:

> These letters having done much in their time to destroy the spirit of indolence for which Bluenose has been rather notorious, and to root out habits so inimical to social prosperity and happiness, may perhaps, by republication encourage our people, by showing the advances we have made and stimulate to new endeavours. The publisher of these old letters was not willing that so much sound, common sense and useful satire, embodied in a quaint, pure, and lively style, should sink into oblivion.[94]

Both the editorial and an advertisement in the same issue announced the availability of the "LETTERS OF MEPHIBOSHETH STEPSURE, Reprinted from the Acadian Recorder, Of the years 1821 and 1822." The book was for sale in Halifax at the office of the *Acadian Recorder* and at "A. & W. McKINLAY, Booksellers & Stationers, Granville Street."[95] Nineteenth-century reviewers, however, made little response to the *Letters Of Mephibosheth Stepsure*.

Although between 20 April and 6 July 1882 the New Glasgow *Eastern Chronicle* serialized the first four letters from the *Acadian Recorder*, there was little further interest in Thomas McCulloch until the private publication in 1920 of the *Life Of Thomas*

McCulloch, D.D. Pictou by his son William. Edited by McCulloch's granddaughters, this biography stressed McCulloch's contribution as an educator and a clergyman but made only passing reference to the Stepsure letters. Interest in the letters was stimulated, however, when in *Thomas Chandler Haliburton ("Sam Slick") A Study in Provincial Toryism* (1924) V.L.O. Chittick compared the Stepsure letters favourably to the Sam Slick sketches. In McCulloch, argued Chittick, Haliburton found

> one who for subtlety and skill in the good-natured indict-
> ment of popular error was easily his master. Every one of
> the social, economic, and agricultural truths which subse-
> quently had to be reimpressed on the easy-going Nova
> Scotians in Sam Slick's strangely fabricated vernacular
> before they would bestir themselves into self-sustaining
> activity was clearly anticipated and expounded in the elu-
> cidation of his neighbors' unnecessary misfortunes by Dr.
> McCulloch's soberly deliberative, frugal-minded, oddly
> named cripple.[96]

D. C. Harvey's seminal essay "The Intellectual Awakening of Nova Scotia" published in the *Dalhousie Review* in 1933 and his "Here And Now" article in the *Halifax Daily News* in January 1935 further enhanced the reputation of the Stepsure letters by placing them and their author at the centre of the province's intellectual ferment after the Napoleonic Wars. "Here again Carlyle would have found a hero," wrote Harvey in the former, "and named him King McCulloch."[97]

In 1960 McClelland and Stewart issued *The Stepsure Letters* in the New Canadian Library series. These included the sixteen letters reprinted by Blackadar as *Letters Of Mephibosheth Stepsure*, the letter from Censor published in the *Acadian Recorder* on 24 December 1822, and Stepsure's responses to him published in the *Acadian Recorder* on 8 February and 29 March 1823. The appearance of this edition and its inclusion of John A. Irving's "The Achievement of Thomas McCulloch," Douglas Lochhead's "A Bibliographical Note," and Northrop Frye's influential introduction finally helped to create a sustained critical response to McCulloch and his humour. Donald Stephens' review of *The Stepsure Letters* in *Canadian Literature* in the autumn of 1961 recognized the comic quality of the work,[98] while Fred Cogswell, Vincent Sharman, Beverly Rasporich, Anne Wood, and Stanley McMullin have subsequently responded to its Calvinist overtones.[99] Robin Mathews has linked the Stepsure letters to the novel of the land, and Gwendolyn Davies to the theme of agricultural change; Janice Kulyk Keefer's *Under Eastern Eyes* has explored their concept of community.[100] A number of dissertations have been written on McCulloch, but at the doctoral level Stanley McMullin's "Thomas McCulloch: The Evolution Of A Liberal Mind" is one of the few theses in literature that discuss the Stepsure letters.[101] A general assessment of McCulloch's literary career published by Marjory Whitelaw in an article in *Canadian Literature* in 1976 was followed in 1985 by her monograph *Thomas McCulloch His Life and Times*.[102]

In spite of the fact that in their own time they "set the hale kintra laughin',"[103] the Stepsure letters have received little critical attention as examples of satire and humour. Yet the enduring popularity of these letters is due as much to their comic effects as to their revelation of life in early nineteenth-century Nova Scotia. According to Northrop Frye, McCulloch's humour "is based on a vision of society and is not merely a series of wisecracks on a single theme."[104] Through his dry comments Stepsure exposes the foibles and frailties of the "bustling, bargaining, running about, sort of folks" (CEECT, p. 38) among whom he lives. Thus, Mrs. Shootem finds her marriage to the Captain to be "all song and no supper" (CEECT, p. 151), Mr. Gypsum was not "by any means a professed drunkard" (CEECT, p. 33), Stepsure sold his "spare wheat to Pumpkin, whose family live chiefly upon pies" (CEECT, p. 101), and the occupants of Mrs. Whinge's cap "increased very fast; and at length, like our townsfolk, they became dissatisfied with the country, and began to emigrate" (CEECT, p. 136). As Frye notes, the "tone" of McCulloch's "humour, quiet, observant, deeply conservative in a human sense, has been the prevailing tone of Canadian humour ever since."[105]

Intensifying McCulloch's comedy are the moments of slapstick and burlesque that punctuate Stepsure's narration. In Letter 2 the episode about "Mammoth the boar" is typical in achieving its comic effects by employing sober or Biblical language to describe a pig rolling around with a butter churn on its head. In Letter 17 the dancing feet, overturned tea tables, and "windysome" (CEECT, p. 182) emission of the Sippit-McCackle tea party fall into the category of genuine slapstick and recall the type of eighteenth-century dramatic and scatalogical humour that reminded William Blackwood of Swift. These elements, combined with the mock heroic and burlesque aspects of Stepsure's responses to Censor, reveal the breadth of McCulloch's comic technique and provide a striking contrast in tone to the irony of Stepsure's other letters and to the sober pathos of the story of William.

Nowhere is the relationship between McCulloch's comic style and his satiric intent better demonstrated than in the stock characters who traverse his pages. Again calling upon his eighteenth-century literary background, McCulloch employs type names to depict the humours of characters like Mosey, Trot, Jack Scorem, Mrs. Grumble, Driddle, and Puff. Callibogus, a New England drink of rum and spruce beer, fittingly becomes the name of the merchant who sells West-Indian rum, and authority figures bear such designations as Squire Worthy, Mr. Catchem, and Mr. Holdfast. The evangelicals for whom McCulloch had little respect are appropriately referred to as Yelpit, Shadrach Howl, and Deacon Sharp. Parson Drone, who frequently represents McCulloch's values in the letters, nonetheless falters in Stepsure's eyes when he too readily addresses each problem with a maxim known to every Nova Scotian of the day: *What can't be cured, must be endured: let us have patience* (CEECT, p. 11). Stepsure has no truck with such patient approaches to life.

Yet Mephibosheth Stepsure, as his first name suggests,[106] is a source of double-edged irony and satire in the letters as he, the norm against whom all others are measured at the beginning of the letters, becomes covetous of position, fame, and respectability by the conclusion of Book One. "Even I myself, too, am beginning to think that I possess more dignity than I was formerly aware of," he muses, "and I have a kind of notion, that, when I get myself seated in stile, with a table before me, covered with a green cloth reaching down to the floor, so as to keep my feet out of the way, I shall make a very respectable looking gentleman" (CEECT, p. 188). The signature "Mephibosheth Stepsure Gent." (CEECT, p. 190) at the conclusion of this letter marks the climax in the shift from modesty to vanity that McCulloch had been developing since Letter 8 when Stepsure "resolved to put Mephibosheth Stepsure into the chronicles of our town" (CEECT, p. 75) and relate the story of his successful apprenticeship. The shift in Stepsure's character also reinforces McCulloch's Presbyterian vision of the fallibility of man.

In the second series McCulloch's mock literalness heightens the burlesque of the Parnassus episode in the retort to Censor in Letter 23 and intensifies the bathos of the moment when Mephibosheth reaches for Apollo's "laurels" and finds instead "that my old woman, perceiving that my head, as she thought, was not very busy, had hung upon it a quantity of worsted which she was winding into balls" (CEECT, p. 259). The constant tension between the sublime and the ridiculous not only creates the energy that informs Book Two but also highlights the difference in comic tone between it and the first seventeen letters.

By the conclusion of Book Two there were few social and moral frailties that McCulloch had left unscathed. Prompted initially by the ills of Nova Scotia in the 1820s, the letters nevertheless exposed the propensity for greed and folly that has informed satire on human nature from time immemorial. It is this characteristic of the letters that Blackwood recognized when he praised McCulloch for his "picturesque sketches of life and manners" and when he proposed that they be revised with the same emphasis on "manners, modes of living thinking etc."[107] McCulloch's decision to retain the particularity of place and the Swiftian humour that Blackwood had found so troubling speaks of both the integrity of his satiric intent and his recognition that human nature is defined by neither time nor place. In Mephibosheth Stepsure McCulloch created a satiric gadfly who has survived in Canadian literature as the conscience not only of his town but also of every town from Pictou to Mariposa, Deptford, and Manawaka.

THE TEXT

The aim of this edition of *The Mephibosheth Stepsure Letters* is to provide the reader with a complete and reliable text of the work that earned for Thomas McCulloch his reputation as the founder of Canadian humour. There are several possible ways of organizing and selecting, as well as editing, the letters that relate to Stepsure and his acquaintances, friends, and foes in Nova Scotia in the early 1820s. This edition takes as its basic premise that the Stepsure letters comprise the twenty-five linked letters that appeared in the *Acadian Recorder* from 22 December 1821 to 29 March 1823. They are the twenty-two letters written by Stepsure, including the three that recount the story of William and the two that are Stepsure's replies to the critic Censor, the letter from the unnamed stranger, and the two letters written by Alexander Scantocreesh. In this edition, therefore, the letters are numbered from one to twenty-five and are presented in the order in which they were first read by Nova Scotians in the *Acadian Recorder*. The letter from the unnamed stranger is Letter 7 in the series; the letter from Scantocreesh to the editors of the *Acadian Recorder* that introduces what McCulloch viewed as the second book of the series is Letter 18; and Scantocreesh's letter to Willy Whooshlicat, his childhood friend in Scotland, is Letter 20.

What Mephibosheth Stepsure called "the first book of the chronicles of our town" (CEECT, p. 185), Letters 1 to 17, exists in two authoritative versions. These are the version of each letter published in the *Acadian Recorder* from 22 December 1821 until

11 May 1822 and the version of these newspaper letters that McCulloch copied and sent to Scotland in late 1822 in the form of the holograph manuscript entitled "The Chronicles of our Town." Neither the 1862 Blackadar edition, based on the letters as they had appeared in the *Acadian Recorder*, nor the 1960 McClelland and Stewart edition, based on the Blackadar and, for the three letters relevant to Censor, on the *Acadian Recorder*, carries any textual authority.

The second book of *The Mephibosheth Stepsure Letters* is comprised of the eight letters, two by Alexander Scantocreesh and six by Mephibosheth Stepsure, published in the *Acadian Recorder* between 28 December 1822 and 29 March 1823. Letter 18, Scantocreesh's letter to the editors of the *Acadian Recorder* that prepares the way for the second series of Stepsure's letters, exists only in the form in which it appeared in the newspaper on 22 December 1822. Letter 20, the other letter by Scantocreesh, survives, except for its last three paragraphs, as the introductory letter of "The Chronicles of our Town"; printed from a second manuscript, now apparently no longer extant, it also appeared in the *Acadian Recorder* on 11 January 1823. Both these forms are authoritative.

Of the six letters written by Stepsure in the second book, Letter 19 is extant only in the form in which it was published in the *Acadian Recorder* on 4 January 1823. Letters 23 and 25, Stepsure's answers to Censor, exist in only one authoritative version, that of the *Acadian Recorder* of, respectively, 8 February and 29 March 1823. The other three, Letters 21, 22, and 24, those that describe Stepsure's visit to Halifax and recount the story of William, are available in three authoritative versions: that of the *Acadian Recorder* of 18 January, 25 January, and 15 February 1823; that of the holograph manuscript of "William," except where leaves of this manuscript are missing; and that of *Colonial Gleanings*, printed from the manuscript and published by William Oliphant in Edinburgh in January 1826. McCulloch prepared the manuscript with the intention of having "William" published as a discrete short story; its opening, therefore, has been revised to make it independent of its context in the Stepsure letters in the *Acadian Recorder*.

In this edition of *The Mephibosheth Stepsure Letters* the copy-text for Letters 1 to 17 is the holograph manuscript of "The Chronicles of our Town." Although it is not the original manuscript (now apparently lost) of the letters that McCulloch sent to the *Acadian Recorder* in 1821-22, "The Chronicles of our Town" contains the version of the letters that McCulloch "corrected and copied" from the newspaper.[108] Between the two versions there are substantial differences in words and phrases, and some sentences have been rewritten in the manuscript. These changes, however, alter meaning very little, and they do not reflect a different intention on the part of McCulloch. The accidentals—especially spelling and punctuation—are significantly different in the two versions, with the manuscript revealing those of McCulloch. The degree to which McCulloch felt these to be important is illustrated in his comment to George Young that until he "began to copy" the letters from the newspaper, he "had not the least conception that they were so inaccurately printed."[109] Because the manuscript contains both McCulloch's revisions and his accidentals, it is the most appropriate choice for the copy-text for the first seventeen letters of *The Mephibosheth Stepsure Letters*. The copy-text for Letter 20, Scantocreesh's letter to Whooshlicat, is also the version of this letter in "The Chronicles of our Town"; the *Acadian Recorder* is the copy-text for the last three paragraphs of this letter that are missing from the manuscript.

The copy-text for the story of "William" in Letters 21, 22, and 24 is the incomplete holograph manuscript that contains the story. Like "The Chronicles of our Town" it is not the original manuscript (now also apparently lost) that McCulloch sent to the *Acadian Recorder*, but the copy of the newspaper version that McCulloch prepared some time after the story appeared in the *Acadian Recorder* originally for submission to the *Edinburgh Christian Instructor* although this intention was never carried out. Like "The Chronicles of our Town" this manuscript reveals

McCulloch's typical habits of punctuation and spelling. This manuscript was the copy for the version of "William" published in *Colonial Gleanings* in 1826. This printed version, despite the difference in its accidentals from those of the manuscript, is, therefore, the copy-text for the parts of the story in Letters 21 and 22 that are missing in the manuscript.

The first eight paragraphs of Letter 21, which deal with Stepsure's journey to Halifax and introduce the story of William, and the introductory passages in each of Letters 22 and 24 are printed from the *Acadian Recorder*. The copy-text for each of Letter 18, Scantocreesh's letter to the editors of the *Acadian Recorder*, Letter 19, Stepsure's first letter in his second series of letters, and Letters 23 and 25, his replies to Censor, is also the *Acadian Recorder*.

Because McCulloch's handwriting is fairly large and clear, the transcription of his manuscripts posed relatively few difficulties. There were some, however. McCulloch used, for example, the long "s," and he began each line of a quotation with opening quotation marks. In this edition of *The Mephibosheth Stepsure Letters* every "s" has been printed in the conventional twentieth-century way, and quotation marks that do not indicate the beginning or end of a quotation have been omitted.

Certain characteristics of McCulloch's handwriting and punctuation also sometimes required interpretation. His uncrossed "t" often resembles his "l," and his undotted "i" his "e." The context usually made clear the word that McCulloch intended, and other examples of the word in the manuscripts confirmed its spelling. One particularly difficult word to decipher, however, was "actively" or "activity" in the phrase "Arouse actively (or activity) to labour"[110] in Letter 13; because "activity" makes better sense in the context of Parson Drone's sermon, this word has been printed in the CEECT edition (CEECT, p. 139). An inconsistency in the amount of space left between words posed a problem if two words could be written as a compound word. If another example of the same possible compound word was found in the manuscripts, then a resolution was based on it; if all the representations of the word in the manuscripts were ambiguous, or if the word appeared only once, then the word was entered according to what seemed its most conventional representation. In the manuscripts italics were indicated by the word or passage intended to be italicized being either underlined or written in a slightly different handwriting, and a line-end hyphen was signalled either by using a hyphen that resembles an equal sign or by slightly extending the last letter to appear at the end of a line. In the CEECT transcription of these manuscripts both forms of italics and line-end hyphens have been accepted; in this edition, however, italics and line-end hyphens are printed conventionally. In a few places in both manuscripts a mark of punctuation remains visible although an elongated ink smudge running down the page from it indicates that the intention was to erase it. These marks have not been printed in the CEECT edition.

During the copying of the first book of letters McCulloch occasionally miswrote a letter or word, changed his mind about a word or phrase, or omitted a letter or word. Intending to emend the passage, he either crossed out what was wrong and entered what was correct beside, above, or below, or indicated, usually with an "x," what should be added. These revisions, all entered in ink on the manuscript, have been accepted in the CEECT edition as the reading in the copy-text since they represent the text that McCulloch intended to have published at the time that he first sent the manuscript to Scotland. The variants among these changes that affect meaning are listed in "Variants in the Manuscript Copy-texts" in the concluding apparatus of this edition. In a few places in "The Chronicles of our Town" there are other alterations and additions in pencil in a hand that is not McCulloch's. In this edition these marks have not been considered either as part of the copy-text or as a source of emendation. They are discussed briefly in the description of "The Chronicles of our Town" manuscript in "Description of Authoritative Versions of the Work."

In the "William" manuscript there are revisions by McCulloch similar to those in "The Chronicles of our Town." These changes, made as he prepared "William" for submission to a publisher, have been accepted in the CEECT edition as the author's final intended reading in the copy-text. The variants among these changes that affect meaning are listed in "Variants in the Manuscript Copy-texts." The revisions that were added to the manuscript by the Oliphant editors and by McCulloch in response to their suggestions are recorded in the "Historical Collation" in the concluding apparatus. Their use as a source of emendation of the copy-text is discussed in the appropriate place in this part of the introduction.

Because of the clarity of McCulloch's handwriting and the condition of the manuscript of "The Chronicles of our Town," relatively few emendations have been made in this edition of *The Mephibosheth Stepsure Letters* to the copy-text of Letters 1 to 17. Copying these letters from the *Acadian Recorder*, McCulloch made a few errors repeatedly. He copied words twice, especially if the first use of the word occurred at the end of a line or a page. Thus, in Letter 1, for example, he wrote of "a habit of of running about" ("Chronicles," *I* [1ᵛ]). Because he may have added punctuation after he had written out a paragraph, a page, or even a letter, sometimes he omitted a period at the end of a sentence, or he misplaced a mark of punctuation within a sentence. In Letter 3, for instance, the statement that the cure for Mr. Gypsum's nose was "worse than the disease" ("Chronicles," II [7ʳ]) does not end with the required period. When McCulloch split a word at the end of a line, he occasionally did not indicate that it should be hyphenated. In Letter 4, for example, the "there/ fore" before "he determined" ("Chronicles," III [5ʳ]) was not hyphenated in either of the two methods McCulloch habitually used. Sometimes McCulloch supplied a word that was close to that of the newspaper but did not fit the context of what he was copying. In Letter 5, for instance, describing the conversation between Parson Drone and the stranger, McCulloch wrote that "They seemed to me to take very learnedly" ("Chronicles," IV [5ᵛ]) although the correct verb was obviously the "talk"[111] printed in the *Acadian*

Recorder. On occasion McCulloch would omit a letter in a word or omit a word entirely. In Letter 8, thus, he wrote "Santocreesh" ("Chronicles," VI [4ʳ]) instead of "Scantocreesh" when he named Alexander's son Jock, and in Letter 13, announcing Mrs. Whinge's belief that "for a married woman to have her head uncovered" was "a grievous sin" (CEECT, p. 136), McCulloch left out the word "sin" ("Chronicles," X [2ᵛ]). In order to correct these mistakes in the manuscript, the reading in the *Acadian Recorder* has been followed.

The last leaf of the manuscript of "The Chronicles of our Town" is torn, and, as a result, a word and part of the following word are missing. At this place in the *Acadian Recorder* Letter 17 reads "to make themselves more angry still,"[112] but in the manuscript the reading is "to keep it up till they [   ]ry angry" ("Chronicles," XIII [8ʳ]). Since the reading in the *Acadian Recorder* does not fit in this revised passage, the editor has supplied the obviously intended "are ve" so that in the CEECT edition Letter 17 reads at this place "to keep it up till they are very angry" (CEECT, pp. 189-90).

For the purpose of emendation Letter 20 is unique in *The Mephibosheth Stepsure Letters*. Its extant manuscript version was prepared by McCulloch for inclusion in "The Chronicles of our Town" some time before November 1822 when he had this manuscript ready for sending to Scotland. At some point McCulloch obviously prepared a second manuscript of Alexander Scantocreesh's letter to Willy Whooshlicat, from which the *Acadian Recorder* printed the version that it published on 11 January 1823. The relationship between the version of Letter 20 in the extant manuscript and that in the lost manuscript used by the newspaper, however, cannot now be established, and, therefore, the substantive differences between the text of this letter in the extant manuscript and in the *Acadian Recorder* cannot be definitively explained. These differences, nevertheless, include reversals of phrases, additions and deletions of words, phrases, and an occasional sentence, and rewritten sentences—changes, in other words, that are typical of those McCulloch made when he recopied Letters 1 to 17 from the *Acadian Recorder*. The emendations made to the manuscript copy-text in the CEECT edition, therefore, are based on the assumptions that the version of the letter prepared for the newspaper was probably copied from the version sent to Scotland and that, where the newspaper version differs substantially from the manuscript version, the text of Letter 20 in the *Acadian Recorder* probably represents revisions made by McCulloch at some time before he sent this Scantocreesh letter to the newspaper. In emending the copy-text of Letter 20, then, all the revised readings in the *Acadian Recorder* text have been incorporated into the CEECT edition. In the last three paragraphs of the letter, which exist uniquely in the newspaper, "kintta's" has been corrected to "kintra's" (CEECT, p. 224).

Because McCulloch worked closely with Oliphant during the editing of "William" for its appearance in *Colonial Gleanings*, the changes that McCulloch obviously approved in the text of "William" that he submitted to Oliphant and that appeared in *Colonial Gleanings* have been incorporated into the text of the story of William in Letters 21, 22, and 24 in the CEECT edition where the copy-text is the "William" manuscript. Most of these revisions involve a change of word or phrase only. The most interesting occur when, in reviewing the proposed editorial changes to his manuscript, McCulloch sometimes decided that he did not like them and, therefore, made further revisions. For example, describing William's initial disgust at the workmen's habit of drinking on the job, McCulloch had originally written, "but such was his view of it, that, in his mind, the fear of temptation never once existed." The phrase "his view of it" was changed by Oliphant to "his horror at it"; this phrase was in turn revised by McCulloch to "his abhorrence of it."[113] In another instance, discussing the state of the business that William acquired from his father-in-law, McCulloch wrote that "a final settlement showed, that, where punctuality in business is wanting, the gain is gone." The clause "the gain is gone" was altered by the publisher to "the profits cannot be expected" and then changed by McCulloch to "the profits cannot be secured" ("William," pp. 25-26).

The changes that were made to "William" during its printing and proofreading have also been incorporated from the text of "William" in *Colonial Gleanings* into the text of the story of "William" in the CEECT edition where the copy-text is the "William" manuscript. Obvious errors in the copy-text have also been corrected from the Oliphant publication. In Letter 21, for example, the word "jealous" in the phrase "jealous care of his improvements" ("William," p. 4) in the manuscript has been replaced by "zealous" (CEECT, p. 231), the word used in the Oliphant version that reflects McCulloch's final revision of the story of "William." The final "ion" in "destruction" (CEECT, p. 232), omitted in the manuscript ("William," p. 6), has been added. The obviously wrong "gentlemen" ("William," p. 7) in the phrase "This gentleman" (CEECT, p. 233) has been corrected. In Letter 22 the few substantive revisions that McCulloch made to the Oliphant version have been accepted, and an ampersand ("William," p. 23) has been emended to "and" (CEECT, p. 245). In Letter 24, the conclusion to the story of "William," five corrections have been incorporated into the copy-text from the Oliphant version. Thus, for example, "women" ("William," p. 26) has been altered to "woman" in the phrase "an agreeable young woman" (CEECT, p. 262); and "conconduct" ("William," p. 31) has been changed to "conduct" (CEECT, p. 266). In addition, four substantive revisions McCulloch made in the Oliphant version have been accepted. In the phrase "in the possession" ("William," p. 29) "the" has been omitted (CEECT, p. 264); "the tavern" ("William," p. 31) has been changed to "a tavern" (CEECT, p. 266); and in the letter of William's father "chastening" ("William," p. 37) has been altered to "chastenings" (CEECT, p. 271) in the phrase "the chastenings of the Lord," and "heart clings" ("William," p. 39) has become "hearts cling" (CEECT, p. 272).

In Letters 21 and 22 in the CEECT edition where the copy-text for the story of William is the Oliphant edition, it has been emended to bring its spelling, hyphenation, and capitalization into line with McCulloch's rendering of Stepsure's usage. Thus, in Letter 21 the passage "from abroad" to "in the way of evil" (CEECT, pp. 234-35), which consists of the three complete and two partial paragraphs that are missing in the manuscript, "mean time," "great grandfather," "reflexion," and "bible" appear in the CEECT edition. Five similar emendations have been incorporated into the text of Letter 22 in the passages where the copy-text is the Oliphant version, that is, from "In a religiously educated young man" to "and he thought" (CEECT, pp. 237-38), and from "formed without a knowledge" to "but, where" (CEECT, pp. 241-43). In these sections "great-grandfather"[114] has been changed to "great grandfather" twice (CEECT, pp. 238 and 242), "Sabbath" (Oliphant, pp. 30 and 31) to "sabbath" twice (CEECT, p. 242), and "Sunday" (Oliphant, p. 30) to "sunday" once (CEECT, p. 242) in order to make these words reflect McCulloch's habitual representation of Stepsure's usage.

Where the *Acadian Recorder* is the copy-text, emendations have been confined to corrections of compositorial errors and to changes to render Stepsure's spelling consistent with that of the manuscript. Thus, in Letter 18 Alexander Scantocreesh's phrase "the stet o' our toon" (CEECT, p. 197), set as "the stet o' our loon,"[115] has been corrected. In this letter, as well as sometimes picking up the wrong piece of type, the compositor, perhaps following McCulloch's manuscript, occasionally doubled a word, omitted a period at the end of a sentence, and dropped a hyphen at the end of a line. All these identifiable mistakes have also been corrected. Otherwise, in spite of Scantocreesh's admission that he is "desperat dowre at the ditin', and nae warlock at the spellin'" (CEECT, p. 197), McCulloch's rendering of the Scotsman's composition and spelling has been accepted. Errors made by the newspaper's compositor have also been corrected in the unique version of Letter 19. For example, in the CEECT edition of this letter dropped punctuation has been added, and each word divided without a hyphen at the end of a line in the *Acadian Recorder* has been emended to a single word. In the first eight paragraphs of Letter 21, where the copy-text is the *Acadian Recorder*,[116] an "a" set instead of an "e" in "were" and a missing hyphen in each of two single words split at the end of a line have been corrected. In Letter 19 the spelling of "ne'er do well," "connexion," and "expence" has been adjusted to reflect McCulloch's habitual representation of Stepsure's orthography, as has the spelling of "expence" and "ne'er do well" in Letter 21.

In both Letters 23 and 25 the bulk of the emendations made in the CEECT edition to the *Acadian Recorder* copy-text have to do with corrections of such obvious errors as a repeated word, a missing hyphen at the end of a line, a dropped period or a comma instead of a period at the end of a sentence, and a dropped or misspelled word. Thus, for example, in Letter 23[117] "heekling" has been changed to "heckling" (CEECT, p. 246) in the phrase "the fearful heckling," and "them" to "theme" (CEECT, p. 246) in the phrase "a serious sort of theme." In Letter 25[118] a period has been added at the end of the sentence "The battle of the pigs . . . exhibits brilliant bursts of genius." (CEECT, p. 278). In both letters "Chronicles," referring to "the chronicles" of Stepsure's town, has been emended to a lower-case word each of the three times it is used in this context (CEECT, pp. 251, 256, and 277). In Letter 23 "Parson" in the phrase "parson Drone's" (CEECT, p. 256) and "Sabbath" in the phrase "keep the sabbath" (CEECT, p. 247), and in Letter 25 "judgement" in the phrase "profundity of judgment" (CEECT, p. 278) have been changed to reflect McCulloch's consistent rendering of Stepsure's spelling of the word.

The address, salutation, and signature of each letter have been emended as necessary to make these aspects of the letters as consistent as possible. Each of these changes, as well as those that have to do with the renumbering of the letters, is listed in "Emendations in Copy-text" in the concluding apparatus. The number of each letter has been printed in Arabic and without a period after it; these changes are also recorded in "Emendations in Copy-text."

In the preparation of this scholarly edition each version of the letters was examined, and a bibliographical analysis was under-taken of each of the books that contained parts of the work. Each version of the letters, except the 1960 edition of *The Stepsure Letters*, was also reproduced for CEECT in the most appropriate way. A photocopy was made by the Public Archives of Nova Scotia of "The Chronicles of our Town" manuscript and the "William" manuscript. A photocopy of each of the letters in the *Acadian Recorder* was produced from the Canadian Library Asso-ciation's microfilm of the newspaper. A photocopy of "William" from *Colonial Gleanings* was provided by Dalhousie University Library. The Public Archives of Nova Scotia provided CEECT with a photocopy of their copy of *Letters Of Mephibosheth Stepsure*. Three copies of *Letters Of Mephibosheth Stepsure*, two loaned by Acadia University (A 819.7 M131 23148 John D. Logan Collec-tion, and A 819.7 M131 32569) and one by Mount Allison Uni-versity (Macleod Collection), were microfilmed for CEECT. Photocopies made from these microfilms, along with the pho-tocopies of the other versions, were used at all the appropriate stages in the establishment and verification of the text of the CEECT edition of *The Mephibosheth Stepsure Letters*.

Both manuscripts were entered on the computer twice, each time by a different typist, and the two versions were proofed by means of a computer program designed to compare one typist's text with the other's. The proofed computer version of each manuscript was then read against the actual manuscript to verify further the accuracy of the former version. The *Acadian Recorder* letters and the *Colonial Gleanings'* version of "William" were entered, proofed, and perfected in a similar manner.

To establish an ideal copy and to identify possible states of *Letters Of Mephibosheth Stepsure*, an oral collation and a light-table collation, both using the four photocopies of *Letters Of Mephibosheth Stepsure*, were performed. One copy of *Letters Of Mephibosheth Stepsure* (NSWA A 819.7 M131 32569) was also entered twice on the computer, and the two versions were then proofed by means of the comparison computer program.

Two collations were done by means of the computer. The first involved Letters 1 to 17 only. It used the *Acadian Recorder* as the standard of comparison, and "The Chronicles of our Town" manuscript and *Letters Of Mephibosheth Stepsure* as comparison texts. It proved that *Letters Of Mephibosheth Stepsure* was set from the *Acadian Recorder* and therefore carried no authority. The second collation included all the letters. The appropriate manuscript, where it existed, was the standard of comparison. The comparison text for Letters 1 to 17 and Letter 20 was the *Acadian Recorder*. For the "William" story the comparison texts were the *Acadian Recorder* and *Colonial Gleanings*. A record of the differences that affect meaning in these various versions is included in the "Historical Collation" in the concluding apparatus. The results of all the collations performed on the various versions of the Stepsure letters are available at the Centre for Editing Early Canadian Texts.

Because the establishment of the critically-edited text of *The Mephibosheth Stepsure Letters* involved the transcription of the material from two holograph manuscripts and the often poorly-inked *Acadian Recorder*, the text of the CEECT edition and its supporting apparatus were proofread many times and in various ways during their preparation. Before the magnetic tape of the CEECT edition was sent to the printer, its contents were also proofread, and the CEECT text of each letter in *The Mephibosheth Stepsure Letters* was frequently compared to its copy-text so that the emendations made to it could be verified. The CEECT edition was also proofread at each stage of its printing. The result of this process is not only an accurate text but also a text that presents for the first time McCulloch's influential work in a complete and authoritative form.

ENDNOTES TO INTRODUCTION

1   H. Northrop Frye, "Introduction," in *The Stepsure Letters* (Toronto: McClelland and Stewart, 1960), p. iii. In this, and in all other quotations included in this introduction and in the explanatory notes, the grammar, punctuation, and spelling of the original have been retained except

in a few cases where the style of the passage makes its sense difficult to comprehend. In these instances the missing letter or word is supplied in a square bracket. When the first letter of a word in the title of a work cited is capitalized, this initial capitalization has been retained.

2 "The Club," *Novascotian*, 15 May 1828, p. 161.

3 Frye, p. ix.

4 William McCulloch, *Life Of Thomas McCulloch, D.D. Pictou* (Truro, [1920]), p. 7. For a recent biography of McCulloch see *DCB*, Vol. 7, pp. 529-41.

5 The Covenanters were originally the subscribers to the National Covenant of 1638 and the Solemn League and Covenant of 1643. These Covenants bound Presbyterian Scots together against royal attempts to impose episcopal church government and a new liturgy on the nation. Around 1650 the supporters of the National Covenant split into two groups, the Moderate Resolutioners and the more extreme Protestors or Remonstrants. When the episcopacy was returned in 1661, the Protestors formed the core of Coventicler or Covenanting opposition. The period between 1660 and 1688 was one of uprising, persecution, and bloodshed as the British government began a policy of breaking this opposition. Reprisals were particularly harsh in southwest Scotland. See Ian B. Cowan, *The Scottish Covenanters 1660-1688* (London: Victor Gollancz, 1976).

6 Bruce's theological classes in "the Old Light Antiburgher Hall" at Whitburn have been described in the following way:

> "There was at Whitburn (says an old student) generally only one meeting a-day, and the hour of meeting was twelve o'clock. The business of each week was as follows. On Monday, a miscellaneous lecture by the Professor; on Tuesday, discourses by the students; on Wednesday, a lecture by the Professor on the system,—the system which he used was Marckii Medulla. On Thursday, examination on the system; on Friday, discourses by the students; on Saturday, a confessional lecture, together with conference on some practical subject stated by the Professor. The duration of the session was eight weeks. Professor Bruce was in many respects highly qualified, and by every student greatly venerated. His examinations and criticisms were very judicious and useful, and himself very pious and amiable."

See David Scott, *Annals And Statistics Of The Original Secession Church* (Edinburgh: Andrew Elliot, 1886), p. 605.

7 On 28 December 1743, following the tradition of their Covenanting ancestors, the Original Seceders of the Secessionist Church renewed the National Covenant of 1638 and the Solemn League and Covenant of 1643. They thus reaffirmed the moral and religious principles of their ancestors, including the belief that Christ, not the King or a bishop, was the head of the church. See Scott, pp. 1-12.

8 William McCulloch, p. 16.

9   Ibid., p. 18.

10   Ibid., p. 19.

11   James Robertson, *History Of The Mission Of The Secession Church To Nova Scotia And Prince Edward Island From Its Commencement In 1765* (Edinburgh: Johnstone, 1847), p. 219. Jotham Blanchard, a Pictou lawyer and close ally of McCulloch, was one of the first graduates of Pictou Academy. See *DCB*, Vol. 7, pp. 81-85.

12   PANS, MP, MG100, Vol. 181, No. 22, ALS, Thomas McCulloch to Rev. Mr. Culbertson, 10 July 1816. In his letters McCulloch often omitted the period at the end of a sentence; he left instead a large space between the end of one sentence and the beginning of another. In the transcription of quotations from these letters in the introduction these spaces have been retained.

13   PANS, MP, MG1, Vol. 553, No. 14, ALS, Thomas McCulloch to John Mitchell, 24 November 1821. The Rev. Dr. John Mitchell (1768-1844) was the son of the Rev. Andrew Mitchell, Secessionist minister at Beith. A graduate of the University of Glasgow, John Mitchell was ordained to the Secession church in 1793 and elected Professor of Biblical Criticism by the United Associate Synod in 1825. He served the Secessionist congregation in Anderston and then Wellington Street, Glasgow, for fifty years. He was the author of a number of religious publications. In 1807 Mitchell received an honorary D.D. from Princeton College, New Jersey; the University of Glasgow confirmed the same degree thirty years later.

14   PANS, MP, MG1, Vol. 553, No. 36, ALS, Thomas McCulloch to James Mitchell, 5 July 1828. James Mitchell, a lawyer, was John Mitchell's son.

15   PANS, MP, MG1, Vol. 553, No. 14, ALS, Thomas McCulloch to John Mitchell, 24 November 1821.

16   George Patterson, *A History of the County Of Pictou Nova Scotia* (1877; rpt. Belleville: Mika Studio, 1972), p. 267.

17   George Patterson, *Memoir Of The Rev. James MacGregor, D.D.* (Philadelphia: Joseph M. Wilson, 1859), p. 370.

18   John Young, *The Letters Of Agricola On The Principles Of Vegetation And Tillage, Written For Nova Scotia, And Published First In The Acadian Recorder* (Halifax: Printed by Holland & Co., 1822), pp. XII-XIII. For John Young see *DCB*, Vol. 7, pp. 930-35.

19   A first-hand account of the depressed conditions in Scotland, "owing to the failure of trade," is contained in a letter written by Thomas McCulloch's brother-in-law, the Rev. James Walker. See William McCulloch, pp. 13-14.

For a description of the conditions facing many immigrants when they arrived in Nova Scotia, see a letter "TO THE EDITOR OF THE RECORDER," *Acadian Recorder*, 26 July 1817, p. [2]. Signed "A RESIDENT MECHANIC," the letter, on the subject of "Emigration into this Province," announces that "in the course of a few weeks not less than *two thousand five hundred and eight* Strangers will arrive amongst us," and notes:

> What Farmers there are, and of others *that would be Farmers*, the number is comparatively small, they have arrived at a season when it is almost too late to obtain employment as husbandmen, much less to take advantageous possession of that "Grant of Land" they were led to believe would be so easily obtained upon their arrival.—Thus situated, it is but rational to presume, nearly the whole must become, in the winter season, a burthen upon the community; for at present, scores are obliged to sleep on the wharves—without a home—without shelter—without a friend, and without money.

20 *A History of the County Of Pictou Nova Scotia*, pp. 293-95.
21 Ibid., p. 295.
22 Young, pp. IX-X.
23 *The Dalhousie Journals*, ed. Marjory Whitelaw (Ottawa: Oberon Press, 1978), Vol. 1, p. 73.
24 PANS, MP, MG1, Vol. 793, No. 69, ALS, Thomas McCulloch to Simon Bradstreet Robie, 9 February 1822.
25 *Acadian Recorder*, 16 February 1822, p. [3]. In 1822 the editors of the *Acadian Recorder* were Anthony Henry Holland, Philip John Holland, and Edward A. Moody; see *DCB*, Vol. 6, pp. 321-23.
26 Ibid., 2 March 1822, p. [3].
27 Ibid., 6 April 1822, p. [3].
28 Ibid., 11 May 1822, p. [3].
29 Ibid., p. [2].
30 Ibid., 2 November 1822, p. [2].
31 Ibid.
32 "To the Editors of the Accaudian Recorder," *Acadian Recorder*, 28 December 1822, p. [2]; rpt. *The Mephibosheth Stepsure Letters*, ed. Gwendolyn Davies (Ottawa: Carleton University Press, 1990), p. 202. All further references to this edition are cited in the body of the text as (CEECT, p. 000).
33 For a discussion of Irving and his contribution to the intellectual life of Nova Scotia, see Gwendolyn Davies, "James Irving: Literature and Libel in Early Nova Scotia," *Essays on Canadian Writing*, No. 29 (1984), pp. 48-65.
34 *Acadian Recorder*, 21 December 1822, p. [2].
35 Ibid., 28 December 1822, p. [2]; rpt. CEECT, pp. 431-35.
36 Ibid., 4 January 1823, p. [2].
37 Ibid., 18 January 1823, p. [3].
38 Ibid., 1 February 1823, p. [2].
39 *Free Press*, 11 February 1823, p. 23.
40 "To Correspondents," *Free Press*, 4 March 1823, p. 29.

41 *Free Press*, 11 March 1823, p. [39]. The "Chief Justice" was most likely Richard Alexander Tucker. Appointed chief justice of Newfoundland in October 1822, he visited Halifax in December of the same year. The arrival "yesterday" of "Richard A. Tucker Esq. Chief Justice for the Island of Newfoundland; Mrs. Tucker, and family" was noted in the *Weekly Chronicle* on 13 December 1822. His departure with "Mrs. Tucker, and family" was announced in the *Acadian Recorder* on 21 December 1822. See *DCB*, Vol. 9, pp. 794-95, *Weekly Chronicle*, 13 December 1822, p. [3], and *Acadian Recorder*, 21 December 1822, p. [3].
42 *Free Press*, 11 March 1823, p. [39].
43 Ibid. For Edmund Ward see *DCB*, Vol. 8, pp. 922-23.
44 *Acadian Recorder*, 22 March 1823, p. [2]; rpt. CEECT, pp. 435-37.
45 *Acadian Recorder*, 29 March 1823, p. [2]; rpt. CEECT, p. 275.
46 *Acadian Recorder*, 2 November 1822, p. [2].
47 Thomas McCulloch, *A Memorial From The Committee Of Missions Of The Presbyterian Church Of Nova Scotia, To The Glasgow Society For Promoting The Religious Interests Of The Scottish Settlers In British North America* (Edinburgh: Oliver & Boyd, 1826), p. 7.
48 *Acadian Recorder*, 11 May 1822, p. [3].
49 Ibid., 24 January 1818, p. [2], 28 February 1818, p. [2], and 25 April 1818, p. [2].
50 D. C. Harvey, "The Intellectual Awakening of Nova Scotia," *Dalhousie Review*, 13 (1933), 18.
51 *Free Press*, 20 June 1820, p. 128.
52 *Weekly Chronicle*, 21 December 1821, p. [1].
53 *Acadian Recorder*, 7 July 1821, p. [2], and 14 July 1821, p. [2].
54 Ibid., 18 August 1821, p. [4]; 25 August 1821, p. [1]; 8 September 1821, p. [1]; 15 September 1821, p. [1]; 20 October 1821, p. [1]; 3 November 1821, p. [1]; 24 November 1821, p. [1]; 1 December 1821, p. [1]; 15 December 1821, p. [1]; 22 December 1821, p. [1]; and 29 December 1821, p. [1].
55 John Galt, *Annals Of The Parish Or The Chronicle Of Dalmailing . . .* (London: Oxford University Press, 1967), p. [201].
56 Mount Allison University Archives, Longworth Manuscripts (Scrapbook), 1-200, ALS, D. McCurdy to Jane, 2 March 1872.
57 *Halifax Journal*, 6 May 1822, p. [2], and 15 May 1822, p. [2].
58 Ibid., 29 April 1822, p. [2].
59 *Acadian Recorder*, 11 May 1822, p. [2].
60 Ibid., 13 July 1822, p. [4].
61 *Halifax Journal*, 20 January 1823, p. [3].
62 *Acadian Recorder*, 1 January 1825, p. [4]; 15 January 1825, p. [2]; 22 January 1825, p. [2]; 29 January 1825, p. [4]; 9 April 1825, p. [4]; 2 July 1825, p. [4]; 13 August 1825, p. [2]; 3 September 1825, p. [2]; 1 October 1825, p. [2]; 8 October 1825, p. [4]; 17 December 1825, p. [4]; 14 January 1826, p. [4]; and 17 June 1826, p. [4].
63 Ibid., 18 February 1826, p. [2].
64 *Novascotian*, 15 May 1828, p. 161.

65 *Acadian Recorder*, 22 March 1823, p. [2].
66 William McCulloch, p. 73.
67 PANS, MP, MG1, Vol. 793, No. 69, ALS, Thomas McCulloch to Simon Bradstreet Robie, 9 February 1822.
68 PANS, MP, MG1, Vol. 554, No. 18, ALS, Thomas McCulloch to George Young, 17 July 1822.
69 PANS, MP, MG1, Vol. 555, No. 82.
70 PANS, MP, MG1, Vol. 553, No. 18, ALS, Thomas McCulloch to John Mitchell, 10 November 1822. John Mitchell's brother was Andrew Mitchell, a writer by profession, who also lived in Glasgow. The "Governor" was most likely Sir James Kempt, who succeeded Lord Dalhousie as lieutenant governor of Nova Scotia.
71 PANS, MP, MG1, Vol. 553, No. 20, ALS, Thomas McCulloch to John Mitchell, 31 May 1824.
72 PANS, MP, MG1, Vol. 555, No. 53.
73 PANS, MP, MG1, Vol. 555, No. 48.
74 PANS, MP, MG1, Vol. 553, No. 58, ALS, Thomas McCulloch to James Mitchell, 29 December 1833.
75 PANS, MP, MG1, Vol. 555, No. 46, ALS, William Oliphant to Thomas McCulloch, 1 January 1826.
76 *"Colonial Gleanings; or, William and Melville," Edinburgh Theological Magazine*, 1 (1826), 136.
77 "ACADIAN LITERATURE," *Novascotian*, 21 September 1826, p. [1].
78 PANS, MP, MG1, Vol. 553, No. 34, ALS, Thomas McCulloch to James Mitchell, 29 [?] June 1828.
79 PANS, MP, MG1, Vol. 553, No. 36, ALS, Thomas McCulloch to James Mitchell, 5 July 1828.
80 PANS, MP, MG1, Vol. 553, No. 38, ALS, Thomas McCulloch to James Mitchell, 29 December 1828.
81 NLS, Blackwoods Letter-books, Acc. 5643/B8, ALS, William Blackwood to John Mitchell, 15 December 1828, pp. 133-37.
82 PANS, MP, MG1, Vol. 553, No. 39, ALS, Thomas McCulloch to James Mitchell, 18 May 1829.
83 PANS, MP, MG1, Vol. 553, No. 42, ALS, Thomas McCulloch to James Mitchell, 4 September 1829.
84 PANS, MP, MG1, Vol. 553, No. 46, ALS, Thomas McCulloch to James Mitchell, 3 December 1829.
85 NLS, Blackwoods Letter-books, Acc. 5643/B8, ALS, William Blackwood to John Mitchell, 31 December 1829, pp. 480-83.
86 P. H. Scott, *John Galt* (Edinburgh: Scottish Academic Press, 1985), pp. 72-73.
87 *Novascotian*, 15 May 1828, p. 161.
88 PANS, MP, MG1, Vol. 553, No. 105, ALS, Jotham Blanchard to Thomas McCulloch, 30 September 1831.
89 PANS, MP, MG1, Vol. 553, No. 58, ALS, Thomas McCulloch to James Mitchell, 29 December 1833.
90 *Acadian Recorder*, 6 April 1833, p. [1]. The McCulloch Papers con-

tain a copy of this newspaper. The paper has the handwritten name "Rev. Dr. McCulloch" across the top and in William McCulloch's hand is written "Father, 1833." See PANS, MP, MG1, Vol. 550, No. 84.

91 PANS, MP, MG1, Vol. 553, No. 58, ALS, Thomas McCulloch to James Mitchell, 29 December 1833.

92 PANS, MP, MG1, Vol. 553, No. 60, ALS, Thomas McCulloch to John Mitchell, 18 July 1834.

93 PANS, MP, MG1, Vol. 553, No. 62, ALS, Thomas McCulloch to James Mitchell, 6 November 1834.

94 "STEPSURE'S LETTERS," *Acadian Recorder*, 21 June 1862, p. [2].

95 *Acadian Recorder*, 21 June 1862, p. [3].

96 V.L.O. Chittick, *Thomas Chandler Haliburton ("Sam Slick") A Study in Provincial Toryism* (1924; rpt. New York: AMS Press, 1966), pp. 378-79.

97 "The Intellectual Awakening of Nova Scotia," *Dalhousie Review*, 13 (1933), 14.

98 "Past Or Permanent," *Canadian Literature*, No. 10 (1961), pp. 83-84.

99 See Fred Cogswell, "Haliburton," in *Literary History Of Canada*, ed. Carl F. Klinck (Toronto: University of Toronto Press, 1965), pp. 92-101; Vincent Sharman, "Thomas McCulloch's Stepsure: The Relentless Presbyterian," *Dalhousie Review* 52 (1972-73), 618-25; Beverly Rasporich, "The New Eden Dream: The Source Of Canadian Humour: McCulloch, Haliburton, And Leacock," *Studies in Canadian Literature*, 7 (1982), 227-40; B. Anne Wood, "The Significance of Calvinism in The Educational Vision of Thomas McCulloch," *Vitae Scholasticae*, 4 (1985), 15-30; and Stanley E. McMullin, "In Search of the Liberal Mind: Thomas McCulloch and the Impulse to Action," *Journal of Canadian Studies*, 23 (1988), 68-85.

100 See Robin Mathews, "*The Stepsure Letters*: Puritanism And The Novel Of The Land," *Studies in Canadian Literature*, 7 (1982), 127-38; Gwendolyn Davies, " 'A Past Of Orchards': Rural Change In Maritime Literature Before Confederation," in *The Red Jeep and other landscapes*, ed. Peter Thomas (Fredericton: Goose Lane Editions, 1987), pp. [35]-43; and Janice Kulyk Keefer, *Under Eastern Eyes* (Toronto: University of Toronto Press, 1987), pp. 39-45 and 67-68.

101 Dalhousie University 1975.

102 See "Thomas McCulloch," *Canadian Literature*, No. 68-69 (1976), pp. 138-47, and *Thomas McCulloch His Life and Times* (Halifax: Nova Scotia Museum, 1985).

103 "The Club," *Novascotian*, 15 May 1828, p. 161.

104 Frye, p. ix.

105 Ibid.

106 After Saul fell to David on Mount Gilboa, the latter spared Mephibosheth, Saul's lame grandson, restored the estates of Saul to him, and maintained him as a guest at his table. David's distrust of Mephibosheth's ambitions, however, eventually forced him to divide Saul's territory between Ziba, Saul's former steward, and Mephibosheth.

See II Samuel 9, 16, and 19, *IB*, Vol. 2 (New York and Nashville: Abingdon Press, 1953), pp. 1092-94, 1129-32, and 1143-50.
107 NLS, Blackwoods Letter-books, Acc. 5643/B8, William Blackwood to John Mitchell, 15 December 1828, pp. 133-37.
108 PANS, MP, MG1, Vol. 554, No. 18, ALS, Thomas McCulloch to George Young, 17 July 1822.
109 Ibid.
110 PANS, MP, MG1, Vol. 555, No. 82, "The Chronicles of our Town," Gathering X [4ᵛ]. All subsequent references to this manuscript are included in the text as ("Chronicles," 0 [00]), where "Chronicles" indicates "The Chronicles of our Town," 0 indicates the number of the gathering, and [00] indicates the number and side (recto or verso) of the leaf.
111 *Acadian Recorder*, 26 January 1822, p. [2].
112 Ibid., 11 May 1822, p. [2].
113 PANS, MP, MG1, Vol. 555, Nos. 53-68, "William," p. 18. All subsequent references to this manuscript are included in the text as ("William," p. 0), where 0 indicates the actual number written on each extant page of the manuscript.
114 *Colonial Gleanings. William, And Melville* (Edinburgh: William Oliphant, 1826), pp. 23 and 32. All subsequent references to this edition are included in the text as (Oliphant, p. 000).
115 *Acadian Recorder*, 28 December 1822, p. [2].
116 Ibid., 18 January 1823, p. [2].
117 Ibid., 8 February 1823, p. [2].
118 Ibid., 29 March 1823, p. [2].

BOOK ONE

"Saw & Grist Mill in the Town of Pictou" by J. E. Woolford, 1817

Letter I. Reading

To the Editors of the ~~Halifax~~ Recorder.

Gentlemen,

Happening some time ago to call upon parson Drone, the clergyman of our town, I found him administering his old standard consolation, to my neighbour Solomon Gosling. The parson has been long among us; and we all know him to be a worthy gentleman: yet, still, I believe, he has fared very hardly; for, though our townsmen respect him, and are the most active people in the world at selling watches and swapping horses, they have never made themselves rich; and, therefore, they have little to give but good wishes. But the parson, except when he is angry, is very good natured, and disposed to bear with a great deal: and having acquired a large fund of patience himself, he has become a quack at comforting, and prescribes it indiscriminately for all sorts of ills. His own life has been spent between preaching and starving: and as he has no resources himself, it never occurs to him, that, for the wants or troubles of other persons, there can be any remedy but patience.

My neighbour Gosling is completely an every day character. His exact likeness may at any time be found in any part of the province. About thirty years ago, his father David left him very well to do; and Solomon, who, at that time, was a brisk young man, had the prospect, that, by means of a little industry, he would live as comfortably as any in the town. Soon after the death of old David, he was married to Polly; and a more likely couple are seldom to be seen. But unluckily for them both, when Solomon went to Halifax with his produce in the winter; Polly went with him to sell her turkeys, and see the fashions: and, from that time, the Goslings had never a day

Page of manuscript of "The Chronicles of our Town"

LETTER 1

To the Editors of the *Acadian Recorder*.

Gentlemen,

Happening some time ago to call upon parson Drone, the clergyman of our town, I found him administring his old standard consolation, to my neighbour Solomon Gosling. The parson has been long among us; and we all know him to be a worthy gentleman: yet, still, I believe, he has fared very hardly; for, though our townsmen respect him, and are the most active people in the world at selling watches and swapping horses, they have never made themselves rich; and, therefore, they have little to give but good wishes. But the parson, except when he is angry, is very good natured, and disposed to bear with a great deal: and having acquired a large fund of patience himself, he has become a quack at comforting, and prescribes it indiscriminately for all sorts of ills. His own life has been spent between preaching and starving: and as he has no resources himself; it never occurs to him, that, for the wants or troubles of other persons, there can be any remedy but patience.

My neighbour Gosling is completely an every day character. His exact likeness may at any time be found in any part of the province. About thirty years ago, his father David left him very well to do; and Solomon, who, at that time, was a brisk young man, had the prospect, that, by means of a little industry, he would live as comfortably as any in the town. Soon after the death of old David, he was married to Polly; and a more likely couple are seldom to be seen. But unluckily for them both, when Solomon went to Halifax with his produce in the winter; Polly went with him to sell her turkeys, and see the fashions: and, from that time, the Goslings had never a day to do well. Solomon was not very fond of hard work. At the same time, he could not be accused of idleness. He was always a good neighbour; and, at every burial and barn raising, Solomon Gosling was set down, as one who would be sure to be there. Indeed, upon all public occasions, he was ready to lend a hand wherever it was needed. By these means, he gradually contracted a habit of running about; which left his own premises in an unpromising plight. Polly, too, by seeing the fashions, had learned to be genteel; and, for the sake of a little show, both lessened the thrift of the family, and added to the outlay; so that, between one thing and another, Solomon began to be hampered, and had more calls than comforters.

When the troubles of life originate in the want of industry, a return to labour is usually the last shift. The habits which my neighbour had been gradually contracting, left him little inclination for the patient and persevering toils of a farming life; nor would urgent necessity permit him to wait for the slow but sure returns of agricultural exertion. But necessity is the mother of invention; and, though the Gosling family were never much noted for profundity of intellect, Solomon, by pure dint of scheming, contrived both to relieve himself from his immediate embarrassments and to avoid hard labour. Though Goose-Hill farm, from want of industry, had not been productive, it was still a property of considerable value; and it occurred to Solomon, that, converted into goods, it would yield returns more prompt and lucrative than by any mode of agriculture. Full of the idea, accordingly, he went down to Halifax; and, by mortgaging his property to Callibogus, the West India merchant, he returned home with a general assortment, adapted to the wants of the town. When I say a general assortment, it is necessary to be a little more explicit. It did not contain any of those articles which are used in subduing the forest, or in cultivating the soil. These he knew to be not very saleable. He was aware, that, though old Tubal Thump supplies the whole town with iron work; he is so miserably poor, that he can scarcely keep himself in materials. The only article of the iron kind which he brought, was a hogshead of horse shoes; which, a blacksmith in Aberdeen, who knew something of the riding disposition of Americans, had sent out upon speculation. From the number of horses and young people in the town, Solomon knew that the shoes would meet with a ready sale.

When a merchant lays in his goods, he naturally consults the taste of his customers. Accordingly, my neighbour's consisted chiefly of West India produce, gin, brandy, tobacco, and a few chests of tea. For the youngsters he provided an assortment of superfine broad cloths and fancy muslins, ready made boots, whips, spurs, and a great variety of gumflowers, and other articles which come under the general denomination of *notions*. In addition to all these, and what Solomon viewed as not the least valuable part of his stock, he had bought from Pendulum & Co. a whole box of old watches, elegantly ornamented with lacquered brass chains and glass seals, in appearance little inferior to gold and Cairngorums.

When all these things were arranged, they had a very pretty appearance. For a number of weeks, little was talked of, but Mr. Gosling's Store; for Solomon, by becoming a merchant, had become Mr. Gosling: little was to be seen, but our townsmen and their families, riding thither to buy and returning with bargains: and, during the course of the day, long lines of horses, fastened to every accessible post and pinacle of the fences, rendered an entrance to his house almost impracticable. By these means, the general appearance of the town soon underwent a complete revolution. Homespun and homely fare were to be found only with a few hardfisted old folks, whose ideas could never rise above labour and saving. The rest, upon sundays, appeared so neat and genteel, that even the Reverend Mr. Drone, though his flock had not enabled him to exchange his own old habiliments for Mr. Gosling's superfine, expressed his satisfaction by complacent looks.

Mr. Gosling, too, had, in reality, improved his circumstances. The most of our townsmen, considering, that, if they carried their money to old Ledger and the other traders to whom they were already in debt, it would only be placed to their credit, took it to Mr. Gosling's Store; so that, by these means, he was very soon able to clear off a number of his old encumbrances; and, also, to carry to market, as much cash as established his credit.

Among traders, punctuality of payment begets confidence in the seller; and the credit which this affords to the purchaser, is generally succeeded by an enlargement of orders. My neighbour returned with a much greater supply; and here his reverses commenced. Credit could not be refused to good customers who had brought their cash to the Store. Those, also, who had formerly showed their good will by bringing their money, now proved their cordiality by taking large credits. But, when the time for returning to the market for supplies arrived, Mr. Gosling had little to carry thither but books. These, it is true, had an imposing appearance. They contained debts to a large amount; and he assured his creditors, that, when these were collected, beside paying them honourably, he would have a large reversion to himself. But, when his accounts were made out, many young men who owed him large sums, had gone to the Lines; and of those that remained, the greater part had mortgaged their farms to Mr. Ledger and the other old traders; and now they carried their ready money to Jerry Gawpus, who, by converting his farm into goods, had just commenced trader. In short, nothing remained for Mr. Gosling, but the bodies or labours of his debtors; and the latter, they all declared themselves very willing to give.

About that time, it happened that vessels were giving a great price; and it naturally occurred to my neighbour, that, by the labour which he could command, he might build a couple. These, accordingly, were put upon the stocks. But labour in payment of debt, goes on heavily; and besides, when vessels were giving two prices, nobody would work without double wages; so that the vessels, like the ark, saw many summers and winters. In the mean time, peace came; and those who owned vessels, were glad to get rid of them at any price. By dint of perseverance, however, Mr. Gosling's were finished: but they had scarcely touched the water, when they were attached by Mr. Hemp, who, at the same time, declared, that, when they were sold, he would lose fifty per cent upon his account for the rigging. Such was my neighbour's case; when happening, as I have already mentioned, to step into parson Drone's, I found that Mr. Gosling had been telling his ailments, and was receiving the reverend old gentleman's standard consolation: *What can't be cured, must be endured: let us have patience.*

"I'll tell you what it is, parson," replied my neighbour, "patience may do very well for those who have plenty; but it won't do for me. Callibogus has foreclosed the mortgage; my vessels are attached; and my books are of no more value than a rotten pumpkin. After struggling hard to supply the country with goods, and to bring up a family so as to be a credit to the town, the country has brought us to ruin. I won't submit to it. I won't see my son Rehoboam, poor fellow, working like a slave upon the roads, with his coat turned into a jacket, and the elbows clouted with the tails. My girls were not sent to Mrs. McCackle's boarding school, to learn to scrub floors. The truth is, parson, the country does not deserve to be lived in. There is neither trade nor money in it, and produce gives nothing. It is fit only for Indians or emigrants from Scotland, who were starving at home. It is time for me to go elsewhere, and carry my family to a place that presents better prospects to young folks."

In reply, the parson was beginning to exhort Mr. Gosling to beware of the murmurings of the wicked; when Jack Catchpole the constable stept in to say, that Mr. Holdfast the sheriff would be glad to speak with Mr. Gosling at the door. Our sheriff is a very hospitable gentleman; and, when any of his neighbours are in hardships, he will call upon them, and even insist upon their making his house their home. Nor did I ever know any shy folks getting off with an excuse. As it occurred to me, therefore, that Mr. Gosling might not come back for the parson's admonition, I returned home; and soon learned that my neighbour had really gone elsewhere, and made a settlement in the very place where Samson turned miller.

This event has not added much to the respectability of the Goslings; nor is it calculated to brighten their prospects. My neighbour's children are as fine a young family as any in the town: but it unavoidably happened, that the apparent prosperity of their father introduced among them habits, not very friendly to regular industry and saving. Hob Gosling, the oldest son, is really a smart young fellow; and, in haying time or harvest, he can do more work than any three labourers. But hard work requires recreation; and, when a young man does any thing uncommon, he generally wishes the neighbours to know it, and to give him due praise. Accordingly, it would sometimes take Hob a week, to tell about the exertions of a day. He would, also, occasionally recreate himself by riding races or playing a game at cards, when he was drinking a glass of grog with other youngsters over Mr. Tipple's counter: and by these means, though Hob is not a quarrelsome young man, his name was frequently called over in court, in assault and battery cases. This, it is true, was not without its advantages. Hob acquired a great knowledge of the law, and the character of being a 'cute young man. But I am inclined to think that the gain ended here; for, I recollect, that, after some of these causes were tried, a few acres of excellent marsh, which Mr. Gosling's trading had enabled him to add to his farm, passed into the hands of Saunders Scantocreesh, a hardfaced, hard working Scotchman; who, a few years ago, came among us with his stockings and shoes suspended from a stick over his shoulder, but now possesses one of the best farms in the town.

My neighbour's daughters, too, are very agreeable young ladies. Every body admits, that, by their education, Mrs. McCackle has completely established her reputation as a teacher. For painting flowers and playing upon the piano forte, they have few equals. Some of my neighbours, indeed, used to complain, that, when Mr. Gosling asked them to dinner, the meat was always ill cooked; and the puddings and pies, mere dough. But the reason was, that neither Mrs. Gosling nor the young ladies, could get the black wench to do as she was bid, unless they were always at her heels; and nobody, you know, can expect ladies to be either cooks or constantly in a kitchen.

But this was not the only hardship which my neighbour suffered by the elegant accomplishments of the young ladies. To be genteel in the country, is attended with difficulties and losses of which you townsfolk can have no conception. Morning visits in the afternoon, dressing, and other things, interfere so often with rural industry, that great show and sad accidents are usually combined. I recollect, when Jacob Ribs married his fourth wife, Mr. and Mrs. Gosling were asked to the wedding; and, as it happened to be on churning day, the young ladies were left to attend to the business. But, when the chaise which carried the old folks to the wedding, returned; it occurred to the young ladies, that, before proceeding to domestic toil, they would have plenty of time to return Miss Trotabout's last morning visit: and off they set, leaving directions with the black girl, to have the churn before the fire by the time they returned. During their absence, it unfortunately happened that the wench descried one of her black cronies going past; and, running down the lane to enjoy a little talk, left the kitchen door open; when Mr. Gosling's boar pig Mammoth, which was always a mischievous brute, finding a clear passage, entered without ceremony and upset the churn. My neighbour's kitchen was immediately converted into the country of the Gadarenes. To guzzle up the contents, was but the work of a moment. The succeeding scarcity, also, aroused that inquisitive disposition for which swine, as well as ladies, are noted; when one of the vile animals, perceiving something in the churn as it lay upon its side, thrust in its snout to explore. In this state of things, the black wench, having descried the young ladies at a distance, returned to her post. Vengeance succeeded amazement; and the first object of it, and apparently the most guilty, was the individual whose fore quarters had already escaped from punishment. Now, it so happens, that no way of driving a pig straight forward, has been yet invented, except pulling it by the tail. As soon, therefore, as it found itself assaulted behind, it made a fair entrance into the wooden tabernacle; and, when the young ladies returned to make butter, it was rolling about the floor, to the utter dismay of the girl, and the complete dispersion of the whole herd of swine. Our country gentlemen, you see, suffer serious afflictions and losses, from which, you townsfolk, who have nothing to do but to eat butter and be genteel, are altogether exempted.

After Mr. Gosling's separation from his family, I went to call upon them; imagining that the countenance of a neighbour would help to soothe and keep up their spirits. Parson Drone, too, had prepared a long discourse upon patience; and, when I was visiting them, came to deliver it. But we found them all very cheerful; and the parson, unwilling to lose the fruits of his study, carried his discourse to old Caleb Staggers; whose mare had just died of the botts. Mr. Gosling's confinement they considered merely as a temporary inconvenience, arising from the spite of his creditors. But when his debts were called in, he would pay every body: and the whole family agreed, that, then, with the rest of his property, they would go to a country better worth the living in. Respecting their destination, however, I found among them a considerable diversity of opinion. Mrs. Gosling spoke of the Ohio; but Mr. Rehoboam declared, that it was a new country without roads; where a young man could not lay a leg over a saddle from the one year's end to the other. Miss Dinah preferred the Cape of Good Hope; but she was afraid of the Caffres, who sometimes carry off white women. To elope with a lord or a duke, she observed, would be a very pretty incident: but, should any person ever write a novel about the Gosling family, to be carried off by a Hottentot, would appear so droll. Upon the whole, they seemed to think the opinion of Miss Fanny most feasible; that it would be best to go to Botany Bay, where every genteel family like the Goslings, receives so many white *nigers*, sent out every year from Britain by Government, to supply the colony.

For the preceding account of my neighbour and his family, I hope, you will find a place in some corner of your paper. To your readers in general, it will not, I know, be very interesting; for they have all seen the like, and heard the like, a hundred times before: and, as it is no fable, but a true story; it will be impossible for them to deduce from it, any sage moral for their own direction in life. Yet, its insertion will gratify a considerable number. By looking over the list of your subscribers, you will perceive that the Gosling family have extensive connexions in every part of the province, and in every kind of occupation; and, I am sure, it will gratify them all, to learn how their relation Mr. Solomon is getting on, since he quitted the farming. I have not been able to afford them a very flattering view of our trading concerns. Yet, still, they will see, that, when they go to live with the sheriff, as the most of them are likely to do, they will get into very genteel company.

Mephibosheth Stepsure

LETTER 2

To the Editors of the *Acadian Recorder*,

Gentlemen,

After Mr. Gosling went to live with the sheriff, I embraced the first spare time to pay him a visit. On arriving at my neighbours new lodgings, I was told that he had just sitten down to dinner with a party of his acquaintances, whom he had invited to see him. Finding, thus, that he had more need of a good appetite than of condolence, I returned home. As our roads are pretty much travelled, I did not proceed far without company: I was soon overtaken by Saunders Scantocreesh the Scotchman, who had been at old Tubal Thump's to get his axe new laid; and was now returning homeward, as fast as his feet could carry him. We had scarcely exchanged salutations, when Jack Scorem the lumberer, whose horse I had seen fastened to Tipple's fence, came gallopping up and joined us.

"So I hear," says Jack, "that old Gosling has got himself into limbo. The old fellow won't poison the town any more with his abominable stuff."

"*An' wha gar'd you drink it,*" replied Saunders, "*It wisna abominable stuff, when your bits o' waens war rinnan wi' ae greybeard fu' after anither. It was Mr. Gosling then; but noo, when you an' the like o' you hae brocht the puir gentleman to ruin, it's the auld fallow wi' the abominable stuff. The foul thief rin throo the guts o' a' sic loons; that I sud ban.*" At the same time, he brandished a new axe handle, which he was carrying home with him. What might have happened, had the conversation been continued, I do not know; for Jack fights

17

a hard battle at times: but fortunately for us all, Jehu, the oldest son of Mr. Gawpus the new merchant, came gallopping along; and Jack, preferring a race to a battle, was soon out of sight.

Having found my old neighbour so comfortably fixed with the sheriff, I was in no haste to renew my visit. A few days ago, however, I received from him a note, acknowledging my former call, and requesting me to eat a beef steak with him at half past five. As Mr Gosling and I had never been upon very intimate terms, this invitation was rather unexpected. But, having all my life dined early, I do not like late hours. Besides, though Mr. Holdfast invites his friends, and never fails to be out of humour when they offer to leave him; I have always thought, that, for his guests to call in their acquaintances, and have dinner parties in his house, is carrying the joke rather too far. I, therefore, sent him my excuse, with a promise that I would see him next day.

Accordingly, after breakfast, having given my boys and servants their tasks, I stepped over to the sheriff's, and was introduced to my neighbour; whom I found so completely involved in a cloud of tobacco smoke, as to be scarcely visible. To account for this circumstance, it is necessary to remark that the inhabitants of our town are all great smokers; and, though the country in general is pretty populous, the sheriff's house is usually the thickest part of the settlement. His house, also, standing in a public place, is very much exposed; and, having more than once suffered depredations from housebreakers, he keeps his windows so well secured, that not even smoke can find a passage; and hence, the darkness in which Mr Gosling was involved.

After surmounting the first impression which the hazy atmosphere of the room had made upon my eyes, I found my neighbour seated at a table; along with a goodly number of our townsmen, who had come to lodge with Mr. Holdfast, till they could be more comfortable at home.

They were all busily employed over a game of whist, and enjoying their smoke at the same time; and, as smoking begets thirst, a few tumblers and the needful stood upon the table. It has been a time of general calamity among us; and, on this account, though our sheriff is really a respectable gentleman, many are now living with him, who, once a day, would have spurned at his invitations. These, as well as Mr. Gosling, have many relations in different parts of the province; and, as they may perhaps hear of their present circumstances, without learning the cause; I shall, for their information, state how my townsmen have been involved in misfortune, which ought rather to be termed unexpected than sudden.

But I must first vindicate myself from the unjust aspersions of some of your readers. It has been affirmed that my account of Mr. Gosling is merely a dry wipe at those, who, not contented with the profits of farming, have grasped at the gains of business, without possessing the knowledge and management which business requires. But have I not affirmed that it is a true story? And surely, I who know best, have the best right to be believed. Besides, I am confident, that there is not one merchant in the country, who will see the least resemblance between Mr. Gosling and himself: And why should they? for there is not the least similarity between their views and intentions, I assure you. All our country traders know better how to manage than Solomon; and as soon as they get rich, they intend to take up their mortgages from Callibogus; and then to live upon their estates, as respectable, independent gentlemen ought to do. Till this happen, I would advise your censorious readers to keep their jibes and jeers to themselves; and to believe that what I have told them, and what I have yet to tell, are true stories in our town.

I formerly mentioned how Jack Scorem set off at the gallop, after Mr. Gawpus' son Jehu. In the course of the race, they arrived at a part where the road takes a sudden turn; when a jostling ensued, which brought man and beast to the ground. At that time, the sheriff happened to be upon the road; when perceiving the accident, and running to lend his assistance, he found Jack both bruised and bleeding; and positively insisted, that, instead of going home to his family in such a plight, he should lodge with himself. Jack now declares himself to be perfectly cured; but Mr. Holdfast is still as careful about him as when he found him upon the road.

About ten years ago, Jack began the world by settling upon a wood lot and marrying a daughter of old Pharaoh Squash. With the exception of rather more legs than one human body has a right to claim, Jack was a likely, clever handed fellow; and could chop more in a day than any of his neighbours. But this was a kind of work of which, except at a chopping frolic, he was never very fond. His wife, too, bating a little glibness of tongue, common to the whole Squash family, was a very engaging and smart young woman.

Jack, having begun the world, was determined to show that he had commenced in earnest. Accordingly, after making a little hole in the woods; that nobody might mistake him for a Pictou highlandman, he raised a couple of good frames for his house and barn; and by chopping for Swing the sawyer, he provided himself with as many boards as would do the outside work of his house. Mr. Ledger, too, who was never known to refuse credit to active, well doing young men, supplied him with paint, glass, nails, and other materials; so that very soon, by dint of labour and the help of a carpenter to make the sashes, the house that Jack built, with its white clapboards and green corners and window facings, had a very pretty appearance. The partitions and ceiling, it is true, were only loose boards; but these he resolved to finish before the winter set in.

When things were in this state, Mrs. Scorem was brought home from her father's; and a happier couple were nowhere to be found. Jack was very fond of his wife. The neighbours, too, showed their kindness by visiting and inviting the young people; so that the time passed pleasantly away. But winter set in before he could get any thing done to the house; and when he began to look after boards for his barn, there were none to be got. The young folks, however, were not easily put out. A few slabs would do very well to shelter the cow in a corner of the frame; and if their house was cold, they were near the woods and could keep a rousing fire.

But Jack's building had produced another inconvenience of much greater magnitude. A few potatoes were the whole of his crop. Every thing, therefore, must be bought at the store; and, as young folk like to be stilish, the day of reckoning was not duly considered. When spring came, Mr. Ledger had a very long account against Jack; but then his farm showed, that, during winter he had been doing something beside visiting: he had slashed down a large piece of wood; and now he determined to raise a crop which would both show his industry and keep Mr. Ledger in good humour.

It happened that spring, that Mr. Ledger's agent at home sent him out more vessels than he knew how to load. Jack was in debt, and known to be a good axeman; and just when he was beginning to clear up his new land, Mr. Ledger's tempting offers interrupted the farming. In the morning he might jump into the woods, and at night return home two or three dollars the richer. This was a prospect not to be despised by one who was in debt; and who, besides, wished to have his house and barn finished.

It happened, also, that, when the vessels came out to Mr. Ledger, they brought a very large importation of goods. These proved a sore temptation to Jack and Mrs. Scorem; who, like other young folks, had gone very bare together. But he was now making great wages, and they could well afford both to live better and dress better; and hence, between finery and their summer's provisions, they had a great many errands to the store. In the mean time, Jack wrought hard and finished his contract; but, when Mr. Ledger balanced his books, he was astonished to find himself deeper in debt than before. At first he was very angry, and would not believe it. But in looking over the account, he found a great many gowns, ribbons, and laces, which he thought might have been spared. He had, also, some twinges about a long line of *dittos*, headed by *1. Gall. Spirits*. But he liked to see his wife as fine as any of her neighbours; and it would be a miserable thing, if he could not afford a glass of grog to an acquaintance when he called at the house. In short the thing was done and could not be recalled. Still, he was a smart young fellow, and had no need to resort to parson Drone for consolation. The house and barn could stand for another year; and, instead of chopping upon his farm, he could have another great lot of timber ready by the spring.

The little timber which had been upon Jack's premises, was now gone. But my cousin Harrow, who lives in the far end of the town and minds only his farming, had an excellent lot of it; and Jack and a few more of the youngsters agreed to pay him stumpage, and make one job of the whole. As they were all far from home; it was necessary to camp in the woods. Now sleeping upon spruce boughs, and living upon hard biscuit and salt pork not very well cooked, do not afford all the comfort requisite for hard working men. Without a little spirits, as every youngster knows, the fatigue of lumbering would be intolerable. Besides, persons who must quit their labour at dusk, cannot sleep all the long nights of winter; and when they are sitting in the camp, they need something along with a game at cards, to make them cheery and keep out the cold.

In the mean time, Mrs. Scorem and the wives of the other young men, found themselves very lonely at home. They, also, felt a little anxious about their husbands; and in order to relieve their uneasiness, they naturally called upon each other; for the double purpose of passing a dull hour, and hearing from the camp. Calls of this kind require comforts; and, as young people have usually a frank disposition, it became a point of emulation among them, who should be kindest. Thus, Jack, living in the woods, had now as it were two families to support; and each of them conducted upon the supposition, that he was making great wages and could very easily afford it.

The large lot of timber was at last made and delivered. But, when a deduction was made for hauling and stumpage; and, also, for the price of a horse to carry his provisions, the remainder left Jack farther in arrears than ever. At first he was confounded. A perusal of Mr. Ledger's account, however, satisfied him that all was right there. His present number of *dittos* had been considerably increased by camping in the woods: but for these he now found a reasonable excuse; they were a part of his supplies, and could not be wanted. The same lenity he found it impossible to extend to many of Mrs. Scorem's items; and, on returning home, disappointed and moody, he could not refrain from muttering something about extravagance, tea, and trumpery. Now, in a case of this kind, it was never known that any of the Squash family did not give as good as they got. Mrs. Scorem could quote with great readiness the number of Jack's *dittos*; so that domestic comfort began to assume a very gloomy appearance. But, as neither of them was ill natured; after a few tears and a little pouting from Mrs. Scorem, harmony was restored; and they both fully resolved to be more careful in future, and to get out of debt as soon as they could. To get out of debt by farming, however, was now out of the question. Another great lot of lumber must, therefore, be made.

It is necessary here to say a few words about our worthy old clergyman, the Reverend Mr. Drone. When the parson first came among us, he was a brisk young gentleman, and preached upon a great variety of subjects. Among other things, I remember, he tried to persuade us, that a person's general habits grow out of his occupation. But almost the whole town laughed at him. One was sure, that, if he had money to lend, he would have more conscience than Gripus the usurer; and another, that he could keep tavern forever, without being such a drunkard as Tipple. None of the young people could see how a little card playing and frolicking could interfere with sober and industrious habits; and the old folks to a man declared, that it was perfectly easy to job about the one half of the year, and to be very good farmers the other. However this may be, I am inclined to think that habits arising out of any particular occupation, are not likely to be impaired by continuing in it. Accordingly, though Jack could not be called a drunkard, for he was seldom seen intoxicated; he used frequently to say, that a good hearty glass of grog along with hard work in the woods, would do no man harm. In proportion, also, as he became more indulgent to himself, his opposition to Mrs. Scorem's domestic management diminished; so that she was at last left to get on in her own way in peace.

In this manner several years passed on without the occurrence of any thing particular to interrupt their quiet; except an occasional reflexion upon Mr. Ledger's debt, which was gradually increasing. At last, one morning when Jack was going past the store, this gentleman called him into his house; and, after some friendly conversation and a hearty glass of grog, observed to him, that, though it was not his practice to tell every body the state of his affairs; he would mention to him, as a particular friend, that he was very hardly pushed. He owed a large sum to Mr. Balance his agent at home; who was become very anxious about it. To satisfy him, therefore, he had just been taking a mortgage from a number of the neighbours; and he hoped that Jack, also, would give him this security upon his farm. The mortgages would satisfy Mr. Balance, that he had not been making bad debts; and thus he would neither be pushed himself, nor be reduced to the painful necessity of harassing good neighbours. He farther assured Jack, when they were taking another glass, that he was the last man in the town that he would be willing to distress. Jack was very sorry to hear that his good friend Mr. Ledger was pushed, and no less so to think that his own farm might be attached. To oblige this gentleman, therefore, and to remove far from himself the evil day, the mortgage was given.

From the time that Mr. Ledger revealed to Jack the secret of his distress and received the mortgage, a sort of intimacy was established between them. That gentleman would frequently take him by himself, and give him a great many advices about care and economy. At first Jack was very proud of this kind of confidence; but, by being often repeated, it became tiresome; and at last he cared for it as little and minded it as little as one of parson Drone's sermons. On the other hand, Mr. Ledger did not bear so patiently as the parson, this disregard of his admonitions. When Jack's greybeard, therefore, to which Saunders Scantocreesh alluded, was in need of replenishing and arrived at the store, it would be frequently sent away as it came. This was usage not to be endured from one whom he had obliged by mortgaging his farm. Jack threatened revenge; and, accordingly, carried his next lot of timber to another trader, and set Mr. Ledger at defiance.

In this manner Jack's affairs went on for several years more. Lots of timber were made, and large debts contracted. In the mean time, the lumbering life had left the farm without improvement. The land which Jack had chopped the winter after his marriage, was again covered with fine young wood. The barn frame, it is true, for it was an excellent frame, had resisted the weather, and still stood its ground; but the house could no longer be known by its fine white clapboards and its green corners and facings. Time had swept away the paint; and the only contrast to its general weather-beaten appearance, was a stripe of white, reaching from the garret window to the ground; occasioned by certain nocturnal distillations, which, in a cold winter's night, it is not always convenient to carry to the door. His windows, too, had suffered the inconvenience of being in the neighbourhood of children and fowls. The want of glass was remedied by a plentiful supply of old hats, trousers, and other articles; at the same time keeping out the cold, and proving that those within had once worn clothes.

From what I have said respecting the outside of the house, it need scarcely be remarked that comforts had not multiplied within. The loose boards had become looser by seasoning. The increase of children, also, had opened up new sources of want; and it usually happens that large wants very injudiciously keep company with little credit. When Jack, therefore, returned from the woods; it was to hear of a long list of particulars which the family needed, summed up with a good deal of grumbling that they had not been provided. Now, family conversations of this kind, when they are often repeated, are apt to become irksome. All persons, also, married and unmarried, contract a habit of going where they are most comfortable. From such matrimonial communings, therefore, Jack would escape to his acquaintances, who neither told him of wants nor plagued him with grumblings; and, as they were generally to be found about Tipple's counter, he became a regular attendant at that place of amusement. A course of this kind was not likely to lessen family grievances. Jack and Mrs. Scorem began to live very unhappily together. That he might forget the past and escape from the present, a resort to Tipple's became every day more necessary; and the thoughts of returning home demanded an additional dose, to prepare him for encountering domestic storm.

I have generally seen, that misfortune which requires a stout heart and strong exertions to overcome it, produces contrary effects. As Jack's prospects of comfort diminished, he became less inclined to labour for comfort; and was no longer that active, hard working fellow, that he had formerly been. In the mean time, from the failure of trade and other circumstances, the price of timber fell so much, that Jack declared it better to go idle than to work for such wages. Go idle he did: but when he was enjoying himself, Mr. Ledger sued out the mortgage, and then capiassed him for the balance of his account; and he is now living with the sheriff, till trade revive, and labour return to its old price. Before I left home, his little boys were at my house, asking a few potatoes to keep them from starving; and when I arrived at Mr. Holdfast's, I found Jack's thoughts and enjoyments, limited to a game at cards and a glass of grog.

Mephibosheth Stepsure

LETTER 3

To the Editors of the *Acadian Recorder*,

Gentlemen,

I formerly observed, that, in our town it has been a time of general distress. This, however, is, by no means, the effect of carelessness or inactivity; for the most of our townsfolk are eager to be rich, and as active as eager. I will venture to affirm that there is not another township in the province, where there are so many bargains every day made. Indeed, the greater part of us spend the half of their time, running about, expressly for the purpose of getting rich: yet by some strange fatality, misfortune has fallen heaviest upon those who were most active. When parson Drone came among us, he tried to persuade us, I remember, that the property of the town at that time, could not make us all wealthy; and, therefore, that, if we would all be rich; we must, by labour, add as much to its value, as would enrich us all. But to the most of us it appeared very plain, that, if every one of us made so many bargains and gained by each of them, he would be so much the richer; and you may depend upon it, no man who can become rich by head work, will ever submit to the drudgery of farming. I am inclined to think that our parson told us the truth; but the Reverend Shadrach Howl, who, being last year tired of chopping down trees, converted himself into a preacher of the gospel, declares, that our calamities are a judgment upon the town for rejecting his doctrine. However this may be; certain it is, that our most active and enterprising townsmen are either living with the sheriff, or from a principle of delicacy, keeping themselves out of the way of his invitations.

After the account which I have given of Jack Scorem, I find that I have little else to do, than to send you the names of the sheriff's other lodgers. Though the life of each of them has been marked by a diversity of incidents; the original situation of the most of them, their views, and the conclusion of their course, have been exactly similar. Respecting them, therefore, I shall send you only a few brief notices.

Whoever looks at the soil of our town, would say that nature designed us to be a farming people; and also, that every man who gives the ground fair play, will be able to live very comfortably. Accordingly, my cousin Harrow, Saunders Scantocreesh, and a few others, who mind only their farms, have every thing about them very snug and thriving; and whoever goes into their houses, is sure to find plenty and cheerfulness. Yet, though our soil is excellent, and farms very easily got; the most of our townsfolk would rather ride two days round the country to make a bargain, than give the ground one day's labour. Whether this proceeds from the waywardness of human nature, or, because being British subjects, we are born traders; I shall not presume to decide. Our parson is sometimes inclined to think that his parishioners are a part of the ten tribes. The only objections to his opinion, he says, are, that, though our townsmen be great traders in watches, old horses, and other kinds of truck; and as eager to be rich as any of the seed of Abraham, not one of them deals in old clothes, or is as rich as a Jew. But Saunders Scantocreesh, who reads his bible a good deal, declares, that, from their disposition to meddle with quiet honest men, they must be the Philistines, or else the children of Ishmael; because, when the court comes round, they are all at loggerheads among themselves.

Along with my neighbour Gosling, I found Mr. Gypsum, the plaster merchant, who once possessed as fair prospects as any in the town. Much about the same time, he married and bought a farm with a good deal of marsh; for which he agreed to pay by easy instalments. The young people were both very active and eager to be out of debt. Now labour in our town is usually succeeded by bountiful returns; so that, in a few years, the farm sent more cattle and hogs to market than that of any of their neighbours; and Mrs. Gypsum's turkeys always brought the highest price. By these means, and using a good deal of thrift, they soon owned an excellent farm, and were out of every man's debt. By pursuing this course, Mr. Gypsum had also acquired a habit of industrious activity; which, in every line of life, is a valuable acquisition. But he had now got his farm in fine order; and not being disposed to clear up any more woodland, he had considerable spare time upon his hands. Still he was not disposed to be idle; and it occurred to him, that, as he had excellent plaster upon his lot, it would be easy for him, when he had nothing else to do, to build a vessel which would carry it to the Lines. Accordingly, the vessel was built, rigged by the help of good credit, and sent off with a cargo. At that time, it happened that plaster brought a great price; so that the rigging was soon paid; and Mr. Gypsum now owned a good farm and a vessel, and had money in his pocket besides. As the best returns were now made by trading, his plaster concern chiefly occupied his thoughts. But money in a man's pocket doing nothing, is of no use. It occurred to him, therefore, that, as he was in the way of business, he might as well make the homeward voyage productive, by bringing flour and corn; which, many of my neighbours having found it cheaper to buy than to raise, are always in demand. Mr. Gypsum was now in very prosperous circumstances. Beside possessing a farm and a vessel, almost the whole town owed him.

It has been rarely found that a state of poverty and hardship, excites the envy of neighbours. But Mr. Gypsum began to be eyed with considerable dislike: There was no reason why he should be growing so fast rich, when every body else was poor. A great many vessels were, therefore, put upon the stocks; and next year, plaster at the Lines was a mere drug.

When a person enters into a trade, he cannot always tell exactly when or how he may get out of it. The vessels were now built; to sell them at a fair price, was out of the question; and to lay them up, dead loss. Still, the Lines afforded a little relief, which our townsmen readily embraced. In the plaster market there are always more goods than money; and frequently a merchant who would not give cash, would be very willing to exchange goods at a fair price. The greater part of goods, it is true, could not be got home without smuggling; but this was easily got over. Were any of my neighbours to be called a rogue, he would be mightily offended; and among us, were one person to take a penny from the pocket of another, the whole town would cry out against such a sinful and shameful transaction. But cheating the whole community at once, was so far from being considered as either sin or shame, that Deacon Scruple, who allowed nothing to be sung in his vessel but hymns, was the greatest smuggler of them all.

Beside flour and corn, there were now brought into the town, gin, tea, tobacco, and a great variety of other articles which persons are apt to think necessary comforts. But, as plaster, on account of the multitude of carriers, had become a mere drug at the Lines; so, in our town, there were more goods than good customers. When goods, however, are on hand; they must be sold. Where the profit, too, is considerable; it is a temptation to traders to make large allowances for the responsibility of purchasers. All my neighbours, who had been buying flour and corn, were equally willing to add the other articles to their comfort; and, as Mr. Ledger who imported for himself, not only paid the duties, but began to be a little scrupulous about crediting, they carried their custom to the new merchants.

The young folks, also, who wrought at the plaster, were always very ready to buy. In the mean time, the new traders, by appearing to own vessels and to do a great deal of business, received credit from every body who had any thing to sell. But, by and by, every body wanted his own; and, when the merchants began to call in their accounts, the young folks had nothing; and the old people, who had found it hard to raise grain, found it harder to raise money: And the new merchants in general, finding that after smuggling in goods for the benefit of the town, they had been dealing with rogues, became dissatisfied; and at the persuasion of the sheriff, retired from business.

As Mr. Gypsum had been a little forehanded, he stood longer than any of them. But no man who is always going back, can always keep his feet. The neighbours, by striving to be rich, had ruined his trade. His smuggled goods, also, like theirs, were sold upon credit. Now, however, the other traders had retired, and there was the prospect of doing something; when unfortunately a great storm in the Bay wrecked his vessel with a large cargo of goods; and at the same time broke through a weak part of his marsh dyke, which, in the hurry of business, he had neglected to mend. In this state, my cousin Harrow, who had long supplied him with beef and other articles, recollecting how much custom Mr. Gypsum had given him, begged of the sheriff to accomodate him in his house, till he could collect his debts.

For the state of Mr. Gypsum's domestic affairs, I must refer you to my account of Jack Scorem's family: Only, Mrs. Gypsum being a trader's wife, conducted matters in a more genteel way. Her husband, she said, was a merchant and kept company with gentlemen; and every thing about his house ought to correspond with his station. One thing I recollect, that, go into Mr. Gypsum's at any hour of the day, you would find the gin bottle standing upon the table. Smuggled gin was cheap: it also helped on trade among the customers; and Mr. Gypsum himself never failed to set them a good example. Not that he was by any means a professed drunkard: but persons deprived of domestic comforts, are apt to become listless; and hence, when he and the sailors were lolling about the deck without any thing to do, they would frequently take a glass to help away the time. I never heard that he was in the practice of taking any thing to do him harm; for, with the exception of a troublesome disease of the nose, he is a sound healthy man. This, he says, is the effect of beating in the Bay, one night late in the fall, against a violent north wester. And here, from Mr. Gypsum's sad experience, I would observe to your readers, that there is nothing like taking a disease of this kind at its very commencement; for, when it gets far on, the cure is worse than the disease. Through neglect Mr. Gypsum's nose swelled and inflamed, and then burned like fire. At last, when it threatened fecundity, and began to show the appearance of a large brood of young ones upon its surface; he got alarmed, and applied to an old lady in our town, noted for curing cancers. But after using for a long time to no purpose, a poultice of cow dung soaked in cold water, he discovered that holding the afflicted member over a glass of spirits, gave him instant relief; and now, as one glass does not produce the same effect twice; I am sure, he will never get over the expence of keeping it easy.

Another of the sheriff's lodgers is Mr. Boniface Soakem, the tavern keeper. Like the rest of us, he began the world by settling upon a farm. At first he was a hard working man, and soon made himself comfortable. But he was eager to be rich; and would frequently compare his hard labour with his little gains, as he called them. At last, one day, going past Tipple's, and observing the great number of horses which were fastened to the fence; it occurred to him that a large proportion of the town very frequently passed his house, and he might as well keep tavern as not:

He would mind the business of the farm, and Mrs. Soakem would attend to the travellers. Accordingly, he applied for a license in the usual way.

When our parson, who was then young and spry, heard of it, he used every argument in his power to dissuade him. He begged him to consider what religion could be in a family, open at all hours to all kinds of company. He entreated him to reflect upon the influence which the profligate conduct of vagabonds must have upon his children. He told him, that a person entering upon any line of life, should view those who are in it; and then asked him how he would like to see himself and his family like Tipple. He conjured him to prefer his religious character and prospects to a little wealth with such fearful hazards: And lastly, he thundered in his ears, that, where one man's sin is another man's gain, the judgment of God is the amount of the profit.

Still Mr. Soakem was not convinced: Houses of entertainment were necessary, and might be very decently kept by religious people; and he hoped that the parson knew him better than to compare him to Tipple.

When Mr. Drone found his arguments ineffectual, he applied to the magistrates. He told them that taverns are at best but necessary nuisances, and ought not to be multiplied. He bid them look round the township, and see how many had been ruined by living in their neighbourhood: And, as he got on, becoming gradually more earnest, he told them that they had received his majesty's commission for better purposes, than to grant a licence to every fool who might choose to ruin himself and his family: that they were the guardians of good order; and, that, if they placed temptation in the way of the unwary, they were the partakers of other men's sins; and might assure themselves, that the wormwood and the gall would be shared between them.

Our magistrates have always been in the practice of granting a licence to every person who asks for it. The town, they say, needs the licence money; and, if taverns increase too much; those who keep them, will get tired of the business. They were, therefore, not well pleased that parson Drone should interfere, and pretend to instruct them in their official duties: They never meddled with his preaching, and he had no right to interfere with them. Hence, partly at the solicitation of Mr. Soakem, and partly from opposition to the parson, the license was granted.

When Mr. Soakem opened his house of entertainment, he was eager to get rich. At the same time, he was really an industrious, honest man; and he commenced with a firm determination to show parson Drone and the whole town, that he was a different man from Tipple, and kept another sort of a house. Accordingly, as his character was generally known in the town, every thing at first went admirably on. The young folks went where they could get cardplaying and fun; and nobody lodged at Mr. Soakem's tavern, except those sober travellers, who wished to take their glass moderately and quietly after the fatigues of the day. As his custom was thus small, and the whole attention of the family directed to have every thing clean and comfortable, travellers never failed to be pleased; and frequently, to show their satisfaction, as Mr. Soakem was a very conversible man, they would invite him to take a glass of grog and chat with them an hour.

When there happens to be a good tavern upon the road, every body soon knows of it. Mr. Soakem's trade began to enlarge very fast. This produced corresponding exertions to please; and every body was pleased. About this time I observed, that, from the attention which the tavern required, my neighbour's farm did not look so well as it used to do. Besides, from the irregularity and bustle, which, in the business of a tavern, cannot be always avoided; family prayers and graces would be sometimes hurried over, and sometimes neglected. But this, at first, happened only in unavoidable cases.

Mr. Soakem was now in prosperous circumstances, and making money very fast. Whether it was on account of his good conduct, or because he was getting rich, I cannot exactly say; but he began to be very much respected, and his friends thought him well qualified to be one of the justices for the town. He was no longer plain Boniface as formerly, but Mr. Soakem; and I have even seen some of his letters from your town merchants with Esq. to his name. Mr. Soakem, having thus arrived at great respectability, now studied to conduct himself with the decent dignity which became him. When a traveller arrived, instead of bustling about as formerly, to get every thing comfortable; as his children were growing up and should learn to do something, the horses were left to the boys, and the cooking and other indoor work, were intrusted to the girls. Mrs. Soakem, too, began to assume a lady like deportment; and, though the very best of you Halifax gentry had stopt at the door, she would not have budged from her seat.

With this new arrangement travellers were not very well satisfied; and, like the discontented in all ages, looked back with regret to good old times. They complained, that, in the house, there were far more attendants than service: and whether it was, that the boys had given the horses too much to eat; they could never get them to start from the door, without a good deal of whipping and spurring. With these things, it must be confessed, Mr. Soakem was altogether unacquainted; for, on account of the enlargement of his business and other causes, he was often from home. I do not know how it is in Halifax; but, in the country, it is really a great hardship to be a respectable gentleman. For the sake of character, such a person must do a great many things which he would otherwise avoid. Accordingly, when Mr. Soakem was abroad; in order to maintain his reputation, he would stop at every tavern upon the road, and show how a gentleman ought to behave. In the mean time, the young people were left to manage both the farm and the house of entertainment. This was more than they could well do; and besides, not very consistent with sober and industrious habits. They had, also, learned whose children they were. Now this is a kind of knowledge, which never fails to influence very powerfully the conduct of youth: They did not see why Mr. Soakem's children should be always drudging upon a farm like beasts, or be the servants of every fellow who chose to come along the road. Of course, when their father was from home, and he was from home very often; they would visit their companions, and their companions would visit them; and travellers, perceiving how affairs stood, passed on to the New Inn, about half a mile distant. In short, Mr. Soakem's gradually became like the habitation of the wicked: he was rarely in it himself; his children were always strolling about; and no traveller came near it. At last, one day the sheriff calling, and finding him at home, remarked that he must now be very lonely; and, therefore, he insisted upon introducing him to the company in which I found him.

When Mr. Soakem began to keep tavern, it happened to be the subject of conversation between parson Drone and myself. "I'll tell you," says he, "Mr. Stepsure, how it will turn out." (Among the neighbours I am plain Mephibosheth; but the sensible gentleman called me Mr. Stepsure.) "I'll tell you, Mr. Stepsure, how it will turn out. Our neighbour Soakem is a well meaning decent man, but eager to be rich, and totally ignorant of the influence of external circumstances upon human conduct and character. He is determined to keep tavern. A tavern must be open at all hours, and to all kinds of company. Irregularity in eating and sleeping requires the comfort of drinking. In a family, too, the want of good order destroys all personal and family religion; and when our neighbour's children are deprived of his present good example, they will learn to imitate his guests. In short, Mr. Soakem, between tasting at home and drinking abroad, will become a mere sot. His fine family of children will become the prey of ill example and idleness: And Mrs. Soakem, poor woman, who dreams of being rich, will come upon the town. It is well for you, Mr. Mephibosheth Stepsure, that you are lame of both feet, and cannot run about like the rest of the town. They are a bustling, bargaining, running about, sort of folks. But depend upon it, it is, as the wise man says, a sore travail and an evil disease. I have generally seen that those who, instead of minding their farms, are always travelling about, need a long rest at last; but, instead of running home to get it, they halt at the sheriff's."

Accordingly, Mr. Soakem's boys are lazy, drunken vagabonds. His daughters, too, and fine looking girls they are, have become pert, idle husseys, without industry or economy. Mrs. Soakem, through the miseries of the family, has lost all heart to welldoing: and, indeed, what can a woman in such circumstances do? And when I arrived at the sheriff's, I found Mr. Soakem, with eyes like collops, poring over the cards and the grog before him.

Mephibosheth Stepsure

LETTER 4

To the Editors of the *Acadian Recorder*,

Gentlemen,

Though your paper affords to your readers instructions of different kinds, I have never observed that you preach to them any sermons. I can assure you, however, that you might be much worse employed; for, to my own certain knowledge, they have been sometimes useful. Though it does not become me to boast of my attainments, I must say, that even I myself have been edified by the discourses of our worthy old parson, the reverend Mr. Drone.

When the parson came among us, he was an active, observing gentleman. He looked at every body, and at every thing they were doing; and when he began to preach, he said, "I have not come among you to tell you merely about your souls. Time stands in relation to eternity. The duties of this life, also, are a step to a better; and he who neglects them, neglects both body and soul. It is my duty to impress upon your minds, that you now belong to this world, and ought to act consistently with the present stage of your existence. I shall, therefore, ascertain your circumstances, and then direct you to those actions which every case requires."

About that time, there happened to be in the town a great many young people; and one day the parson took for his text these words of scripture, *It is not good for man to be alone.* I was then thinking of my old woman Dorothy; and, as I at first imagined that the parson had heard of it, I felt a little confused. On recovering myself, I observed most of

39

the young men looking at Peter Pumpkin's large family of daughters; who, at that time, were the most noted bundlers in the town. All the young women of the congregation seemed wonderfully pleased, and kept their eyes attentively fixed upon the parson, who was then a fine looking young gentleman. I cannot say, that, among the old people, there was the same general appearance of satisfaction. A few of them edged closer to their wives: but the greater part looked very grave; and Mrs. Grumble's husband Job, who is a quiet inoffensive man, assumed a length of visage, which, had he been standing beside her coffin, I am sure, would not have been greater.

As I was then thinking about Dorothy, I was very attentive to what the parson said; and though it be a long time since, I recollect some notes of the sermon as well as if it had been preached yesterday. He told us, that man, by the constitution of his nature and by the external circumstances of his lot, was evidently designed for society; and by the diversity of sex, for domestic life. "It is, therefore," says he, "to *home* that human beings must look for the commencement and perfection of social duties and social enjoyments. Nature has established a relation between male and female, which constitutes a basis for duty; and a feeling of duty produces exertions of energy, which exalt the mind and give it exalted pleasures. My dearly beloved brethren, honour the relation and cultivate the duties of the matrimonial life. Live in its society; study to please each other; and, by the help of a little mutual good nature and exertion, you will enjoy as much happiness as human beings have a right to expect. But let me earnestly beseech you to beware of every thing which interrupts domestic society; for I tell it to you from this sacred book, (and he gave a rap upon the bible, which made many of us start,) I testify to you, that the person who is often from home, whether upon business or from any other cause, is in danger of returning a worse man and to fewer enjoyments."

As it is foolish to pay a parson to instruct us and not follow his advice, I married Dorothy; and I must say, that, though my spouse and I have lived long together, our greatest affliction is, that we must by and by part. The young folks in general, also, were very well pleased; but some of the old people went away with melancholy faces. Mrs. Grumble's husband Job observed, that the parson was a young man and did not know the world. Israel Doubleribs said, that, when Mr. Drone had like him worn out a couple of wives, he would know better about it; and Caleb Castup, who was then newly married, declared that it was all humbug and nonsense; for whether he stayed at home or went abroad, Mrs. Castup and he were equally happy.

Caleb was a very good sort of young man; only a little fond of riding. After his marriage, however, he became much more steady; and gradually acquired a very pretty property. In course of time, also, as is usual among us, his family contained a number of fine stout boys, who were very useful about the farm. On considering with himself that his family were getting up, and would need a little help when they settled upon lots of their own, he began to feel an anxiety to get rich faster than his farm in its present state would permit. When he was turning the subject in his mind, and had almost resolved to take in a few new fields, a contested election happened in the town. Caleb, by being in snug circumstances, possessed a good deal of influence. In a case of this kind, too, he was very willing to show it; and, as he took an active part in the business, the candidate of his choice was returned.

During the hurry of the election, the management of the farm was intrusted to the boys; and nothing was said about taking in the new fields. It happened, also, as was natural where things are intrusted to boys, that, on returning home at night from electioneering, he saw a great many reasons to be dissatisfied: One thing was done wrong; and another, neglected. Being a little hasty, he would scold the boys; but Mrs. Castup, who was a very considerate woman, would take their part and tell him, that he should not look for old heads upon young shoulders: And at one time, when he was very angry, she plainly told him that it would be greater wisdom to be at home minding his farm and his boys, than gallopping round the country about other people's affairs. But, when they both cooled a little, they were not disposed to quarrel, and the matter was dropped.

Caleb, by electioneering, had not improved his circumstances. Of this the new member was sensible; and when the House of Assembly divided the road money; though there were almost as many applications as pounds to be expended, he was appointed commissioner. Accordingly, when the spring opened, he and the boys were very industrious; and had their ordinary crop in the ground, rather sooner than usual. When the road work commenced; as he had good stout teams and boys of his own, much of the labour was done by himself; and as it was near his house, he could be at home in the evening; so that upon the whole his gain was considerable. No person, however, must imagine, that, because the work was done by himself, it was finished in a sham way. The new member's word had been pledged for him, and all the neighbours were watching him. Besides, he looked forward to future employment; and, therefore, he determined that nobody should have cause to find fault. When the money was expended, every person agreed that a piece of road, finished so reasonably and so well, had never before been seen in the town.

His farm, it is true, had not succeeded so well as the road making. His potatoes were badly hoed, and his grain ill taken care of. Mr. Bullock's breachy cattle would get into his grass, and neighbour Snout's hogs rooted out his corn; so that, when he returned home in the evening, it was usually to witness new depredations. Now, in a farming life, there is nothing so irritating as the destruction of crop. On entering his house, therefore, it was generally in ill humour: It was a strange thing that when he was from home, toiling like a beast to make the family comfortable; every thing about the farm was allowed to go to ruin and destruction.

At first Mrs. Castup, who knew that the little boys were to blame, would only say she did the best that she could. But, as the tresspasses were repeated, so were the ill natured remarks; till at last she plainly told him, that, when a farmer puts a crop in the ground, he should consider how he is to get it out: that it was faring with him as with old Tubal Thump, when he had two irons in the fire: and, that, if he wanted the farm better managed, he might take care of it himself. In this humour they would go to bed; and in the morning, neither of them was well pleased. During the day, however, good nature would return; and thus, without any real dislike to each other, they began to find that they were both most comfortable when apart. The approach of evening brought with it the prospect of bickering, and a corresponding depression of mind; and they were always glad when the morning was past. Still, in the fall, notwithstanding their little family disputes and the losses upon the farm, he was considerably a gainer.

The general satisfaction which he had given, procured for him corresponding favour. He was now considered as a faithful servant of the public; and, as such, intrusted with a much larger sum; but this was to be expended in a distant part of the town. By these means, the farming became of less consequence, and was less regarded. From the occurrences of the preceding summer, also, to be from home, was not upon either side viewed as any great hardship.

Caleb had been hitherto rather a sober living man; and kept his family in such excellent order, that there was some talk in the town about making him a deacon. But, after he had been some time upon the roads, the notion was dropped. Every body knows that working upon the highways in the heat of summer, is a scorching employment; and, were it not generally known too, that a little spirits qualifies cold water; from the parching thirst of the labourers, dreadful accidents would often ensue. Accordingly, even the young people, though not the most careful about their health, being fully aware of the danger, always take care to be well provided. When these, in the course of the day, were quenching their own thirst; they would, from respect to Mr. Castup the commissioner, ask him to taste; who, though he did not care much about it, was not willing to offend by refusing; so that, between one and another, he would sometimes be induced to drink a great deal. As commissioner, too, he would occasionally treat them; and then, to show that he was not niggardly, he set them a good example. Besides, sustaining the character of Mr. Castup the commissioner, he was a man of some consequence; and, on this account, though his boys could camp in the woods with the rest of the youngsters, his respectability required him to lodge in Mr. Soakem's tavern. Here, when his boys were enjoying themselves in their own way, he would spend his evenings with Mr. Soakem and those who frequented his house.

To make a long tale short, from being a sober industrious man, he became a mere sot; and his boys are getting on after him as fast as they can. The farm, from neglect, became of little use to his family. The late sudden decrease of our revenue, also, made his profits by the roads a mere song; and at last, one day, as he was passing the sheriff's, that gentleman invited him to walk in and see Mr. Soakem. This was partly a relief to his mind; for, though his gains were gone, his business was more pressing than ever: almost every body in the town wanted to speak with him. His home also had lost its charms. At first, when he occasionally returned to Mrs. Castup intoxicated, she considered it merely as a circumstance unavoidable in the life of a gentleman. But frequent recurrence produced weeping and entreaties, and at last reproaches: And it was even said, though I cannot affirm it, that they proceeded as far as a battle. Certain it is, that, between poverty and quarrelling, home was a torment to them both. His family, also, and a fine family they were, are fit for nothing else than strolling about and drinking; and poor Mrs. Castup curses the day which made her husband a commissioner of roads.

In the same company I found my neighbour Steer, whose course requires only to be mentioned. Neither a snug farm nor every reasonable domestic comfort could satisfy him, without becoming suddenly rich; and to effect this purpose, he became a dealer in cattle. Being thus often from home and exposed to a great variety of companies and hardships, he would at last drink as much as Soakem, without being the worse of it. When he began the business, he was a civil young man, and religiously disposed. But whether it be that cattle, like sailors, will not get on without swearing; or whether, that those who associate with brutes, become brutes themselves, I do not know: but Steer became the most profane person in the town, and did a great deal of harm among the youngsters. Being often in Halifax, he was supposed to see and know more of the world than some of us; and when any of the old people reproved him, he would laugh at them, and say that he used the language of a gentleman. But Saunders Scantocreesh used to declare that it was the language of Ashdod: that parson Drone should cast him out of the church; as Ezra did the mongrel Jews: and, that, if our magistrates did their duty, they would put the villain to death for his blasphemies.

Steer's trade seemed to go on wonderfully well, and became gradually larger; till at last, having collected all the disposeable cattle of the town into one large drove, and sent it to Halifax; he declared that he had gone too much abroad for his good; and that, for a long time to come, nobody should see him from home. This resolution produced in our town a great deal of running to visit him; but whether he was at home, nobody could tell. The general report was, that the devil haunted his house; for listeners on the outside heard strange noises, as if Steer were swearing, and his wife crying and calling out for help. Whether the devil had really become a lodger with Steer, I cannot tell; but I am rather inclined to think that our townsmen mistook the one for the other; as it does not comport with the general practice of the devil, to be found either where persons expect him, or where his labours are not very necessary. In passing his house, it is true, Mr. Gawpus the new merchant got himself terribly frightened by something in the dark; but it turned out to be Mr. Gosling's boar pig Mammoth.

At last, one day, when Steer's boy was returning home with a bottle of spirits; a strange looking gentleman bid him tell his father, that he had on hand a large lot of cattle, and wished to speak with him. As he had not completely overcome the habit of bargaining, he ventured abroad; and was immediately addressed by the sheriff, who assured him that all his cattle were stall fed; and, as some of them had been kept up for years, they were in excellent order. But to give him fair play, he carried him along with him, that he might judge for himself.

Along side of Steer, I found his old servant Peter Longshanks. Peter, in his early days, was a nice young fellow; though, in the opinion of the girls, not the best model of a man. In the formation of the upper part of his frame, nature had been very sparing of materials. She had, however, given him an offset of extremities, which beat Jack Scorem's by at least four inches, and procured for him the nickname of *Nobody*. Peter was a good natured and obliging fellow; and, on this account, his legs had frequently a great deal to do in places where he had little business himself. At last, like the rest of us, he married, settled upon a farm, and was beginning to live comfortably. About that time, Steer's droves required an additional hand to manage them. Peter could run like a carriboo; and the offer of large wages tempted him to quit the farming. Of course, the habits of the master became the habits of the man. In Halifax, indeed, their manner of living was considerably different. When Steer was spending his evenings with Brisket the butcher and other gentlemen; Peter, being a servant was forced to look out for companions. By chance he heard of Seignior Caperini, at that time famed for his skill in improving the paces of the human species; and Peter, having from the quality of his limbs a natural gift that way, concluded that by a little improvement it might become a source of profit in the country. Accordingly, by taking lessons as often as he was in town, and drilling a good deal by himself, he became an experienced dancer, forsook Steer, and advertised for a school in parson Drone's congregation.

To the old religious people, the prospect of Peter's school gave general offence. They remarked, that, beside the improvement of his dancing talent, he had been taking lessons from Steer. Parson Drone, too, assured his congregation, that dancing frolics did harm without good. But Saunders Scantocreesh, whose girls wished very much to attend, was furious. He declared that all such doings were against the bible and the Confession of Faith; and that none of the seed of Scantocreesh should with his will ever enter the synagogue of Satan: And farther, that Peter Longshanks, instead of capering about the country, corrupting the youth, had better be minding his poor starved family, and considering what account he would give of the use of his legs at the day of judgment.

Still the business of the school went on: the night for its commencement was fixed, and Peter had engaged old

Driddle the fiddler; who, by the by, having played at all our weddings for these thirty years, is now fit for nothing but fiddling and drinking. Unluckily, commencement night happened to be the coldest of all last winter. All our young folks, however, and Driddle, were there. But, after a great deal of screwing and twisting and trying, and as much wondering what could have become of Mr. Longshanks, no Mr. Longshanks appeared: And the young people, after waiting as long as the cold would let them, returned home disappointed and angry. In the morning every body learned, that Mr. Longshanks, in coming to the school, had got both his feet frosted; and, on this account, had stopped at Mr. Soakem's. There is scarcely another employment in life, exposed to such a sweeping calamity. A dancing master with frosted feet, has his whole trade cut up by the roots; and for any purpose which they can serve, he might as well want them. Neither nimbleness nor grace can reasonably be expected from frosted feet. Like a hen upon hot coals, it is true, they receive the sympathy of all who hear of them: but what does this avail a benevolent dancing master, who knows how much the grand interests of rational beings depend upon his labours?

Time, however, cures a great many sores; and Peter's were beginning to mend; when, one morning, Mr. Holdfast stepped in, expressed himself happy to hear that he was getting well, and begged him to try if he could walk as far as his house.

But overlooking, in the mean time, the rest of my townsmen, I shall just introduce you to our schoolmaster, Mr. Pat O'rafferty; who had become their comrade in the sheriff's. Pat was born in the county of Tipperary; and, as he said himself, come of a genteel family: for his father's establishment consumed more butter milk and potatoes, than any of the neighbours. In due time he was put to school, and learned to write a good hand; with which his father was so much pleased, that, one day, he declared himself resolved to make him a priest. Pat said that he did not like to be a holy father; because he liked Judy O'flanagan: but, if his father wished him to be a spiritual man, he was very willing to be clerk to Mr. Wort, at the whiskey distillery. To the distillery, accordingly, he went; and, in a short time, was the best judge of whiskey about it. Pat married Judy; and they soon loved each other so well, as to be rarely without the proofs of mutual affection: Judy had black eyes; and Pat, a great many scratches. In the course of clerking, also, he became so dexterous; that he would write all that he was ordered, and sometimes a little more. This could not be done long without the knowledge of his master; and when Mr. Wort heard of it, he was so full of it himself, that he could not avoid telling the whole affair to his friend Justice Choakem. Now, the Justice was a curious sort of man; and whenever any thing out of the common road was done; the person who did it, was sure to be sent for and rewarded. He, therefore, expressed a very strong wish to see Pat; and to prevent disappointment, the best way, he thought, would be to issue a warrant.

Beside being a great rewarder of merit, the Justice loved bacon better than any other kind of food. In order, therefore, to have it to his taste; he was accustomed to cure his own hams. Now it happened one day, that, when his worship was thinking about a large hog which he had lately purchased, a servant stepped in and told him, that he was just come: And, says he, a stout fellow he is; for he took three of us to bring him along. The Justice immediately gave orders to kill and hang him up: but, when the servant returned to see what they should do next, it turned out to be Teddy O'Leary, who had been sent for to show the squire how he contrived to make the neighbours' hens disappear when he pleased. Pat soon learned that Justice Choakem wanted to speak with him; and would have been very glad to oblige his honour: but he was a little unwilling to expose himself to such fearful risks. He, therefore, shipped himself off for Newfoundland; where, during the course of the summer, the codfishing afforded him abundant amusement. But, though the grog in summer was very much to his taste; the prospect of starving in winter was not so agreeable. This induced him with a cargo of his countrymen, to land upon our coast late in the fall a few years ago. Pat found his way to our town; and, as there is among us a general taste for education, we employed him to communicate to our youth the true tone and accent of the English language. Here, of course, he became a lodger with Tipple. But, though he paid very punctually for his grog, (for Tipple gives no credit,) his board was for some time entirely overlooked by them both. At last, his landlord being anxious, as he said, to preserve the reputation of his house, and also to guard the town against the ill example of drunkards, requested the sheriff to take charge of Pat and prevent him from going at large.

Mephibosheth Stepsure

LETTER 5

To the Editors of the *Acadian Recorder*,

Gentlemen,

Since my last letter I have experienced so many vexations, that I had almost resolved never to write to you again. Both the incredulity and belief of the world are so capricious, that no man who writes for the public, is sure of getting justice. For example, when it was told last winter, that a worthy old gentleman of this province boldly girded himself with his armour, and slew a bear at that season of the year, every body believed it: And now, when I have stated the exact truth; it is the current report, that there is no such township as ours, nor in the whole province any such characters as I have described. Now, I am not willing to have my word questioned; for, as my old woman says, the word of Mephibosheth Stepsure will go much farther than some of his neighbours' notes of hand. But this is not the worst of it: I am reviled at home, as well as discredited abroad. The sheriff's lodgers in particular, are very angry at what I have written about their grog drinking and that gentleman's kind treatment. So far from being grateful for his good offices; Mr. Pat O'Rafferty declares that he is a perfect Polyphemus; only he does not eat them, when he has got them into his den. Jack Scorem, too, says that I am a censorious old rascal, and deserve the stocks for writing such stuff about him and his family; and that it is well for me that no stocks will take in my abominable clubs.

For my own part, I do not care very much for Jack's revilings. But to have met with such general discredit, is a

51

little trying; for no man likes to be disbelieved and belied, when he knows that he is telling the truth. I was, therefore, inclined to discontinue my communications: but my spouse will not give her consent; and we married people, as worthy parson Drone teaches, are bound to study family peace. She has always had a great respect for her husband, and cannot think of his being reckoned a story teller; and she affirms that to drop the business, is to plead guilty. Besides, the reproaches which Jack has thrown out against the extreme parts of my outward man, have made her very angry. My feet, she says, and she has seen them often, are as seemly feet of the sort as could be fastened to any man's legs: and that they have never carried me the roads which some people's have been obliged to go: That lame as Mephibosheth Stepsure is, he can go about at large; when some folks, who have as many legs as a spider, are obliged to lay them up in the sheriff's.

On consulting Mr. Drone upon the business, he appeared to be very much at a loss. Our parson has been, by poverty and depression, so completely shut out from society, that he has become almost an entire stranger to the ways and even language of the world. His principal comfort, he says, is derived from the perusal of the old Scotch and English divines; and some how or other, he has become very like them himself. He seemed inclined to think that I ought to write; but advised me, in the mean time to exercise a little patience.

What was wanting in the parson, however, I found my neighbour Scantocreesh very forward to supply. When Saunders heard the reports that were going, he threw down his axe, and came over to our house; and finding me at a loss what to do, he declared that I should write; though he should kill every goose in his yard to furnish me with pens. My word, he said, was not believed; because the country was swarming with a set of idle vagabonds like the sheriff's people, who were not willing to see themselves described: That, if they got what they deserved, instead of being allowed to go galloping about, they would be put under saws and harrows: That they were no better than the remnant of the Hittites and Perizzites, who were left in the land to be thorns in the sides of honest men: and what was worse, in prosperous times they had been allowed to multiply; till decent folks could not live in the country and bring up a family, without mingling with the villains and learning their ways: That, in short, the good of the province required that all such ne'er do well vagabonds, whether in the possession of the sheriff or out of it, should be hunted out from Dan to Beersheba: And finally he concluded with saying, that, if I would not write; though he was dead ill at the spelling, he would rub up a little and do it himself. When he was gone, my old woman observed that Saunders Scantocreesh was a solid, sensible man; and I resolved to continue my relation.

You will recollect that I found the sheriff's lodgers playing a game at cards and the grog before them. They all declared themselves very glad to see me; asking me at the same time to be seated and take a glass along with them. In these dull times, they said, spirits were a rare article with them: but I had had the good luck to hit the right time, and was intitled to a share. As an invitation to drink in such cases, is usually an invitation to something else, I declined the offer; remarking to them, that people who have little, should be sparing in the use of it. After some general conversation, Mr. Gosling took me to a remote part of the room and told me, that, as he had sent for me upon a very particular business, he was glad that I was come. His creditors had agreed to relieve him upon condition of finding security till his debts were collected. This, he thought very reasonable; and, accordingly, he would have applied to his cousin Sheldrake: but, as I knew, the poor gentleman, not being able to endure the rigour of a Nova Scotian winter, had gone to the south for the benefit of his health. In his cousin's absence, he had spoken to some of the rest of his friends, when they were dining with him lately; and they had all agreed to do it at once. But unfortunately, when the bond was prepared, one of them was taken sick; another, obliged to go down to Halifax; and, through some unexpected accident or other, he had not been able to see any of the rest. All the creditors, however declared Mr. Stepsure's signature to be perfectly sufficient. This, he had assured them, he could easily get; as there was no risk in the case: and he had just sent for me to put my name to the bond.

My neighbour, it would appear, had more friends to eat dinners than to sign bonds. As I had neither been feasted nor made promises, I was not altogether sure, that, in the division of Mr. Gosling's business, the signing was my share. At the same time, I felt a little to give him a positive refusal: but just when I was considering about an answer, notice was sent to us by the sheriff to look sharp; for parson Drone was coming in. This was a relief to me; but, among the rest of the company, it produced a sad bustling. In a moment the cards disappeared; the bottles and tumblers were clapt under a bed; and Jack Scorem picked up a piece of an old bible, which was lying upon the floor, and laid it on the table.

Every thing was scarcely in order when the parson entered; and I do believe that the whole company received him with unfeigned respect; for the breath of a religious man fans the embers of affection in the very worst of the human race. After Mr. Drone was seated, he expressed his sorrow at finding them where they were. He observed farther, that he had frequently seen those who lived long with the sheriff, instead of becoming wiser or better by tribulation, leaving his house, utter malignants and enemies to a seemly walk and conversation; and, therefore, to guard them against lukewarmness and neutrality, the usual beginnings of such wickedness; if they would vouchsafe to yield an ear to his doctrine, he would tender them the word of exhortation. Immediately they all expressed their gratitude and readiness to hear; and, I must confess, that, after what Mr. Gosling had told me, I fervently wished that our parson would give us one of his longest discourses.

We had now placed ourselves in a hearing position, and the parson was just about to commence; when *O tempora, O mores,* or something like it, was exclaimed from a dark corner of the room. Jack Scorem jumped up instinctively; and clenching his fist, cried out, "Keep your slang to yourself, and give us none of your Gaelic; else I'll lend you a sneezer upon the snout, that will bring the ill blood out of you." But recollecting that the parson was present, he again sat down.

Our attention was now directed to the dark corner from which the voice had issued; when the person who had spoken, conceiving, I suppose, from Jack's last motion, that no danger was at hand, stepped forward and showed us a thin sharp faced, dark coloured man in a threadbare coat, which had once been black. He assured Mr. Drone that he had got among the very goats of his flock; and, that, if, instead of giving them an exhortation, he would give each of them a halter, it was what they deserved. The fellows, says he, from morning to night, except when the grog is running down their throat, abuse the country; but the only misfortune is, that the country is cursed with such wretches: And, to satisfy the parson, he turned up the bed which concealed the bottles and tumblers; at the same time assuring him, that, if every man's pockets did not contain a pack of cards, he would retract what he had said.

Our worthy old clergyman, lifting up his hands, declared that he did not think there had been such wickedness upon the earth, and that verily our lot had been cast in the very dregs of time. But neither of us had much leisure to moralize; for, as the conduct of the company was now blown, Mr. Drone's presence commanded less respect; and to protect the poor gentleman, we were obliged to call for the sheriff, who reduced them to order, and conducted the stranger and us into another apartment. Here we soon learned how he had got into the possession of the sheriff. He would neither tell us who he was, nor whence he had come: but he informed us that he had arrived in the township upon Saturday evening, and lodged in Tipple's; and that his landlord, finding him without funds, had turned him out next morning before breakfast. In passing along, he happened to meet Deacon Sharp, who was going to sermon. The deacon was a grand juryman, and mindful of his oath; and rightly judging that this was neither a Halifax gentleman, who might be affronted and injure the town, nor any of the neighbours, who regularly travel from necessity with their teams upon the Lord's day, he resolved to make him a warning to others; and, when he found that he had nothing to pay the fine, he conscientiously put him into the hands of the sheriff.

The parson, though he observes the sabbath better than any of us, thought it a hard case, and promised to speak to the magistrates about him. Afterward, they entered into a long conversation about something which they called Political Economy. They seemed to me to talk very learnedly; but I could not understand them. I only remember, that they mentioned a great many names which I had never heard of before; such as Adam Smith, Ricardo, Du Say, and the French Economists. When we left him, Mr. Drone took the sheriff's promise to give him something comfortable to eat, and to keep him by himself. Afterward, as the parson and I were going along the road, he appeared to me to be as lively as in the days of his youth; and, in speaking of the poor gentleman in confinement, he remarked that he was a very learned man, and the only person he had met with in the country, who knew its interests.

Next morning, I was a good deal surprised to hear that the stranger was dead. Had he remained with the sheriff's other lodgers, I would have been disposed to think that he had not received fair play; but, as things were, I was at a loss to account for it. To satisfy myself, therefore, I stepped over to the sheriff's; and sure enough, the poor man was dead and very much swelled. When an inquest was held, the jury were exceedingly puzzled about what to make of it. Whether he had been poisoned, there was no evidence. At last they determined to look into the business minutely; and sent for the doctor, who at that time happened to be attending the wife of my neighbour Scantocreesh. When the message came for the doctor, Saunders grasped an axe handle; and vowed, that, while he had the breath of life in his body, none of the seed of Adam, living or dead, should be the means of calling his child, when it was born, Ichabod; and, that, if the doctor offered to go, he would fell him upon the floor. The jury were then very much at a loss. But Mr. Pat O'Rafferty said, that, in Newfoundland, he had split up codfish many a time, and could do the business completely. Accordingly, the poor man was opened by Pat; when it was discovered that his stomach was crammed with cabbage, and the rest of his bowels very much distended with wind. The sheriff had been boiling a quantity for his pigs; and recollecting his promise to the parson, had sent a large mess of them to the stranger; who, having eaten nothing since Tipple turned him out, took as many of them as finished a life upon which the sun of prosperity did not appear to have beamed.

When the jury proceeded to make up their verdict, there was a violent dispute among them, whether it should be *Died by the visitation of God*, or *Died by the visitation of the sheriff*. It happened that Mr. Gawpus, who is the sheriff's cousin, was upon the jury; and it occurred to him, that, if the last decision were adopted, Mr. Holdfast might be brought in for manslaughter. Besides, he thought that the present accident afforded him a good opportunity for displaying his medical talents; for, by reading the directions upon a large package of quack medicines, which he brought up from Halifax with the rest of his goods, he has lately become so skilful that our old doctor is now very much neglected. He, therefore, insisted that the stranger was not killed by the cabbage at all; but had died merely because the breath was gone out of his body; and, that, if he had continued to breathe; which no doubt he would have done, had his belly been rubbed with his Steer's Oppodeldock, he would have been alive still. Mr. Gawpus' opinion had much weight with the jury, who were mostly his customers. They, therefore, returned their verdict, *Died; because he could not live any longer*; and the overseers of the poor were directed to get the body put under ground, as quickly and with as little expence to the town as possible.

The burial happened to be upon the day which was to decide a bet of twenty guineas upon the comparative merits of Mr. Gawpus' grey mare and the sheriff's bay gelding. On this account, nobody could attend except Saunders Scantocreesh, myself, and one or two more. The sheriff's lodgers would very willingly have lent us a hand; but, some how or other, before he went to the race, he happened to turn the key of their room door; so that they could not get out. When we were waiting about to see if any more would come, my neighbour Saunders observing Jack Scorem and Peter Longshanks looking out of the window, walked up to them, and said that he was glad to see them so comfortably lodged. They should consider it, he added, as matter of daily thankfulness, that they had fallen in with a gentleman who took so good care of them; for, had they lived in persecuting times; they might have been obliged, like the Scotch Worthies, to wander among moors and mosses; and at last been taken up by some of the Highland Host or of Claverhouse's dragoons, who would have shot them or hanged them. He asked Jack how the old fellow with the abominable stuff was coming on in limbo; and advised him to take good care of himself, and never to ride a race with Jehu again, till he was sure that the sheriff was upon the road. To Peter he remarked, that, after such a long rest with Mr. Holdfast, his feet must be in excellent trim; and that his girls were anxious to attend the school, when the cold weather was fairly set in. He advised them both, that, since the stuff was abominable, they had as well leave it to Mr. Gypsum's nose: and when they felt an inclination to drink, to eat plenty of cabbage; which, he said, were an excellent quencher of thirst, and far better for them: And he concluded with exhorting them not to spare the cabbage; for he had abundance; and when the sheriff's were done, he would send them over a load. By this time, there was a good deal of noise among the lodgers. As I was standing at a little distance, I could hear only the words, *Scotch rascal* and *oatmeal*, frequently repeated. I had, however, no time to inquire; for it was now far in the day, and we proceeded to carry the poor stranger to his grave.

By the time we returned, the sheriff also had come from the race in very ill humour. His gelding had stumbled, when a few steps more would have won the twenty guineas. For his part, he did not know what the world would come to. Money had disappeared from the country; and he verily believed, the devil had come in its place; for he had seen as much fighting at the race, as was enough to put racing out of fashion: And in return for all his trouble in preserving the peace, his only reward was to have every strolling vagabond turned in upon him, to die on his hands and bring discredit on his establishment. Had the fellow, says he, been able to pay, it would have been nothing; but he and all that belonged to him, are not worth a groat. At the same time, he held up an old black silk handkerchief, and shook out a parcel of papers, which he began to pick up, for the purpose of throwing them into the fire. On requesting a sight of them, I found them filled with a variety of marks which I could not understand. But recollecting what our parson had said, about the stranger, it occurred to me that he might be gratified by a sight of them; and, therefore, instead of throwing them into the fire, I put them into my pocket and carried them to Mr. Drone. On looking over them, he said that they were letters addressed to the Recorder; but unless they were transcribed, it was of no use to send them. This, at my solicitation, he has engaged to do: but when you may receive them, I cannot exactly say; for our worthy parson is very poor and cannot keep a servant; and on this account, between tending his flock and looking after his cattle, he has a great deal to do.

P. S. Since writing the above, a variety of alterations has occurred in the town. Our sheriff is a very genteel man; and, as he sees a great deal of company at home, he is forced at times to be abroad in the evening, along with Mr. Cribbage, Mr. Pool, and a few other gentlemen. Accordingly, in his usual way, he stepped over one evening to Mr. Trumph's; partly to spend a spare hour, and partly to settle with Mr. Gawpus about the twenty guineas. When he returned home pretty late, which was some time before day light, he found his house standing exactly where it was before; but his lodgers were gone. Nothing remained but Mr. Goslings bond, a number of empty bottles, and a note from Mr. Pat O'Rafferty. The note informed him, that they had gone to the New Inn to spend the evening; and designed early next morning to take a look down the Bay: That, if he wanted to speak with them, he must make haste, and be sure to borrow Mr. Gawpus' mare; for his own gelding was a stumbling brute: And lastly, that, if he wished his lodgers to stay with him in future, he must give them plenty of cabbage. The sheriff rode every way but to the New Inn; and at last learned, that, had he gone there, he would have found them snug. Since then, he has secured his house well; and told his securities from a window, that no man in future shall enter his doors.

This event has increased the afflictions of Mr. Gosling's family, who were rather in need of comfort. Upon the day before the old gentleman left the sheriff's, his son Hob and Mr. Gawpus' son Jehu, agreed to ride each others horses for a wager. Hob started upon the grey mare; soon distanced Jehu out of sight; and since that time, has never been heard of: And poor Miss Dinah is in a very bad way. Some time ago, along with a number of the youngsters, she went to Miss Sippit's tea party and frolic, in very good health and spirits. After a good deal of dancing, the young folks, as it was a wet night, agreed to bundle; and the poor girl has never been well since.

In the midst of all these saddening events, my neighbour Saunders is almost the only rejoicer. Respecting the sheriff's lodgers he declares, that the country is well rid of the vagabonds; and that they will be a warning to the generation to come: That their flight is one of the best signs of the times; and he hopes to see the day, when the last remnant of the Canaanites will be driven out of the land.

Mephibosheth Stepsure

LETTER 6

To the Editors of the *Acadian Recorder,*

Gentlemen,

According to promise, I have herewith sent you the first of the stranger's letters. Our parson says, that, as far as he has gone, his reasonings are perfectly conclusive. But of this you and your readers must judge for yourselves.

Since I wrote you last, nothing of consequence has happened among us; except that Mr. Catchem has been appointed sheriff. For the comfort of our town, it was really necessary that the office should be immediately filled. Our parson looks after the souls of his flock: but they have bodies too; and I do assure you, that, in these times, the most of people's bodies cost them far more trouble than their souls; so that such a man as the sheriff, who kindly takes charge of them, is both very useful, and has a great deal to do. As far as I can see, Mr. Holdfast will not be missed. Mr. Catchem has got a large house; and he has already been going a good deal about, expressly for the purpose of inquiring after those who are uncomfortable at home.

As soon as the new sheriff undertook the office, he proceeded to take charge of the farm of my neighbour Fairface; and, as he had several others upon his hands, and could not manage them all; he judged it best to sell the farm, and apply the price for my neighbours benefit. The most of us imagined Mr. Fairface to be very well to do. Neither he nor his family, it is true, were ever great workers. But they owned a fine farm, kept a very genteel

62

house, and drove the best chaise in the town: And you may depend upon it, the chaises in our town are neither few nor shabby. It would appear, however, that my neighbour is one of those, who, as Saunders says, cannot walk upon their feet like other sober folks; but trust in chariots and in horses, and go down to Egypt for help; and at last get themselves drowned in the Red sea: for so he calls Mr. Ledger's large book with the coloured lines; in which that gentleman records those events, that the rest of the town are most apt to forget.

Thinking that the farm might suit my son Abner, I resolved to attend the sale; and knowing that my neighbour Saunders wanted it for his son Jock, I called in at his house upon the way, and took him along with me. When we arrived at the farm, riders and sleighs were turning in from every part of the town. Not that our townsmen in general intended to buy; for, in talking together before the sale commenced, they all agreed that money was money now, and no where to be got: but having nothing to do at home, they rode over to see how the farm would go, and who would get it.

The farm is really a fine property; and a few years ago, would have given fifteen hundred pounds: but, though the sheriff did ample justice to the sale, it was at last knocked down to Saunders for four hundred and ninety. When the sale was over, our townsmen began to joke him about living with the sheriff; and Mr. Catchem, too, asked him pretty sharply about his mode of payment. Saunders replied, that, before he could pay him, he must try to find out where all the cash had been going to in these hard times; and pulling out the leg of an old stocking tied at both ends, he told out of it as many doubloons as satisfied the sheriff and made all the jokers marvel. After tying up the remainder, he told us that he had been turning up his fields and found it there. He, therefore, advised us all to do the same thing, and perhaps we might be as fortunate; but withal, to follow his plan, and not do like the Chester folks; who once dug for money, and at last got so deep that they arrived in the other world; and falling in with the devil, were glad to get away with the loss of their tools.

When we were about to separate, Ehud Slush, one of our townsmen, arrived; evidently at the expence of a great deal of kicking and spurring. Ehud's mare is old; and withal, not very well fed. Besides, when he alighted, he told us that he had been out at his fox traps; and having found parson Howl's dog in one of them, he had been detained a little; so that he could not get forward to the sale: For his part, he had no intention to bid: for there was no money in the country; and it was a strange thing where it could be all gone to. Our townsman Slush is sometimes in Halifax with his furs; perhaps, you may have seen him. He is a squab little man, with large prominent eyes and lips unusually thick; which, according to the fashion of the world, because they are neighbours, keep as far apart from each other as possible. I am inclined to think that the human face divine of Ehud Slush is so configured from the nature of his employment; for hunters must always keep a sharp look out; and every body knows that the mouth administers great help, when the eyes are in earnest. But some of the neighbours affirm that it is in consequence of his intimacy with a bear, which scraped acquaintance with him one day in the woods; and shook hands so often, that he could scarcely get away.

About twenty years ago, Slush was a good natured young fellow. In due time, according to the practice of our town, he married and settled upon a lot of good land; and really had the prospect of being very comfortable. He had never, indeed, been guilty of hard work: but he had now got a wife in addition to his mare; and working or starving were his only alternatives. Ehud boldly chose the first, sharpened his axe, and determined that no son of the forest should resist its strokes.

When he began to cut down, he observed a great many fox tracks; and it naturally occurred to him that he had a trap in the house, and might as well set it as not. Accordingly, the trap was baited and set, and next morning he owned a black fox. The fox was brought home in triumph, and skined and dried and carried to market and sold; and Ehud put sixteen dollars into his pocket. Such an easy way of getting rich was not to be overlooked. In imagination he was already an extensive dealer in the skins of black foxes. But no man is lucky forever. Though the traps were managed with care and regularly visited, nothing sable came near them; except the little brother of Mr. Gosling's black wench, who happened to be strolling in the woods and got himself caught: And in the spring, Slush owned the skins of three red foxes and of as many martins. Hunters, however, as well as fishers, are a persevering generation: and hence, with a variety of luck, he has ever since continued to lie in wait for foxes.

In such a case good farming or, indeed, farming at all, would be contrary to nature; for, in every country, fox hunters are the avowed enemies of every thing in the shape of crop or inclosure. Besides, though Slush had been disposed to farm, it was not in his power. The man who sets a number of traps, has a great deal to do. In addition to visiting them, he must look after bait; and hence, when Ehud was not in the woods, he was wandering about the town, in search of dead animals, tripes, and other garbage in the way of his profession. In stating his toils, I cannot say much about the amount of his gains. I am inclined to think that it is not very great; for his family are always in rags and wretchedness. In going about the town, he gets an occasional bellyful among the neighbours; which, like all hunting folks, he contrives to make sufficient for a long time to come. Mrs. Slush, in her own way too, is a very industrious woman; so that, between making occasionally a little soft soap with the help of the bait, doing dirty jobs for the neighbours, and getting now and then a rabbit, they make out to live. Even in this way, however, they have not been able to get on, without contracting a great many small debts; which have made Slush wonder fully as much about the scarcity of cash, as about the scarcity of foxes. Indeed, necessity has rendered the former a subject of daily admiration; for he rarely meets with any of the neighbours without being reminded that they are very needful of money.

Ehud had come to the sale without much consideration. It had entirely escaped him, that, when money is scarce, men and beasts are very much alike; upon the least alarm, some run like foxes, and others are as familiar and crusty as bears. He was, therefore, in the middle of a scrape, before he was aware of it. He had scarcely got off the old mare, when my cousin Harrow began to inquire how he liked the potatoes which he had sold him last year; and Slush had just wondered where all the cash had gone to: but here the conversation was interrupted by Mr. Catchem, who bid Ehud come along with him and he would show him.

I hope, however, that Ehud's ill luck will deter nobody from setting traps. This country needs labour; and catching foxes is a laborious trade. They are, also, a destructive animal; and, in a particular manner, ruinous to *geese*. Besides, in these days, catching black foxes is a lucrative employment; and it would be a pity, if civilized people were to let the Indians get them all. Every body, therefore, should catch black foxes: and, I am sure, if we were all running about with dead pigs and pieces of old horses, we would be a more industrious people than we are. For my own part, I wish the trade encouraged; and, therefore, I give notice to all fox catchers, that, by and by, when they want potatoes, or begin to wonder about the scarcity of cash, my cousin Harrow has the first for sale, and Mr. Catchem will tell them about the last.

Mephibosheth Stepsure

LETTER 7

STRANGER'S LETTERS

LETTER 1

To the Editors of the *Acadian Recorder*,

Gentlemen,

The Province has now arrived at a state with which almost every man is dissatisfied; and, indeed, at a state in which it cannot possibly remain. In the midst of our golden dreams, disappointment has beset us; our imaginary mountains of gold have become mountains of embarrassment; and every honest mind is awakened to feelings of debts and deprivations, which render it a stranger to peace. Merchants, it is true, have large books; and farmers, large properties: but, in these days, a transfer of property is usually a loss upon the one side, and ruin upon the other. But description is unnecessary: every man knows our state, and every man feels it.

Still, by deploring the badness of the times, nothing can be gained. It is more requisite to inquire what has made them bad, and how they may get better. But, as these are questions which all your readers may not be both able and disposed to answer, I shall attempt to do it for them: and, as I am in a state which sets the world at defiance, I shall do it with boldness. If any person among us can do it better; we need his help, and let him not withhold his exertions.

There are some countries in which, from their very nature, the inhabitants must have few comforts. That is always a bad country, which does not contain resources to supply the wants of those who reside upon its surface. But to Nova Scotia, this remark does not apply. I will venture to affirm, that few parts of this continent possess such a combination of advantages; and advantages too, which must ultimately enrich it at the expence of its neighbours. The wealth of the sea is in profusion upon its coasts, and its mineral productions of value are inexhaustible. Nor have the farming part of the community any just cause of complaint. Idle people, it is true, are always meeting with bad land, hard labour, and poor returns; and hence it is, that we hear of the Ohio and Upper Canada, where the soil is far better. Yet when such worthies give these countries a fair trial, and at any time happen to return; which, I believe, is just as often as ability and shame will permit; they return with tidings that Nova Scotia is not the only country where comfortable living rests upon the labour of industry. Taking this province as a whole, it contains more soil adapted to the purposes of farming, than any country around it of the same extent, Prince Edward Island only excepted. But the best way to ascertain its value, is to look at those who have done it justice. I never yet heard of a good farmer, who blamed the country or complained of his returns. We do not possess the most fertile part of the world; but we possess a country whose soil will enable a judicious farmer to live, and to enjoy as many comforts as in other nations are usually connected with the farming life. If we grasp at these without farming as we ought, or if we grasp at more and feel disappointment, let us not blame the soil.

Nor have the complaints which are occasionally uttered against the climate of Nova Scotia, any better foundation. We have long and hard winters, it is true; and we have also short springs. But is not the luxuriance of the summer's growth, an antidote which nature itself affords against the length of winter? And surely, our long and delightful falls do not admonish farmers to indulge in idleness, during that season of the year; and then to cram the cultivation of the soil into the short period of spring. Besides, a farmer's whole life is not spent in plowing and sowing and gathering into barns. If the different parts of his labour be judiciously arranged, long as the winter is, it does not contain one day in which he might not be profitably employed. Our neighbours in New England, with a similar climate and a worse soil, have arrived at wealth and no mean station in the scale of society: we, instead of coping with them in improvement, are drowned in debt. How does this happen? Is it because our neighbours have a better government?

A fine country and want of comfort, are not unfrequently combined. The most fertile are often the very home of poverty and depression. As if to counterbalance superior advantages, providence has cursed them with a government which crushes comfort in the bud. But, upon the subject of dissatisfaction with government, where is the dog in Nova Scotia that dares to move his tongue. I do not believe that there exists a legislature, more zealous to promote the general interests of its subjects. I do not mean to say that the Legislature of this province have either done all that they ought to do, or all that they know ought to be done. At present, they have not the means of doing what the country needs. But judging by their means and expenditure, it will be hard to find a community in which the revenue is more judiciously applied. Nor, certainly, have we any reason to complain of the executive. This province needs a governor who will neither be indolent, nor regulate his measures by the suggestions of prowling individuals: And his Majesty has sent us one, who does business in a business like manner; who shrinks from no labour, where labour is requisite; who sees with his own eyes; and acts with an order and promptitude of decision, which gives activity to inferior offices and life to government.

But in relation to government, a more enlarged view must be taken. We are a dependant country: we are a colony of Britain; and, as such, under a variety of restraints with respect to trade and other things connected with the prosperity of a nation. Now a great deal has been said about a free trade, and about the cheap articles which we would by means of it obtain. But, I doubt, it has been said chiefly by persons who neither know the principles of commerce, the real state of this province, nor the source of its difficulties. Perhaps, in some instances, our trade is under restrictions which might be profitably removed; and, perhaps too, proper representation would produce their removal. In the mean time, it becomes the friends of free trade and cheap articles to consider, that a great trade and a trade of great profit are not exactly the same; and also, that articles are cheap, not because they cost little, but because that little can be easily commanded: And hence, before we arrive at the conclusion, that a free trade would better our circumstances; there are points to be proved, which, I doubt have hitherto escaped general observation.

But the point to be ascertained at present, is, whether our connexion with Britain be the cause of our depression. Has the British Government made us poor? or has Britain become poorer by a connexion with this province? Now let it be admitted here, that we are in debt to British merchants; and I doubt very much, that, if every man had his own, we would have little reason to be proud of our share. Still this is foreign to the question: exactly the same thing might have happened, though every creek and corner of the earth had been open to us for speculation.

With respect to the trade of this province, two points must be admitted: our lumber in the British market enjoys a preference; and in return, we receive a great variety of goods, at a price which almost annihilates the manufactures of other nations. From some markets, it is true, we are excluded; and must take through the medium of the British merchant a number of articles. But still the question recurs: Are they really articles, which, if imported cheaper, would leave a gain to the province? With respect to a number I do not hesitate to say, that, if their price were doubled, we would be a great deal richer. Cheap articles are sometimes troublesome guests in a house: when they are not carefully watched, they will turn the owner out of doors. Is it any hardship upon this province, that it cannot import crapes from Canton and laces from France?

Admitting, however, that in some instances we might go with advantage to a cheaper market than Britain; the question then is, has our extra expenditure on this account reduced us to our present situation? And to this question the reply is not difficult. Great Britain sells us a few articles at an additional price. In return she gives our timber a preference. She expends large sums upon our civil government, education, and religion. She provides the fleets and armies which protect us. Yet with all these advantages we are involved in embarrassment. These the preceding remarks have not traced to their source. They must, therefore, be the subject of farther investigation.

XXX XXXX

LETTER 8

To the Editors of the *Acadian Recorder*,

Gentlemen,

Calling upon our parson to day, I found that he had nothing transcribed. Mr. Drone, as I formerly mentioned, is very poor and cannot keep a servant. On this account, he has usually a great deal to do; and this week it happened, that, between additional parish duty and killing some pigs for the winter, he has been very much hurried. Not that the reverend old gentleman kills them and scrapes them with his own hands; for of this I am not assured. But, in this country, even when a farmer gets a little help, the work goes ill on without his presence; and you may depend upon it, our parson has hard work to make the two ends meet. Indeed, if he did not, beside feeding his flock, occasionally rear a few pigs, he could not live among us.

From these remarks, however, you must not conclude that our parson is disliked in the town. On the contrary, he is very much respected; and upon all occasions of good cheer in our own houses, we send for him and give him a share: but kindness beyond this the most of us have not in their power; for, as I told you before, the greater part of the town are in debt to the merchants, as well as to the parson; and, as these have not so much patience as Mr. Drone, they are always first paid. You may depend upon it, however, that he has the good wishes of us all; and, accordingly, at all our parish meetings, when nobody has paid him, every body cries shame; and in order to preserve some respect for religion among ourselves, and to support our clergyman decently, a resolution is every year entered upon the parish book, that he shall be well and regularly paid in all time coming.

On conversing with our parson, I found him considerably at a loss what to do with the stranger's letters. Mr. Drone says that he upbraids every class of the community with so much boldness, and at the same time with so much justice, that his statements will sting in every direction; and the parson is not willing to bear the odium which will naturally fall upon the transcriber. Neither traders nor farmers have escaped his censures. He says that the distresses of the province originate in the idleness, extravagance, and ill applied labour of the community: "And, indeed," says Mr Drone, while at the same time the tear was trickling down the cheek of the worthy old gentleman, "we clergymen have not stemmed the torrent of corruption as we ought. Partly from necessity, and partly otherwise, there is among us a great deal of ill spent time and unprofitable labour. For myself I can say, that I have often fed cattle, when the flock of Christ needed my services; and my conscience tells me, that, had I never entangled myself with the affairs of this life, I would have warred a more successful warfare against the vices of the town." What, therefore, may become of the letters, I cannot yet inform you. The parson says, that what can't be cured, must be endured; and then patience should be exercised: but, that no man ought to subject himself to reproach, merely for the sake of showing patience under it; and, therefore, he will take time to consider. He has been pleased to say farther, that my life illustrates the very doctrines which the stranger inculcates; and, lest the letters should not be sent, he insists that I shall transmit to you an account of the various steps of my progress.

When a person proposes to write the history of his own life, every body expects that he is going to tell lies; and, on this account, I, whose word has been questioned already, was not willing to comply with Mr. Drone's request. But my old woman insists upon it. She says that Mephibosheth Stepsure need not be ashamed among decent folks like himself at any time; and farther, that, if I will not do it, she will employ Saunders Scantocreesh, honest man, and help him with the spelling herself. Saunders also vows, that, though he is desperate ill at diting a letter; and, after getting on as far as these words, *hoping these few lines will find you in the same,* would rather work a hard days work than write another sentence, it sha'nt fail on his part. He says that I have been writing the chronicles of the town; and, that chronicles, to be properly written, should contain the history of some good men among a great many bad: And he farther affirms, that I have now a fair call to lift up a testimony against the whole seed and generation of those ne'er do well villains who are pestering the country; fellows, who are ignorant of every thing but the doctrine of Balaam; and exactly like their master, constantly running unlawful roads; and ruining themselves, by trying to get rich at honest men's expence. Saunders, also, assured me, that, in other parts of the province, people were beginning to call the whole of us in our town, a generation of vipers; and, that the credit of the town required me to show, that at least worthy, honest Mephibosheth Stepsure and a few others, are sober, industrious men, and live as comfortably as farmers could desire. My old woman insisted that Mr. Scantocreesh should stay and dine with us, and I resolved to put Mephibosheth Stepsure into the chronicles of our town.

With respect to our townsmen, I have not at present a great deal to communicate. If what my neighbour Scantocreesh says, be true; they are in the fair way of improvement. A number of them are already living with Mr. Catchem; and Saunders affirms, that the Jews gathered a large stock of wisdom when they went into captivity. At present, I shall only mention Bill Scamp;

whose history deserves the attention of all fathers who have active young sons, with whom they expect to live comfortably in their declining days.

Old William, the father, was an industrious, hard-working man; and by dint of perseverance and moderate living, acquired a very pretty property. I rather think, however, that our parson judged him too eager about providing a property for his son, to be sufficiently mindful of other points no less necessary; for I have frequently heard Mr. Drone tell him, that, when he was striving to leave a farm worthy of his son, he should take care to leave a son worthy of his farm; and neither be like old Stot, who wrought like a beast all his days, and left a beast behind him; nor like the father of Gibeon Trick, who ran through the old man's property, and lost both his ears before he was of age. William usually replied, that his son's education was not neglected; for he got more schooling than any boy in the town; and he was sure that he saw no ill example at home: he did not, indeed, spend much time in counselling him; for he could not spare it: but Bill was a smart chap at uptaking; and, as he was not given to bad ways, he did not need much advice.

The old man was always eager upon the work. By these means, he was both able to work a great deal, and do it well too; and, on this account, it frequently happened, that, rather than see a job badly done, he would do it himself; so that Bill had a great deal more spare time than his father. William, also, had a strong affection for his son; and, knowing that too much hard work is hurtful, particularly to young, growing boys; when Bill was not steadily employed, he would say little about it.

It must not, however, be imagined that Bill was lazy. He was a smart little fellow; and could get upon the mare and go an errand better than any boy of his age. To the father this was particularly gratifying; as it both showed the activity of his son, and saved himself a great deal of time and toil. To the neighbours, who would be occasionally complaining of heedless children, he would remark, that he did not know how it was; but his Bill was an uncommon boy for his age, and might be intrusted with any thing.

In this manner things moved on for a number of years; when, at last, the old man was a little startled by the appearance of a seal hanging down below Bill's waistcoat. On being questioned about it, he told his father, that he had been down, as he had bid him, to Mr. Gosling's store; and, that, just when he was getting upon the mare to go away, he thought of taking with him the skin of the black fox which he had caught last winter. This he had sold to Mr. Gosling, and received the watch in payment. Though the old man thought that the watch might have been spared; still he was not displeased to see that his son had a little spirit. The watch appeared to be a good one: besides, it had a fine chain and seal; and, therefore, as he seemed to have made a good bargain, he was rather praised than blamed. By and by it was discovered that the watch did not go very well. On this account it was exchanged; and a great many changes occurred, in search of a better. Sometimes, Bill had no watch at all; at other times, one; and frequently, two. All this the old man viewed with little concern, or rather with a feeling of satisfaction at the good management of his son; for Bill always assured him that he had gained upon every bargain.

For a considerable time this trading course continued without interruption or apparent change; when at last old William, one day, going out from his dinner, descried a young gentleman of very genteel appearance, approaching the house. Wondering a good deal, who he could be, and what he could be wanting, he waited his arrival, and was introduced to his own son Bill, in a fine fancy vest and a long coat and pantaloons of Mr. Gosling's superfine. The history of Bill's transformation was soon told: Having made a little by his watches, he had thought of buying himself a suit of clothes for sunday; and he had just been at the tailor's to get them. William had never before seen any thing in his family but homespun; and still he thought that homespun was good enough. But Bill assured him that he had got a great bargain of the cloth: it was also paid for, by his own profits: and besides, the old man was secretly so pleased with the improvement of his son's appearance, that, for the sake of seeing him so fine, he would have almost paid for them himself. Bill, therefore, found no difficulty in adding to his stock, boots, spurs, and all the other habiliments of a gentleman.

Soon after Bill's defection from the homespun, his father was one morning a good deal surprised at finding a strange horse in the barn, instead of his own mare. On returning to the house to inquire about it, he learned from Bill, that of late he had been thinking a good deal about the mare; she was getting old and not fit for the work; and he had just exchanged her and a couple of tons of salt hay, for an excellent young horse which their neighbour Swap had bought at an officer's sale in Halifax, and which could ride and draw equally well. The old man thought with himself, that he ought to have been consulted. But it was an excellent bargain: the mare was really getting old; two tons of salt hay were nothing; and the horse was a capital young beast; so that, all things considered, William was very well pleased, and viewed his son as an excellent manager. From this time, Bill made great proficiency in the knowledge of horse flesh; and apparently added so much to his gains, that, upon the farm, there would be sometimes more horses than cows.

Soon after the homespun was forsaken, Bill's occasions to be from home in the evening, began to be pretty frequent. At what time he returned, was never exactly ascertained by old William; for, like every other hard working man, he went early to bed; and his wife was what the world calls a very prudent woman, and said nothing about it. When questioned next morning about his absence, he had either been at the mill or the blacksmith's shop, or at some other place where farmers must occasionally go; except when he happened to be from home all night, and then he had stepped up to his uncle the deacon's; and staying rather late, he had been persuaded to stop and sleep with the boys.

It has been always said that late hours from home are injurious to health. Accordingly, Bill was at times not so able to rise in the morning as usual. Sometimes, he had been all night very badly with the colic; but most frequently, he was afflicted in the morning with a violent headach. The old man had been all his days very healthy and stout. On this account, Bill's ailments at first received little attention. But, at last, their frequent recurrence made his father think more seriously about them; when going to his bedside one morning to see what was the matter, he found a great deal of ugly looking stuff upon the floor, which plainly showed that the stomach from which it had proceeded, must be in a very bad way. The old man was very much alarmed, and spoke of sending for the doctor; but Bill would not hear of it: he hated doctor's stuffs; and besides, doctors were so dear, that a man might as well die as employ them. At length his father recollected how much good a little bitters in the morning had done himself, when he was not very well. Bill was persuaded to try them, and they had a wonderful effect.

Much about the same time, William received another unexpected alarm. One morning when the family were sitting down to breakfast, Bill, having occasion to use his handkerchief, pulled it from his pocket; but instead of coming alone, it brought with it a pack of cards, which the sudden jerk of the handkerchief showered upon the floor. To his father a sight of Satan would have scarcely been more confounding. But whatever astonishes, produces a dead pause; and before rage could find utterance, Bill had collected the cards, and thrown them into the fire: He knew exactly how it was; he had called last evening at Mr. Gosling's store, where young Cribbage was purchasing cards. Cribbage knew very well that he never played at cards, because his father hated them; and for the fun of the thing, had slipped them into his pocket: but the first time they met, he would make it dear fun to him. Where the mind wishes to believe, it is easily persuaded. William was glad to receive such a feasible account, and the affair passed off without doubt or inquiry.

Soon after the joke about the cards, Bill, as was now frequently the case, had stopped all night with his cousins the deacon's boys: but in returning home in the morning, he brought along with him a pair of black eyes. When William learned where he had been, he was not a little puzzled to make out how black eyes had come in Bill's way at his uncle's. He knew that the deacon himself was no fighting man; and his boys had never been known to lift their hand to any body. He was, therefore, disposed to think that all was not right: but just when he was getting into a rage, Bill put him in mind of the cards, and told him, that, happening to meet young Cribbage at the store, the fellow was not satisfied with making game of him before a great many people, but began to throw out wipes against old codgers who hate cardplaying. Bill could not bear to hear his father abused, and was proceeding to give Cribbage a good hiding; when young Pool and Trumph struck in, and bruised him so much, that, in returning home, he could not come farther than his uncle's. William was very angry, and for being off without delay to a lawyer. The town, he said, was come to a fine pass, when sober decent lads could not go about their business without being insulted by vagabonds; but if there was law in the country, they should remember the old codger as long as they lived.

Along with the black eyes, Bill seemed to have acquired a great deal of wisdom. He told his father, that he did not like to go to law; because, when young people's names were called in court, it sometimes did no good to their character afterward: besides, that lawyers are as bad as the doctors; and farther, that young Cribbage was a spiteful fellow, and might do them harm in some other way. William was very proud to find such an old head upon young shoulders; and partly to gratify Bill, and partly to avoid the costs of a suit, he let the business sleep.

The remainder of Bill's carreer may be stated in a few words. After getting rid of his black eyes, he married one of our neighbour Puff's daughters. Puff, by mortgaging his farm to Mr. Ledger, kept a very genteel house; and his daughters were well bred, flashy young women. Soon after Bill's marriage, his father began to feel the infirmities of old age. He used frequently to say, that, though his judgment was as good as ever, his memory was gone. Amidst the infirmities of age, it is a great comfort to old folks, that whatever destruction time works in their memory, they never find it affecting their judgment. I am, therefore, inclined to think that he who called old age a second childhood, must have been some foolish young fellow without experience: and, doubtless, if he lived to gather wisdom like old people, he afterward found his judgment as good and even better than before. My neighbour William showed the soundness of his, by giving up the farm to Bill, upon condition of supporting himself and the old woman comfortably, as long as they lived.

Bill was now a man of more consequence than ever. Being also a married man, the neighbours began to call him Billy; and some of them, young William. But even at the last of these names, he had a way of looking sour; for he was a good customer to Mr. Gosling's superfine; and on this account, among strangers, he was always Mr. Scamp. Indeed, both Mrs Scamp and he, were genteel young people. They kept good company too; and, I dare say, would have been ashamed to be seen with homespun boys, such as Jock Scantocreesh and my son Abner.

It seems, it is a law in genteel life, that every thing must correspond; and in general it is really a good law. When any person does happen to see one of your longtailed, superfine gentlemen, swinging an axe or holding the plough, the sight never fails to disgust. It always reminds me of what my old woman says of those poor unfortunate people who are lame of only one leg, that they have something unnatural about them; for they can neither make out a genteel limp nor a seemly walk. But Mr. and Mrs. Scamp, who moved in a circle where the law is observed, both understood and obeyed it. When they had dressed themselves out for visiting, it was impossible to ride upon horseback, without being covered with hairs or bespattered with mud. Besides, nobody in our town rode upon horseback, but Ehud Slush, old Trot, and the like of them. Fine clothes, therefore, needed a fine chaise, a fine house, and a long list of et ceteras. But, then, beside farming, which by the by was not much, no man in the town made so many bargains in the course of a year.

Neither bargaining nor farming, however, can withstand overwhelming calamity; and it usually happens that such misfortunes as Mr. Scamp's come upon people when they are worst prepared for them. Indeed, it was not possible to be prepared; for though he said himself that he was always gaining, he gradually got in debt to every body. Whether it was that other people cheated, and then abused him, I cannot tell; but along with his debts, he acquired the character, that for a penny he would cheat his father. I will not say that this is true; but, sure enough, the sheriff has sold the farm; for my son Abner has got it; and William and his wife are likely to come upon the town.

My neighbour Scantocreesh says, that nothing better could happen the villain: that he was made a man of, before the shell was off his tail: and that he was learning to be one of the drunkards of Ephraim, when he should have been learning his *carritches*. Saunders hopes to see the day, when every cheating, lying, huckstering vagabond, instead of being allowed to run about, making the shekel light and the ephah small, shall be carried away into utter captivity. But Saunders comes from Scotland, where the young folks are naturally dull; and on this account, snooled and kept down the half of their days: And he does not consider that our boys are sharp and active, and always take up a great many things without any teaching. Every sensible father among us knows, that, between his son and those Scotch dolts, there is a very great difference. It would, therefore, be just as absurd to give our boys a Scotch education, as it would be to try Scotch farming upon the land of this province. On the contrary, as soon as they can crawl about, they should be set upon the mare and be made to go errands. Above all, they should get something to begin the world with, such as a fox skin; for really experience shows that every body in this country has not been able to make out by his farming. Prudent mothers, also, will consider, that, when young people are pushing to be rich by trading, they cannot keep early hours, like hard working folk in the farming way; and, therefore, when the youngsters are late out and come home a little disordered, they will say nothing about it. By these means, the boys will soon become able to manage for themselves and to take care of the old people. Fathers, too, who are getting old, should consider that age brings with it a decay of strength and memory which renders them unfit to take care of themselves, and much less of their farms; and, therefore, they should show that their judgment is as good as ever, by giving up all to young active sons, and then spending their last days along with them, comfortably and without any care. My neighbour Scantocreesh vows, that, as long as his name is Saunders, none of his seed and generation shall lay a finger upon his farm: but for my own part, as soon as I feel myself to be an old dotard; which will be, exactly when I think of parting with my property and depending upon others, I design to give up all without the least security to my youngest son; for I shall then be able to say, (and every old dotard can say the same of his son,) that there is no danger of my boy using me, as Bill Scamp did old William.

Mephibosheth Stepsure

LETTER 9

To the Editors of the *Acadian Recorder*,

Gentlemen,

I have read somewhere in an old book, that Jupiter being in a great rage, as fathers sometimes are, tossed his son Vulcan neck and heel out of heaven. The poor fellow, between terror and tumbling had a sad time of it. Whether it was, that the gods of those days could not tumble upward, I cannot tell; but sure enough, he came down just as any of us would have done. If any body think that I am telling an incredible story, I can only say that it is nothing to what happened in Scotland, when it rained old wives and pike staves. Vulcan, poor lad, had, in the course of his descent, recovered himself considerably; for like the cats, that always contrive to fall in the most comfortable posture, he came down feet foremost. But, even though he was a god, such a terrible tumble could not be experienced without some damage; and, accordingly, when he began to gather himself out of the mud, into which he had sunk pretty deep, he was lame of both legs.

For my own part, I can give no such honourable account of my origin and lameness. I neither came down from Jupiter; nor am I, to the best of my knowledge, of royal descent like old Mephibosheth, but the son of Jabez Stepsure, of whom I only know, that, along with his wife and my cousin Harrow, who had been left upon their hands a little orphan, he came about the time that I was born into our town, very poor; and died soon after. Nature, in conferring upon me the due quantity of lower

85

extremities, had been sufficiently bountiful; but somehow she had omitted the last finish; so that, though by a little care I became pretty sure footed, my gait was never the most graceful. Of my mother I know as little as of my father; for she did not survive him long; and on this account, by the time I was able to crawl about, my cousin Harrow and I, came upon the town. As is usual in such cases, we were publicly advertised; but, when the day of sale came, though my cousin went off for a triffle, nobody would bid for me; for who, it was said, would take the trouble of bringing up a creature that would never be worth its victuals? When the crowd were about to disperse, old Squire Worthy arrived; and understanding how things stood, he told them, that, though they had all seen a good deal of hardship since they came into the town, they had yet some humanity to learn; and, that, if the poor boy was disformed, he had the more need to be taken care of. He then told the overseers of the poor, to allow him a reasonable sum; and lifting me upon the horse before him he carried me to his house.

Squire Worthy or the Old Squire, as he was afterward called, was a man very different from the squires of the present generation. There were then no offices of profit nor expenditures of public money, which, in these days, make honour, the ladder to advantage; and the old gentleman, instead of trafficking in writs for the sake of fees, was the peace maker of the town. When neighbours quarrelled and threatened to sue each other; Squire Worthy, instead of sending the constable, used to get upon his horse and visit them; and somehow, by good natured remonstrances, for he was a very good natured man, he generally prevailed upon them to cease from strife. In short, he had been made a magistrate, because our governor at that time knew him to be a good man and likely to do good, not by dealing out law, but by promoting good neighbourhood. When the Squire settled in the town, he had brought considerable property with him; so that he could afford both to live better and to show more hospitality than those around him: and as he did not seem to have a worldly wish beyond the desire of seeing every body about him comfortable, his family always enjoyed abundance; and the neighbours looked up to him in all their little straits.

By the time that I entered into the Squire's family, his own children were young men and women; and I must say for them, that, as they lived very affectionately among themselves, so they all used me with a great deal of kindness. As far as I recollect, the only hardship which I experienced, was the occasional difficulty of serving many masters at once. Every syllable of my name would be put into requisition at the same time. Meph must bring one thing, and Phib take away another; Bosh come here, and Sheth go there. But, as nature had given me only one person to four names, Mephibosheth could do but one thing at once; and, of course, where one was pleased, there were three angry. Still, after their little pet was over, they were as kind as before. They knew that I was willing to serve them all; and easily saw that to be in four places at once, was too much even for one who had his feet in good order.

The history of my apprenticeship I shall make very brief. It contains little which can amuse your readers; and, I am sure, just as little which could afford them instruction; for the world is wonderfully changed since I was an apprentice. This province in particular, is fast growing in importance. The proposal which was made some time ago, to adapt the state of the country to its ideas, by making all our militia men captains and colonels, very plainly shows, that, with few exceptions we are a nation of gentlemen; and what instruction could gentlemen derive from the apprenticeship of a bound servant?

With the exception of the youthful griefs of being called the lame boy, and then the lame lad, my time passed very pleasantly away. As soon as I was of any use, I was set to do little jobs about the house; and by and by, to work upon the farm. One thing I recollect, that, being at first a good deal with my mistress, who was an excellent woman; she used frequently to tell me, that I was a poor orphan, without parents to take care of me; and, therefore, I must learn to take care of myself. The good lady's drilling upon this subject, had all the effect which she could desire. Who am I? was a question which I frequently put to myself; and, as the answer never contained any account of rich parents and fine prospects, my humility suffered no violent attack; and it regularly recurred to me, that I who had nobody to do any thing for me, must learn to be my own helper.

Nature had not qualified me for runing races. There is, however, scarcely any disadvantage in life, which may not be turned to some good account. Nimble young men like Peter Longshanks, are apt to have their business in one place and their legs in another; but to me, to whom even a moderate pace was always a painful exertion, it soon became a subject of study, when walking was necessary, how many steps might be saved. Here your readers must not suppose that I am going to praise myself, by telling them, that, like young Bill Scamp, I had an old head upon young shoulders. On the contrary, this calculating disposition arose out of hard necessity; for, in the Squire's, we conducted the farming very much upon the old plan. But as some of your readers may not comprehend how the old system of farming could have any connexion with my lame legs, I shall explain the point.

Every body knows that farmers keep cows. Now, according to the new mode, some house them as carefully as Mr. Catchem does his lodgers; and others put them within as good fences, as if they were going to pound them. But the Squire's cows had the range of the whole province before them; and when milking time came, we would sometimes seek them a couple of days; and, perhaps, not find them at last. As for loss of time, we did not care any thing about it; for we had got the crop in the ground; and except hoeing the potatoes and a little corn, we had nothing else to do. But when the finding of the cows came to my share of the farming, as it frequently did, my feet would remonstrate mightily; and this usually introduced a great deal of communing with myself, how such an evil might be prevented.

It generally happens, also, that, as the crop gets forward, pasture becomes scarce; and then cattle are breachy. Now, in the old farming, it is a standing rule, that the fences will do for another year; so that at last they need a great deal of mending; and every body knows that cattle have always an antipathy against the mended part of a fence. On this account, half a dozen of repairs left the seventh no less necessary. This was a source of sore travel to my lame legs; for, as the Squire's sons were often from home, to look after the fences was a part of my business: and you may depend upon it, that it cost me no little hobbling about and mending, before I learned that much journeying and time and labour, are saved by doing a thing well at once.

Another part of the old farming consists in doing great day's works: And here I must say for my master's sons, that few young men could either work harder, or do more in the same time. But then, after the job was finished, the least additional labour would have been contrary to all law and custom. If we had been ploughing or harrowing; at the conclusion of the business, the cattle were loosed; and the implements remained stationary, till they were again in demand. Hoes, harness, and every thing else about the farm, were managed much in the same way; except the axe, which, being every day needed, kept its own place pretty well. This kind of economy, I recollect, was no great help to us; for when we set about a job, every thing was out of order; and the labour of repairing or running about to borrow, was frequently greater than the rest of our toil. By the by, when I mention borrowing, it is necessary to remark, that, according to the old farming, to return a borrowed article, would be such a violation of established order, as was scarcely ever known: And as my master was much better provided than any of the neighbours, we had usually more lending than borrowing, and of course this additional travel. But these things I did not, at that time, regard very much. My master's sons were more nimble than I; and upon such occasions, always employed; for who would send a lame boy upon an errand, when people are in a hurry? and you may depend upon it, there is nothing done without hurry, according to the old farming.

The only thing in which I had then a particular interest, was, the finding of the articles which were to be used. Nobody knew any thing about them; but I, as the servant of the family, was supposed to have the care of every thing; and whatever was wanting, it became necessary for me to find. In those days, I was just as heedless as other young people; but the pain of doing in a hurry what nature had not enabled me to do as fast as other folks, at last taught me that keeping every thing in its own place, is both an excellent preservative of articles, and a great saving of time and labour to those who use them. For the sake of my lame legs, therefore, my master's farming implements were always where they ought to be; and this simple particular had such an influence upon the prosperity of the farm, that the very man who had declared me to be a creature not worth my victuals, tempted me with an offer of great wages, to get away from the Squire and to live with him. But I loved my master: and I must say for him, that he always treated me like a son; and used frequently to say, that he did not know what he would do without Mephibosheth.

These remarks will show the connexion between the old farming and my lame legs. It is scarcely necessary to add, that the state of my lower extremities saved me from the errands of the family. These fell to the share of my master's sons, who were smart active young men; and never at any time needed two hints to go upon an errand. At that time I frequently wondered what could make them so anxious to be from home; for, as I said before, the whole family lived very affectionately together. Since then, I have heard parson Drone say that it is foolish for parents to complain of strolling children: that this disposition is altogether a habit which might have been prevented, by sending them fewer errands and keeping them steadily employed upon the farm: and, also, that any parent of common sense might, upon this subject, learn a lesson from the very dogs of our town; which go regularly to church, whether there be sermon or not. The parson also affirms, that it is a measure of sound policy, very much needed in this province, to provide every part of it with tolls; not only for the sake of the roads, but also to counteract that wandering disposition, which, he says, is a principal cause of our immoralities and distresses. However this may be; certain it is, that I have many a time seen my master's sons, leaving agreeable entertainment at home, perhaps for the sake of hanging about a blacksmith's shop; even when there would be nobody there but themselves: and I, on the other hand, was rarely from home, and never felt an inclination to go.

Whether I ever made any havoc in the hearts of the young women of our town, my knowledge does not enable me to affirm. I am rather inclined to think that my atchievements in this line were not very great; for, when I happened to be in the company of any of them, which by the by was not often, my feet seemed to be the only part about me which attracted their attention; and though my old woman says that they are very becoming feet of the kind, they are not the most comely portion of my frame. This only I recollect, that, when any frolicking was going on, I was never asked to be there. To be so overlooked by the young folks, was to me a sore affliction; and I would often wonder, whether it was that I was a bound servant and could not dress very finely; or because, being no great hand at the dancing, it was supposed that a frolic could not give me much enjoyment. I must, however, do the young people the justice to say, that, though I was overlooked at their frolics, I was not always neglected: for I recollect that when any of them were sick or dying, they would often send for me to come and chat with them; which the rest of the youngsters had seldom leisure to do.

These things I mention, principally for the purpose of showing you, that I had fewer occasions to be from home in the evenings than other young people. Indeed, I was rarely from my master's; except when he sent me to chop a little firewood for Widow Scant, and see how she was coming on. The widow and her daughter lived upon my master's farm, in a little log hut by the edge of the woods. She was a very religious, sensible woman; and on this account, as well as because she had seen better days, the Squire was very kind to her: And when any thing nice was in his own family, he took care that the portion of the widow and the fatherless, was always sent. Indeed, the whole family considered kindness to the widow, as an indispensible duty. My master's daughters in particular, who were excellent young women, would have parted with almost any thing for the sake of seeing her comfortable.

Being, thus, generally at home in the evening, I had a great deal of spare time upon my hands; and often in the winter, like other boys, I did not know what to do with myself. At last, my master advised me to try the writing and cyphering, and all the young people promised to help me. It was fortunate for me that my worthy master was so considerate; for, otherwise, I must have remained without these useful branches of learning. Our town, at that time, happened to be in the same state, as many parts of the province at present: no two persons could agree about a place for the school house; and, therefore, they all resolved to prevent their neighbours' children from receiving education, by having no school at all. With a little help and perseverance I learned, as you see, to write a legible hand; and got through with my Dilworth, without much difficulty.

After getting on thus far in my learning, I was again very much at a loss how to dispose of my spare time. I was past those days in which windmills and bows and arrows gratify the mind. It happened that Widow Scant, out of the wreck of the world, had saved her husband's books; and when I would step up about dusk, to see how the firewood stood, she frequently put a book into my hand, and asked me to read for her. Though the widow was a very good woman, she did not restrict her reading to religious books. Young people, she used to say, should know something about this world as well as about the next; and when she employed me to read, it was generally some book of voyages or travels, of which she had a number. Of this kind of reading I became at last so fond, that she would sometimes be obliged to remind me of home; and finally to get rid of me, would allow me to put the book into my pocket. By these means, I contracted such a habit of stopping at the widow's, that my master's family began to joke me about the daughter. But they might have easily seen that a lame lad like me, who was another man's servant, had no use for a wife.

Here, again, I must introduce you to our worthy old parson, the reverend Mr. Drone. The old gentleman has often told me, that, next to my lame legs, my acquaintance with Widow Scant is the best gift which I ever received from a bountiful providence. He says, and from experience I know it to be true, that an inclination to read, is an incalculable gain; that, beside the information and enjoyment which reading affords, it leads to those sober and steady habits which constitute character, and qualify persons for the duties of the social life.

At one time, I recollect, the parson was so impressed with the importance of this point, that he exerted himself to get a small library begun among us; and he so far succeeded, as to persuade a number in the town, after grumbling a good deal and abusing the parson, to give a triffle for the sake of the youth. It was of no use, they said: the boys of this country had no inclination to read; and it was needless to throw away good money upon parson Drone's nonsense. Accordingly, when the books were bought; those who had paid for them, recounted their predictions; and those who had abused the clergyman most and given nothing, laughed at their neighbours: for not a youngster would look at them. In the selection of the books, the parson's voice had no influence. Every man who gave any thing, was determined to have a book to his own taste. Deacon Scruple, who had found the benefit of hymns when he was smuggling, insisted upon getting a great many hymn-books: some of the magistrates wanted Burn's Justice; and Mrs. Grumble's husband Job voted for the Crook in the Lot. Mr. Drone told them that they were doing wrong: that, if they wished the youth to read, they must provide books which are engaging to youth: and, that, if they did not render amusement an introduction to rational and religious information, they would not succeed.

As the parson had predicted, so it fared with the library. The only readers are a few religious old people, who still make a point of conscience to read so many pages to their family upon sunday evening; and it generally happens, that the young people, when the reading begins, lay themselves back upon their chairs, and are soon fast asleep. Saunders Scantocreesh says that there is no wonder though the young people in our town be as ignorant as his stots; for the most of their parents have just as little sense: they encourage their children in card playing and frolicking and every kind of folly; but where is there one of them that ever bought for them a diverting story book to entice them to read? Saunders farther affirms, that almost every village in Scotland has its library; and that the thing speaks for itself. Every body, he says, reads except ne'er do well vagabonds; and that, not only diverting stories, but the bible too. As a proof of this, he tells me, that, in his country, a decent sober lad would almost as soon be catched stealing, as without his bible at the sermon; and, as an effect of this reading disposition, he declares that he has known many a farmer, who never had any thing upon his head but a blue bonnet, that could run through the kittle names in the Chronicles, and handle a point of doctrine almost as well as the minister. For myself I can only say, that my disposition to read was acquired exactly as the parson stated; and also, that, by means of it, I have passed with pleasure and profit many an hour in the evening, when my neighbours were in Tipple's.

The period of my apprenticeship was now drawing near its conclusion; when one day my master put me in mind of this circumstance. At the same time he told me, that, if I would consult my own interest as carefully as I had attended to his; I must look out for a good lot of land, settle upon it, and get married: for he had generally seen, that, in this country, if young people acted otherwise, they rarely turned out well. He then said, that, as a reward for my fidelity to him, I might either have the money which he had received from the overseers, or one of his wood lots; and, that, if I chose the last, I might take a little time to myself, and get a few acres down before next spring. The land was by far the best offer: it was, therefore, my choice; and next spring, with my lot of land, a few acres chopped, and a pair of lame legs, I began the world.

Mephibosheth Stepsure

LETTER 10

To the Editors of the *Acadian Recorder*,

Gentlemen,

   In the subsequent part of my life, none of your readers must expect a relation of surprising events. I was not, like Robinson Crusoe, cast upon a desolate island; and forced to try shifts which nobody had ever tried before me. On the contrary, I was in a christian country, and in the midst of neighbours who kindly spent a great part of their time, in preventing one another from being lonely. Not much of the visiting, it is true, came to my share; for, in those days, I was lame Meph, and not of much consideration among our great folks. Besides, when I was out of bed, I was generally doing something; and on this account, as well as because in those days I neither smoked nor kept grog in my house, it was supposed that I did not need to be visited. My only visitors were a few young people, who would lay their heads together to go to Meph's in the evening and have a little fun. But when I understood their drift, I used to read to them a sermon. Of my gift at preaching I can say very little. It has been often remarked, that read sermons rarely do much good; and sure enough, though I read good sermons, and very distinctly too; the young people profited so little under my ministry, that none of them ever came back a second time.

   Before I proceed to the history of my life, I must remind your readers of the apprenticeship which I had served to my lame legs. As I formerly stated, necessity kept me at home; and there, the same necessity forced me to keep

96

every thing in its own place, and to do every thing well and at the proper time. By pursuing this course, though I was seldom hurried, I had little leisure in working hours; and at last I contracted such a habit of doing one thing or other, that, when I had nothing to do I felt myself uneasy. The only additional particulars in which I differed from the rest of the youngsters, were, the habits of reading in the evening, and going pretty often to Widow Scant's; for whom I had contracted the same affection as my master's family.

When I was about to clear up my few chopped acres in the spring, a number of the young people proposed to make a frolic of the business and do it for me. This would have been a great help to me in the mean time; and, at first, I was very much inclined to accept the offer. But a little consideration showed me that the profit of a frolic would be dearly purchased. At a business of this kind, a number attend principally for amusement. In return, I would owe each of them a day when his frolic came round; and in order to pay my debt, it would be necessary for my lame legs to travel to every part of the town; perhaps too, at the very time when I might be most needed at home. Besides, young people, upon such occasions, expect something better than ordinary eating and drinking: but feasting I could not afford without running into debt. Mr. Ledger, it is true, had told me to come to his store for whatever I wanted: but a conversation which I had with my old master a few days before, convinced me, that applying to that gentleman in a strait, was, as my neighbour Saunders expresses it, like going down to Egypt for help; instead of finding myself better off, I might be drowned in the Red Sea.

The Squire had stepped over to learn how I was getting on; and when about to leave me, he said that he was going to give me a very serious advice. The evening before, I had been to see Widow Scant, and thought that he intended to speak about the daughter; but he had a different subject in view. "Never," says he, "Mephibosheth, allow yourself to get into a merchant's books. Debt hangs about the neck of an honest man like a millstone; and, in this country, it requires no ordinary uprightness and activity to prevent him from sinking under the load. Running into debt and long credits, have been the destruction of both property and religion among us. The person who has credit in a store, is apt to feel wants which his circumstances do not warrant him to gratify; and to gratify these propensities, he involves himself in debt; which, perhaps, never leaves him, till he has lost his little property and his character too. There is Puff, who has credit with Mr. Ledger; and he is living, not by his labour, but by sinking his farm: And there is old Guess; who, for these thirty years, has been telling his creditors when he would pay them; and, you know, he has nothing left him but the name of a notorious liar. Merchants are very useful; and we cannot do without them: but they live by the labour of other people; and they usually live well. Those, therefore, who employ them, must support them; and, in order that a merchant may live, he must lay the loss of bad pay upon the purchases of good customers. In short, according to the way in which business is carried on in this country, the one half of us are obliged to pay the debts of the other. If a farmer, therefore, wish to thrive, he must take care to have much credit but little debt." The old gentleman's advice was not lost; and from that day to this, though I have often rejected Mr. Ledger's counsels as obstinately as Jack Scorem, my greybeard was never sent away empty from the store.

About the time that my farming commenced, the suits which had been long pending between Mr. Bullock and young Quirk, were decided. Quirk was what our townsfolk call a 'cute young man. Indeed, he was a smart chap; but some how or other, he was very poor and not much respected. When he began the world, by settling upon a farm like the rest of us, he happened to be made a constable. This led him to acquire a great knowledge of the law; which was at times useful to him in the way of his profession: for, as he had the counting of other people's money, he often found it much more easy to tell how the cash came into his hands, than how it got out of them. He was, also, very helpful to the neighbours in the way of giving them advice. This, as it saved them a guinea at the commencement of a suit, was often acceptable. But, though I speak it to the shame of our town, I must say, that those who followed Quirk's cheap counsels, were always very ungrateful when their suits were decided, and abused him without mercy.

Quirk, by his new occupation made a great deal of money. On this account, his little clearing was not in very good order; and one day when he was from home serving an ejectment, Mr. Bullock's oxen came along; and seeing within a little brush something very inviting, they stepped over it, and took peaceable possession of Quirk's little patch of grain. When he returned, he was in a great rage, beat the oxen unmercifully, and then drove them to the pound. The case had now become complicated. Mr. Bullock, who is one of our great people, spoke big; and Quirk, who thought that the beating of the cattle could not be proved, answered him with abundance of law. Suits were entered; and on account of the intricacy of the case, as the lawyers said, protracted from term to term; till, at last, Quirk had justice done to him, and then sold his farm to cover his expences. To me this was a useful lesson. Before planting, I put a good fence around my few acres; and I must say, that, though both Mr. Bullock's cattle and neighbour Snout's pigs, were often about; I always found them very civil. Since that time, I have had much experience of both beasts and fences; and I have uniformly found that good fences make good friends and safe crops. Many persons believe that cattle break down fences, because they have no sense.

But, I assure you, that they are more sensible animals than a number who try to keep them out. As far as my experience goes, no ordinary beast tries to get into a field, after a farmer has fairly convinced it that he intends to keep it on the outside of the fence; and I have never seen any who proceed upon this principle, either quarrel with their neighbour about trespasses, or acquire the protection of the law by selling their farms.

My clearing was small, and therefore easily managed: and, as I was always at home, to do every thing about my little crop in the proper time and way, it throve wonderfully well. The satisfaction of viewing it, I recollect, was greater than the pleasure which I derived from considering its value. My old master, too, was so well pleased with my success, that he brought a number of the neighbours to see what industry would do. They all agreed that every thing was excellent and in excellent order; but to account for appearances, each had a different reason. When Deacon Scruple saw how my potatoes were hoed, he was sure I must have wrought upon sunday. Old Pumpkin, who has a large farm, and expends his labour chiefly in hunting the cattle from his fields, remarked, that lame people are lucky: And Mrs. Grumble, who, out of curiosity, had come with the rest, complained that there had always been a crook in Job's lot and hers; and, that, if providence had been as kind to them as to Meph, they would have had a very different life of it. My old master, I could see, was very much displeased. After hearing them out, he told them, that, though they had seen Mephibosheth's fields, they had never yet taken a proper view of himself. Every person's eyes were now directed to my lame feet; which the Squire perceiving, told them that that was not what he meant: and observing Mrs. Grumble feeling for her spectacles, he asked them, if they did not see about Mephibosheth, good sense directing labour and care to their proper ends. Here my visitors left me, displeased; and all speaking loudly, that I might hear them. Deacon Scruple declared that Deacon Sharp and he would see into the business; for such doings must not be permitted in the town. Old Pumpkin wondered that the Squire was not ashamed to hint that they had less sense than a lame creature: And Mrs. Grumble said that she wished me no ill; but it was a hard case that lame Meph should be so well off, when her Job and other decent men had such bad crops. This little pet, however, did not last long; for next spring I sold my spare wheat to Pumpkin, whose family live chiefly upon pies; and Job, who is obliged to live very meanly, bought my potatoes.

For myself, I was so pleased with my success, and so encouraged by my master's commendations, that I resolved to get on as I had done; and during the whole of my life, I have never had the least reason to complain of my returns. Many of my neighbours, it is true, have not been so successful. Still, though we differ in our modes of farming; I must say for them, that they are in general a good sort of people, and very helpful to one another. Indeed, if they did not assist each other, their life would be very miserable. I am always at home looking after my affairs, and never fail to have good crops: but my neighbours so often meet with bad land, hard labour, and poor returns, that they are obliged to spend much of their time in mutual visits, for the purpose of unburthening their minds and keeping each other in heart.

The man who settles upon a wood lot, has, during the first year, a great deal to do; and, if he be not disposed to get into debt, he must take care to lose no time. Yet, if he employ himself with ordinary judgment and steadiness, it is wonderful how much he will do without doing great days works. After getting in my seed, I began to think about my house and barn. By the help of the Squire's team I had got the logs upon the spot; (for I could not, like Jack Scorem, venture upon two frames;) and just when I was considering who would assist me to put them up, young Loopy came past. Loopy lived then, as he does now, in a little log hut covered with spruce bark. Neither the outside nor inside of it, I recollect, presented any inducement to visit it twice. His door was always beset by a couple of starved pigs, which occupied this station for the double purpose of enjoying the benefit of the puddle, and of being at hand to make their entrance good when the door happened to be opened. Loopy and his wife were good looking, flashy young folks; and on sundays and other public occasions, few dressed better or carried their heads higher. But, in speaking of them, our old parson used to say, that, if you trace a butterfly to its shell, you will find it a maggot; and sure enough, if there was any cleanliness or comfort about Loopy's house, the pigs had got them. His whole furniture was a large looking glass, a cross legged table, a few broken chairs, a number of nails driven into the walls; and, for a bed, a couple of blankets laid upon a little straw. As his articles were few, they were of course pretty much used. Mrs. Loopy was frequently from home, and required to be dressed. On this account, the eating apparatus was not much looked after. They usually stood upon the table, amidst scraps of pork or fish and piles of potatoe skins; of all which, also, the chairs very frequently contained a proportion. The nails were very useful for keeping their clothes out of the pigs way; and for showing how many gowns, petticoats, trousers, and other finery the young people had got. As for the bed, it was in constant use, and served the whole family. In Loopy's it was the standing order, that the dog jumped out, and Loopy and his wife jumped in. When he was finely dressed, I remember, he had a particular way of twisting his shoulders. Not that he carried any of his stock about with him; for I never knew him have more than one cow and the two pigs; except when he happened to be in the horse trade. But some people's clothes, you know, do not sit easily upon them, and then they are fidgetty. I make this remark; because some flashy young people may think that I am pointing at them; when I am only describing Loopy, who came past at the time that I was considering how I should get up my log house and barn.

Loopy, stopping a little for the purpose of offering me a great bargain of a horse, gave me a very discouraging view of the farming life. "Meph," says he, "I'll tell you what it is, you have got a world of hard work before you. Upon my word, the farmer has got a laborious life of it. I do assure you, it takes a great deal of toiling to maintain a family by a farm; and after all, it won't do." But, as Loopy had never been guilty of working hard; he could know the toil of it only by tradition, which is not a very sure guide. I was not, therefore, discouraged completely; though I refused to buy the horse: and when he left me to call upon his aunt Mrs. Grumble, I began the preparation for getting up my house and barn.

A log house is easily finished: and where its owner has any taste, it is susceptible of a degree of neatness and comfort, which comparatively few farmers in this country, can afford to unite in a larger building. For example, my neighbour Pumpkin, whose ideas were always large, in order that his buildings might correspond with his farm, raised a huge frame; and really, when the outside was finished, it had an imposing appearance. Travellers admired it very much; and Pumpkin himself, from the praises bestowed upon his good taste, began to look big. But, in building the outside to please travellers, he forgot that he had the inside to build for the comfort of his family. As I formerly stated, much of his farming labour is expended in hunting the cattle from his large fields: on this account, he was never very forehanded; and when passengers were admiring Mr. Pumpkin's fine house, he and his family were living in a corner of it, which had been partitioned off by a few loose boards. The rest of the building was found very handy for holding odd things. Now, about a farm house, this is a discovery which the owner cannot keep to himself. Pigs, dogs, cats, and fowls, all make it, and make use of it too; and my neighbour's house, beside the finery of the young ladies, suspended upon nails and pegs around the walls, generally contained a great variety of articles and smells, very useful to a farmer. Pumpkin had resolved to finish by degrees; but fighting against time, is often a hard battle. The other day, I had occasion to pass by his house; and came home very thankful, as I have often been, for my lame legs. I found the family, emptying the windows of the old hats and trousers; and one of his sons, who was tearing the clapboards from the end of the house, told me, that, had I been any thing else than a lame old rascal, he would have given me a beating. By the by, since I wrote you about Jack Scorem's house, there has been a violent revolution among the white stripes upon the clapboards of our town. Some of the youngsters have got wooden spouts erected; which you will see projecting out from the houses, when you come up the country. How the rest intend to conduct the distillation in future, I have not yet learned. But with the exception of Jack's house; and those of old Stot, Ehud Slush, and one or two more, the buildings of our town are very much altered.

Where every thing is done in a hurry according to the old farming, there are a great many little parts of improvement omitted; because they can be done at any time. For example, when a new settler builds a log house, he often leaves the ground about his door in a state of nature; and the chimney top, roof, or corners of his house, remain unfinished. This part of the old system of farming my master could never endure; and, indeed, I have generally seen, that, where these things are without, there is a corresponding want of comfort within. The farmer who does not finish his jobs, has either too many of them for his profit, or wants that industry which insures comfort. I, therefore, at once finished my house as it ought to be; and by doing so, found myself a gainer. The additional labour was triffling. In return for this triffling labour, I was relieved equally from smoke and puddle; and when my neighbours, in their large open houses, during winter, were shivering over huge fires; my little hut, well stuffed with moss, rendered me snug with a small quantity of fuel.

After finishing my house, I began to think about a garden and orchard. In visiting Widow Scant, who derived a great part of her living from a little garden kept in excellent order, I had seen its importance to a family. In my masters, too, whose house was surrounded with fruit trees, we never went to the door in summer, without being delighted; and upon his table, I have often seen a dinner, derived from his own premises, which would have gratified a prince.

With respect to my garden and orchard, however, as I was in no hurry, I did not proceed according to the old farming. The most of my neighbours had tried to raise an orchard; but had given it up in despair. Either the trees would not grow at all; or, if they did grow, it was only for a year or two; and then they died, or were destroyed by the cattle. But upon these points, I never found any difficulty. Pigs and fruit trees are very much alike: starvation brings leanness; and good feed, a flourishing appearance and profit. As for my cattle, after looking at the fence of my orchard, they always went away abusing the trees for being as sour as crabs; and now, the only difference between many of my neighbours and me, is, that they have not been able to raise orchards, and I sell them fruit.

When my garden and orchard were put into good order; with the addition of a few flourishing polls of hops, rose bushes, and honeysuckles, planted around my little hut, my premises looked very well. My good old master, who always took an interest in my success, was so pleased, that, when any of the great folks from Halifax came about, he never failed to bring them, as he said, to see industry rewarded with prosperity and comfort. These gentlemen, too, would sit down in my house or at the door, with as much cheerfulness and familiarity as any of the neighbours; and in conversing with the Squire, would draw a great many comparisons between my little hut and Mr. Pumpkin's large white castle, surrounded by ill cultivated fields and miserable fences.

Many of your readers may not believe that a stout active person, and much less a lame lad, could get on so well. I shall, therefore, explain the business to their satisfaction in a few words. I was no visitor myself, and few came to see me. Here was a large saving of time and expence. I was neither a great man nor a great man's son. I was lame Meph, whose highest ambition was to be a plain decent farmer. Here the whole habiliments and expences of a gentleman were saved; and being a gentleman, I assure you, is a trade which requires costly tools. But though I was lame Meph, I had a good stout back and good hard hands, and a disposition to keep them both out of mischief, by giving them something useful to do. I was always at home to do every thing properly and at the proper time. On this account, though I was rarely in a hurry, and seldom needed to work hard, I was able to do a great deal; and I must here observe, that I never accounted any kind of labour too mean or slavish, if I saw it to be useful. Besides, though I was a farmer, I was a lumberer too. I did not, indeed, like Jack Scorem, make great lots of timber. But knowing that I owned trees as well as land, I judged that I had a right to turn them to my advantage; and, therefore, rarely entered the woods without laying them under contribution. It was easy to arrange matters so, as to carry home a companion; and whether it was a junk for shingles, staves, or axe handles, my shoulders never grumbled. All these I deposited at home; and, during the long winter nights, when my neighbours were at Tipple's or visiting each other, some little article was added to my stock. These, according to my usual custom, I always made well; and, as my neighbours generally found it cheaper to buy than to make, my articles met with a ready sale, and brought ready money too. At first, also, I lived hardly; for what right had I to live otherwise? But the time slipped past; and I soon found myself surrounded by every comfort which a farmer ought to desire.

Mephibosheth Stepsure

LETTER 11

To the Editors of the *Acadian Recorder*,

Gentlemen,

During the first year of my farming, as I formerly mentioned, I had a great deal to do. But, in the warfare of life, exertion and perseverance fight a hard battle; and unless the odds against them be very great indeed, they never fail to be rewarded with victory. Before my crop was ready to be removed from the ground, my barn and cellar were in order; and long before the winter set in, my house was as snug and comfortable as a little log house could be.

I am not going to tell your readers every particular which occurred in my batchelor's hall. My cookery, you may depend upon it, was not very fine, nor my varieties numerous. I was never a great hand at stews and hashes and frying and brandering. As for those little preserved vegetables which set out a table and help better food; though I liked them very well, I had something else to do than look after them. Besides, in those days, they were not necessary. All that a hard working young fellow needs, is, to bring his hungry stomach into the company of food; and if it be clean, coarseness is no ground of quarrel between them: they stick as lovingly together as any new married couple. Indeed, I have generally seen that your men cooks have more belly than head. Abroad they are of little use; and at home, the torment of their wives. There is our townsman Pickle; who is a great hand at sauces and preserves. He can fry pork with the face of clay; and his wife, poor woman, ever since they were married, has been

108

serving an apprenticeship to him; and a very uneasy one too: for he is always in his kitchen, and always finding fault. Nothing but the cooking prevents him from living well in his family. About that he is so much employed, that little time to labour for the materials remains. Pickle frequently remarks, that every wise man will see into his kitchen affairs: but Saunders Scantocreesh says, that the man's god is his belly, and his idolatry has rewarded him with famine.

With respect to my little hut I must observe, that whoever came into it, never found the house running out at the door. My old master's family lived very neatly; and I myself, too, you will recollect, had served an apprenticeship to keeping every thing in its own place. This I have found to be a principal source of my success in life; for the abuse of articles is the chief cause of their destruction. Whatever belonged to the inside of my hut, stood in its proper place; and every thing which had no right to be there, was condemned to exclusion. Though I had not many clothes, I always liked to be decent. On this account, as I had resolved to keep myself out of debt, I could not afford to have a shirt lying here and a pair of trousers there, nor yet to hang them upon nails and pegs; for I have generally seen that clothes have no great notion of hanging any more than their masters; and if they can only get down, they are not very nice about where they go afterward. At the expence of a few hours work, therefore, I made myself a couple of chests; which saved me a great deal of money and a great deal of confusion.

My bed is the only additional particular which deserves to be noticed. My old master used to say, that a good bed is one of the best enjoyments of life; and whoever slept in his house, was sure to lie comfortably. Indeed, a good bed is not only a comfort, but a great saving to a labouring man. Whoever sleeps upon a little straw, as many of our dashing youngsters are obliged to do, must sleep in his clothes during the cold nights of winter; and where clothes are not allowed reasonable rest as well as their owners, not a few of them, I assure you, are requisite to keep flashy young people genteel.

You must not, however, imagine that all our townsfolk lie down like cattle. It is the boast of my neighbour Puff, that whoever sleeps in his house, sleeps on a feather bed. This I know to be true; for, being a gentleman, he would allow no other kind of beds in his house. Yet I have often heard his visitors remark, that they would rather hear parson Drone's longest sermon, than be in Puff's feather bed. When the parson is preaching, his hearers can take a nap at their leisure; but, in Puff's feather beds, the loud and incessant conversation between the ribs of his lodgers and the boards below them, sets sleep at defiance. For my own part, though I liked a good bed, I had few articles of dress; and, therefore, could not afford to lie upon straw. I had frequently heard too, that neither lectures nor conversations in bed, are comfortable things; and, as I had as often observed, that great talkers are not great workers, I resolved that my ribs should neither interrupt my peace by night nor my labour by day; and, therefore, when my oats were threshed, I made myself a bed of chaff which put the talkers out of each other's hearing: and, as I did not keep a dog, nobody slept in it but myself.

Summer had now fled, and with it all that variety of prospect which charms and cheers. The fading beauties of the autumn, also, had fallen before the stern blasts of the north; and rain, sleet, and snow, had perfected the desolation of nature. But none of these harbingers of winter took me by surprise. These I have always considered as the preparations of a bountiful providence, to renew those supplies which are necessary for the enjoyment of life; and, as the exertions of nature are made for the benefit of man, it appeared to me foolish, that, amid so much activity, he alone should be idle. When winter comes, the most of my neighbours find a great many days in which no man can work out of doors; and then they spend the time, smoking their pipe and talking about the storm. With me this was never the case. In summer and fall, I considered that winter was coming on; and being a poor lad who could not afford to go idle, I had laid the forests under contribution, and had more work before me than I was well able to do. By these means, in spring, beside supplying my neighbours with axe-handles, yokes, and other little articles, I carried to Mr. Ledger's store, such an assortment of lathwood, shingles, oars, handspikes, and staves, as he had rarely received from one hand at once. This established confidence between us; and I, as well as Jack Scorem, looked upon that gentleman as my very good friend. If any person doubt Mr. Ledger's friendship and mine; I can only tell him, that, when that gentleman would wrangle with the rest of the youngsters for attempting to impose upon him their plugged timber and other bad articles; mine, made well in my usual way, were taken at my word; and whenever I wished to see how our account stood, Mr. Ledger, instead of speaking of his straits and Mr. Balance, would tell me that he was in no hurry.

Still it must be confessed, that neither my industry nor reading made me so comfortable as I wished to be. In the long winter nights I felt very lonely; and, though I dreaded neither ghost nor witch, I often wished to have somebody along with me. To relieve myself, therefore, from solitude, I often stepped over to Widow Scant's, and spent a spare hour. The Widow was a sensible and cheerful woman; and, in her company, the time passed so agreeably away, that occasionally she would be obliged to remind me that the night was getting late.

Toward spring when Mrs. Grumble's husband Job was buying my potatoes, I began to be less lonely at home. The old lady would frequently come to speak about them; and not being in a hurry, (for our townsfolk are never in a hurry; except when they are farming, going from home, or getting out of church,) she would spend an hour, deploring the hard lot of some decent, sober folks. I do not know how it was, but every thing about me pleased her exceedingly; and, after praising my farm and my house, she would compliment myself, by wishing that her daughter Leah might get a husband like Mephibosheth Stepsure.

Though Job's family lived chiefly upon potatoes, Leah was a flashy young woman. When she issued out of Job's poor hovel to go to a frolic or a sermon, many a traveller has received an unexpected surprise. Nature had designed Leah to take the lead in every thing; for she was mistress of the family, and very harsh to the old people: and, though every one who followed her, admired her person; those only who met her, could feel the force of her charms. It is true, there were no dimples in Leah's cheeks: but still she had all the expression of a commanding beauty. To compensate for the want of those useless pits, which some chuffy-cheeked, good natured young people have in their faces; she could see two ways at once, much more distinctly than Venus; and possessed a nose, evidently intended for finding its way into very small crevices: And, as for the charms of her voice, nobody in the town could sing treble like Leah. When the old lady then wished her daughter as good a husband as Mephibosheth, you may depend upon it it was no small compliment; for you know I was lame. But Mrs. Grumble's friendship and mine did not last long. Since that time, too, I have often thought that it did not fail upon my part; for, when she used to wish Leah as good a husband as myself, I never failed to wish her a better. Whether it was that I did not praise the young lady enough, I cannot exactly say: but Mrs. Grumble ceased to visit me; and declared among the neighbours that I was a deceitful fellow to whom providence was too kind; and I, for company, was again obliged to return to Widow Scant's.

About the commencement of my second summer's farming, parson Drone was settled among us. As I told you before, he then preached a sermon which proved to my satisfaction that it is not good to be alone; and having always a disposition to enjoy as many comforts as possible, I married the Widow's daughter Dorothy. The habit of visiting them had become so inveterate, that I could not do without them. I, therefore, concluded that to have them in my house, would save me much time and travel; and so I got a wife. For many reasons I liked Dorothy, and Dorothy liked me; not because I made a handsome figure upon the floor at a frolic; for when my feet were born, the Graces, who had been invited to the ceremony, fled with precipitation as soon as they saw them; and, on this account, I was never a great dancer. Indeed, the Highland Fling is the only dance of which I could ever make any hand. But Dorothy liked me, because I was a sober industrious lad, good natured and kind to her mother: And here let me give a private hint to all good young ladies who are looking forward to matrimony. No man can be always cutting figures upon a floor for the happiness of his wife; and to make up for this deficiency, nothing but a great deal of sober industry and good nature will do. Without these, therefore, the married life becomes a warfare; in which female charms and exertions to please, instead of being repaid with domestic enjoyment, must grapple with a host of miseries. Marriage changes states but not dispositions. What a man is, such he is likely to remain: And, therefore, my good young ladies, if you do not wish to waste life in putting sloth to shame and soothing down crossness, take care not to marry them. But, as every body who hears of a marriage, asks about the bride; I, who was present and saw every thing with my own eyes, will give you an account of Dorothy.

My spouse was a good looking little woman; but as unlike the young ladies of these days, as our townsman Tun is unlike Peter Longshanks. Females, now a days, have lost all dimensions but length. The time has been, when I could have swung any of them around me with my finger and thumb. Dorothy was a round faced, red cheeked, junky little woman; and had good bottom in her too, I assure you: for I recollect very well, that, when I used in those days to lift her over a bad step, she was a good heavy load for any ordinary working man. About the bride's dress I shall say but little. Dorothy owned neither gumflower nor notion of any kind. Still she had good decent clothes, such as became the daughter of Widow Scant; and they were paid for too. As for our wedding, nobody was present but my good old master and mistress, who always rejoiced in my prosperity. Among us it is the practice to set off the young folks with a general meeting of the town, and a dinner which would keep the new married couple comfortably for a number of months; and though starvation should follow, this must not be omitted. But such feasting I could ill afford. Besides, though I, as well as my neighbours, liked a good dinner; I was not sure that Dorothy and I would come so well on with the starving part of the business. Some of the youngsters told me, that they wished to come to the marriage and get a little fun; but, though I assured them that I would be as glad to see them as ever, not one of them came. They expected, I suppose, that I would give them another word of sermon.

Beside Dorothy's person, there were several other reasons which induced me to make her my wife. These I shall state in order, for the benefit of all young men who have a notion to be married.

My spouse, as you know, was Widow Scant's daughter; and nobody could be long in the company of the Widow, without being the better for it. As I told you before, she was a very sensible and religious woman. About her religion, it is true, she said very little herself; and what she did say, was not much to her credit. But the neighbours pointed to her conduct, and agreed that she was an excellent woman. Mrs. Sham and Miss Clippit, indeed, who are two of parson

Howl's hearers, called her the barren fig tree; and always affirmed that she had no life. In mentioning these two ladies, I must give you a little sketch of their character; for they well deserve a place in the chronicles of the town.

Mrs. Sham and Miss Clippit were exceedingly religious in their own way, and zealous too in proportion. Accordingly, they spent the most of their time, running about the town to tell every body their experiences and how they felt. How many believed them, I cannot exactly say; but, as people by practice improve in religion as well as in other things, these ladies at last became so acute, that, by looking into a person's face, they could ascertain his state precisely; and when they found it bad, they could even do a great deal for his conversion. When my neighbour Scantocreesh came to our town; because he wrought pretty hard, Mrs. Sham declared him to be in a natural state. But Saunders was not easily alarmed: he said that slothfulness in business is no mark of fervency of spirit. At last the two ladies sent him word that they designed to hold a meeting in his house, in order to pray for him and convert him: And, as Mrs. Sham could recount something very like miracles, as seals of her ministry, she was pretty confident of success. Saunders did not know very well what to make of it. He said that in Scotland neither the Stuarton sickness nor the Cambuslang work, had done much good; and he doubted that his conversion would come slowly on in their hands. He let them know, however, that, as they seemed to think his house nearer heaven than their own, it must, of course, be the best place for praying in with a prospect of being heard; and, therefore, they were welcome to come and try their hand at the business. At the same time he gave notice to a few of us, that he was going to be converted; and he asked us to step over and witness the process.

When the time arrived, we were all there, to see what would become of Saunders; and, really, every thing looked as if some strange event were about to happen. My neighbour is a hard faced Scotchman; but, as if he had set his face against conversion, it seemed harder than usual. The two ladies, also, when they arrived, along with a few others to assist them in holding the meeting, appeared exceedingly solemn. Instead of being cheerful and chatty, as Widow Scant usually was; they looked as grim, as if they had been going to hang Saunders. Before they had well sitten down, Mrs. Sham began to tell him what miserable sinners she and sister Clippit had been; to which my neighbour nodded a cordial assent: but when she recounted the joys which succeeded their conversion, he seemed to examine their countenances with a great deal of care. She then ran over with much volubility, what she called marks of grace and the experiences of gracious souls; and was just beginning to tell him about the day of judgment and its consequences to himself; when Saunders interrupted her by saying, that he did not expect his conversion to be an easy job; and that before proceeding to it, we had better take something to eat. To such a reasonable proposal nobody objected. My neighbour, who is a very hospitable man, gave us his very best cheer; and I could easily see, that, though the ladies perceived nothing to be commended in Saunders, they had found something very good about his house. After our repast, my neighbour observed that about a business of this sort, he understood, there was always a good deal of tumbling and roaring. He, therefore, proposed, that, as his house was small and the evening very fine, we had better all go to the smooth green before his door; where we would have plenty of room. Accordingly, we turned out, one after another, as fast as possible.

When we were all upon the green, Saunders said to the two ladies, that he had now got them out of his house; and would tell them a little of his mind, before they began: And first of all, that, if he needed to be converted, he was resolved that it should be done by the word of God and his own minister, who had some sense and religion; and not by silly women like them, ladened with sins, and as ignorant of true godliness as his stots. He told Mrs. Sham, that, before running about the country, pretending to convert sober, industrious folks; she had better show a little christianity at home, by lessening that misery in which her idleness, ill management, and ill nature, had involved her family. As for sister Clippit, he advised her to find a husband for herself, and get children as the bible bid her. This, he assured her, would be more to her credit, than tattling through the town about her experiences and marks of grace; when every body could see nothing about her, but marks of corruption; and on this account, concluded her to be one of Solomon's foolish women, who are clamorous and know nothing. They and the like of them, he said, were a disgrace to religion. Instead of minding their own affairs, and living comfortably like other decent folks; they ran about the country in idleness, preying upon their neighbours the one half of the year, and starving the other: And, if it fared ill with themselves, it fared worse with their religion. Every fool among them was a preacher and a converter; and when a decent minister who could put a little sense in them, happened to come among them; they soon starved him away. They would give him plenty of prayers; and long stories which they had learned from one another, about their conversions and experiences and marks of grace. But when necessity forced the poor gentleman to remind them, that the labourer is worthy of his hire; his whole congregation would forsake him, to run after the like of Shadrach Howl, whom no careful man would trust with the feeding of his swine. With their groaning, and whining, and slang about religion, he said, they had made decent people, who have some sense of it, almost ashamed to mention many of its doctrines. At last, Saunders concluded with advising them to go home, read their bible, and mind their own calling; and let ministers mind theirs. This, he said, would help them to redeem their character; which they would soon find to be necessary: for he hoped to see the day in this province; when every body, instead of running after them, would, according to the bible, believe them to be silly women who had turned aside unto Satan. Thus ended all hope of my neighbour's conversion by the ministration of Mrs. Sham and Miss Clippit. For my own part, I was something of Saunders' mind. I have always thought that kind of female religion which speaks little and does much, both the most graceful and the most beneficial. I, therefore, married Dorothy, because hers had been learned in Widow Scant's school. What this means, will be by and by explained. In the mean time I would observe to all young men, that, as none but a fool will account female religion to be no ornament nor source of domestic enjoyment; so every wise man, before he slips with a female into a noose from which there is no escape with the life, will consider where she has learned her religion, and what are its fruits.

Mephibosheth Stepsure

LETTER 12

To the Editors of the *Acadian Recorder*,

Gentlemen,

I formerly told you that I had married the Widow's daughter. Indeed, I might be said to have married the Widow too; for neither Dorothy nor I, could think of parting with her. Our worthy old parson used to observe, that wherever Widow Scant was, there would be a blessing along with her; and, therefore, as I had married the daughter, it would have been foolish to have left the blessing behind. What the parson said, I have found to be true. I have now a good farm; I have, also, every comfort which a farmer should desire; and as times are, I cannot be called a poor man; for, as you know, I lately bought Bill Scamp's farm for my son Abner. But, after all, these are the least part of the blessing which I received with the Widow. I enjoyed her conversation daily; and instead of those grudgings and grumblings, which, in this country, are usually found at family consultations about how the old people are to be kept; making the Widow comfortable, was my principal enjoyment. Many a time, when I was working about the farm, the wish to keep her, as good old people ought to be kept, has strengthened my back, and made it willing to run faster than my legs would carry it. Indeed, almost the only symptom of hurry which ever appeared in our family, was, when the children knew that grandmother wanted any thing; and then, there were more servants than jobs.

When Dorothy and I, were married; Mr. Drone made a solid and sensible discourse, of at least an hours length; in

119

which he explained the reasons and grounds of matrimony. Then he gravely laid before us the duties of the married life; and among other things he told me, I remember, that, if I wished to have comfort for a lodger in my house, I must keep want on the outside; for, says he, a husband's house is the home of his wife; she clings to him, as the vine clings to the elm; and when he willingly gives her poverty for a companion, he kills affection by the roots, and domestic comfort dies along with it; so that even when they have something to eat, they eat it with bitter herbs. As I had, therefore, married Dorothy and the old woman, expressly with a view that we might all be comfortable, I could easily see that I had no time to lose, and must work harder than ever. To me, a return to labour after marriage was an easy task; for I always liked to be doing something. Besides, our marriage was succeeded by a great many savings in those very things which at times bring ruin upon promising young people. Neither calls nor visitings wasted our time, exposed us to expence, or supplanted habits of industry by those of a worse kind; for, to tell you the truth, the marriage of lame Meph and Dorothy, made less noise in our town, than the death of Caleb Staggers mare, when she died of the botts. I, therefore, returned quietly to my work; and I recollect very well, that, when I was slashing down the woods, thoughts of card playing and frolicking, horse racing and drinking, never crossed my mind; but my affection for Dorothy and the Widow, made the strokes fall thick, and made every stroke tell.

By these means, fields and crops rose very fast about my little hut. Whether it was, that I was now a married man, I cannot exactly say; but at that time I observed, that the increasing civility of the neighbours kept pace with the enlargement of my farm. I was no longer lame Meph and lame Bosh, but Mephy or Boshy; and some of the old and sensible people even called me Mephibosheth. To me this was gratifying; for every decent man likes to be respected. I did not, however, get too proud. Some doubts which hung upon my mind, prevented me from running about the country with my respectable new name. Having no superfine, longtailed coat, like Bill Scamp, I was not certain but I might yet be mistaken for lame Meph, instead of arriving at the higher appellation of Mr. Stepsure. I, therefore, stayed at home; and in the mean time pleased myself with the hope, that, as my name had grown with my farm, a few more fields would at last bring it to its full stature and due number of syllables. Nor have I been disappointed: All the neighbours call me Mephibosheth; except when they wish to borrow from me; and then I am Mr. Stepsure. But it is now time for us to look at the inside of my little hut. I formerly told you that I married Dorothy, because she was Widow Scant's daughter, and had learned her religion in Widow Scant's school. This last point I shall now explain to you.

When worthy Mr. Drone, at our marriage, tendered me the word of exhortation, he did not forget Dorothy. Whether it was that he was particularly anxious for our comfort, or thought that my spouse needed a little additional admonition, I do not know. But when he was leaving us after dinner, he told her that he was going to give her a very serious advice. "Dorothy," says he, "you have got a very good lad for your husband, (so the clever-spoken, sensible gentleman was pleased to say;) and if you do not find yourself comfortable, it will be your own fault. Remember, however, that you must derive your comfort from your husband's happiness. If you seek it elsewhere, woe will betide you. Many of the females of our town experience, that an unhappy husband makes a wretched wife; and they have themselves to blame. Young women are not sufficiently aware of the connexion between female happiness and home. Their enjoyments are scattered among the neighbours: of course, they must go in quest of them; and when a husband, after toiling all day, returns to his house, he finds his wife absent from her post and every thing in confusion; and because he loves his wife, and sees no means of comfort without her; in order to bring her home, he follows her to one or other of the neighbour's houses. Now, our townsfolk, upon all visiting occasions, are very hospitable; and both the young people soon learn that a neighbour's house and not their own, is the place of enjoyment. For a little while this does very well; but I have generally seen that the husband who is bound by no tie to his house, in the course of straggling after his wife, loses the chain of attachment which linked them together; and then, instead of going all the way to bring her back, he gets no farther than Tipple's. Dorothy, if you wish to enjoy true comfort yourself, make your husband happy, by making his house his home. You have been a good daughter; the old woman too has richly repaid you, by instilling into your mind the principles of religion; and I am now going to tell you the use of them. Religion qualifies people to go to heaven, because it prepares them to do their duty in the mean time; and that is always a bad sort of it, which does not draw the mind to social relations and social duties. Our duty in this life is a trust from God; and whoever looks forward to the true riches, must take care to be faithful in that which is least. You must, therefore, bring your catechism to bear upon the matrimonial state: And, as I told Mephibosheth to chace want from his house, I now tell you, that domestic happiness, though helped by plenty, depends very much upon who lives in the house, and upon what use is made of plenty when it gets to the inside. In short, Dorothy, if you wish to live a comfortable life, be a domestic woman; and when your husband shows industry without, let him see that beside the old woman and you, he has got contentment, cleanliness, and economy within."

As I knew this to be the education which my spouse had been all her life receiving from the Widow, I thought the parson's discourse rather long; particularly, as his last sentence contained the substance of the whole. Many of your readers, too, I dare say, will feel very glad that they do not belong to Mr. Drone's congregation. In our town, we are now pretty well used to his ministry; yet it must be confessed, that, even among ourselves, when he formerly discussed topics of this sort, which nobody cared about; the sermon always required a great deal of sleeping, in order to get through with it. But I thought of setting down the advice, that you might see what our parson was when he was young and spry. Of late years, indeed, the poor gentleman is very much changed; and rarely gets beyond the doctrine of patience. This he prescribes even in cases which appear to need immediate relief. When Tubal Thump's young daughter in law came, the other day, with black eyes, to the parson, complaining of her husband; he only told her, that what can't be cured must be endured; and that, even though her husband should beat her frequently, the best way was to stay at home and take it; for patience might bring a blessing along with it, which would do her good in the end. Under all the calamities of our town too, the only comfort which he administers, is, that when the state of society gets wrong to a certain extent, it then begins to get better of itself; and that those who exercise a little patience in the mean time, will see better days. Our townsfolk cannot comprehend him: but my neighbour Scantocreesh affirms, that the parson's doctrine is both true and plain. Though Saunders does not try the preaching; (for you know he was not converted;) he pretends to know a little of the signs of the times; and really he seems to have no sympathy for our distressed neighbours. He says that the calamities of the ne'er do well villains, are the dawning of a bright day for Nova Scotia; when every huckstering, swapping, cheating, running about vagabond will be driven into the woods; and a race of decent, industrious folk like Mephibosheth Stepsure will inherit the land. But I must now conduct you back to my little hut.

When I was living with the Squire, my spouse served an apprenticeship to the Widow, which made compliance with the parson's advice, a very easy business. Like myself, she had been habituated to domestic life. She was not lame, it is true; but she was a poor widow's daughter; and, as she could not dress finely like the rest of our young ladies, she was not much in repute. By these means, her mother became her principal acquaintance: this fanned the flame of affection between them; and, thus, by domestic life and domestic enjoyments, a habit was formed, that to Dorothy home and her mother were every thing.

Some of your readers will, perhaps, say, that all this is plausible enough; but how could a young woman learn contentment in the house of a poor widow? But the Widow and my spouse were not its only inhabitants: religion lived there; and where there is religion like the Widow's, industry and contentment are always its companions. For things which most of people despise, I have seen in Widow Scant's little hut, more gratitude than ever entered the door of a rich man's mansion: and gratitude hates grumbling; it is the companion of comfort. But beside religion, my spouse had found a home in the Widow's; and, strange as it may appear to many of your readers, whoever finds a home, has gained the grand point in the business of life. It will take very hard fare indeed, to kill contentment and drive him from his home. Having, therefore, married the Widow, as well as the daughter, my house was home to Dorothy. Besides, she was very good natured; and good nature is not only willing to be pleased itself, but when it draws affection to itself, it deals out contentment and cheerfulness to others with a liberal hand. Indeed, I never see my spouse angry, except when any body meddles with the configuration of my feet; and really she has discovered about them so much decent seemliness, that she has no great opinion of the judgment of the Graces.

But when I am upon the subject of contentment, I must make a few remarks for the benefit of young folks. Many of the ills of life are unavoidable; and wherever this is the case, a discontented mind bears the calamity and has the grumbling to the bargain. Others again, may be surmounted; but neither praying nor grumbling pulls the cart out of the mire: the sure way is to set a shoulder to the wheel. In most cases this brings relief; and even where it fails, it in the mean time frees the mind from its broodings of misery. A discontented disposition is an everlasting plague. It both kills comfort, and destroys the only means which could again bring it to life; as Job's wife Mrs. Grumble and all her connexions know. They are a large family in our town. Indeed, they have spread out so as to be the chief part of its inhabitants; for somehow discontent never impedes the progress of population. For different reasons they deserve a place in the chronicles of the town; and, therefore, as Mrs. Grumble and her father are samples of the whole, I shall give you an account of them.

Mrs. Grumble is the daughter of old Whinge, who was once a leading man in parson Drone's congregation. The old gentleman is still alive; and though his daughter has seen a great many years, he is healthy and stout, and likely to live a long time. In his own way he is exceedingly devout. Our parson often says that Whinge has wonderfully mistaken the nature of religion; yet still he hopes that the old man has some gold among large heaps of dross. He is among the oldest settlers in the town; but whence he came, and where he learned his religion, I cannot exactly say. Being always very poor, he has never known many changes of raiment; and at last his dress has become a part of his religion. His sunday's apparel is a legacy from his grandfather; who, as I can see from some old pictures, must have been a first rate buck about the days of Queen Ann. The tails of his coat meet before; but as for the rest of it it sets description at defiance. Perhaps, you know some poker made, dandy looking chap, he could creep through the sleeve of Whinge's coat, with a great deal of ease.

Besides, in every part, it has as many buttons and button holes, as would cost any of your town taylors a whole week's work. His waistcoat is remarkable for nothing but its flaps and pockets; in each of the latter, a pig six weeks old would lie snug and comfortable. As for his lower habiliments, the less that is said about them the better. When Whinge has his sunday's dress on, he has a venerable appearance; and among our youngsters he is generally known by the name of Methusalem. During the course of his long life he had observed, that dandies and other creatures of the same cast, have neither sense nor religion. On this account he has acquired a notion, that his own dress is the religious fashion; and when he sees the young people upon sundays, he never fails to rail against the foolish vanities of the present generation, and to lament the degeneracy of the times.

Before parson Drone was settled in the town, Whinge, among our religious folks, was a kind of oracle. The most of his time was spent in their houses, praying and giving them advices about their souls. The amount of his doctrine was, that time and time's things are nothing; and that every religious man must live above the world, and derive his comfort from his religious frames. Of course, his farm was in a very bad state. Indeed, if our religious people had not been kind to him; one giving him a little grain; and another, a few potatoes; he could never have made out. But it was often remarked, that, though Whinge lived above the world when he was giving advice, if any of the neighbours offered him a little help, he always showed that even good men may fall before temptation. After the arrival of the parson, these helps were naturally withheld; and since that time he has stayed mostly at home, not labouring his farm and living comfortably, but bewailing that since Mr. Drone began to preach, religion has no life, and that the church has fallen into very bad times. Some of our sly folks used to hint that Whinge was lazy, and liked much better to talk about religion than to do any thing for it; but this is only report. All that I can say from my own knowledge, is, that the old gentleman always seemed to me to like time's things very well, when he could get them for nothing: and though at home he lived, I believe, pretty much above the world; in his neighbours' houses, he never found fault with earthly things for being too many or too good. I have frequently heard parson Drone tell him, that, though a religious man care nothing about worldly comforts; industry, as it affords the means of doing good, is an indispensible duty. In reply, Whinge as often professes a great love for bible societies and other good institutions: but he has nothing to give them; nor does he conceive giving to be any part of his duty. The work, he says, is God's; and he will carry it on in his own way, if we only pray about it.

As Whinge had no industry, want lived in his house; and where want does not scrape acquaintance with industry, it becomes the companion of discontent. In Whinge's house every thing went on with a grudge. But discontent generally put on the form of religion; and when the family entered upon serious conversation, their standing topic was the poverty of religious men, and the hard lot which they must expect in the world. Whinge in a strait, never thought of exerting himself and making his young people work a little harder: all his comfort was derived from the parable of the rich man and Lazarus. In this school Mrs. Grumble received her education; and Job, poor man, and his family, are reaping the fruits of it.

Job was a simple honest young fellow. In those days, too, he wanted neither hands nor heart to employ them; and though the youngsters played upon him at times, he had good nature and industry sufficient to make any ordinary woman happy. Job was a sober lad too. Instead of running about taverns, he used frequently to visit old Whinge, to hear him talk about religion. Whether his present wife had taken a fancy to him, I cannot say; but when some mischievous boy slipped a hornet's nest into Job's trousers; there was no end to her dissatisfaction, that providence should allow such doings. Though the thing happened about Whinge's house, it did not terminate his visits. Job was not superstitious; and, therefore, did not consider the visitation of the hornets, as an evil omen. Some time after, as he was passing through the woods, his foot slipped in stepping upon a windfall; and on reaching the ground, he found himself seated very snugly in one of Ehud's fox traps. This Whinge's daughter declared to be no ordinary visitation; and, indeed, it was a long time before he was cured. It, therefore, called forth her discontent and her kindness; and Job, judging that such an affectionate young woman must prove an excellent wife, made her Mrs. Grumble.

Job was fond of his wife, and resolved to make her happy. After his marriage, therefore, he wrought hard upon his farm; and as he was a stout young fellow, he was likely to get on very fast. Mrs. Grumble too, was an affectionate wife; and, in her own way, exerted herself to make Job as happy as possible. When he came home from the woods, it was to hear her lamenting that her Job who wrought so hard, should have such hard fare; when all the neighbours enjoyed so many fine things. For some time this did very well. It made Job happy to hear her; and, in the overflowings of his affection, he would tell her that he would rather have her and hard fare, than all the fine things of the neighbours. But the truth is, that, along with the daughter of old Whinge, he had married the spirit of discontent, which gradually extended itself to every thing that came in its way, not even excepting Job; so that at last, with a wife who really liked him, he became very miserable. Besides, a mind which sees every thing wrong, sinks under the load; and feels little inclination to put any thing right. On this account, Job's hut began very soon to resemble

Loopy's. By these means he lost his home, and with it his
love for his wife. Now, the married man who has no home,
is like a stray sheep, ready to go one way as soon as another.
Every mind pants for enjoyment; and when a wife
withholds it, her husband looks for it in some other place.
Accordingly, many of our townsmen have discovered
Tipple's, to be the happiest house in the town. But Job was
a sober lad; and when he lost comfort, he did not part with
decency: he only became heartless. This, however, was
sufficient to destroy all progress. Though he still stuck to
his farm; he wrought but little; and that little, not much to
the purpose. He spent the most of his time, poking about
his small clearing; and when he happened to turn his eye to
his house; he viewed it with dislike, and hated to come near
it.

Thus, Mrs. Grumble, who could not be contented with a
kind and industrious husband, has passed through a pretty
long life; whose only comforts have been recounting hard
dispensations of providence and eating potatoes. Our old
parson says, that Job is the only man in the town who has
been edified by his sermons on patience. My neighbour
Saunders affirms, that Mrs. Grumble is one of the foolish
women who torment husbands, because they have not been
taught a little sense at the outset; and, that, if honest Job,
instead of submitting to be henpecked and miserable for
life, had laid a few cross dispensations upon her back; she
would have soon become thankful for small mercies, and
repaid him with smiles all the days of her life. For my own
part, I have never needed to try this experiment; and I
would advise all young wives to keep themselves out of the
way of it; for, though it might do them good, it must be
something like the rest of doctor's stuffs, not very pleasant
in the taking. Young folks had better do like my spouse and
me. My neighbours remark, that, when I am going home, I

gradually quicken my pace; and when I arrive, Dorothy and Mephibosheth are always glad to meet.

Mephibosheth Stepsure

LETTER 13

To the Editors of the *Acadian Recorder*,

Gentlemen,

At our marriage, as I stated in my last letter, Mr. Drone delivered to my spouse an admonition upon the subject of cleanliness. Imagining that the parson had seen something about her which he did not like, I was not altogether pleased; for new married folks, you know, are not willing to find fault with each other themselves, and much less to bear patiently the censorious remarks of the neighbours. On turning the subject in my own mind, also, I recollected that both Dorothy and I, had, before our marriage been improving in this point. When I happened to go to the Widow's a little earlier than usual, I would sometimes catch her putting herself or the house in better order; and then, as if something had been wrong, she seemed to be mortified. On this account, I thought that he might have kept his advice to himself; or, if he would reprove dirty people, carried it to Loopy's or old Stot's, where it was more needed. But a discourse which he made to her a short time afterward, convinced me of my mistake; and satisfied me, that our parson, in his early days, was a shrewd, observing gentleman. Perhaps, some of your readers would like to know what it was: I shall, therefore, set it down. If they can only get through with it without sleeping; as our people generally do when the parson preaches upon subjects of this kind, it may do them good: for my old woman, I assure you, has been none the worse of it. At any rate, in your paper, it will be like a doubloon in a poor man's pocket; it will beget admiration how it happens to be there.

131

A few weeks after our marriage, Mr. Drone stepped over one day, to see how we were coming on in the matrimonial state. When he arrived, he found my spouse mending the elbows of an old jacket; which, you may depend upon it, she could do to very good purpose. Every thing about the house, also, was in order; and herself, as trig and tidy, as when she was only Widow Scant's daughter. "Dorothy," says he, "I am glad that you understand and practice the duties of religion so well. This is better than singing hymns in the midst of rags and dirt, as many of our young folks usually do. People who have a home, should strive to have in it every rational enjoyment; and cleanliness and economy bring along with them a great many comforts. Indeed, I have generally seen, that, where cleanliness and economy are wanting, there is no domestic happiness and very little religion. It is a miserable life and a foul kind of piety, which do not try to keep the door between dirt and duty. As examples of this, I might mention the wife of our townsman Whinge, Mrs. Drab, Mrs. Slabber, and many others in the neighbourhood. Whinge, from his poverty, is obliged to stay at home, with no other comfort than the grumblings of a discontented mind; but the husbands of the rest live chiefly in Tipple's, or travel about the town without any business.

"All our unmarried females understand the subject of neatness exceedingly well; and, though I say it, I question if there be another township in the province, which contains as many pretty and neatly dressed young females as ours. Yet I doubt if there be another, in which, there are so many filthy houses and slovenly wives. When the lawyers, who are a jibing generation, visit our town, upon the circuit; I am often ashamed to hear them ask the meaning of the white stripes upon our houses, and to see them pointing to our windows, and then offering to send us up a cargo of old hats and trowsers. The wives, I know, are not always to blame; for many of them have husbands, who would depress the heart and industry of the best of women. Instead of minding their farms, as industrious men ought to do, they are constantly running about, looking after every thing but their own business; and their poor wives are left to fag on with poverty and wretchedness; first to bear the ill humour of husbands who return home to miseries which they have taken no care to prevent, and then to receive the character of bad wives from strangers who do not know their difficulties. Females were given to be helps; and I do believe, that, when husbands give them fair scope, they add more to the amount of human happiness than is usually ascribed to them. Many a young woman, who, in good hands, would have proved the ornament of her husband, has, through his own ill management, become his torment and shame."

"Still it must be admitted, that a number of wives are unhappy through their own misconduct. When they were candidates for marriage, it never occurred to any of them to trust solely to the force of their charms. On the contrary, I have often thought them more eager for dress, than became their station. But scarcely have they entered upon the married life; when, as if neatness and cleanliness were unnatural things, they forget the ornaments of a maid and the attire of a bride; and present to their husbands, not the appearance which contributed to gain his heart, but what, had he seen it before marriage, would have killed affection forever. Remember, Dorothy, that affection gained is not affection secured. To gain and to secure, require the same means; and the wife who desires domestic happiness, must, by the neatness of her person and house, take care to prevent her husband from harbouring a suspicion, that, before marriage, she had cheated him by false appearances. A woman of taste is always an engaging object. Mere beauty will never secure the heart of a husband; and wherever it is combined with slovenliness, it is, as the wise man says, like a jewel in the snout of the vilest of animals. Many of our young wives dress only for the benefit of their neighbours; and their husbands, because they see nothing pleasant at home, are always running about. Dorothy, if you wish to enjoy the company of Mephibosheth, use those means which brought him to Widow Scant's."

When your married subscribers read these admonitions to their wives, I hope they will likewise tell them, that to be angry and call me lame old rascal, is of no use. If there be any blame, it is the parson's. But to blame even him would be unreasonable; for his discourse, you see, refers only to the people of our town: and I, who know the wife of old Whinge, Mrs. Drab, Mrs. Slabber, and, indeed, the whole of the neighbours, know likewise, that he had just cause for all that he said, and for a great deal more.

Mrs. Whinge, as well as her husband, is, in her own way, a very religious woman; and like some other folks who think themselves uncommonly religious, the state of her neighbours who are not doing as she does, gives her much uneasiness. One source of her dissatisfaction, is, what she calls the stinking pride of our young people; who, as I told you before, dress very genteely; and who, as they think it of no use to dress for the sake of home, are always running about the town. Indeed, of late years, I have frequently thought, that the old lady has both reason and religion upon her side; for our youth are wonderfully altered, since I was a boy. Though many of them live upon potatoes, and sleep upon straw; the very poorest of them have their gumflowers and notions of all kinds, silk gowns and superfine longtailed coats; as you may learn from Mr. Ledger and the other merchants; who are very observing gentlemen, and for the credit of our town, keep an exact list of its finery: And when any of them, such as Bill Scamp, are dressed and gallopping about; did they happen to meet the very best of you Halifax gentry upon the road, they would stare at you, as if they intended to tell you how thankful you ought to be, that they allowed you to get out of the way without giving you a beating. But it was not the debt of the young people, their want of industry, nor their want of economy, which troubled Mrs. Whinge. It was merely their neatness, compared with the appearance of her own family, who were neither the best dressed nor the most cleanly in the town.

Were I to consult the credit of our town, I would stop here; but he who writes chronicles, should tell the truth; and in writing about religious people, such as Mrs. Whinge, he should be particularly careful to record those truths which illustrate the nature of their religion. This, our worthy old parson calls trying the spirits: And I recollect, that, frequently, in his younger days, he would exhort us never to receive any kind of religion, which did not tend to make us wiser and better, to exalt human nature above the inferior creation; and particularly which did not draw us to home, and make it the abode of rational and religious enjoyment. At present, therefore, overlooking Mrs Drab and Mrs. Slabber, whose character originates in pure laziness and want of thought, I shall restrict myself to a brief notice of Mrs. Whinge.

As old Whinge had grafted want of industry and discontent upon religion, it was easy for his wife to mistake dirt for humility. Accordingly, when the old lady expatiated upon the stinking pride of young people; their gentle stomachs usually came in by way of an appendix. Indeed, much squeamishness could never have lived in the family of Whinge; for it will be generally found, that, where want arises from habits of indolence, cookery does not arrive at its highest perfection. That it takes a great deal of dirt to poison poor people, was one of the old lady's favorite sayings. Of course, a mouse drowned in the milk, or hairs and other little straggling articles in food, were nothing: And even one day at dinner, when Whinge observed, that providence had sent them more meat than the family knew about; and the old lady examining, instead of finding death in the pot, only drew out a frog; though it proved a considerable stumbling block in the way of the young people's hunger; it was not, in the opinion of the old folks, sufficient to spoil good broth. If any of your readers suppose that no living creature could ever submit to stay in such a family, they are altogether mistaken. Many of our townsfolk, it is true, were not fond of lodging with Whinge: but when they did happen to sleep in his house, they were not without bedfellows; and some of them would even remark, that they had never seen so much company before. At one time Mrs. Whinge took a notion, that for a married woman to have her head uncovered, is a grievous sin. On this account, the practice of many of our young wives gave her great offence; and in order to be in the way of her own duty, she was accustomed to bring her clean cap into contact with the foul, and thus to remove the one and slip on the other at the same time. By these means she kept herself free from transgression; but what quieted her conscience, excited a sad commotion in her head. The population there increased very fast; and at length, like our townsfolk, they became dissatisfied with the country, and began to emigrate. Whether they were going to the Ohio or Upper Canada, nobody could tell: but I recollect, when any of our youngsters were obliged to sit beside Mrs. Whinge at church, they were particularly careful to leave a clear passage for the departure of the travellers.

If any of your readers disbelieve this account of Mrs. Whinge, let them only consider that I have given it in black and white, and in the chronicles of our town too; which are not like other chronicles, written about dead folks, who, when they are belied, cannot speak for themselves. Should they still bogle at believing, send them to me; and though Whinge lives in a far out settlement, I will conduct them thither, and procure them a night's lodging. But remember, I do not promise to stay with them; for I may be needed at home. In the mean time, I hope all your female readers will be persuaded, that domestic cleanliness is much better calculated to secure family comfort, than Mrs. Whinge's plan of covering the head and finding frogs in the broth.

But beside contentment and cleanliness, parson Drone, in his younger days, was a great hand for recommending economy; and at one time, after visiting the town, he preached a sermon upon the subject. As he has acquired some credit, particularly among the young people, by his discourse upon marriage, I shall show you how he treated the doctrine of economy; for, as he himself observes respecting patience, it is, in a family, a comfortable doctrine; yea and moreover, very seasonable and suited to the times. But I must first show you what is meant by his visiting the town.

You must not imagine that our clergyman ever spent his time in going about to make morning calls. The visitation of parson Drone was a season of much solemnity among our religious people, and of no less quaking among transgressors. In those days, the worthy gentleman feared nobody in the discharge of his duty; he divided the word of truth as every man needed; and as he regularly visited every house in the town for this purpose, each family heard from him those truths which he judged best adapted to their case, whether they needed encouragement or reproof. But as I formerly stated, after one of his general visitations, he appointed a week day's sermon for the female part of his flock. Whether he was going to praise or blame, nobody could tell; but every body was agog: and though we men folks had not been invited; male, as well as female, the whole town were there.

For the service of the day, Mr. Drone gave out that portion of scripture which says, *I will, therefore, that the younger women marry, bear children, guide the house.*

On observing my neighbour Pumpkin's large family of daughters, I could see that they were wonderfully pleased.

Some of them had stayed long upon his hands; for I have generally seen, that bundling is not the short road to marriage. When a lad of sense looks out for a wife; it is never among those who have been in bed with a great many young fellows. Pumpkin's young ladies imagined, that the parson, having formerly shown it to be not good to be alone, was now going to prove that it is good to marry. But Mr. Drone by commencing, set conjecture at rest.

"There are," said he, "three points contained in the text. With respect to the first, I must refer you to my former discourse: And be assured, that the young woman who seeks to avoid solitude, without taking marriage in the way, is in great danger of getting company which will bring her to shame."

Here, the countenance of the whole Pumpkin family fell. The oldest, in the course of bundling, had acquired a good deal of brass; but it was not possible for one young woman to outstare a whole congregation.

"The second topic," subjoined the parson, "stands in connexion with the first, and ought not to receive a separate illustration. At present, therefore, I shall direct your attention solely to the third, which is, *Guide the house*."

Here, with the exception of a little fidgetting and shifting of position among the Trotabouts, who are pretty numerous in the town, we became all very attentive, and Mr. Drone proceeded.

"It was not good for man to be alone; and divine beneficence provided for him a companion and helper. But she who was given him to be the joy of his life, helped him to sin; and labour and sorrow became the allotment of both. This is a fair statement of the case: let us now observe its result."

"Every mind shrinks from pain; and because the exertions of labour fatigue, many foolishly conclude that an escape from toil is a relief from sorrow. But are those of you who work least the happiest in the town? They have the fewest means of enjoyment; and their idle life gives them time for pursuits, which at last load them with misery."

At this part of the parson's discourse, a number of our townsmen who had come to enjoy themselves at the expence of the females, began to get very long faces. The wives of Tipple's customers, all looked at their husbands; and the head of my neighbour Trot required a great deal of scratching. As for the young ladies of the Trotabout connexion; by their smothering a laugh, I could easily see that none of them believed travelling about the town to be a journey of sorrow.

"Many," said the parson, "view labour, only as the wages of sin; and without quarrelling with the sin, they avoid the labour. But to man in his present state, industrious exertion is one of heaven's best gifts. It is the wise arrangement of a merciful providence, to curb his vices and protect him from misery. It is the means to collect around him an abundance of individual and social enjoyments. But those who escape from the activity of an industrious life, do not escape to a life of happiness: they become the debased and profligate; and at last, the wretched dregs of a miserable world."

"A life without care would not satisfy man; and thorns and thistles and barren land, were sent to give him something to think about. He would not limit his activity to the service of his creator: now, his duty arises from his sin; and his activity must relieve his own wants. Here is a correct view of the case: upon the earth transgression has entailed a curse, which man must remove by an industrious life. This and this only, will gladden the wilderness and solitary place, will make the desert rejoice and blossom as the rose. Do you wish the excellency of Carmel and Sharon to adorn your fields? Arouse activity to labour; and then, in the restoration of beauty and fruitfulness to the face of nature, and in the return of rational and religious enjoyment to your home, you shall see the glory of the Lord and the excellency of our God."

With this part of the parsons discourse, our females seemed wonderfully pleased. But Tipple's customers began to yawn a good deal; and Trot, who, for several days before, had been running every where and asking every body, what Mr. Drone was going to preach about, fell fast asleep.

"With these introductory remarks," subjoined the parson, "I shall now proceed to the immediate subject of discourse."

"As labour is thus a general allotment, females must not expect an exemption. In the business of life they are still the helpers of men; and nature itself marks out the sphere of their activity. With the rugged toils of the field, the strength of man coincides; and for the delicate frame of the female, there are domestic labours, in which prudent management is more availing than strength. By the misconduct of a female, labour and sorrow have become the portion of man: hers, therefore, is the duty of sweetening his toil and soothing his sorrow: and when he turns to his home as the retreat of comfort, and gathers into it the means of enjoyment; she must *guide the house.*"

"The female, then, who would be the guide of her husband's house, must make it her abode: she must be a *keeper at home*. I do not mean, that, between females or families there should be no mutual visitings. Well regulated social intercourse is a sweetner of life; but, recurring too often, it is the destruction of morals and of all domestic enjoyment. The female who views home as a prison, and escapes from it with pleasure, is unfaithful to her trust. When she is straggling about the town, there must be ill management in the house of her husband; and be assured that the heart of a husband is never linked with the misconduct of a wife. Home hated by the wife, has no charms for the husband. When necessity forces them to make it their abode, misery dwells there."

"Remember, also, that the female who lives with a husband, is not a mere *keeper at home*: she is the *guide* of his house; and whether she have the management of little or much, economy is the parent of permanent comfort. By economy I do not mean that niggardly disposition which grudges the very comforts for which labour is expended. It embraces the whole range of female exertion in *guiding the house*. Economy sees the mistress of a family and every thing connected with domestic management, in their own places; and every part of domestic labour, done at the right time. It takes care that the desire of pleasure contract no debt. It restricts itself to the means of enjoyment which a husband provides; and when it proceeds to expend, it squanders not upon transient pleasures: its first care is the solid and permanent comforts of domestic life. This is economy: And now let me tell you, that, because many of you want it, you want every thing which can make home desirable to either husband or wife. Through inattention to time and place, you are always in confusion, always in a hurry, and always behind with your work. Besides, there is among you a sad mismanagement of the means of domestic comfort. With some of you, I know, there is alternately feasting or famine, dressing with finery, or living in rags. To your elegant appearance and feasting, as far as they are consistent with a christian deportment, I do not object. But, surely, for the sake of fine clothes and frolicking, either to involve your husbands in debt, or to be deprived of the real comforts of life during the greater part of the year, discovers a disregard of domestic happiness, which cannot fail to produce ill doing husbands and wretched wives: And—"

How far the parson might have proceeded I do not know; for upon topics of this kind he was always longwinded. But, just at this part of his discourse, an alarm was given, that the pipe of the stove had caught fire, and had kindled the roof. To preserve the church, therefore, we turned out as quickly as possible; and, indeed, the most of our females now needed to be cooled. The wife of my cousin Harrow, Dorothy, and a few others, agreed that Mr. Drone had given us a solid and sensible discourse; but it was a long time before the rest of the females would be reconciled to the parson, or even hear his sermon upon economy mentioned.

Thus, by means of a religious education, beside the old woman and Dorothy, contentment, cleanliness, and economy, lived in my house. I must do my spouse the justice to say, that the prosperity of our family is not more indebted to my labours without, than to her thrifty management and economy within. She has been a good wife to me; she is, therefore, mistress in my house; and whatever she says about domestic affairs, is law in the family. Some of your readers may, perhaps, suspect, that she has got into the trousers. You may tell them, that, were their wives there, they would perhaps be better men; and their families, more comfortable. But to prevent all misrepresentation and mistake, I shall give you the history of the trousers from beginning to end; and I request all your farming readers to ponder it well: my sheep produce the wool, my family spin it, and weave it, and dye it: my wife makes the trousers, and I wear them.

Mephibosheth Stepsure

LETTER 14

To the Editors of the *Acadian Recorder*,

Gentlemen,

At our marriage, as you may recollect, the parson told me, that, if I wished to have comfort for a lodger in my house, I must keep want on the outside. To me the advice appeared to be reasonable; for want gives no scope to the domestic talents of a wife. When it arises from a husbands indolence, it represses female desire and exertion to please; it arouses feelings which make home, the habitation of misery. Determined, therefore, that my spouse should have fair play, I considered with myself that I was a stout young fellow, having so much time, and able to do a certain quantity of labour; and then I resolved that neither lost time nor ill employed labour, should stand in the way of her domestic management. Every man who works for his neighbour, knows time to be money. I, therefore, determined to make it money by working for myself. Upon this point, the experience of my neighbour Trot afforded me a useful warning.

Trot, in his younger days, owned an excellent farm; and was a very good sort of man. Many a hungry belly he has filled; and he has lodged many pennyless travellers, who have long since forgotten that he ever showed them kindness. Nature had given Trot a very long nose, which was always in his way, and gave him great annoyance when he began to work. Indeed, I may say that his life has taken its direction from this member of his body; for, when it was kept out of his own way, it usually got among his

143

neighbours' affairs: and at last the habit of thinking and talking of other folks' business, became so inveterate; that, unless compelled by necessity, he would never submit to the painful exertion of bridling his nose duly, and working for himself. Had Trot's curiosity been properly directed, he would have become a sensible and well informed man: but his desire of knowledge rarely looked beyond the occurrences of the day. Respecting these, however, it became by habit insatiable. If a stranger passed, when he was getting out of bed; he has been known, for the sake of learning the news, to run after him with his trousers in his hand. When his own farm needed his presence, he would get upon his horse and ride twenty miles to learn what his acquaintances were doing: and many a long day he has spent with Ehud, travelling through the woods to see what was in the traps.

With such a life, Trot's farm could not be in very good order. He had always more work than he was able to overtake. This could not escape his observation; and, in thinking upon the subject, he discovered, that, in this country, the winters are so long as to leave very little time for the labour of farming: and many a day he has spent, and many a mile he has ridden, to tell his neighbours about the shortness of summer and the length of winter. At last the sheriff persuaded him, that, as the short summers prevented him from managing his farm to his liking, it would be better to give it up: and now, the poor old man, without property or even a horse to ride upon, wanders about the town hunting for news. His large family too, (and a fine family they would have been, had a domestic father been the guide of their youth;) are mere strolling vagabonds. Though they may be found in every part of the province, they live nowhere. They are noted for doing one great day's work, drinking two, getting into debt, and then decamping to some remote part, to begin another great day's work.

Trot had warned me that the summers are short. I, therefore, concluded that not a day must be lost; and, in adhering to this rule, I found my lame legs of essential service. In this country there are many public duties and private necessities, which call a farmer from home; and which require to be carefully watched, if he would wish to avoid contracting a disposition to wander. For myself, I had found a *home*, and had no desire to be abroad; and my feet excused me from a variety of services. I was not fit to be a constable; for the people of our town are pretty long legged, and run amazingly when a constable comes in sight. In those days, also, it was not supposed by any body, that lame Boshy was qualified to be a juryman. I question if there be another township in the province, which maintains as conscientiously the dignity of the courts. When the sheriff summons so many to attend; the rest, except my cousin Harrow, Saunders Scantocreesh, and a few others, summon themselves and their horses; and, indeed, it is a fortunate thing that our people are so public spirited; for otherwise the lawyers would get it all their own way; and then I do not know what would become of the town. But my neighbours are all aware of the danger; and whenever the attorneys come round, every man gets upon horseback and gallops to the court. Here, the whole of them, as often as they can be spared from Tipple's, abuse the lawyers for ruining the country. By these means the lawyers are watched, and the country well taken care of. With respect to myself, in those days, the voice of lame Boshy would have been less regarded than the grunting of one of Snout's pigs. Instead of going to court, therefore, to abuse the lawyers, I stayed at home and wrought many a good day's work upon my farm; and this had a wonderful effect upon its improvement. I have generally seen that the farmer who is often away from his business, finds a return to it up hill work. When he does work; because his mind is elsewhere, labour goes on slowly. On the contrary, I, who was always at home, moved on like a clock, and with a hearty good will. By these means, when my neighbours, by taking care that the lawyers should not ruin the country, became poor and embarrassed; I, by degrees, got pretty forehanded, and could relieve them in a strait.

But the increase of my property had almost subjected me to those public calls from home, which, by means of poverty and lameness, I had been hitherto enabled to avoid. When a number of the neighbours whom I had relieved in their difficulties, found it inconvenient to repay me; there was a good deal of talk in the town, about getting me made a magistrate. Had any of your readers been in my situation; doubtless, they would have felt highly gratified: for, as our townsman Justice Grub, who sits in his bed till he mend his trousers, frequently affirms, it is a high honour to be a magistrate. But the thing was scarcely mentioned; when Pumpkin and Puff set their faces against it, and the affair was dropped. Pumpkin, who had long imagined that his large house and farm intitled him to the office, looked big; and affirmed, that, were lame Meph, who had been brought up by the town, to be set over it to rule, it would be disgraced forever; and Puff, who is a gentleman, declared that blind Bartimeus Beetle, our townsman, was fitter to distinguish colours, than a lame creature like me to sit in judgment between man and man. My friends then had no way of exalting me to honour, except by getting me made a captain of militia; but this the nature of my paces would not admit.

Thus, notwithstanding the good wishes of my friends, my lame carcase was excluded from dignities: it could neither ascend the bench, nor be adorned with a uniform and epaulette. But to compensate for the want of honour, I was at liberty to stay at home as long as I pleased; and I recollect very well, that, when our magistrates and militia officers, for the sake of honour, were neglecting their own business, my snug farm was in excellent order; and every thing about my house, comfortable. Let no person, however, conclude that I either despise dignities, or would discourage those who are not lame, from mounting to them as fast as they can. On the contrary, laudable ambition is well intitled to praise. When, for the sake of king and country, it submits to such hardships as many of our magistrates and militia officers endure, it transforms the man into the patriot or hero; and these, I am sure, every loyal subject would wish to be as plentiful as potatoes. For the credit of our town be it told, that, though I be a lame creature, there is among us abundance of legs and feet too, ever ready to run when king and country call; and not only to run, but to make the body which they bear, submit to every kind of privation and hardship which comes in their way. Many there are, as brave, public spirited, and persevering as Captain Hector Shootem: but, perhaps, you do not know the captain.

Captain Hector Shootem or Hecky, as our youngsters usually call him when he is not upon duty, about ten years ago, was a nice, good natured young fellow. About that time he settled upon a lot of land, and got married; and no man among us was more likely to do well. Hector possessed an active disposition; and could swing an axe with any young fellow in the town: and, as he was a stout, well made lad, of at least six feet high; there was every appearance that trees would fall before him, as reeds before the wind. But his stately form procured for him a sergeantcy in the militia of our town; and, then, the ardour of his genius soared far above chopping and rolling. Hector was rather a genteel young man. With the spirit of a gentleman, also, he possessed the ambition of a soldier; and now looked forward to his present commission, as the most desireable object in nature. At last, by the usual means, his desire was gratified; and, by selling his oxen, he was enabled to clothe himself in what he conceived to be martial glory. My neighbour Saunders used often to tell him, that it was folly for a poor man like him, whose comfort depended upon his labour, to spend his time as he did: that, if he wished to be a man of renown, he was a stout young fellow; and might easily make himself famous, by lifting up his axe against thick trees: and, that, as for swords, a farmer had nothing to do with them; unless he could lay his hand upon a piece of a broken one; and then, by putting it into a wooden handle, it might be very useful in the fall when the pigs were to be scraped. But Hector's military ardour was not to be repressed. His head was full of marches and countermarches, wheeling, halting, and charging. As for the sons of the forest, they did not belong to the enemy, and were never attacked.

None of your readers must conclude that this was empty parade; for Hector was a valiant man, and never feared an enemy in his life. It is true, he was not a bloodthirsty man; as no brave man is. Except killing a rabbit or a partridge occasionally, and at one time a weasel which had dared to commit depredations among his poultry, I never heard of his shedding the blood of any living creature. But this was because the enemy never faced him. Had he been at the battle of Waterloo, or any other great battle, the whole world would have heard of him; for, upon a muster day, he and his men would charge as boldly as if the enemy had been there; and if they had only dared to be there, and waited till Captain Shootem's company put them all to the bayonet; I am sure, they would have been skewered every man of them. This is not mere conjecture; for in the Battle of Scorem's Corner, which the company fought with Snout's pigs, they acted with a cool and determined bravery, which excited the admiration of the whole battalion, and procured them the thanks of the commanding officer. The affair well deserves to be recorded; and were I writing despatches, instead of chronicles, I would send you an account of it, as long as one of parson Drone's sermons upon economy.

It happened, that, as Captain Shootem and his men were marching from the field after a general muster; my neighbour Pumpkin was hunting Snout's pigs from his fields. The whole herd, headed by Mr. Gosling's boar pig Mammoth, were in full retreat; and just as the company advanced to the sudden turn of the road, where Jack Scorem's horse fell; Mammoth, who was ever at the head of all swinish mischief, rushed forward; and turned the left flank of the company, before they were apprised of the approach of the enemy. The squeeling of Mammoth and the shouts of the soldiers, were as good as scouts to the herd; and instantly, according to the tactics of swine upon reconoitering occasions, there was a dead stand and a dead silence through the whole army. But, in a moment, the brave Captain Shootem was in the post of danger; and the cool behaviour and bravery of his men, were beyond all praise. Halt, Dress, March, Charge, were uttered and executed in the same breath. Terror and confusion pervaded the enemy; and such grunting, and snorting, and blowing, and throwing up of heels, had never before been witnessed in the town. Had the cowardly rascals only waited for the charge, the carnage and bloodshed would have been terrible. As it was, it covered Captain Shootem with glory; and from that day's atchievement, he obtained the character of a brave and experienced officer.

That your readers may justly appreciate the merits of the Captain, they ought to be informed that his military ardour and gallantry had to struggle with a great many hardships; hardships too, which would have made my cousin Harrow, Saunders Scantocreesh, and even myself, lose all ambition for martial glory. In the pursuit of military honour, the pursuits of husbandry had been considerably overlooked; so that the Captain's means of domestic comfort did not keep pace with the increase of his family. The sale of his oxen, it is true, enabled him upon field days to make a warlike appearance; but it added little to the produce of his farm. In the mean time, the expence of treating his company and of occasional dinners with his brother officers, was an unavoidable tax arising out of his military carreer; a tax, which, when brought into connexion with his farming, was not easily borne.

But beside these difficulties, the Captain submitted to a great many hardships which the world never dreamed of. When he himself, upon public occasions, was gracefully adorned with the insignia of war; his little children at home were covered with coats of many colours, so assorted and sewed, that it was impossible to tell to what battalion they belonged. Even the genteel appearance of the Captain was not made, without resorting at times to extraordinary shifts. Happening one night to step over to his house about a little business, I found him in bed; because next day being a general muster, Mrs. Shootem was washing his trousers. As my business was a little urgent, I called next morning; and found him still in bed, and the whole family in confusion. The trousers had been hung out all night to dry, and in the morning they were gone. This was an event more appalling to a brave man, than the Battle of Scorem's Corner or any other great battle. To be absent from the muster, would disgrace him; and to appear upon the field without trousers, might put him under arrest, or at least send him to Coventry. But Mrs. Shootem, who is a nice, handy body, possessed a white petticoat; and in a trice, the Captain was rigged out in trousers as good as new: And I must say, that, in a petticoat, he was just as good a soldier, as when he wore his own trousers. Nobody could discern the least difference. For the credit of our town, however, it must be stated, that the Captain's lower habiliments were not stolen by any of our people. Among us it was never known that any person would pick up at his neighbour's door, even so much as a millstone. But that night, some of Snout's pigs happened to be out upon a scouting party, and carried them off. Whether this was done to revenge themselves upon the brave Captain Shootem for their disgraceful defeat, nobody could tell; but sure enough, they were afterward found in one of Snout's pens, administring to the cleanliness and comfort of a numerous offspring. After their discovery, it became an inquiry in the battalion, how the Captain happened to be better provided with trousers than his brother officers. This led to a discovery of the affair of the petticoat; and ever after he received the name of a place in the next province, of which some of your readers may have heard.[1]

At first Mrs. Shootem was wonderfully elated with the honours of her husband, and ate her potatoes with a great deal of pleasure. When the Captain, also, returned a little gay from a muster or militia dinner, he would kiss her gallantly and sing,

None but the brave deserve the fair:

And Mrs. Shootem was a very happy woman. At last, however, finding it all song and no supper, she got a little discontented; and when the Captain commenced his music, she would interrupt him with a stanza of grumbling. But he was none of those valiant men, who are brave in the field, and henpecked at home. He who had discomfited a whole herd of swine, was not to be snooled by a wife. After the affair of the petticoat also, imagining that since its transformation into trousers, Mrs. Shootem was plotting to wear them, he resisted her boldly; and henceforward, neither kiss nor song entered into their family communings. In this state matters continued till lately; when a number of the neighbours began to complain to him very loudly of the scarcity of cash. Captain Hector did not like to be troubled with either their grievances or grumblings; and in order to be out of the way of them, he

---

[1] Petit Codiac, usually pronounced Petticoat Jack.

resolved to take a look at the Lines, and see what the enemy were doing. But Mr. Catchem, hearing of his intention, assured him that the villains who used to annoy us at the Lines, were all reformed now, and peaceably minding their own affairs. The sheriff farther declared, that he himself really needed the presence of the Captain exceedingly; having got into his house Bill Scamp and a number of vagabonds as bad, who regarded neither law nor gospel; and, therefore, he begged him to accept a lodging in his house, and keep them in order.

For my own part, though I had always a wish to be respected; I was never satisfied that honour abroad would make my spouse and me so happy, as a snug farm affording us every means of domestic comfort. On this account, I left public honours to others who were more willing than myself to enjoy them at the expence of a hungry belly, a starved family, and a burden of debt: And when these were abroad, as honourable men often are; I kept at home, improving my farm, and advancing step by step to that abundance of domestic enjoyments which I and my family possess. For this I am indebted, partly to my lame legs, and partly to the advice of our worthy old parson.

Some time after our marriage, Mr. Drone stepped over to see what we were doing. At the house he found every thing in excellent order as usual, and my spouse busily employed about her domestic affairs. Having learned that I was clearing up a new field, he came out, and found me as black and dirty as burnt logs could make me. At first I felt a little ashamed, and began to apologise to the parson: but he interrupted me by saying, *Blessed is that servant, whom his lord, when he cometh, shall find so doing.* When Mr. Drone used these words, I looked at him with surprise; and said that when Christ came, I hoped he would find me about better employment. We then sat down upon a log together; and as nearly as I can recollect, the following is the amount of what the parson said:—

"Many of our townsmen sadly mistake both the nature of religion and the road to respectability. They, perhaps, say their prayers, read the scriptures, and attend the public ordinances of religion; and in the discharge of these duties, they would wish Christ to find them. In the mean time, there are about them a want of industry, an eagerness for amusement, and an ambition for what they conceive to be honour, altogether inconsistent with a religious life. The deity has endowed man with active principles; he has placed him in circumstances, in which activity expended upon industrious pursuits, acquires property; and property enables him to enjoy the comforts of life, and to be the friend of every good and benevolent design. Intrusting the human race with all this beneficence, he has also said to them, *Occupy till I come.* Can he, then, who has disregarded the injunction of his master, say at his appearance, *I have been glorifying thee upon the earth: I have been finishing the work which thou gavest me to do?* It is the industrious and benevolent christian, whom his lord esteems; the man who combines religious principle and worship with active industry and diffusive benevolence. Whether he be found prostrate at the altar of God, or rolling logs in his field, *Well done good and faithful servant,* will be the salutation of Christ.

"Mephibosheth, if you wish to be a respectable man, attend to this course; and connect it with the words of inspiration, *them that honour me, I will honour; and they who despise me, shall be lightly esteemed.* Many of our people are eager for honour; but they *seek not that honour which cometh from God*: they neglect their duty; and, of course, look for reputation in paths where they find only the want of respectability. They conceive that were they justices or militia officers, they would be honourable men. But a fool exalted to dignity, is merely a fool more conspicuous. Besides, where there is either a want of means to maintain the dignity of an office, or of talents to discharge its duties;

the office is disgraced; and the holder, contemptible. Hence it is, that Grub, with the high dignity of his office, is the jest of every body; and many of our militia officers too, with their show abroad and their wretchedness at home, are very little better. They think themselves to be great men: but, for the sake of a little empty parade, to sacrifice industry and domestic comfort, proves them to be great fools; and, with the sensible part of the community, this is their character. On the other hand, the course in which you are employed, is a life which the deity honours with the means of domestic enjoyment; and these means, used as every religious man ought to employ them, never fail to secure both respectability and influence."

Our parson seemed to me to speak very sensibly. I, therefore, stuck to my farm; and, sure enough, every thing turned out exactly as the parson said. Old Grub is old Grub still; maintaining the high dignity of his office, and sometimes mending his trousers in bed: Captain Shootem has gone to live with the sheriff: And I, whose friendship both magistrates and militia officers are now very willing to cultivate, am

Mephibosheth Stepsure.

LETTER 15

To the Editors of the *Acadian Recorder*,

Gentlemen,

I formerly stated, that, in this country, there are many public duties and private necessities, which call a farmer from home. I showed you, also, that, being neither a constable nor juryman, justice of the peace nor militia officer, I was considerably relieved from the first. I shall now explain to you, how I managed those private necessities which lead so many of our young people astray.

It has often occurred to me, that our townsmen and Snout's pigs resemble each other very much. Whether pigs derive any instruction or amusement from their mutual gruntings, I do not know; but, though they are often quarrelling and fighting and tormenting each other, they always keep in company. Exactly in the same way, though our townsmen are needed at home; and might, with good management, be very comfortable there; they would rather meet at Tipple's, the court, or any other place of general resort: And though, on this account, they suffer many domestic privations; and occasionally, when abroad, get themselves beat and abused like pigs; they return to the same places and company, with as much eagerness as if nothing had happened. On mentioning to parson Drone this feature in the character of our people, he observed, that the causes of it are simple, and the cure very easy; if they were only willing to be cured of a disease which had destroyed the industry, domestic comfort, and religion of the town.

155

"Man," said the parson, "is, by the principles of his nature, attached to society. He cannot live alone, without a perversion of mind, or a deprivation of those social enjoyments for which he was formed. But the most of our townsmen, though married, have no *home*. The link which attached them to the wife of their choice, has been broken; and hence, the society which they cannot find in their own houses, they expect in Tipple's or other places of public resort."

"Besides, in the human constitution, a principle of curiosity or the desire of knowledge, as philosophers term it, is an ingredient of powerful operation. When the mind is not adding to its stock of information, it becomes dissatisfied. But our people, in general, have not acquired that intelligence which can enable them, by reflexion and reasoning, to deduce from the stores of their own minds additional knowledge; and they have no disposition to acquire by a perusal of books, the valuable information which these would afford them. Still, their desire to know something continues in operation; and to allay the uneasiness which always attends ungratified desire, they will neglect their business and travel about the town, merely to learn what their neighbours are doing: And when a few of them meet, a conversation about Snout's pigs or any other triffle, as it fixes their attention and removes the uneasiness of the mind, becomes, in the mean time, a sufficient gratification. But this is not the worst of it. Repeated absence from home ingrafts upon the mind, habits which are stronger and more pernicious than the perversion of original desire. Many of our people are often abroad, when they have really no cause. They can no more stay upon their farms, than their dogs can stay at home upon sundays: And along with their wandering disposition, some of them, you know, have contracted a habit of drinking, which, in the face of reason and religion, and at the expence of true enjoyment in time and happiness in eternity, now forces them abroad."

"Married persons who would avoid such terrible evils, have only to unite in making their house a *home* to them both. Whoever does so, will find society there, which will reduce within reasonable bounds all inclination for other kinds of social intercourse. With respect to the desire of knowledge, no man who gives it a rational direction, finds it necessary to quiet its uneasiness by running about the town. When he cannot enjoy useful conversation with his neighbours, he will, by the perusal of books, converse with both the living and the dead; and from the stores of his own mind he will derive topics of reflexion, which will leave him no taste for the company and gratifications that draw other persons to Tipple's."

How far the parson was right, I shall leave your readers to judge. For myself I can only say, that, having found a *home* and society there, I had no wish to wander. I gradually furnished myself also, with a good collection of books and a newspaper; and though no man enjoys a rational conversation with more relish than myself, I have never felt the least inclination either to go to Tipple's, or to talk about Snout's pigs. By these means, my necessities to go from home were considerably abridged.

In the course of my life I have frequently observed, that, as a domestic disposition delights in *home*, it has really fewer occasions to go abroad. Every person endeavours to be near those things upon which he imagines his happiness to depend; and, in proceeding upon this principle, a farmer of domestic habits who manages well, easily relieves himself from a great deal of wandering. Not a little of the straggling of our town, arises from domestic wants. Whatever necessaries a farmer does not derive from his own land, he must collect from a different quarter. Now, among us, there have been always a great many articles, which our townsmen have judged it cheaper to buy than to raise. To provide themselves, therefore, with what a family needs; much time and running about, are unavoidably expended. You are aware also, I presume, that, in this country, purchasing and paying belong to different sides of a book. One of our townsmen would sooner think of asking parson Drone to preach his longest sermon upon a week day, than he would think of purchasing an article without six or twelve months credit. On this account, after a great deal of running about and lost time, a necessary article is bought at a high rate, (for all our townsmen stand out for great prices,) and then it makes a fair entry upon the one side of the book. But before it find its way to the other, much additional lost time and travel, I assure you are indispensible; and after all, the high price must be paid. But though my legs, as I formerly stated, are pretty long; I was never any great hand at the running; and, indeed, I have rarely tried it, except when I was going *home*. Besides, I did not like to be from home. I have always had a notion too, that time is money. I, therefore, concluded that it would be best for me to raise upon my own farm, the provisions which others collect from different parts of the town. By these means, no time was lost. Labour, also, was expended as it ought to be; and, upon my fields and crops, this had a wonderful effect. But after all, I must give our townsmen the praise of being to an industrious farmer, a very useful and accommodating sort of folk: they find it cheapest to buy provisions, and I sell them. Thus, by the produce of my farm, my travelling necessities were farther reduced.

But a number of our people raise considerable produce upon their farms; and of course sell occasionally: and when this happens, I do assure you, it costs them no little labour and travelling. As they are often going about, they cannot be expected to have a very great deal to spare. On this account, it is requisite to dispose of what they have to the best advantage; that is, to sell it for the promise of a great price and the payment as soon after as possible. But, in our town, those who have money in their pocket, are very shy

about promises; and when they do make them, they are
rarely of a size sufficient to please persons who need and
expect great prices. The people of our town, therefore,
generally deal with such as Moses Slack, who is poor from
thoughtless ill management; or with the like of Trot's sons,
who, when the day of payment arrives, are not easily
found. By proceeding upon this principle, some of them
become rich in promises and notes of hand, which, by the
by, are among us a staple article of trade. But, though they
expend much time and travel, looking after the promisers
of great prices, they usually remain still rich in promises;
and as for the notes of hand, they are at last sold for what
they will bring to Truck and other chaps; who put them
into some lawyer's hands, merely to keep him out of
mischief and prevent him from ruining the country.

From all this labour and loss of time and trucking, I
relieved myself by very simple means. As I owed no man
any thing myself, I was not willing to keep a register of
other peoples debts; and, therefore, though I have been
always as forward as any of the neighbours to help a poor
settler beginning the world, the expectation of a great price
could never induce me to sell to idle folks or to ill doing
vagabonds. My dealings have uniformly been with those
whose payments gave me no trouble. But, as some of your
farming readers may not believe that I could always meet
with good and ready pay, I shall show them my
management.

Some farmers go to market with a bad article; and
perhaps meeting with an ignorant purchaser, obtain a
price which they do not deserve. By and by, they carry him
a better; but the good article brings rogue along with it.
Other farmers again, are uniformly noted for the inferior
quality of their produce. In both cases, they must hawk
about for a customer; receive a low price; and then return
home, complaining of dull markets and poor pay. I, on the
other hand, considering that the world generally treats

men as it finds them, was careful in the first place to establish a character. Whatever I sold, I sold as it was and at a reasonable rate; for good payers always expect to buy reasonably. During the whole course of my life, also, quality, as well as quantity, has occupied my attention. On this account, my produce of every kind has been generally good: And this, you may depend upon it, is a great help to me in these dull times; for now, it is bespoke. These remarks I hope will satisfy your readers, that a farmer, by much running about, does not always arrive at the best market at last.

But beside the preceding causes of absence from home, the store, the mill, and the blacksmith's shop, are serious items among the travelling necessities of our town. As for the church, it scarcely deserves to be mentioned. Though our people generally go there, I never knew it give any of them a habit of travelling. On the contrary, were they obliged to hear a sermon from our parson, every time they go abroad; I do think, that they would become a very domestic sort of folks: for Mr. Drone has scarcely finished upon sunday, when they all hurry homeward with as much haste as Snout's pigs, when the dogs are at their heels. But if any of them go to the other places which I have mentioned, the case is altogether different: then nobody can tell when they will be home. When they leave their own houses, it is true, they are in a great hurry; as our people going from home, usually are. But, as they get over the road, they get over their hurry too; for, except my cousin Harrow, Saunders, and a few others, I never, at those places, found our townsmen in haste. On the contrary, they will very contentedly hang about them the whole day, discussing the news, and a number of half pints which they fetch from Tipple's; and then, toward evening, instead of sending for more, they adjourn to his house, and perhaps stay all night.

But neither the store, the mill, nor the blacksmith's shop, ever cost me much travel or lost time. The produce of my farm saved me many a journey to Mr. Ledger's. My spouse and I, were a homespun couple; so that neither silks nor superfine produced travelling from home: And, when I did go to the store; I must say that I always found Mr. Ledger, a very considerate gentleman. To the neighbours who were crowding about his counter, he would say, that, as they were in no haste, he would serve Mephibosheth first. To the mill, my journeyings were comparatively few. I did not, like many of our townsmen, for the purpose of being often there, carry my grain thither by a bushel at a time: And as for old Tubal; when he saw me enter his shop, he knew that my pocket contained the money to pay him for the job; and if even Puff's horse was there; he was put out, till Mephibosheth's was shod.

As yet I have said nothing about borrowing and lending; which, in our town, are both causes of no small travel. With respect to borrowing, this, in ordinary cases, was with me out of the question. Without the necessary tools, a farmer can no more work to advantage than a tradesman. My first care, therefore, has always been, to provide myself with every farming implement; and these I keep in good order, and each in its own place. By these means, when I proceed to do any thing, I save myself the trouble of travelling about to borrow bad articles; for borrowed articles are usually in bad order; and need a great deal of repairing, before they can be used, But my tools carefully kept, enable me to go to work at once. Thus, my job is always well done; and, in the same time, I can do much more than any of my neighbours.

With respect to lending my farming articles, I confess, I have ever been very shy. I consider them as a part of my farm; and except to a poor settler beginning the world, I have never been willing to let them out of my possession. At first, this procured for me the name of being a particular kind of man; but it saved me a great deal of travel; (for no man in our town ever thinks of returning a borrowed article:) And, as I am in other things, as obliging as any of the neighbours, they are now used with my way and do not take it ill; and my farming tools keep at home pretty well. Upon this subject, and indeed upon farming in general, I derived much useful instruction from the experience of my neighbour Moses Slack.

Mosey, as we usually call him, is a good natured easy man. Unlike the most of our townsmen, who, as I said before, are pretty long legged; Mosey, from his youth, was a squab little fellow. Nature had given him a good broad face; and a quantity of nose, which equalled old Trot's: but some how or other, she put her foot upon this last member after it was made; and ever since, its breadth has been much more remarkable than its length. Mosey, of course, cared nothing for news; nor indeed, did he care a great deal for any thing else. My neighbour Saunders frequently says, that nature never intended Slack to be his own master; and, that, if he had only got his face blackballed, when he was young; and then, been put into the hands of some decent master, who would have provided for him, and made him work; he would have been a very good negro. Certain it is, that Slack has never managed well for himself. But still, Saunders may be mistaken; for he says exactly the same thing of many of our people, who have as long legs and as sharp noses as any in the town.

Though Mosey could work very well in company, he would just as soon let it alone. Yet he cannot be called lazy; for he has spent a very busy life, and wrought a great deal. About the time that I was married, Mosey also was joined in wedlock to one of Mrs. Drab's daughters; and, as he settled upon a lot not far from mine, I had frequent opportunities of observing his progress. Before his marriage I helped him to put up a little log hut, which, he said, would do very well for a sheep house, when he raised his new frame. Into this the young couple entered; and there they continued, till it came down about their ears. Both he and his wife, were fond of fine clothes; which, like all the Drab family, they were better at having on, than taking care of. Like most of young people, too, they were inclined to live pretty well; so that, by the beginning of next summer, Mosey, instead of labouring upon his farm, was obliged to work the greater part of his time to Mr. Ledger and the neighbours who had supplied him with provisions. On this account, his own crop was small and ill taken care of. Now, a life of this kind is much more easily begun than altered. He who spends his wages before they are due, is always behind with his payments. He is, of course, the servant of his creditors; and when he happens to work for himself; every thing which he does, he does to a disadvantage. What should have provided Mosey with the necessary articles for getting on with his farm, had found its way to the back and belly of the young couple: And even those things which he had, as he was often from home working for other people, were always out of order. When he needed a little firewood, a horse must be sought among the neighbours. After finding the horse; perhaps, finding a collar cost him a great deal of running. Then his own traces were lost; and when these were found, and Mosey had got to the woods, probably the first stroke separated the axe from the handle, which had been split before. Mosey never thought of going to the mill, till there was no flour in the house. Then, in a great hurry, a bushel was threshed, carried thither, and brought home at the expence of a day's waiting and a half pint or two. In this manner he managed the whole of his business.

Where farming is so conducted, little can be raised. Mosey had, therefore, a great deal of travelling about the town in search of provisions; and, as may be supposed, he traded with those who expect great prices; so that, at last, he became very poor. With this kind of life, however, he dragged on till he owned a few fields; which, partly from want of thought, and partly from necessity, received from him a miserable kind of cultivation. Mosey, in the management of his land, was a rigid adherent of the old system of farming. This some of your Halifax readers may not understand. I shall, therefore, explain it.

During winter, every farmer, by means of his cattle, makes about his barn so much manure, which, when he can find sufficient leisure in the spring, he lays upon his lands. I say when he can find sufficient leisure; for the manure is not always used. A number of years ago, I recollect, our parson advised old Stot to lay lime upon his fields: but the old man very justly observed, that to toil himself burning lime, would be folly, when he could never find time to carry out the dung of his cattle. If a farmer's hurry, however, permit him to lay his manure upon his fields; they first yield him potatoes, and then wheat as long as it will grow. When the wheat fails him, the ground is fit for oats; and after the oats refuse to grow any longer, it is in good state for laying down in grass. But it somehow happens, that, though our people who follow this rotation, sow very good grass seed, it turns always into sorrel. A few years after, the land is again broken up; and yields a special good crop of weeds; which, as our townsmen did not sow them, produce a great deal of wondering how they happened to get there. This is the system of farming which Mosey employed; and, indeed, I may say that it is the general system of the town. How it may fare with the rest, I cannot exactly tell; but Mr. Ledger, after long forbearance, has been forced to sell out Mosey and be satisfied with partial payment; for to put him in jail, was of no use: And now, he is jobbing about among the neighbours; till he can get away to the Ohio, Upper Canada, or some other country better worth the living in.

From the experience of Mosey, as I formerly observed, I derived much useful instruction. Though he laboured his little fields so mightily, that he rarely gave them rest; his crops were miserable. The principal part of them was weeds; and even these were not like the stout healthy fellows which I occasionally pick out of my own grounds. All Mosey's ploughing and harrowing, could not bring even weeds to perfection. I could, therefore, easily see, that fields, like cattle, unless they be well fed and well taken care of, have a beggarly appearance and are very little worth: And, during the course of my life, I have uniformly treated them in a similar way. For my cattle I provide abundance of fodder; and for my ground, as much manure as possible: And, as I expect from my cattle only reasonable work; from my fields, I never seek more abundant nor more frequent crops, than nature and good heart enable them to afford. By pursuing this plan, I have always plentiful returns; and, as I labour for profit, I take care to raise only what is saleable. Though our townsfolk purchase a great many useless articles, nobody buys weeds; for they have all plenty of their own; and therefore I never raise them.

The experience of Mosey, and also of my neighbour Pumpkin, showed me, that neither labour nor large fields are sufficient to make a farmer wealthy. No man in our town ploughs so much, nor, in haying time, goes over more ground than Pumpkin. Yet he is obliged to purchase flour for his pies; and his cattle are half starved in winter. I, therefore, resolved to try how a less farm kept in good heart would do. This diminished the toil of fencing; and, indeed, labour of every kind: but, strange as it may appear to some of your farming readers, it increased the produce of my land wonderfully: and now, beside maintaining my own family well, I supply Pumpkin and many of the neighbours.

Thus, by getting on in my own way, I own a good farm. I have also bought a snug property for Abner; and I can yet tell a pretty long and feasible story about where the cash has been going to in these hard times. Let no person, however, suppose that I am one of the great folks in our town. On the contrary, neither Mr. Cribbage nor any of the Sippit family, would demean themselves so far as to ask the like of me to visit them. Still, among our folks, I pass for a remarkable kind of man: *I have a pair of lame legs, I stay at home, I mind my own affairs, I wear homespun, and I have become wealthy by farming.* In short, as I have been all along telling you, I am

Mephibosheth Stepsure

LETTER 16

To the Editors of the *Acadian Recorder*,

Gentlemen,

Since I wrote you last, I stepped over one afternoon to converse an hour with my neighbour Saunders; who, as you may perceive, does not want rough good sense. Upon the same day, Puff's farm happened to be sold by Mr. Ledger. Puff is one of our great folks; and, as he says himself, has done a great deal to keep up the credit of the town. Indeed, few among us carried their heads higher than the Puff family; or expended so much upon dress, chaises, and other sorts of finery. But Mr. Ledger, who has also the credit of our town very much at heart, took a different view of the subject; and, by foreclosing the mortgage upon Puff's farm, interrupted his exertions to make us a respectable people.

When I was sitting with Saunders, the neighbours were returning from the sale in very gallant stile; some in sleighs, and others on horseback; and all hurrying to Tipple's or some other public place; in order to enjoy themselves a little, before they returned to domestic life. As they were gallopping past my neighbour's; one of his little boys, who was wonderfully delighted with their appearance, came running in, and asked his father to buy him a horse. Saunders, though a good natured man, is a little hasty; and withal, a deadly enemy to our townsmen's general practice of riding in chariots and upon horses; which he calls the abomination of the Egyptians. All at once, therefore, his hand was raised high for correcting uses: but, in looking at

167

the size of the little chap, he forgot that he had been angry, and brought it down gently over his head; telling him to be a good boy till spring, and when Mortar the mason came to build the chimneys of his new house, he would get him a *mare*. At the same time Saunders observed, that, though I had written a great deal about the management of my farm, the chronicles of our town would be incomplete, if they did not contain an account of the management of my children. Many fine young families among us, he said, were ruined through the thoughtless folly and ill conduct of their parents. The youth of this country, he added, are acute and active; and, if they were only brought up as they ought to be, they would become judicious and respectable men: but many of their parents were fools; and their children, as might be expected, turned out to be rogues and vagabonds.

You must not, however, imagine that all our young people are wickedly inclined. Miss Clippit, though formerly a miserable sinner, is now, as she says herself, a very religious young woman. In her own opinion, she knows more about experiences and marks of grace, than parson Drone himself; and some of those who have attended her ministrations, even say that she can preach a better sermon. I could also mention many others, who, when they have no opportunity to frolic or play at cards, very punctually attend those night meetings where miserable sinners like Miss Clippit, all at once become uncommonly religious people: And, you may depend upon it, they do not attend without profit; for, when they go to Tipple's, which they do very often, they sing so many hymns over their grog; that he frequently declares his own house to be as uncomfortable to him as parson Drone's church upon sunday.

Indeed, our people do a great deal for the instruction of youth. All the Cribbage family, as soon as they are able to crawl about, acquire the first principles of arithmetic, the art of castle-building, and a world of ingenuity of different kinds, by means of the cards. The Sippits, too, as soon as they can handle a cup, are initiated into the mysteries of genteel life, by having tea parties and frolics for their little companions. When our youth get a little farther on, the boys are taught to saddle the mare and go errands; and also, to read and write a little under the tuition of Mr. Pat O'Rafferty or some other teacher as good. As for the girls, they are intrusted to Mrs. McCackle, who, I assure you, does ample justice to their education. Though this lady has never been at court; nor, indeed, farther into what is called the world, than to edge in at Sippit's of an evening, she knows all about fashionable life; and can teach our young ladies to talk as glibly, to sit as uprightly, and to walk as much according to rule, as any boarding school mistress can teach a boarding school miss. Besides, she gives them many other accomplishments no less valuable. When they return home to get husbands and manage families, they can paint flowers and make filligree work to admiration. They can also sing and dance delightfully; and some of them can even play upon the piano forte so well, that in frolicking times old Driddle is occasionally out of employment. As for cookery and other things connected with housekeeping, Mrs. McCackle and her pupils are careful to leave them to vulgar folks. Indeed, to act otherwise would be a violation of common sense; for were any rational person to see one of our fine young ladies in her Canton crapes, stooping over a tub, scrubbing a floor, or cooking a dinner; it would not appear less contrary to nature, than the sight of one of our genteel young farmers in his superfine longtailed coat, ploughing or harrowing on a fine summer's day.

With respect to the religious instruction of youth, also, our town is provided with a variety of means. Our old parson upon sundays, preaches to all who are willing to hear him; and, indeed, upon other days too, he labours among us as much as the care of his own cattle and pigs will permit. Mrs. Sham and Miss Clippit, as I said before, are likewise labourers in word and doctrine. In addition to these, our town enjoys the ministrations of parson Howl; and also of young Yelpit, who lately converted and called himself to the preaching of the gospel; so that, upon the whole, our youth are by no means destitute of religious instructors. Mr. Drone, it is true, does not seem to relish the assistance of these helpers in the word; and Tipple, who dislikes the parson, says, that our clergyman has been all his life praying that labourers might be sent into the vineyard; and now when they are come, he is not satisfied. But my neighbour Saunders, who, since his conversion failed, holds them in utter abhorrence, declares that the whole seed and generation of them, are under the delusions of satan; and no better than Muckle John Gib and Mrs. Buchan, who, with their ravings and nonsense, tried to lead silly people off their feet in Scotland: And that providence has sent them and their erroneous doctrine into our town, not for the improvement, but for the destruction of youth. Old fools, he says, gallop about the country, after them and their meetings; and, in the mean time, their children at home have liberty to run into every kind of mischief: And young people, too, who follow them, get into a notion that they are converted; when they are only lazy, idle vagabonds, fit for nothing else but singing hymns and cheating: That, if he had got his will, when Mrs. Sham bit her husband's thumb to the bone, he would have made her eat her own tongue to the root: And that, as for Howl and Yelpit, fellows as ignorant as his stots, he would send them to the house of correction; where, if they did not learn some sense, they would at least get the laziness squeezed out of them, and be of some use in the world.

How far Saunders views and plans are correct, I shall not pretend to affirm: Nor, indeed, will any of your readers be well qualified to judge; till they peruse that part of the chronicles of our town, which directly records the life and ministrations of parson Drone and his helpers. From what I have stated, however, they will all perceive, that, if our youth be not very religious, it is not for want of public instructors.

In addition to these means of knowledge, many of our young people receive also reproof and correction in abundance. Some parents, it is true, do not flog their children at home; nor would they permit Mr. Pat O'rafferty to correct them: And, indeed, no wonder; for when Pat was giving Judy her schooling, it cost her many a pair of black eyes. Puff and others of our gentlemen frequently say, that the poor little dears are not sent to a teacher to be snooled and beaten, but to get on with their education. It is certain, however, that all our youth do not serve such an easy apprenticeship. In Mrs. Grumble's family and among all her connexions, every thing begins with a grudge and ends with a scolding. When Mrs. Sham, too, returns from her meetings; her girls, as they well deserve, receive both scolding and beating for their neglect of family affairs: and Trot's sons, who always left the work when he went after the news, were, at his return, sure of a good pounding.

With some of these means of education our old parson was never well satisfied. For the cards in particular, he was at no time an advocate. In discussing this point he has frequently told us, that, before a religious man admit them into his house, he should be sure that their admission originates in a degree of good sense and piety, superior to the principles of those who have reprobated cards, as an amusement unfriendly alike to personal religion and the sober education of youth: And, also, that, before any parent employ them as a domestic recreation, he should ask himself, if, along with them, he be willing to grapple with his share of that misery which they have entailed upon the world.

How it is with you in Halifax, I do not know; but the experience of our townsmen presents no encouragement to any rational man to be a great player at cards. Cribbage and a number of our gentlemen have frequent evening parties in each other's houses by rotation; where they empty the pockets of each other with much apparent good humour upon all sides. But the losers invariably return home in a rage; abusing the winners, and declaring that they had been invited, merely for the purpose of swindling them out of their money, in order to pay for their supper. Not that any of our genteel people are swindlers; for, you know, a cardplayer may fleece and even ruin his neighbour, and yet be as honest and honourable as any other gentleman like himself. But losses beget ill humour; and some how or other, ill humour discovers successful gamesters to be rogues.

In our town, also, Swap, Truck, and other chaps of the same sort, are great hands for the cards; and between their amusement and drinking, swearing and fighting, frequently spend whole nights in Tipple's. But, though the happiness of a life of this kind be great, it is at times exposed to unexpected interruptions. Not long ago, it was reported among us, that, in the heat of one of their broils, the devil himself was so scandalised at their conduct, that he appeared personally to command the peace. The poor fellows, of course, were dreadfully alarmed; and talked of going to parson Howl to get themselves converted. But it turned out to be the brother of Mr. Gosling's black wench; who happened to be going past pretty early in the morning, and hearing the noise, looked in at the window to see what was the matter. When the truth spunked out, the chaps returned to their cards; and deferred their conversion, till they would be more at leisure.

With the frolicking part of the education of youth, our old parson was always displeased. In adverting to this point he has frequently said to us, "Young people need amusement; but both the nature and extent of their pleasures should be carefully watched. The youthful mind pants for enjoyment; and what it desires, it is prone to consider as the grand object of life. But in the present stage of human existence, beside enjoyment, there is much duty to be performed and adversity to be endured. Parents, therefore, by their own reason and experience, should correct the views and regulate the passions of youth; not mislead and inflame their minds, by the overweening indulgence of injudicious affection. Amusements ought not to be withheld from children: but every parent who loves his offspring so as to consult their happiness, will study to render their youthful pleasures subservient to the duties of life, and to that rational enjoyment for which life is designed. Parents who act in any other way, are the worst enemies to the happiness of their offspring; and their children will repay them with retributions of misery. It grieves me to say, that, in the experience of many of you, truth speaks for itself. What are those whose youth has passed away in frolicking amusements? Have they arrived at religion? at respectability in life? at the enjoyment of happiness? They are the idle, wandering, drinking, bundling part of the town; in youth, characterised by their follies; in old age, loaded with contempt and misery."

Though our people enjoy many a comfortable nap at church; whenever the parson preached upon this topic, almost every one imagined that Mr. Drone was pointing at him, and not preaching to other people only, as in ordinary cases; and, on this account, anger set all disposition to nod at defiance. To vindicate their own conduct, also, they would abuse the parson, as by far too hard upon young people. The Sippit family in particular, never failed to revile him for a bigot; whose narrow contracted mind made no allowance for the sprightliness of youth. He was of no use in the town, they said; except to give young people a dislike to religion: for he was never satisfied unless they were praying or poring over their bibles. Religion, they would add, was not intended to make men miserable: And, accordingly, to show that they knew better than the parson, and would not be priest-ridden; when Mr. Drone preached upon training up children, the Sippits improved his doctrine by a tea party and frolic, which usually concluded with a bundling.

When the remarks of the Sippits were repeated to the parson; he would merely reply, that, perhaps, he might be a bigot: but that the point for them to consider, was, whether he had told them the truth; and whether, when they were misrepresenting him, they might not be cheating themselves out of that religion which they would find very necessary when affliction or death knocked at their door: "And let me tell you farther," he would say, "that a great deal of frolicking and a life such as human beings ought to lead, are utterly incompatible. Those who give the heart to pleasure, are not lovers of God; and so it fares with them. They take the frolicking first; and leave their poring upon the bible and their prayers till a period, when these may afford them neither the improvement nor peace which their situation needs:" And sure enough, when Miss Sippit was lately attacked with the pleurisy, there was a sad to do in the family.

I formerly told you that Miss Dinah Gosling began to droop after Miss Sippit's tea party and frolic. This young lady, too, by dancing and bustling about to make her company comfortable, had overheated herself; and was in consequence seized with a cold, which terminated in a pleuritic affection. At that time, along with the disease, the thoughts of dying naturally occurred. Now, the person who contemplates the grave, endeavours also to look beyond it; and from a consideration of the future, insensibly turns to the recollection of the past. But to poor Miss Sippit the remembrance of frolicking times did not link itself with the grateful and desireable hope of future enjoyment. Her pleasures had perished with the using; and their place was occupied by a variety of thoughts, which neither brightened her prospects nor soothed her mind. Gladly she would have turned to evidences of her religious improvement; but memory interposed, and supplied her with the recollection of times in which a view of religion, as the essence of life and a preparation for death, made her miserable; and as a rude intruder, was banished by amusement: And though she had formerly supposed, that dying persons have only to be sorry for their sins, receive forgiveness, and then leave the world; now, she was very sorry indeed, and yet a stranger to hope.

Old Mr. Sippit, who is an indulgent parent, perceiving his daughter in this state of mind and upon the brink of the grave, was very much grieved. He told her not to distress herself: that she had always been a dutiful child; and was now going to a merciful father, from whom she had nothing to fear. But her own judgment marked her out, as a lover of pleasure, and not a lover of God: and though of religion in general her conceptions were crude; some how or other, she perceived distinctly, that death introduces retributions of justice, which are not blended with the forgiving fondness of doting affection. On this account, the cheering consolations of her father were administered in vain.

To relieve her mind, therefore, he next proposed to read to her the bible. This, indeed, was an employment of which he was not very fond; for, when a boy, he had experienced that it always made him dull and melancholy. But he had heard that it was of use to persons who are dying; and though he did not exactly see how it could cheer up the mind of his daughter, he was very willing to try it, however disagreeable to himself. From what I have stated, you will perceive that the old gentleman was not very well qualified to make an appropriate selection of parts; and, indeed, when he was going to begin, he found himself puzzled. He recollected, however, that, when he and his friends had occasionally discussed religion over their wine after dinner, it was frequently remarked that the book of Proverbs contains a large fund of sound morality. It occurred to him, therefore, that, as his daughter was perplexed about her sins, he could not do better than teach her about her duty; and, accordingly, as an introduction to spiritual relief, he read to her the first chapter.

It is not necessary to tell your readers what the first chapter of the Proverbs contains; for, as they are not going to die soon like Miss Sippit, they do not need to be instructed. Besides, I am not sure, that any of them have the least curiosity to know. I can assure them, however, that, as the old gentleman proceeded, his daughter listened with increasing eagerness; and when he had concluded the lesson, he found that all the long speeches of Job's three comforters, did not produce so much misery, as the simple reading of the first chapter of the Proverbs, had planted in the breast of his child. She told him that it marked her character and sealed her doom. "I never," said she, "attended to the instructions of Mr. Drone: I am falling into the hands of the living God."

When matters were in this state; though the Sippits do not like the parson, they were glad to send for him: and, indeed, I may say, that, in our town, all who revile Mr. Drone, are very anxious to enjoy his presence, when adversity or death visits their families. By means of his instructions, the poor girl's mind became considerably composed. She was very penitent for the past, and hopeful for the future; and firmly resolved, that, if providence spared her, she would live in a very different manner. In a short time, her disease assumed a favourable appearance, and she began to recover. The parson then told her, that he had always viewed a death bed repentance, as a suspicious kind of religion; and now it became her to prove that her penitence had not been forced out by fear. The young lady's mind was in that chastened state which every person feels, when the cessation of severe affliction administers relief. She was, therefore, profuse in her professions and promises. At last, complete health returned, and with it the absence of all those gloomy thoughts which had alarmed her mind; and tonight, she is going to have a large tea party and frolic, to celebrate her recovery. Our old parson does not seem to be much disappointed. On mentioning to him the result of his labours, he only said, *Education which begins with frolicking, is not likely to terminate in godliness. But, though frolickers should live an hundred years, and rejoice in them all; let them remember the days of darkness; for they shall be many.*

With respect to my own children I would only observe, that I have always endeavoured to conduct their education, according to the directions of our worthy old parson; on which account, as well as for other reasons that were formerly stated, our townsmen consider me as rather an odd sort of man. The most of our people keep Mr. Drone, not to instruct them, but to preach to them upon sundays; and except when they are sick or dying, they take special good care, I assure you, that he attend to his own duty, without interfering with any part of their management. I, on the other hand, have always been anxious to receive from him instruction as well as preaching; and I must say for our parson, that, in following his advice about the management of youth, I have every reason to be satisfied with the result. My children, though not perhaps as white as the old crow imagined her brood to be, are strangers to those habits which have forced many of our people to accept the sympathy of the sheriff; and from their general conduct, my spouse and I derive as much satisfaction, as reasonable parents should expect from youth. What instructions our clergyman occasionally gave me upon the subject of education, I may probably, at some future period, put upon record in the chronicles of our town.

Mephibosheth Stepsure

LETTER 17

To the Editors of the *Acadian Recorder*,

Gentlemen,

Since I began to write the history of my own life, there has occurred a variety of events; some of a pleasing, and others of an afflicting kind. But the greater part of them it is not necessary to mention; for your readers would care about them just as little, as our people care about the society which Saunders and a few others have begun, in order to improve the agriculture of the town. I shall, therefore, send you only a few brief notices: And first of all I may observe, that, for any thing I can see, Mr. Catchem, poor gentleman, is likely to be ruined. I do not mean that he neglects his duty; but nobody will employ him: creditors now say that it is of no use, either to sell property or put debtors in jail.

On the other hand, our townsmen, who have been allowed to go at large, have, I assure you, been active in no ordinary degree. Between travelling to Mr. Gawpus' store, (which, by the bye, is now pretty well emptied,) attending the courts, looking into Tipple's occasionally, assisting each other to deplore the badness of the times, and going about their ordinary business, such as hanging all day about the mill or the blacksmith's shop, they have been very seldom at home. You must not, however, imagine that our people want industry. On the contrary, they rarely go abroad without making great bargains; and in the mean time, they suffer no damage at home: for except during spring, haying time, and harvest, they have nothing to do upon their farms. Indeed, I must say, that, in having winter and misfortune together, we have been extremely lucky; for, during that season of the year, our people can both talk about their troubles at leisure, and do a great deal to make them sit lightly. Winter is the time of good cheer, which you may depend upon it we have not been neglecting; and good eating and drinking, you know, are a great comfort to persons who have hard times to bewail.

Nor have the youth of our town been less actively employed. But, as I have lately explained the nature of their education, it is not very requisite to detail what they have been doing. I must remark, however, that they, as well as the old people, have been experiencing hard times and misfortunes. Miss Sippit's tea party and frolic have not passed off with all the eclat which the young lady anticipated. Never had a meeting of our young people excited such high expectations; and never before, was there a meeting attended with so many serious disasters. In particular, old Stot's son Hodge, poor fellow, is not likely to get over it soon. To record calamities, is a disagreeable task: but in the present case, it is an act of justice to our town, which ought not to be omitted. It will show you that we have society as elegant and refined, as any other part of the province: and I am sure, it will convince all your readers, that, when the children of farmers become ladies and gentlemen; they have a great deal to do and suffer, and deserve a great deal of praise.

I formerly stated that Miss Sippit, being relieved from the disagreeable necessity of preparing for death, had resolved to redeem her lost time, and celebrate her recovery by a tea party and frolic. This, of course, required a great deal of preparation and bustling about; such as borrowing a little flour here, and a little butter there: for, though we are a very genteel township, and before company make an elegant appearance, it would be foolish to suppose that our country gentlemen in general, possess every thing requisite for the entertainment of a large party. Indeed, I may say that the preparation extended to almost the whole town. Near every house, the fences indicated that our young gentlemen were getting their ruffled shirt in order; and the ladies, their gowns or some other part of dress, for the joyful occasion.

At last, the expected evening arrived; when our youngsters and Mrs. McCackle, who had been appointed mistress of the ceremonies, convened in Sippit's. In commendation of this lady, I must observe, that, for conducting the business in genteel stile, a better choice could not have been made. With the exception of Mr. Peter Longshanks, I question if there be another who knows half so much about the manner in which young people should behave in company. Under her direction, therefore, every thing was conducted with due decorum. Indeed, it was the general opinion, that our young ladies had never sitten so erectly, nor displayed such a lady like appearance before. The young gentlemen, too, exerted themselves mightily to find out the best position for their legs and arms; which, I assure you, is not easily discovered by a young country gentleman, when he gets into a company where he thinks every body looking at him. Upon the whole, however, Mrs. McCackle was very well pleased; and declared, that, as how, they were the most gracefullest assembly she had ever beheld: and how could it be otherwise? for all our young people and all their finery, were there.

Having never myself been in such polite company, I must, of course, be ignorant of the general modes of proceeding; and, therefore, I shall not attempt to describe them. I understand, however, that it is the ordinary custom for the gentlemen to go about taking care of the ladies. In conformity with this order of things, Mrs. McCackle had requested old Stot's son Hodge, to have the goodness as to be so kind as to hand round the fried pork to the ladies. Hodge was upon the alert in an instant; and, as politeness required, determined to present it with an elegant bow; which, in our town, consists in pushing out the right foot and then bringing it back with a scrape upon the ground; at the same time, bending the body forward with suitable solemnity. Now it unfortunately happened, that the young gentleman's shoes, which he had sent to the mending, were not ready in time. But, in order to be at the frolic, he had put on a new pair of his father's; which the old man had carefully fortified with an abundant supply of hobnails: and scarcely had Hodge entered upon his bow, when a shriek from Miss Sippit admonished him that he had begun his scrape at her shin, and was subjecting her satin slipper to an unmerciful visitation. In such a case, it was natural for him to draw back his foot as fast and as far as possible. But, in his haste, it escaped him that where the head goes one way and the feet another, there is always a violation of the order of nature; and, before he was aware, he had placed the fried pork, melted and unmelted, in the young lady's lap; and was himself fast following. Emergency, however, will at times produce wonderful exertion. One powerful effort relieved him from the apparent danger. But no man can think of two things at once; and, of course, he who is falling forward, does not consider that there may be danger behind. Hodge only thought of getting back from the young lady; but, in his haste to retreat, forgetting to take his legs along with him, he unfortunately overturned the tea table and its contents upon Mrs. McCackle's new poplin. Whether this unusual combination of accidents had produced a sudden convulsion of nature; or whether Hodge had been dining upon cabbage, which, you know, is a windysome kind of food, I cannot tell: but the poor fellow, in falling, made a lengthy apology, which scandalized the whole assembly of our young ladies amazingly: and, indeed, no wonder; for such a speaker was never introduced into any genteel company, and much less allowed to lift up his voice.

Hodge is a stout hearted fellow; and can, with perfect equanimity, bear any ordinary trial; such as losses upon a bargain or getting himself capiassed: but here was an accumulation of sore adversities; adversities too, which brought with them the loss of character. One spring placed the door between him and the rest of our young ladies and gentlemen; and since that time, he has never been seen by any of them.

When matters in Sippit's were restored to a little order, the young people agreed to get on with the frolicking; and, accordingly, Driddle was called. But the old man, having been obliged to fill himself with tea instead of grog, was seized very badly with the belly ache. Here was a real disappointment; for, you may depend upon it, that a fiddler with the belly ache, has got other concerns to mind than either music or dancing. As Miss Sippit's piano was out of order, all hope seemed to be gone; when young Kickit recollected, that he had seen Mrs. McCackle sing and dance at the same time. He, therefore, proposed that she should officiate in the place of old Driddle; and, as a compliment to the lady, he insisted upon opening the ball with her. Mrs. McCackle, from the recollection of her damaged poplin, was not in a very tuneful mood. Still, she was willing to gratify the young folks, and no less willing to display her own talents. To it, accordingly, they went; and an elegant couple they must have been, I assure you. Kickit is one of our tallest young fellows; with legs like rafters, and as nimble as Peter Longshanks. Mrs. McCackle, too, is a handsome figure; only, not being a native of our town, she is a little differently formed. Nature, in the construction of the upper part of her frame, had forgotten that legs are an indispensible appendage; and, afterward, in order that the whole might be of a reasonable longitude, she was necessitated to add such extremities as suited the case.

Of the exhibition of this uncommon couple, you must not expect me to give you a scientific account; for I am not very far seen in the dancing; and, besides, I was not there. I can only say, that, in the opinion of our young people, between singing, and turning, and wheeling, and shuffling, and leaping, and skipping, it was truly enchanting. But, just when delight was wound up to rapture; Kickit's foot, in one of its high leaps, thought of taking a look into Mrs. McCackle's pocket; and afterward, like every other violent possessor, positively refused to renounce its claims. Now, it would be unreasonable to expect that any lady would either sing or dance, with a gentleman's foot in her pocket. I must, however, do young Kickit the justice to say that he was still, if possible, more ready than ever to gratify the delighted spectators. Having parted with one foot, he was even anxious to make the other do the business of two; and the more eager Mrs. McCackle became to withdraw from the enchanting scene, the more earnest he was upon the dance, and hopped around the old lady with surprising diligence; till at last a wrong step from the want of music, brought them both to the floor.

After such a specimen of superior stile, none of the other youngsters was willing to exhibit. They, therefore, agreed to disperse: but scarcely had they left Mr. Sippit's, when the violent rain of last week overtook them, and subjected the gumflowers and other finery of the town to a sweeping destruction.

Our young ladies and gentlemen, you see, are, as well as their parents, meeting with hard times. Still, great as their disappointments and misfortunes are, it is well for them that they are not in the hands of my neighbour Scantocreesh. Saunders declares, that, if his foot had been in old Stot's shoe; instead of kicking Miss Sippit's shins and tearing her slipper, he would have broken the leg of the brazen faced limmer. The old vagabond Driddle, he says, with his fiddling and drinking and corrupting the youth, deserves to be fed upon tea all the days of his life; and, as for the rest of the ne'er do wells, instead of letting them off with the loss of their trumpery, he would have applied a cudgel to their back and sent them home with their buttocks bare; and then, instead of junketting about the town, they would be glad to stay at home and wear homespun, like other decent folk.

I have now arrived at the end of the first book of the chronicles of our town; and, for a number of reasons, winter must return before I enter upon the second. In the first place, I have resolved to make the ensuing summer the busiest of my life. The exertions of you Halifax gentlemen to promote the agriculture of the province, have suggested to me a great many improvements which my present system of farming needs. These I have resolved to make; and, when my neighbours are lamenting the badness of the times, and executing their present determination to raise nothing upon their farms till the prices rise, I will banish all discouraging thoughts by working a little harder; and if better times come, or if bad times continue, my good crop will be in readiness to meet them.

Secondly, I have got myself a great deal of ill will from many of the neighbours; who say that I have made them and our whole town a laughing stock to the rest of the province. Old Grub, in particular, is very angry about the mending of the trowsers. He says that the high dignity of his office ought to have been treated with greater reverence; and that, as clouting the covering of his nether extremities, was no part of his magisterial duty, I had no right to meddle with it. He says, also, that things in our town are come to a fine pass, when even the lame despise dignities: and he hopes to see the day, that, when worthy gentlemen are sitting upon the bench to maintain the honour of the town, Mephibosheth and others like him will be sitting in the stocks, as a warning to revilers.

That the worthy gentleman should be offended, has grieved me sorely. In vindication of myself I must say, that the story of the trousers was told, expressly for the purpose of showing how careful he is to maintain the high dignity of his office; for this honourable member of the bench does not always mend his trousers in bed. The truth is, that some of our young ladies, happening to pass his house, resolved to pop in and see what old Squire Grub was doing. But the worthy gentleman descried them coming, and buried the unseemly parts of his frame among the blankets; which was surely more becoming the high dignity of his office, than if they had found him in his ordinary way, as my neighbour Saunders expresses it. Indeed, he is, as I may by and by show you, a pattern of industry and economy worthy of imitation.

Our reverend old parson, too, is not altogether satisfied. He says that touching the matter of the swine, I have allowed my waggery to overrun my judgment: that albeit he did nourish and maintain a few of those unclean beasts for the sustenance of himself and his household, it was not for edification to hold up his labours among them as a spectacle to the world, and much less to place them before the other part of his ministrations. Now, I positively aver that Mr. Drone is not even related to the Trulliber family. He does not feed pigs for sale; he has no delight in feeding them; and in dividing his labours, would, if possible, place the people of our town before them. But when our folks starve him, necessity has no law; pigs must be reared; and, of course, the feeding of the town restricted to the remnants and husks of his time.

In the third place, I have now got a character to maintain, and must take care not to lose it; as persons who are perpetually writing, very generally do. Trudge, the pedlar of our town, has just come from Halifax, with a large assortment of notions and news. Among other things he tells me, that, when he and Tug the truckman were taking a glass of grog together, they were both of opinion that my letters were a very clever thing: and farther, that a number of their friends were going to use their influence with government to get me a pension. This, you may be sure, was very gratifying to me; for every decent man likes to be respected by respectable persons, such as Trudge and his acquaintance Tug. At the same time I must confess, that, when Trudge told me the news, I had some misgivings about its truth; both because pedlars are privileged talkers; and because, when he was speaking about the pension, he was persuading my spouse to purchase a great bargain of a shawl which would cost her only ten dollars. On this account, when my old woman was telling him that the first ten dollars of the pension should go for a shawl, I resolved not to believe all that he said; till I had learned the truth of it from some other quarter. Still, I was very anxious to believe. You may judge, then, how much I was gratified, when Saunders came running over with the Weekly Chronicle; and, in the speech of that worthy, clever spoken, sensible gentleman, the Honorable the Attorney General, pointed out to me the following words: "Turn where you will, folly and extravagance stare you in the face. That GENTLEMAN, Mephibosheth Stepsure, had given us a picture of ourselves, which he was sorry to say was too true: but he did not approve of its being hung up in the newspapers for all the world to look at. But he should be obliged to him, if he would go to every door in the province, and sound his reproofs in their ears. For his own part, he was surprised to see our extravagance in dress. The east and the west, the north and the south, the whole world was ransacked to collect the rags which were to be thrown upon a young woman's back."

Who could have believed that lame Boshy would ever be called a GENTLEMAN, at a public meeting of the grandees of the province. To say nothing of my own feelings, my old woman is wonderfully pleased; and says that honour will not be brought to shame, by getting into the company of Mephibosheth Stepsure: that I am not like

Puff and others of our poor gentry, who wear fine coats, and nothing in their pockets but an account from Mr. Ledger or a summons to the court. On the contrary, that, having arrived at great respectability, I have something which will help to maintain the dignity of my character. Even I myself, too, am beginning to think that I possess more dignity than I was formerly aware of; and I have a kind of notion, that, when I get myself seated in stile, with a table before me, covered with a green cloth reaching down to the floor, so as to keep my feet out of the way, I shall make a very respectable looking gentleman. My spouse seems to think that now, when I have become somebody, reading the chronicles of our town at every man's door, would confer upon me more notoriety than honour; and upon the whole, I am rather inclined to shift the business: for I am no great hand at the running; and you know, it would be necessary to get away very nimbly from every door, as soon as they were read. Old Trot, when he is going after the news, could do it very well: but the poor man is getting feeble; and could neither run very fast, nor stand much beating.

Could the clever spoken, sensible gentleman, the Honorable the Attorney General, be induced to comply with the plan of my neighbour Scantocreesh, it would do the business completely. Saunders is delighted with his speech. He declares that it is as good as one of parson Drone's best sermons; and that the decent gentleman understands the ne'er do wells of our town better than they understand themselves. But to put the speech into the newspapers, he thinks, will do them no good; as they never read any thing from the one end of the year to the other; except, perhaps, an advertisement at the store or the blacksmith's shop. Could the worthy gentleman, however, be induced to come to our town and say the same things over again; by advertising a cattle show or a town meeting at Tipple's, our people would turn out to a man: Or, he says, that, though it be no credit to a decent farmer to be a constable; he and the rest of the hard working, homespun neighbours, will get themselves sworn in to catch the villains and force them to the meeting: and as he will then be clothed with authority and have the law upon his side, his staff of office shall be faithfully used, to command attention and to apply the doctrine. He thinks, also, that, as our females will of course be there, to see that their husbands get full justice when the doctrine is applied; it would not be amiss to tender them a word of exhortation too. Not that he wishes to have any hand in the application; but he thinks that when their husbands are receiving instructions about industry, a few hints upon the subject of economy might be useful to themselves. Nothing, he says, has prevented our town from being one of the wealthiest places in the world, but want of industry and want of economy. But as the execution of Saunders' plan is rather to be desired than expected, there is still another scheme which might be equally successful. Were every person who could stand an examination upon the chronicles to be made a magistrate or militia officer, the most of our people would soon have them by heart.

Gentlemen, after telling so many truths about the people of our town, I must now beg leave to say a few words to your readers. Some of them, I have been told, are a good humoured, laughing sort of folks; and others are just as crusty and angry at the chronicles of our town. To the first I would observe, that they have a right to laugh at themselves as much as they please; and when they get their laugh out, to reform as fast as they can. But when they meet with their angry neighbours, they should consider that laughing is a very serious thing, and ought to be tempered with a great deal of gravity; for no man in a passion likes to be laughed at. As for your crusty readers, they have just as good a right to be angry, and far more reason. I would advise them, therefore, to keep it up till they are very angry; which they may easily be, by telling every body their complaints: and when they have thus learned that every body is laughing at them, they might transfer their rage against the exposure of folly, to the fools who needed to be exposed. I am sorry that the chronicles have affronted them; very sorry, indeed, that their neighbours should be laughing at them; for I must say that all your readers, if they had only good management, would be a very decent sort of folks. But they begin at the wrong end; and so it fares with them. They are not willing to be like lame Meph, whom every body despised; nor like lame Boshy, whom nobody cared about: but before they have well fixed themselves upon a wood lot and raised a few potatoes, they wish to be like

Mephibosheth Stepsure Gent.

BOOK TWO

"Perspective View of the Province Building [Halifax] from the N.E." by J.E. Woolford, 1819

To the Editor of the Christian Instructor.

Sir,

By inserting the following little narative in your valuable paper, you will afford useful information to parents who feel inclined to send their children abroad. It is part of a series of sketches originally published in this province, and generally ~~acknowledged~~ admitted to be an exact representation of North American manners. They that will be rich fall into temptation and a snare, and into many foolish and hurtful lusts, which drown men in destruction and perdition.

~~Pictou, Nova Scotia.~~

William

Some time ago, a little business called me to our metropolis. As I had never been in Halifax before, curiosity induced me to devote a few hours to the inspection of its various parts. After a great deal of strolling, I found myself in the street which contains the poors' house and jail. Accident has placed them together, as if for the purpose of showing at one glance, the different results of a life of thoughtlessness and folly; for such in general are the charac-

Page of Manuscript of "William"

LETTER 18

To the Editors of the *Accaudian Recorder*,

SIRS—

This cums to let you kno that I and my concerns are a' in gude at present, hoppin' these few lines will find you in the same. Tho I am aye desperat dowre at the ditin', and nae warlock at the spellin', I hae taen in han' to put a few thochts thegither anent the stet o' our toon; and, in an espeshal maner, anent that onest man Mephibosheth Stepsure, wha, last winter pat out a wheen letters o' yeur prentin', about our neighours and their neerdoweel gaets.

It's a sair peety that our fok canna' be perswadit to keep to their ferms and live like their stashon. They hae a gran' kintra aneath their feet; and if they wad only gie't moderat labour, and then tak care o' their earnins; insteed o' the beagles grippin' and puttin' them in the tabooth, they wad be rowin' in the comforts o' life and hae siller beside. The distresses o' our toon, and they're no sma', hae sprung frae naething but idleset and wastery. Ane o' them's aneuch to ruin ony body; but our fok wadna be setisficed without the twa thegither. In war times, when they sud hae been layin' by a penny for a sair foot, they did naething but stravaig and gallop about the kintra, like the Laird o' Todhole and ither ill doin' gentry in Scotland; and when they war abrod spennin' like gentlemen, their families at hame war liven' at heck and manger. It was fill and fetch mair wi' them a'. There's nae wonner, that, when the peace cam, naething was to the fore but Maister Ledger's muckle red beuk weel filled and a kist fou' o' mortgajes, which, the onest

197

gentleman fand, war o' nae use to him; for nae body coud buy.

There maun be a great alterashon in our toon, afore it cum to ony gude. We maun gie ower our idleset and wasterfu' gaets or be spued out o't like Jock Scorum and that lang spault villain Pate Langshanks. We hae ower mony gentlemen, as they think themsels, galloppin about the kintra wi' horses and shaises. It's an abomination no to be borne. If Wull Scamp and the like o' him, wha hae nae means o' livlihude but cheatin' onest fok, war in Scotland; instead o' ridin' in gran' shaises, they wad shune be grippit and tied ahint a cart wi' the hangman at their backs. But in this kintra, sic neerdoweels hae neither fear nor shem. Ye'll see them ridin' in their shaises to the vera coorts, whar they hae been summoned for det, as gran' as the judges. There they'll stan' up afore the worthy gentlemen as bauldly as if they war their equals; and when they can jouk the peyment o' a just det, they think themsels clever fallows. A wheen o' our fok will do nae thrift, till the judges cum amang us, as the lords do in Scotland; whar they ride thro the kintra wi' a trumpet blawin' afore them, as if the day o' judgment war cum; and whar they gar gentle and semple trimle when they speak. War Wull Scamp and the like o' him there; instead o' galloppin' to the coort in shaises when the judges cam roun', they wad be puttin' up their han's to fin' if there was nae rapes about their necks, and vera thankfu' that they gat leave to stay at hame.

Then agen, if the kintra wad thrive, there maun be less kert playin' and frolickin' and drinkin' amang baith gentle and semple. There's nae seriousness nor sobriety whar thae things are gaun on; and there's as little gude cums out o' them. Naebody ever saw a douce, sober man that wantit to do weel, a great player at kerts. Every body kens, and mony ken by fearfu' experience, that they're the destrucshon o' youth. Yet in our toon, parents, by their ain exemple, encourage their vera waens in a coorse which lan's them in meesery. If our merchants wad only consider the peyment o' their ain debts, they wad bring nae kerts to the kintra. But if they will help to corrup and ruin their neibours; they needna tak it ill whin our youth get deep in their beuks, and syne rin the kintra wi' a pak o' kerts in their pouch.

This endless frolickin' about every thing maun be gien up. It's a scandal to the kintra and the ruin o' youth. I wiss parents wad learn to keep their waens at hame and gar them work. They hae mair need to be helpin' to pay their ain and their parent's dets, than to be stravagin' about in ban's, and eggin' ane anither on to a' sorts o' wickitness. There's ane Sippit and his dochters in our toon, wha are aneuch to puzion a hail kintra side wi' their fuleries. Tho they're sae puir that they're aye rinnin' about borrowin'; they maun set up for gentles, and feed the hail toon wi' their tea and trashtry. The doless things o' dochters sit a' day, skirlin' and bumiain' on a thing they ca' a penny forty; and syne at nichts they hae gatherin's o' the young fok, that lead to nae gude. It wad better fa' them to hae a pair o' woo' cairds or a kirnstaff in their han's, or be learnin' to fill pirns and ca' a shuttle. This wad mak them usefu' in a family, and gie them less to murn ower when they happen to tak the host and are like to dee; as ane o' them was last winter. They think themsels leddies; and when afore fok, they sit as mim as May puddocks: but for a' that, when they're waukened, they hae tongs like kail wives. Ye'll no beleeve that the ane that was seek, when she becam better, grew shemed o' religion, and abusit baith the minister and that decent man Mephibosheth Stepsure. It's nae wodner that she ca'd me an auld Scotch beast. The tinkler hizzy sud get a rice to her back till the wants stood on't, to learn her mair maners. There's nae gude cum o' frolickin' nor o' frolicken fok.

Anent the drinkin' o' our toon, it's no beleevable. It's the beginin' and the en' o' every thing: and to croon a', our magistrats keep up that neerdoweel Tipple, tho they ken weel that he has been the ruin o' the ha'f o' the toon, and is ilka day bringin' our youth to destrucshon wi' his ill doin' gaets. The villain gies auld Grub and some mae o' them a dram for naething when they're gaun by; and then they stan' up for him and say, that the toon needs the leeshens siller, and that if our youth will drink, it's needless to keep it frae them. They dinna lay duly to heart how mony drunkards they are helpin' to mak. Our minister Maister Drone has aften tauld them, "That the vices which they patronize, are marked as theirs in the book of remembrance; and that the groanings of wretchedness from every part of the town, have ascended on high, and, with irresistible supplication against them, press into the presence of that Being who declares justice and judgment to be the habitation of his throne." But our magestrats think themsels a' great men and dinna care a snuff o' tobacco for what the minister says.

I hae't upon gude athority, that the maist pairt o' our public revenue arises frae drinkin'. It's judgment like. I wiss that a' wha bring drink in the kintra and a' that buy't, wad consider what accoont they hae to gie.

A' this neerdoweel sort o' doin in our toon, springs frae idleset. Naebody ever saw a carefu' workin' man, rinnin' about the kintra wi' kerts in his pouch, and gettin' himsel fou' at ilka changehouse. It's a sair peety that our fok hae sic an avershon to what's gude for them. There's nae perswadin' them that moderat wark upon their ferms, is the shure way to walth and comfort. They're aye for tryin' out o' the way gaets to be rich; and now there's a fallow they ca' Medium cum amang them, makin' a great sugh about a bank, and perswadin' them that they can mak siller. It wad be wiser like, if he wad advise them to mind their ferms and hae something to sell. He'll cure our fok o' poverty, as that fule Gawpus wi' his quackery cured auld Peter Punkin and Cawleb Staggers. Wha ever heard o' a bank doin' gude to fok that earn ae penny and try to spen' twa? They say there's nae siller sirclatin' in the kintra. Whas faut's that? Carefu' fok are no without a spair penny; and the rest has been sent awa' to keep up wasterfu' craters in their neerdoweel gaets. Our fok maun hae their silks and satins and shaises; they maun hae their tea and tobacco and wine and spirits o' a' sorts; they maun hae their butes and spurs and supperfine langtaild cots, as if they war gentles: and yet the maist o' them canna keep themsels in bannocks, but maun sen' to the Stets for the very bread they eat. The like o't was never heard o' in ony decent kintra. We maun lay by thae fuleries, and labour and live as fermers sud do; and there's nae fear o' walth o' siller sirclatin' amang us. Our wives and dochters maun spin and weave their ain claes. We maun sneck the lang tails aff our ain cots; and no shem o' them, when they're cloutit at the elbocks: and syne, instead o' spennin' praishous time doin' naething and war than naething, we maun spit in our loofs, and gar our axes and ither tools do their duty. This will put it in the power o' our merchants to send something out o' the kintra and bring back the siller, and then, if we want a bank to help us on wi' our improvements, it'll do us some gude. Till a' this happen, our fok maun put up wi' hard times. Let them do like that decent man Mephibosheth Stepsure, wha keeps nae hard times about his house. Ye'll no see him rinnin' races whar he has nae erran', nor gaun out to the wars when he has nae breeks to gang wi'. Naebody ever grippit him at a frolic, dancin' amang neerdoweels. The douce, sober man stays at hame and leuks after the wark; and his auld wife Dorothy taks care o' the spennin'; and atween them, I'se assure you, they keep a bein and blythe house. They hae aye plenty to eat and plenty to put on them, and a bickerfu' o' gude ale to tak to themsels and gie a neibour. Isna' that aneuch to setisfice ony raisonable fermer?

Touchin' the hard times, I canna' say but I like them weel. They're a gran' thing fur the kintra. They hae cleered our toon o' a wheen o' the neerdoweels; and the lave o' them are takin' to the wark, like their decent neibours. Ae yeer o' hard times has done mair gude amang us than the hail time o' the war, when our fok did little but rin about drinkin' and droonin' themsels in det. I think, if we had only twa three mae hard yeers and twa three treadin' mills set up at Sippit's and Tipple's and some ither places, we wad a' cum roun' yet. Thae treadin' mills are a gran' thing for idle gangrels. Our youth are a' keen o' the dancin'; but if, when they are stravaigin' about, they war grippit and set to the mill; ae dreich job at it wad gie them as mony steps, as wad setisfice them for a twallmonth to cum. If young fok will wallop and fling wi' their feet; there's naething better for them, than to gie them as mony steps as will mak it sair wark.

Anent our neibour Mephibosheth Stepsure I maun neist mak some observes. I dout ye maun gie him some heartnin' afore he sen' you ony mae letters. He's in a great swither about it, I ken; and there's nae wonner. Ye'll no beleeve what abuse the neerdoweels o' our toon hae gien him. Ca'in' him lame auld rascal's the best o't. The onest man, it's true, is a wee shaivly about the legs, and no vera tosh in the feet; but, as our minister says, whaever fins faut wi' the walk and conversation o' Mephibosheth Stepsure, has gude sense to learn. Tho he never tries the waltzin', as they ca't, wi' Sippit's dochter Jezebel; he has as mony feet as enable him to gang a' his onest gaets, and as muckle gumshon as keeps them frae places whar they hae nae business. Tho he's fou' o' droll jokes, he's a douce, sober man.—He's in naebody's det; he's aye afore han' wi' his stipens; (sae the minister says;) and when ony puir body cums the gaet, he has something to gie and gies wi' gude will. If our fok, instead o' leukin' aye at the crookit shanks o' the decent man, wad leuk at his behaviour, and tak a lesson frae t'; they wadna' need to grumle about hard times, nor rin like grews, at the sicht o' a beagle.

I hae been ower the gaet, perswadin' him to gie us anither screed o' his letters; but he disna like to lie oonder the ill will o' auld Trot, that chirmin' body Girzel Grumle, auld square Grub, and a wheen mae o' them: (they ca' them a' maisters and mistresses and misses in our toon: it ill fa's the craters) I maun say that he has some raison; for there's nane o' them pleased. The minister himsel is no ower weel setisficed, tho he says little about it. But auld Grub, the meeserable body, is cleen wude about the steekin' o' his claes. He's neither to ha'd nor bin, but rins about roarin' that the dignity o' his office is contem'd, and that lame Stepsure the rascal sud get his back weel scored. I wad like to see wha wad attempt it. He wad shune ken whether my auld axe handle or his hurdies war hardest.

But amang them a', there's nane that misca's the onest man mair than a chiel they ca' Glunch, a neerdoweel loon frae Scotland; the mair shem till him. They tell me that when the king was at Embro', he ca'd the fok in Scotland, a naishon o' gentlemen. It was weel for Scotland, that Glunch cam awa' afore the king gaed there. Had he kend the misleered fallow, he wad hae tell'd anither tale. It's weel kenn'd what is the raison o' his ill will against our weeldoin' neibour. The villain ca's himsel a gentleman; and gangs sloongin' about, gettin' a dinner here and a supper there: but like the maist o' our toonsfok, he disna like the work; and he likes naebody that puts him in mind o't. He maunna ca' himself a gentleman when I'm by. I kenn'd the chiel afore he cam here. A fine gentleman! he was whipper-in to the Laird o' Todhole's jowlers.—When he hadna a fecket to his back, the laird teuk him and gied him a ben leather kep and a pair o' buck skin breeks; and the fallow's fine claes pat him out o' his wits. When they're worryin' the tod jowlers and lairds and whippers in, are a' tumlin' throuther; and because Glunch hadna' four feet like the dogs, but a ben leather kep and buck skin breeks like the laird, he thocht himsel a gentleman. But the laird ran thro his means; and Glunch, because he wadna work, was obleeged to cum awa' to America, whar he thinks every body sud respeck his ben leather kep and his buck skin breeks, and upha'd him in idleness. The fallow keeps awa' frae our house: it's weel for him. They tell me that auld Luckie Sham, our puir simple neibour Solomon's wife, is gaun to convert him as they ca't, and gie him ane o' her dochters. It's like aneuch ye'll hear o' his preechin' some o' thae days. The neerdoweel has as muckle laziness as either Howl or Yelpit; and he was sae used gowlin' amang the laird's dogs, that he's as able to preech as ony o' them. He has been gaun roun' the hail toon telling, that, when onest Mephibosheth put out his letters, nae body read them but the riffraff o' the kintra. I hop ye'll no let the villain gang wi' his lees. Ye maun let our fok ken that they war read whar Glunch and the like o' him, darna' put in their noses. This'll put some smeddum in our decent neibour; and let a' the toon see, that, when Glunch leuks ower his nose at what his betters like, he's but a gumshonless fellow.

Finally, and lastly, and to mak an end for the sake o' breefness, and no to multiply words without meenin', as our minister aften says a long while afore he gies ower, I maun gie you a sma' word o' advice about the prentin'. I wiss ye wad keep your sma' teeps that are no readable, for adverteesements about rum and ither wasterfu' things, and put our neibour's letters in prent that we auld bodies will be able to mak use o'. About the paper, tho it's no vera gude, I'll say naething. They tell me ye mak it yoursels; and canna mak it better, for want o' the rags which the thriftless craters thro the kintra dinna' think it worth their while to gether and sell to you. It's wise like to mak your ain paper. Ye hae mair wisdom than our fok wha raise their ain wasterfu' neerdoweels; and then sen' a' the siller out o' toon, to buy floor to feed them.

No more at present, but remains your humle servent,

ALEXANDER SCANTOCREESH.

LETTER 19

To the Editors of the *Acadian Recorder*,

Gentlemen,

The importunity of my neighbour Scantocreesh has induced me to drop you a few lines. With the solicitations of Saunders I am the more willing to comply; because it enables me to specify the reasons which have hitherto rendered my correspondence with you in future, a subject of weighty consideration and doubt.

Since I was made a gentleman, I have endeavoured to maintain that decent demeanour which becomes my station. My present rank in society was fairly and honourably acquired: and I have been very careful to show that my old woman knew something about her husband when she said, that honour would not be disgraced by getting into the company of Mephibosheth Stepsure. But somehow or other, I have not been so successful in my genteel as in my farming labours. When I was only a plain countryman, every exertion of labour added to my comforts: since I became a gentleman, the troubles of high life have beset me sorely. Whether it be, because I am envied, or because, as our neighbour Puff's son Totum when he stretches himself out, is accustomed to observe, it is not easy for a man who rises in the world to keep up his dignity, I cannot exactly say: but sure enough, though, in our town, lame Meph ingrossed less attention than Snout's pigs; genteel Mephibosheth is reviled by almost every body: and those who in passing scarcely knew me before, have now a great deal to tell about limping Boshy who was brought up by the town.

205

With respect to my original poverty, though it be a source of grievous affliction to my girls to hear it mentioned so often, there is no dodging the reproach. The only comfort which I can give them, is, that to their father before them it was the cause of bitter vexation in his early days. Many a time when I was hunting for the Squire's cows, I have asked myself, why my father did not leave me a large property of marsh and money and other good things; and I, as often, summed up the pleasures which our dashing youngsters enjoyed. But after perplexing myself to no purpose, my meditations usually terminated in this point, that having no inheritance, if I wished riches and pleasures, I must work my way to them. To the work, accordingly, I set; and finding property of every kind hard to be got, I learned to take care of it. Had I been, like Bill Scamp, born a gentleman; and then, according to the usual practice of our town, after entering upon a fine farm, passed through the varied incidents of high life, from a fine chaise to a capias; there would have been, in the gentility of the Stepsures, no stigma of disgrace. As things are, I can see no help for my girls but to comfort themselves with their father's wealth, till, like other great families before them, their origin and reproach be forgotten.

As for my lameness, being myself a living witness of its reality, it cannot be denied. If our people, however, knew the half of the grief which it caused me in my youthful days; they would all be satisfied, that, for the crime of being lame, I have long ago endured the due quantum of punishment. Often and often I used to turn my lower extremities into every possible position, hoping to discover in them unknown beauties; but all was in vain: for it must be confessed, as Miss Sippit says, that such legs and feet as Mephibosheth Stepsure's, were never before seen upon either man or beast. How I happened to get them, I could never find out: and were it not for a hint that Saunders has given me, I might have still been ignorant of their use. My neighbour says that horny stumps like mine would never do for old Trot or Peter Longshanks; but, upon Mephibosheth Stepsure, they are the grandest thing in the world for treading upon the sore heels of the ne'er do wells of our town: and farther, that if I would only consent to go to old Tubal and be shod, they would strike such terror in our people, as would make them glad to stay at home. How this may be, I cannot exactly say; for, though Snout's pigs often get themselves lamed by their straggling about, nothing but the want of legs keeps them at home and from mischief.

Still I must observe, that I do not see the connexion between my gentlemanship and lameness. Every body knows or may know, that, when I became what I am now, I was not made a lame gentleman. Before I arrived at honour, I had arrived at wealth. Your readers, therefore, I hope, will always keep in mind that it was only when I was Mephibosheth, that there were defects about me. Indeed, my old woman says, that I am the only man in our town who has no slouch in his gait: Our people claim the honour: Saunders and the other homespun neighbours have got the wealth: And, as for old Cruikshanks the Scotchman, who goes about among us doing little jobs, he has neither got the one or the other. But my spouse is not like the rest of our wives; she was always a little partial to her husband.

It is of no use to detail to you how I have been reviled and threatened. I shall only observe, that the danger of writing chronicles requires careful consideration. Indeed, the displeasure of Squire Grub alone, is enough to make any thinking man pause. Did the worthy gentleman get his will, my back would be bereaved of its best ornament. Now, were any thing of this kind to befal me, it would be a serious business; and, therefore, I must not omit the opportunity of putting in my objections which now presents itself.

As I only praised the Squire, I do not well see why he should be so angry. Perhaps he thought that I did not praise him enough; and indeed, I must confess that the half was not told. My neighbour Scantocreesh was a careful man; but he is nothing to the Squire. Saunders thinks that roads were made to help travellers, not to wear stockings and shoes; and, therefore, when he goes upon a journey, he carries his upon his shoulder. The Squire, when he goes to court to maintain the high dignity of his office, does not take the roads alone for the basis of his calculations. He considers the danger of tear and wear in rubbing through the bushes, and also the expence of mending; and then he exemplifies a care of his habiliments, which astonishes every body.

But though all this and a great deal more were formerly omitted, I am not exactly sure that it is equal to the dimensions of my back. As I formerly told you, I have good broad shoulders; and you may depend upon it, I am none of your dandy chaps, that may be grasped about the middle. If the ends of justice, therefore, require the scoring of a gentleman's back; I would much rather that the Squire should give it to little Totum or some other of our young gentlemen. Crime and punishment would there be exactly proportioned; and I am sure that a due administration of justice in this way, would be a great help to my patience and fortitude.

Under all these discouraging circumstances and a great many more which I shall not mention, I have frequently thought that it would be better for me to renounce honour and writing together, and to limp peaceably about my farm in my former way: And were it not for the gratifying encouragements which our family occasionally receive, my mind would have been long ago made up upon the point. Mrs. Stepsure, (for you must recollect that Widow Scant's daughter has now become a lady,) Mrs. Stepsure, it is true, has not yet got her shawl. She has, however, received what is far more gratifying: she knows that her husband is respected in the very capital of the province. Beside accidental notices, Trudge the pedlar on his return from Halifax in the beginning of summer with a large assortment of notions, came to our house expressly for the purpose of telling her, that, if I should ever go down to town, Tug and his friends had resolved to put me upon one of their trucks, and drag me through the streets like other great men: And farther, that, but for a mere accident, my health would, at one of their public meetings, have been drunk with a burst of applause, both louder and longer than any three times three that ever were hurraed. Tug had risen pretty late in the evening to propose the health of Mr. Stepsure: but it seems, that, for the preservation of good order, it is a standing law of the club, that no more than thirteen must speak at the same time: and, as Mr. President is obliged to be very much upon the alert, he happened to knock down Tug with his hammer of office, before counting heads. When my friend recovered his feet, he knocked down the president in his turn; and then began to insist that there were only twelve speaking before him. Whether this was really the case, was never exactly ascertained; for a general engagement ensued: and though after a good many wounds and bruises, complete harmony was restored; such a number had fallen to Tug's share, as left him not very well qualified to see when it would be safe for him to get a second time upon his feet; and on this account, the drinking of my health was unavoidably postponed.

To me all this, you may be sure, was exceedingly gratifying; for what gentleman is not pleased by knowing that his worth is duly appreciated? or what author is not gratified when good judges applaud his works? Mrs. Stepsure too, I believe, would have been actually induced to purchase the shawl, had it not been that the trucking part of the business was not exactly to her mind. She is very jealous of her husband's honour; and it occurred to her, that, were it ever reported through the medium of your paper, (as it undoubtedly would,) that Mephibosheth Stepsure was carted through the streets of Halifax; opinions not much to his credit, might be formed at a distance. She, therefore, told Trudge that she would keep the ten dollars till her husband went to town; and then perhaps, she might hire for him our neighbour Tandem's gig; that he might be drawn as decently as other great men before him. In her opinion, Mephibosheth Stepsure Gent. in a truck, would be rather a heterogeneous kind of conjunction. At some future period it might be a doubtful point, whether he was a patriot honoured or a vagabond going to the workhouse.

Since all this happened, I have put our pedlar's veracity to the test. Necessity forced me in the course of last fall to visit your town; and considering what was before me, you may depend upon it, that, in our house, the journey was the subject of no little preparation. My girls had been working hard to make a web of homespun, which, they had resolved, should reach from the house to the barn; which is no small distance. At last, after many an evenings calculation, it was agreed without a dissenting voice, that all was ready for the weaving, and, accordingly, a warp of the due length and a little over, in order to be sure, was put upon the loom. But my eldest daughter Becky had scarcely arriven at the middle of the web, when we all perceived that my Halifax journey must be undertaken in the fall. To my girls it would have been no common pleasure, to have seen the distance between our house and barn completely covered with cloth of their own making: but their eager importunity induced their mother to cut the web out of the loom and put it to the dyeing; and, as they all thought, never web in our house had dyed so slowly. At last, after much anxiety, I was rigged out from top to toe, as the saying is, (for, to tell you the truth, where my toes are, is a little doubtful:) and, as none of my children ever think of the cut of my lower extremities, I was, in the opinion of the whole, a very respectable looking country gentleman. They all agreed that at a distance my coat looked as well as Mr. Ledger's superfine; and the old lady observed, that it had no accounts from that gentleman in its pocket. Even our neighbour Saunders participated in the general satisfaction. Happening to stop in, when Buckram the taylor was proving his job, he surveyed me minutely in every dimension; and rubbing his hands most cordially together, declared that bating my shavely legs and ill made feet, he had never in his life seen any body so like the douce, bein goodman of Muckmidden, when he was dressed out for the fair of Buchlyvie. My wife, who has more respect for Saunders than for any half dozen of our gentlemen, having sent for his family when we were trying on the clothes, insisted that he should spend the evening with us; and never was evening spent with more unalloyed satisfaction. No symptom of gloom appeared, till my neighbour rose to go home; but this he immediately dissipated, by exacting a promise that, young and old, we should spend the next evening with him.

When any of our neighbours go from home, perhaps the first notice which the family gets, is, that the horse is missing. Then it is naturally concluded, that they have gone to Tipple's, or some other place of general resort. My journey to Halifax was altogether a different sort of thing. In our family it seemed to assume the solemnity of a burial; only, as it wanted the grog, none of the neighbours except Saunders cared any thing about it. To see me go from home, was an event so unusual, that, among my children, it had linked itself with the idea of never returning; and this produced such saddening effects, that, when my neighbour Scantocreesh, who seemed to enjoy the thing wondrously, suggested to me, that his father being once obliged to travel forty miles to Edinburgh, took care to make his will before he went away, the pipes of my younger offspring were immediately put in tune.

As going, however, was unavoidable; all were determined that I should go comfortably. On talking over the business of the chaise, we all agreed that it would be downright wastery: and, as a previous knowledge of the measure of Trudge's tongue had enabled us to ascertain, that, between the risk of a carting and the worth of ten dollars in these times, there existed no proportion whatever; it was unanimously resolved, that I Mephibosheth Stepsure, gent. should neither like Trudge walk before a horse, nor like the most of our townsfolk be pulled behind him, but, as becomes a man of my high station, be mounted upon his back.

Every body knows that one of the miseries of human life is packing up for a journey.—But in such a family as mine, it is always a comfortable kind of calamity. When the trouble is over, it leaves behind it recollections of endearing regard, which never fail to impress upon the mind the privations of travelling and the comforts of home. In our house all hands were busy; and it must be admitted, that, though there was some needless running about, and more mistakes committed than the abundance of help authorised, a good deal of work was done upon the whole; for, when I at last contrived to get upon my horse; saddle bags and every pocket about me, between clothes and cakes and other little comforts, were as well replenished as any of Mrs. Gypsum's crammed turkeys. My neighbour Saunders, who had stepped over to bid me farewell, after surveying the various protuberances about me, declared that he had never in his life seen any body so like old Creels the cadger of Kippen, when he was rigged out for the market. At last, a little exertion enabled me to begin my pilgrimage, and enter upon the feelings of a domestic man; which, you may depend upon it, when he is going from home, are not very comfortable. I had, however, scarcely begun to moralize, when the cheering shouts of one of my little boys admonished me to wait for his arrival. The little fellow had been able to devise no offering of comfort for the general stock: but recollecting afterward, that the object of my particular taste had been omitted, he had contrived to smuggle away a spacious pork ham; and was now in pursuit of me, exulting in his prize. When he was handing to me this substantial proof of his affection, one of Jack Scorem's boys happened to be passing, and seemed to me to view it with a wishful eye. Now, I would rather at any time make two human beings happy than see one miserable. No part of my stock, therefore, was more gladly received: and the rest of it put together, I am sure, did not produce half so much happiness.

I am not going to give you a statistical account of the roads and taverns. To your readers this would be like carrying coals to Newcastle; for who has not been at our town and in every tavern upon the road? At once, therefore, I shall enter myself into that long street with which Halifax on the side next our town, commences: and here I may observe, that, as I had given Tug no notice of my approach, I could not expect him to be waiting with his truck. Indeed, as Trudge afterward told me, he had been obliged to wait at the police office about some fighting affair. Eventually, however, never great man entering into a town, had less reason to deplore the want of attendants and admirers. I had scarcely made my appearance, when one little fellow shouted to another to come and see what funny feet a countryman had got; and in a short time, Mephibosheth Stepsure, gent. was accompanied by a goodly assemblage. I think, it may without vanity be added, that never were any great man's followers so generally or so wonderfully pleased.

Thus, you see, I at last arrived safely in town. Some of your country readers will, perhaps, ask what I was doing there. In reply I can only tell them at present, that I saw a great deal, heard a great deal, and did a great deal of business: but whether I shall again write chronicles, is not so easily told. On balancing my encouragements with my troubles and dangers; the result is so doubtful, that I question whether the wise men of Gotham, though they were all present, would know which way to turn the scale. In the mean time, as your readers wish news, along with this I have sent you the copy of a letter, which my neighbour Saunders has been writing to one of his acquaintances in Scotland. He says, that, though the diting and spelling are none of the best, it will let our ne'er do wells see themselves: and for his part he cares for none of them: no man shall attempt to score his back without such a taste of his axe handle, as will put other thoughts in his head.

Mephibosheth Stepsure, gent.

LETTER 20

Copy of a letter from Alexander Scantocreesh, farmer in our town, to Willy Whooshlicat, Residenter in the Puddockdib, Parish o' Balfron.

Auld and respeckit frien',

This cums to let you kno that I and my concerns are a' in gude helth at present, hoppin' these few lines will find you in the same. To learn by your letter, that auld neibours and acquantances haena forgotten me a' thegither, gies me great plesur in this strange lan'. Tho I didna cum to America because I was het and fou' at hame, my heart warms to Scotland and a' that belangs till't; and in this I am no singwaler: the vera waens that are born here, speak o' this kintra, as if it war the lan' o' cabteevity; and, when they hear o' ony body ettlin' to gang to Scotland, they say he's gawn hame. I wiss we coud only meet agen, to hae a crack thegither about auld lang syne. I haena forgotten the days when we war neibour herd callans; nor how, when we becam runty chiels, we used to forgether at the fair o' Kippen and the Balloch, fou o' daffin and mishief, ready at a wink to tumle ower a sweetie wife's stan'; or, like twa fules, far readier to gie crackit crouns than gude advice to ither fules like oursels. The thochtless follies o' youth aften bring manhude to sorro and shame. You and I hae great matter o' thankfu'ness, that we hae been spaired to be what we are. Wha wad hae thocht ance a day, that ye wad be an elder in the Kirk; (they ca' them deekins in this kintra,) or, that I wad be in America, doin' raisonably weel. We micht hae been like our auld crony Jock Spluter, wha, after drinkin'

215

himsel out o' wark and credit, gaed awa' wi' the sodgers, and gat himsel stickit in some drucken quarrel in Spain; or, like Geordie McCleekit, wha began wi' gingebread and sweeties, at the fair o' Buchlyvie; and frae less to mair, at last pat han' to the gudewife o' Muckmidden's piner pig and the siller; and was banisht the kintra, after a sair facht for his life.

Anent an anser to your letter about the state o' this pairt o' the warl', I dout it'll cum ill on. I was aye desperat doure at the ditin'; and as for the spellin', you and I, ye ken, gat our schulin' frae auld dominie McDoit, afore spellin' cam in fashon. It's but a sma' account that I can sen' you in ae letter. A descripshon o' this kintra and o' the gaets o' the fok that live in't, wad requare a hail beuk. To ane that cums here, every thing's a ferlie. The vera taeds and puddocks are no like the Scotch anes. They ca' them Nova Scotian nichtingells; but they micht as shune ca' them leviathans. They are grewsome leukin' craters; and in the spring time, mak a whustlin' and whurrin' that wad deave a miller.

Ae thing I may say, that the accounts which Jograffies gie o' this kintra, are no to be heedit. They are nae mair like the trowth, than the wilderness was like the lan' o' Canaan. On the south cost o' this Province, there's naething but stanes; but alang the north side, the soil is as gude as ony industrious man wad wiss to set his face to. As to what is said about the fearfu'ness o' the cauld, it's a' a blaflum. Twa or three times in a winter we hae't desperat doure for a day or twa at ance; but few o' them are sae ill as to hinner a carefu' man frae travellin' or gawn about his wark. Winter is the time when the vera weemen gang stravaigin' about, visitin' as they ca't. Touchin' the mist, about which Jograffies mak sae muckle ado; in our pairt o' the kintra there's nae sic thing.

The hail kintra, excep what has been cleered by the han' o' man, is kivered ower wi' woods, for ocht I ken, as auld as the flude; and the grun', in its naitral state, is a' heichs and hows, wi' the withert trees tumlin' out by the roots. Afore it can be made into decent fiel's, it taks a hantle o' wark.

When ony body cums to this kintra to settle, by applyin' to comishoners appointit by the Governor, he gets a hunder ackers o' lan'; and if he hae a family, aiblins he'll get mair. This is noo far back in the woods; and unless he hae brocht something wi' him, he has a hard doonsittin', and maun work to ither fok the maist o' his time. A' that he can do the first yeer, is to get a wee piece lan' clear'd o' the woods, and a house and barn up. In his clear lan' he sets taties amang the rutes wi' a how; and if he can get mair grun' cleared, he may hae some vittle. For the first yeer this is his hail crap. The next spring the tatie lan' is sawn wi' some kind o' grain, and laid out in gress: in this state it continues for aught or nine yeers; and then the stumps ha'f rotten are taen out, and the grun' plewed and levelled. The house and barn are made o' trees wi' their ens laid over ane anither. The holes atween them are filled wi' fog; and the roof theekit wi' spruce bark, which can be taen aff the trees in great blawds in the spring. But whaever brings to this kintra a penny siller, needna gang to the woods exceptin' his ain plesur. By leuking cannily about him, he'll at ony time get a chep bargen o' the mailen o' some neerdoweel, wha has run thro the carefu' gatherins o' his father. It's the way o' this kintra, that the youngest son for common gets the estate; and a puir han' he aften maks o't. As the aulder anes grow up, their father helps them on wi' a piece lan' o' their ain; so that in his auld age he is left wi' the youngest; and uswally, like a fule, gies ower every thing to him, expeckin' to be keepit comfortably as lang as he lives. Being the youngest, for a great chance he has been dawtit and indulg't in neerdoweel gaets; and when he gets things in his ain han's, he neglecks his parents, rins throo their means, and at last lan's himsel in the han's o' the beagles. Auld fok, they say, are twice bairns; and it leuks vera like it: for, tho they see the maist o' their auld neibours meetin' wi' rough usage frae their ain, they're sae doitit that they'll no tak warnin'.

This is nae place for gentlemen that haena abeelity or will to work. It's the puirest bred in the kintra, as may be seen amang our militia cornels and cabtens and our majestrats, wha are a' squares after their kind; and amang mony mae without ony teetle. They a' want to be great men, and for the sake o' onour that's no worth a winlestrae, they negleck their ferms, and drown themsels in det. Were ye to hear the fok in our toon speakin', or to see them at the kirk wi' their shaises and ither bravery, ye wad think them lords and leddies: but the maist o' them haena a bawbee in their pouch; and at hame, some hae scarcely a caff bed to sleep on.

When I speak o' our toon, ye maunna think that I am livin' in a ceety. They hae a sayin' here, that a kirk, a changehouse, and a smiddy, mak a toon in America. A toon or toonship means a place twall or saxteen miles square, laid aff by Goverment.

But tho this be a puir kintra for gentry, it's a gran' place for ony sober, workin' man that's willin' to lay his han's about him. I cam here, as ye ken, wi' little; and noo, I am as bein as ony o' your wee moorlan' lairds in Scotland; and my auldest son Jock has a gude mailen beside. But ye maunna think that every body in our toon cums on sae weel. The maist o' our neibours are keepit frae han' to mouth wi' their ain ill management. Tho they like to live weel and dress themsels granly, they hae a naitral avershon to work upon their ferms. When they maun do't, they flee to't like furies till the job's done; and they gang idle, or hing about doin' little the rest o' their time. Their fermin' is something like what we used to see about Fintry when we war herd callans. They powter in the same bit grun' till it bear naething but weeds, and syne they compleen o' the lan'. When needcessity cums upon them, they'll do ony thing but ferm. Ane pawns his mailen and turns merchan, anither taks up changehouse, and a thrid gangs to the woods to mak timmer, or bigs a gabert and carries what they ca' gypsum doon the Bay o' Fundy to the Lines, and sells't to the Americans to put upon their lan'. Tho' they're no willin' to work, they a' want to be gentlemen; and mony a strange gaet they try to mak themsels rich. If they can only get ha'd o' an auld horse or an auld watch, they'll sell and swap them roun' the hail kintra; and every fule that gets them, thinks he has fun' a fortun. Some o' them even expeck to mak themsels rich by dreemin'. About twenty yeers back, ane o' the fules dreemt that anither o' them wi' a mark upon his nose, was to fin' a trasur, said to be buried on the cost o' this province by ane o' the auld pyrats. Anither o' the fules wi' a plooky nose, beleev't that his anser'd the descripshon; and shune dreem't, that, by howkin' at a place ca'd Chester, he wad get the siller. This was aneuch to set the hail kintra asteer. To the howkin' they gaed; and every nicht, expeckit to get the trasur in the mornin'; for they heard their tools rattle upon the kist. But, in the nicht time, the Enemy, as they said, wha was takin' care o't, aye pat it out o' their gaet, and gied them anither day's wark; till at last, when they had gotten down a hunder feet and mair, the water brak in and was like to droon them. Then they began to howk anither hole, expeckin' to get aneath the water. But frae the way they howkit it, it grew sae mirk that they coudna see to work; and when they teuk a caunle doon wi' them, the hole teuk low and gaed aff like a cannon: And the puir fules, after workin' a hail simmer, cam hame wi' their tails atween their feet, droon'd in det, and laucht at by every body that had a mouthfu' o' sense. Here and there amang them, there's a considerat man that minds his ferm; and ane o' this kind for common baith lives like a king and has siller to len'; but the maist o' them are sae keen to be gentlemen that they're no willin' to work as fermers sud do. If they war in Scotland, they wad hae to rin the kintra, or gae 'wa wi' the sodgers.

Even what they do get aff the lan', is ill taen care o'; and tho it war a gude deal mair, they wad be puir and in hardship. Their sinfu' and wasterfu' gaets o' makin' awa' wi' their earnin's, are scarcely beleevable. Tho the kintra's but thinly inhabited, they canna gree amang themsels, and are aye at the law. Atween bargens and fechtin' the young fok hae a rowth o' quarrels to red; and the auld anes are never without some stramash or ither, about their cattle breakin' ower fences, or about some bit grun' that's no worth a bodle. Ony clishmaclaver's aneuch to set them by the lugs and gar them rin to the coort. Then agen, they're aye in debt to the merchans; sae that atweesh ae thing and anither, the beagles hae a thrang time o't. Every yeer our wee toony thro's awa' as muckle siller upon the lawwers, as wad burden the estate o' ane o' your Scots lairds.

Still I maun say for them, that they're vera ceevil to strangers; and excep when they're quarrellin', kin' to ane anither. Whaever gangs to their house, gets the best that's in't. But there's nae thrift amang them. Every thing gangs to their back or their wame, and then they grumle that there's nae siller in the kintra. The maist o' them hae nae mair forethocht than waens or the tinklers in Scotland. When they hae, they hae; and when they want, they want. Naething 'll sair them but gran' claes and shaises and ither sorts o' bravery; and this lests till the beagles grip them and put them in the ta'booth.

When they get the crap aff the grun', there's naething amang them but gallantin' and feastin'; and then, the neist simmer a wheen o' them will be rinnin' thro the kintra in their shaises wi' pocks, seekin' to borro' or buy a pickle floor frae their neibours. The maist o' them are great han's for their wame; and their wives and dochters, excep when they're dressin' or stravaigin', are aye aboot some hashtry or ither. I canna gie you an accoont o' their cuikery; for the like o't was never heard o' in Scotland nor in ony decent kintra. What the scriptures say o' the locusts, is troo o' them: they devoor every green thing. The vera bean shaups that we wad gie to the kye, is ane o' their favorite dishes. They fry lumps o' raw daich in swine ceme, and ca' them Yanky cakes. It's aneuch to gar a soo scunner to think o't. They mak a great wark wi' pies made o' pumpkins; which, if it warna for the eggs and shugar and spices put into them, wad be nae better than a piece o' a fosy turnip. Instead o' livin', as carefu' fermers sud do, upon parritch, and brose, and hackit kail, and pease bannocks, and crowdie, and drammock; naething 'ill gang down wi' them frae mornin' to nicht, but tea and fried pork or some ither kind o' flesh, spirits o' a' kinds and mony mae extravagancies. Ae family in our toon, will devoor as muckle flesh as a hail baronry in Balfron. There's nae wonner that they're aye puir and in det.

The families here are maistly large, and as gude leukin' young fok as ye wad wiss to see; only they hae ower muckle glibness o' tong, which is said to arise frae their eatin' a fosy thing they ca' squashes. But they're ill brocht up, and sae's seen o' them. Their parents indulge them wi fine claes and idleset, and they're aye galloppin' about frolickin' and drinkin'. Amaist every thing in our toon is done wi' a frolic, that is, when they want ony job done, they gather a' the young fok and gie them plenty o' rum to drink; and when the wark's ower, they send for Driddle, an auld drucken neerdoweel, to fiddle to them at nicht; and after they're tired wi' the dancin', a wheen o' them gang to the bundlin' as they ca't. Nane o' my seed and generation, I hop, will ever be guilty o' sic Babylonish gaets. I hae gien the young fallows here a lesson that they'll no shoon forget. Ae nicht, when our dochter Eppy, wha is a snod weel far'd lass, gaed to her bed, she terrifit the hail house wi' an unco skreichin'; and when I ran to see what was the matter, I fand a chiel amang the blankets. Hoo the villain got there, I ne'er kend; but my auld axe handle and his hurdies can tell hoo he gaed awa. After I had done wi the neerdoweel, I inveetit him to cum back anither nicht and bundle; but ane was aneuch.

Ye inquare hoo this lan' is providit wi' the ordinances. I dout no sae weel as it needs. In maist pairts o' the kintra, the peeple are sair dividit amang themsels; and because they canna gree about ae minister, they grow up in ignorance and delusion. The kintra's owergane wi' lazy vagabonds, wha pretend to veesions and revelashons. Then they tak up the preechin' at their ain han' and wanner about, livin' on silly fules and promisin' to convert them. Ye'll no beleeve what havers they tell about their convershons and experiences. Ane says, he gaed into the woods; and, after warslin' three days and three nichts wi' a bear, which turned out to be the Enemy, he cam out a new man and coudna keep himsel frae preechin'. Anither tells hoo he facht the deil wi' a bar o' airn; and strak about him sae manfu'ly that sathan, frae dreed o' sair banes, was fain to mak a pair o' cleen heels and rin like a maukin. I coud tell you ither stories about them, just as lee like; but they're no worth the comin' ower. They're no just sae ill, sin ane o' them in the neist province, that ca'd himsel John the Babtist, endit wi' cuttin' his sister's throt, and gat himsel hang't for the deed. Ye'll hardly credit that sic things coud happen in a christian lan'; yet there's neer a vegabond o' this sort but gets some puir deludit bodies to beleeve and rin after him: and when they think themsels convertit, they set up the preechin' and gather ither gowks like themsels to their meetin's, whar they waste prashous time, singin' hims and preechin' to ane anither, and tellin' great pockfu's o' lees about their convershons and experiences. Even weemen that haena a mouthfu' o' sense, will stan up in public to tell their fulish clavers; and it's no uncommon for them to ha'd meetin's for prayin' decent sober fok into their fuleries: And wi a life o' this kind, they think themsels great sants.

In our toon, I canna say that we're ill providit. Our minister Maister Drone is a troo frien' to the cause; but the onest man, atween gangrels intrudin' into the office unsent, and his ain poverty, is sair ha'den doon. Amaist every body here is in det; and because the minister disna like to crave, and has naebody to do't for him, he's aye last paid. If he hadna paishens forbye ordinar, he wad hae been broken heartit lang syne. The auld fok say that he's no what he used to be. When he cam first to the toon, every body alloo'd that he was a clever spokesman in the pu'pit; but noo, whenever he holds furth, he's sair fashed, which maks him lang o' tellin' his tale and no vera takin'. Yet, I maun say for him, that, when he does get his observes out; they're aye soun' and sappy, and weel worth the waitin' for. I hae aften wonner'd hoo our minister sud be sae afflickit when he munts the pu'pit. It's no for lack o' matter; for every body alloos him to be a dungeon o' diveenity; and when he tauks wi' ony o' us about kintra affairs, he discoorses stracht on, without hostin' or hampin'. Tipple, a neerdoweel that keeps a changehouse in the toon, manteens that Maister Drone's infirmity and dreich way o' speakin', are a pairt o' the preechin'. But the villain's no to be heedit; for he hates the minister, because he lifts up a testimony against him, for corruptin' the youth wi' his card playin' and drinkin' and ither illdoin' gaets. Some are dissatisficed, and compleen that the minister disna study as he used to do. But hoo can the onest man do't? If he didna spen' his time, leukin' after his cattle and swine, like the rest o' us, he coudna live in the toon.

I see, it's no possable for me to gie you sic a descripshon o' this place as it needs. But to mak up my defecks, I hae sent you hame a wheen letters, which a decent neibour o' ours put out last winter in the public prents, describin' the fok in our toon and their ways o' doin'. They'll do as weel for ony ither pairt o' the kintra; for amaist every body's tarr't wi' the same stick. Trudge, anither o' our neibours, a canny man, wha has made a hantle o' siller at the packman tred, and is ettlin' to gang to Glasgow to lay in his gudes afore he turn merchant, has promis't to gie the letters carefu'ly to Watty Langtrams, the Balfron carrier. I needna' say how gled it'll mak me, if they perswad you to cum out. It's a gran' time for ony fermer wi' a penny siller to cum to this kintra. Amaist the tae ha'f o' the ferms wad be sould, if ony body wad gie a bod for them. In war times the fermers gat twa prices for every thing; end the maist o' them lived as if they war gettin' three. Some coft dear ferms that they had nae use for, and naething to pay for; and ithers coft fine shaises and fine claes, or drank themsels out o' credit. Because siller was then plenty, they thocht naething o' det. But when the peace cam, the siller gaed out o' sicht like sna' aff a dyke; and then the thochtless craters war ruined, and the merchans that trustit them little better. Noo, they're as angry at the sma' prices and scarcity o' siller, as if somebody war cheatin' them; and because they're puir, they think the kintra's no worth the livin' in.

As mony a body in Scotland wants to ken something about America; ye had better gie the letters to auld Bauldy Benks, when he cums your way sellin' his ballads and carritches. He'll aiblins get some prenter body about Fa'kirk to put them out. The sellin' o' them may help the puir crater to a mouthfu' o' meat; and whaever likes to read them, will learn a hantle about this pairt o' the warl'. No more at present but remains,

Your lovin' frien' and humle servant to command till death,

Alexander Scantocreesh.

LETTER 21

To the Editors of the *Acadian Recorder*,

Gentlemen—

Through the importunities of my old lady, I have reconsidered the subject of our correspondence; and am now disposed to view compliance with her wishes, as the least of two evils. Not that I am like Mrs Grumble's husband Job, a man subject to rule; for, as I told all your farming readers before, my wife makes the trowsers and I wear them. But it is very reasonable you know, that, when she allows me to govern, I on my part should always consult her, and follow her advice. Indeed, she has been a goodwife to me; and I may safely affirm that I never rejected her counsels without feeling afterwards uneasy.

With respect to the present point she says, that there is no dropping your correspondence without disgrace: that already, by writing, I have arrived at honour; and that, if I wish to get on, I must walk straight forward. In going about, I have, you may depend upon it, taken many a crooked and unprofitable step, sometimes one way and sometimes another. If, for the information of your readers, I might be allowed to state the amount of my travelling expences in the course of my life, I would say that I have always found getting on as straightly as possible, to be the nearest way to the journey's end. I never yet made progress by going backward; and when I did happen to take side steps, they always led me into the ditch. The advice of my spouse, therefore, aided by a little inclination of my own, and sanctioned by so much experimental knowledge, has

225

induced me to put it out of her power, at any future period to say to me what Mrs Grumble is always sounding in honest Job's ears,—I told you so.

In forming this resolution, the suggestions of my neighbour Saunders, I must confess, have not been without their influence. Saunders is a deadly enemy to all our townsfolk who try to live without working, or who grasp at a station to which they are not entitled. Our town, he says, will never be what it ought, till all those huckstering, idle vagabonds and ne'er do well gentry by whom it is overrun, be cut off root and branch: And farther, that since our worthy old pastor has not been able to make them religious and useful men; the next best is to hunt them down like wild beasts, till the very sight of an honest man make them run like foxes as they are: and that, as I am the only writer who has attempted to make our people see and be ashamed of themselves, my credit is pledged to stick to the point till a better appear. My neighbour has also supplied me with an additional hint, which is never lost upon an author. He says that Lord Byron and Sir Walter Scott show me how renowned lame writers may be: and he does not see why Mephibosheth Stepsure might not become as famous as them both. To a lame author nothing, you may depend upon it, could be more gratifying; for Saunders is an excellent judge. My mind, therefore, is fully made up: and though I have some lurking suspicion, that neither Lord Byron nor Sir Walter has so much difficulty in making headway as myself; if I do not overtake good company and fame, it shall not be for want of exertion to get forward: And that, in the mean time, I may not give offence to any body; I shall continue my own life, by stating some additional particulars connected with my journey to Halifax.

On my arrival in town, I took up my lodgings at Mr. Guzzle's; who, as you know, keeps a house of entertainment at the mouth of Swallow street. He is a nephew of Tipple's, and the only man in Halifax with whom I was at that time acquainted. These considerations induced me to prefer his house; for I am never at home among strangers; and besides, I anticipated the convenience of having an acquaintance to whom I could freely apply for information about places and persons: And I must say that I found him a very pleasant and communicative landlord. In the evening in particular, except when his wife had persuaded him to go to bed and rest away the fatigue of his extra exertions, he was sure to devote to his guests his whole time and conversation. From Mr Guzzle I soon learned, that, in Halifax, the times were very bad. The same thing also, I heard frequently repeated by a number of very social gentlemen, who having nothing to do at home, were accustomed to meet in the evening at my landlord's, for the express purposes of mutual bewailing and comfort. All seemed to agree that they had never experienced so dull and distressing times: and indeed, I am inclined to think that they all felt them sorely; for I recollect very well, that their sittings were long; and a great many sorts of comfort were requisite, in order to prepare them for facing the pressure of the succeeding day. At my outset in life, when hard times beset me, I used to live more sparingly at home; and then, instead of going abroad to Tipple's to spend, I took care to bring from the woods a back load of hoop poles or something else, which, in the evening, left me no leisure to think of the times. By pursuing this plan, I uniformly found that a little saving and a little additional industry would drive the greatest pressure before them. But in Halifax, I conjecture, my scheme of facing hard times has never been adopted; for as far as I remember, I did not see one gentleman with a load of hoop poles upon his back. But a mind in hardship is fertile in shifts; and I suppose, they must have discovered in Guzzle's, the comfort which they were reluctant to carry from the woods.

As a number of gentlemen with whom I had business, belonged to the club, I was very glad to find them so near home; and I promised myself that what I had to do, would be easily and soon completed. Next morning accordingly, I commenced my calls; when obstructions which I had not anticipated, presented themselves. One had just gone to the lakes upon a fishing excursion; another was over at Dartmouth shooting; a third was taking a ride to the Nine Mile House; and a fourth had just sailed down the harbour with a few acquaintances, upon a party of pleasure. In short, nobody whom I wished to see, could be found but Mr. Stickatit. On remarking to the old gentleman, that he was a better housekeeper than some of his neighbours, he replied, that, though he was not doing much, he could not afford to be doing nothing, and much less increasing his expence. Hard times, said he, require to be watched; for a little trade neglected, always becomes less; and a declining business is a death blow to hope, which few ever surmount.

As my business was not of much consequence to any of those gentlemen; and besides, could suffer nothing from the delay of a few hours, I was not disposed to find fault: And, as this was my first journey to town, I determined to devote the day to a general view of it.

What different courses I took, or what remarks occasionally occurred to me, I shall not at present detail. After a great deal of wandering about, I found myself upon the road which leads past the poors' house and jail; which, in your town, are wisely placed in the same neighbourhood; doubtless, that your young people may at one glance perceive the different results of a life of thoughtless folly. As I was proceeding slowly along, engrossed by these musings which naturally occur to the person who has for the first time seen what is properly called a town; one of your young gentlemen, upon a high spirited horse, came gallopping along, and unexpectedly hailed me to get out of the way, old codger. In cases of this kind, I have never found the decisions of my will and feet equally prompt. Whether it be that the latter looking, different ways, do not take the same view of things; or because, being near neighbours, they cannot readily agree, I shall not say: but sure enough, to this day they have not acquired that quick cooperation which sudden danger requires; and in the present instance, I was, without any real injury, overturned, at the very moment when my feet had resolved upon exertion.

On attempting to get up, I found myself assisted by a decent looking old gentleman, whom I had previously seen proceeding from a gate which opens into one of the above mentioned buildings. Proceeding in the same direction, we naturally entered into conversation; and had travelled over the ordinary topics, as far as the hardness of the times and the difficulty of maintaining a family, when the old gentleman observed, that these things gave him no uneasiness. "Discontent and despondency," said he, "are the companions of unreasonable desire. Where the mind grasps at little, hope is easily cherished. For my own part, when my means are small, I have learned to be content. For all that I need, I have the best security: *'His bread shall be given him, and his water shall be sure'*."

"Religion," I replied, "is doubtless a sure ground of confidence; and to the mind which lives under its influence, its consolations are peace: but a parent's comfort depends considerably upon the members of his family; and young people, even when convinced of the excellence of religion, are not always willing to be content with its provisions."

"I have no family," said he: "my partner in life I have laid in the grave; and I bless God, that, when I shall be laid beside her, I shall have neither son nor daughter in this place."

"Your opinion of our metropolis," I replied, "is not much in its favour. Hitherto, I have known it only at a distance:

but, from the numerous examples of the benevolence of its inhabitants with which I am acquainted, it has had my esteem. Among themselves, much is said to be done for the relief of the poor; and, though impostors from the country have often deceived them, still no unfortunate settler ever tells his distresses in Halifax, and tells them in vain."

"To condemn this town collectively," said he, "would be a violation of justice. With much to be reprobated, it contains much that is valuable. In this place, the rewards of industry are adequate to the rational enjoyments of life; nor is it without men whose principles and deportment adorn society: and I trust, it contains some, who, in the great day of account, will be adjudged worthy to walk in white. But, with all this goodness, it contains enough to alarm the mind of every parent who makes it his abode. Its allurements to vice are fearful: it is not surprising that youth fall before them: it is strange that the integrity of any is preserved. If your leisure permit, I will give you an example by which you may judge." Accordingly, having just arrived at a rivulet which flows behind the town, we seated ourselves upon its brink; and I received from the old gentleman the subsequent narrative.

In the vicinity of one of those numerous villages by which the city of Glasgow is surrounded, an ancient family, a number of years ago, had contrived to finish the remains of their paternal estate. This event occurred opportunely for a gentleman who had just returned from this continent to his native country. A long series of years devoted to business in one of the southern States, had enabled him to retire with a splendid fortune; and when this estate was advertised for sale, he was looking out for a place where he might display his affluence, and enjoy that nursing which a constitution shattered by the luxuries and diseases of a warm climate, necessarily requires. The estate, therefore, was purchased; a mansion in the modern stile, quickly erected; and every thing about it, adorned with a degree of splendor which astonished the whole village. His zealous care of his improvements also, increased their fascinating power. He would have very gladly dispensed with the presence of the village. Had it been a negro village upon any of his American plantations, a word would have swept its last vestige from the face of the earth. But though it belonged to the estate; as its inhabitants happened to be white men, and each in the possession of a good lease and under the protection of law, every house and inhabitant remained unmolested. His defence against the danger of trespass, extended only to prohibitions and threats. These, however, were not always a sufficient barrier against the principle of curiosity: and whenever any daring little fellow did venture into prohibited ground, he was bewildered amid walks and arbours, where the honeysuckle and the rose perfumed the air with their fragrance, and the lilac and laburnum adorned the scene. In the youthful minds which contemplated this profusion of the beauties of nature, it was the uniform conclusion, that he who possessed them, must be the happiest of men.

As it was generally known that this gentleman had been only the son of a poor widow, one consequence of his splendor soon exemplified itself, in frequent emigrations of the youthful villagers to different parts of the world. To many families this was a source of grievous affliction. In Scotland, the religious sentiments which are cherished by the mass of the people, fan the flame of parental affection; and in many, the combined operation of principle and feeling produces such dread of the contamination of their offspring, that often the affliction of a father when his son goes abroad, is not less acute than if he had laid him in the grave. Still the ambition of youth, inflamed by a daily contemplation of the splendor which emigration might procure, occasioned in the village a disruption of the unity and peace of many of its families. Hope, it is true, rather than the actual experience of any of the emigrants, cherished the ardour of those whose minds turned them to the same course. Of those who had gone abroad, some, soon after their arrival in foreign parts, had died; and others, in a few years, had returned with their constitutions destroyed and their habits depraved. But, as nobody knew how it fared with the rest, the young people concluded that they were amassing a fortune, with which they would soon return to the village in splendor.

At last, by the same means, the family of one of my old acquaintances was threatened with the destruction of domestic comfort. Though he was only a tradesman in ordinary circumstances, his conscientious deportment had, by the general voice of the village, marked him out as a pattern worthy of imitation, and raised him to the office of an elder in the parish; and, in the opinion of the whole, it was never filled by a worthier man. His family consisted of his wife and their only son William, who, like many others before him, had now resolved to make his fortune abroad.

To the parents of William, whose sole ambition was to exemplify that religious and peaceful life whose brighter prospects are beyond the grave, and to witness their son, the resemblance of themselves, his determination was a dreadful stroke. In the prospect of declining days, he was the earthly pillar of their hope. Beside their son, they had none to care for them, and none to comfort. But this reflexion was the least cause of their grief. With the fire and ambition of youth, he was about to launch into a world of snares, where the warning voice of religion might not be heard; and, in their estimation, the soul of their son was more valuable than the wealth of worlds. To shake his resolution, therefore, the persuasives of religion and parental affection were alike employed: but they were employed in vain. To those filial sympathies which turn the heart of children to their fathers, William was by no means a stranger. The grief of his parents and the prospect of separation, had wounded him deeply: but the fairy dreams of ambition bewildered and perverted his mind. He felt firmly assured that he would never forget his parents nor their worthy example: abroad, he would retain his integrity; and when he returned to cheer their declining days, he would return both a wealthy and a religious man.

When his father found his own influence unavailing, he applied to the clergyman of the parish for his friendly interference. This gentleman was one of those worthy men, who, by their instruction and example, have conferred upon Scotland, riches more valuable than silver and gold. His heart dwelt upon the comfort of his flock: in all their afflictions he was afflicted. At the request of the parent, accordingly, he walked over one evening to his house. It was one of those evenings in the blooming season of the year, when the peaceful stillness of nature tranquillizes the mind to the contemplation of her beauties. The abode to which he was proceeding, was less remarkable for the splendour of its appearance, than for the worth of its inmates. It was one of those rude habitations with which the older villages in Scotland abound. It was the house from which William's great grandfather had been taken, to cement with his blood in the Grass Market of Edinburgh, that noble structure of civil and religious privilege which is the glory of Scotland. This worthy martyr, at the end of his little habitation, had planted an ivy, whose tendrils now spreading in every direction, supplied it with an unfading mantle of green. Around its little window in front, a blooming honeysuckle had been guided with care; while the spot of ground by which it was separated from the road, surrounded by a neatly trimmed hedge, had, by the taste and industry of William, become an emporium of flowery beauty.

When the clergyman arrived at the little gate in front of the house, the evening sun receding from the view, faintly cast upon the verdant memorial of the martyr a parting ray. William was in the midst of his flowers; and his mother, sitting upon the rude seat which is the usual companion of the door of the older houses in Scotland, was gazing upon her son.

"William," said the clergyman, "you have made this a very beautiful spot. How gratifying it must be to your parents, to sit at their door on such an evening as this, and to contemplate their son, caring for their comfort even in his amusements. Your father's house has long been the habitation of the just: its ivy is the plant of four generations. It deserves the ornaments of nature. To strew flowers in the path of religious parents, is fit employment for a son. But, William, where will your mother sit, and what will rejoice her, when she has nothing left but the recollection of such an evening as this?"

William's mind was oppressed by compunction and shame; but he made no reply: he thought upon the lawns and groves of the gentleman who had returned from abroad; and he resolved, that in a few years, his parents, whenever they pleased, should be shaded by groves as fine and lofty as those which adorned the neighbouring demesne.

"If," resumed the clergyman, "the visitations of the Almighty afflict the habitation of the just, when the child of their bowels has forsaken them, who is to comfort? If the last enemy assail them, who will put his hand upon their eyes, and bury them with their fathers, when they are gathered to their people?"

As William's parents were in moderate circumstances, and neither very old nor in ill health, he was disposed to view these as improbable events. At any rate, a few years hence he would return; and in the mean time, he should take care to let them want for nothing.

"Your great grandfather," subjoined the clergyman, "was dragged from this house, and persecuted to the death, for the testimony of Jesus: you, William, are hastening to parts where, perhaps, the testimony of Jesus has never been proclaimed. When you thirst for the wealth of a foreign land, are you willing to be tarnished by its vices and crimes? Have you considered the character of the man whose riches have inflamed your ambition? His vices are productions of the countries where his wealth was gained. When, in similar circumstances, you grasp at wealth, you must grapple with temptations which have bereaved him of the mind's best feelings and hopes: And what has he gained? He has brought home riches; splendour surrounds him; he may fare sumptuously every day. But what are these to a man whom skill cannot cure? Better it is, William, to tread in the footsteps of your fathers. Seek not great things; seek them not. You may get wealth in a foreign land; and with it you may get the gloomy reflexion, that you have spent your strength for nought and in vain. What is the man profited, who gains the world and loses his soul?"

William turned from the clergyman with that sullen obstinacy which the determined mind feels, when it conceives itself to be unreasonably opposed. In short, a few weeks after, he was standing upon one of the quays at Greenock, whither his father had accompanied him, to bid him farewell. The moment of separation had arrived: William's hand solicited the parting pressure of a parent's; but, instead of the hand of a father, it grasped a bible.

"William," said his father, "it was my highest ambition, to inspire you with the love and the fear of God, to witness you a worthy member of his church, and to be cheered with the hope that you would at last mingle with the company of our fathers who are around the throne. You are putting yourself in the way of evil. Here is the rule which I have taught you to observe. We may never meet till the heavens be no more. May the God before whom our fathers walked, the God who has fed me all my life long, bless you and keep you! I desire not your greatness. My heart yearns for the soul of my son. Listen to the last and best proof of my love: In the name of my God, the God of my fathers, I charge you: *Read your bible; obey its voice; and on the great day of account, take care to meet me at the right hand of Christ.*"

LETTER 22

To the Editors of the *Acadian Recorder*,

Gentlemen—

Your readers will recollect that they left William in the possession of the parting charge of a father. In a religiously educated young man, who was forsaking his parents, and might see them no more, the preceding charge was not calculated to produce lightness of heart. But there was no time for serious moralisings. The vessel was under weigh, and all was bustle; and though William resolved that he would never forget the last words of his father; circumstances forced him, in the mean time, to postpone their consideration. On entering the vessel, he found himself in the company of a number of young men, who, having felt poverty at home, were, like himself, going to meet riches abroad.

In the opinion of the youth of Scotland, to go abroad and to get rich, are terms nearly synonymous. The qualifications requisite in order to the acquisition of wealth, and the influence of external circumstances in the formation of character, are rarely considered. Hope carries them abroad: disappointment gives them knowledge. As the youthful voyagers, therefore, were satisfied with their prospects, they were disposed to be pleased with themselves and each other, and mutually to exemplify that frank and obliging disposition, which, by communicating kindness, conciliates affection.

A pleasant breeze had wafted them gently down the Firth; behind them the towering mountains of Arran had gradually disappeared; and, in every direction, the eye met only the clouds of heaven and the swell of the western wave. Of such a scene, the first effect is a feeling of grandeur; the next, a state of listless depression, which the want of employment never fails to cherish. When William and his companions were in this condition, the indications of the sky suggested to the master of the vessel, the propriety of preparing for an approaching storm. In cases of this kind, seafaring men are seldom deceived. A tempest succeeded; which, though attended with much less danger than dismay, was sufficient to alarm the minds of young men who had never before been where the deep alone meets the horizon, and where only a few boards, incessantly lashed by the fury of the waves, preserved them from an unfathomable abyss. The sailors, too, diverted by their fears, were careful to magnify the danger; so that between sickness and terror, each of the young adventurers would have gladly exchanged his splendid prospects abroad for a safe footing upon the land of his poverty. William's mind turned to the tranquil enjoyments of his paternal home. When his great grandfather left it, it was upon a pilgrimage of glory: he felt that he himself had fled from the presence of his father, and he thought upon Jonah. He had his bible, it is true; but its consolations were sealed. By and bye, more agreeable weather reanimated his mind; he learned to laugh at his fears; and his feelings of remorse were exchanged for the enjoyments of hope. At last, without any accident or unusual adventure, the vessel arrived upon the coast of this province.

Though a passenger from Britain be aware that he will see a great deal of wood in Nova Scotia; the continuous succession of forest which almost every where exists, rarely fails to give his mind an unexpected shock. He had pictured to himself a diversity of lawn and grove, which would cheer and delight: his eye meets tree towering above tree, till the horizon terminate, not the succession but the view; and when it seeks relief in the habitations of men, only a few wretched huts, scattered along the coast, diversify the scene. He had anticipated the indications of affluence and social enjoyment. From the immense solitudes of the forest, therefore, his mind shrinks within itself, and feels as if it stood alone in the midst of the earth. Nor is a nearer approach to the coast at all calculated to remove these saddening impressions. Rock appears piled upon rock; and where a tree is interspersed, it is the hemlock or spruce, upon which the occasional visitations of the spray have conferred the aspect of old age unpreceded by the vigour of youth. It seems the very home of desolation and despair. Under the influence of kindred feelings, William and his companions entered our spacious harbour.

No person from the parent country, I presume, ever approached Halifax by sea for the first time, without a mingled sensation of surprise and delight. With the appearance of the coast, it forms a contrast which has the effect of enchantment. Upon a mind brooding over previous prospects of dreary desolation, its commanding position and its numerous indications of strength and splendour, have an overwhelming influence. When the vessel entered the harbour, it was one of those days in the fall, in which the beauty of the sky compensates for the decay of the green mantle of spring. It was a day, too, devoted to the celebration of one of those victories which have elevated Great Britain to the pinacle of nations. At that time, a number of the bulwarks of the ocean floated in our harbour; and the wharves were crouded with the trophies of their superiority. In every direction, therefore, the signals of exultation waved proudly in the breeze; and when the vessel anchored before the town, it was amid the thundering of cannon, which responded to the shout of rejoicing. William's mind was completely bewildered. His first thought was of Vanity Fair: but he thought not of

Yielding. The glare of magnificence which dazzled his eye, lighted up the blaze of ambition within; and he felt the sensations of a son, bearing proudly home to his parents the trophies of his splendour. In the mean time, his whole resources consisted in a few tools and the art which he had learned from his father.

In those days, the difficulty of a master tradesman in Halifax, was not, to find business, but, to secure workmen who might enable him to fulfil his engagements. Among the labouring classes extravagant wages had produced their usual effects, the dislike of steady employment and a spirit of dissipation; so that to the masters a supply of new hands was always a relief. William, therefore, was immediately engaged; and, as he was an excellent tradesman and wrought by the piece, he could, by moderate exertion, earn almost as much money in one day, as with his father in a week. To be in such a situation, had been the object of his wishes: he had resolved to be rich; and now he was determined not to spare labour. At the same time, he was not of that grasping disposition which has no feeling but the desire of wealth. Educated as he had been, religion kept a hold of his mind; and filial affection, fortified by this superior principle, and cherished by endearing recollections, induced him to view wealth as the means by which a dutiful son might gladden the heart of a parent. At the conclusion of a few weeks, accordingly, he remitted home the greater part of his wages and at the same time a letter, in which he gave an account of his situation, his prospects, and his hopes. His parents he particularly enjoined, to expend the money upon their comfort and to fear no want. He spoke of his flowers, and of the wrens and robins which nestled with confidence under the sheltering protection of his great grandfather's ivy; and concluded with a cheering encouragement, that he would soon revisit the verdant covering of his father's abode.

In William's situation, however, there were other particulars which he was less willing to bring under the review of his parents. The shop in which he wrought, was not without those incentives to dissipation which fascinate the thoughtless, and cast entanglements around the mind, before it is aware that vice stings as an adder. In the morning, his shopmates preceded their labours by assembling around the bitters; and, during the course of the day, the bottle was often re-visited. The conduct of the master too, was of that conciliating kind which pleased his servants. He was eager to have his work completed: it was, therefore, his interest to keep them in good humour; and when he happened to step into the shop, he would freely take his glass along with them; and in contributing to their comfort, he was never a niggard. By these means, general good humour was maintained; and the work went on with a degree of merriment, which, though often less allied to wit than to obscenity and profanation, was highly amusing to minds of a corresponding cast.

To William, who had been accustomed to the sobriety and religious deportment of his father's house, these things appeared in their true hideous forms. He felt that he had made himself the companion of vice; but such was his abhorrence of it, that, in his mind, the fear of temptation never once existed. He resolved that though, for the sake of peace, he might share the expences of his shopmates, their profligacy should be their own. But this determination was formed without a knowledge of himself and of the nature of vice. The religion of the youthful mind courts concealment: vice is bold and obtrusive. It is not satisfied with the neglect of religion: it drives it from its presence. William soon found himself subjected to those odious epithets and jeers, which the depraved heart uses, to deface the beauties of religion, and to veil its own crimes. In a workshop, to be an object of dislike, is a painful situation. For the sake of peace, therefore, he found it necessary to taste with his neighbours; and, without apparent dislike, to listen to conversations which his mind abhorred.

The character of a sunday in Halifax, too, he had not anticipated. He had never before associated with men to whom the Lord's day was the season of unrestrained amusement, or, at best, devoted to mere cessation from toil, an occasional attendance upon public worship, and the quiet enjoyments of what are termed the comforts of life. In his father's house it was a sabbath to the Lord; a day in which public instruction was followed up by private improvement; when the domestic circle was entertained, not by a detail of the events of the week, but by a relation of the painful sufferings and triumphant exit of sires, who loved not their lives unto the death; when hearts thus warmed with the holy fire of religion, ascended to the Lord of the sabbath in the melody of praise.

Though William lodged with a sober and decent family; it contained none of these things. As he could not, therefore, enjoy his father's house, he resolved to be alone; and accordingly, upon the Lord's day, he walked out to the valley beyond these heights before us. It is a region which nature has doomed to perpetual sterility. Its continuous accumulations of stony masses defy the labours of man. He seated himself on the shelving projection of a rock, shaded by a stunted hemlock, upon which no hatchet had deigned to descend. Nature, however, had stamped it with decay; and the hoary locks of the moss, in profusion occupied the room of its former verdure. Taking from his pocket the last gift of his father, it opened at a leaf which parental anxiety had doubled down upon these words, "Herein is my Father glorified, that ye bear much fruit, so shall ye be my disciples." William's eye wandered over the scene before him; his mind turned to the place of his labour and its moral waste; and a tear dropped upon the words of inspiration: he resolved that he would never forget his great grandfather's glorious example; and replacing in its proper position the leaf which his father had folded, he arose and returned to Halifax.

Such scenes and reveries are well calculated to cherish religious sentiments and feelings; but, where temptation is incessant, and serious impressions rare; there is against religion an overwhelming odds. The season of the year, congenial to solitary walks and musings, glided past; nature resigned her sway to the fell blasts of the north; and the return of spring found William prepared to listen to the jests of his shopmates, in which meagre attempts at wit were eked out by obscenity or profanation; and upon the Lord's day, equally prepared to enter into the quiet conversations and amusements of his landlord's family.

It must not, however, be supposed that he was addicted to his shopmates' vices. On the contrary, by all who knew him, he was recognised as a pattern of a correct deportment. To be rich, was his ambition: every day, therefore, witnessed a steady renewal of exertion; and evening never found him in the depraving haunts of dissipation. His spare hours were usually spent in the company of a few young men like himself, who, abhorring the gratifications of profligacy, quietly amused themselves with a simple game at cards. These, it is true, had always been the object of his father's marked disapprobation; and, on this account, he at first felt a reluctance to be where they were. But the amusement which the game seemed to afford to his companions, and the apparent absence of every thing criminal, induced him to receive a few lessons; and by the time he had acquired a moderate knowledge of the game, he felt perfectly satisfied that his father's aversion was one of those groundless prejudices, which religious men are apt to entertain with unreasonable obstinacy. Still, he was no gamester. He had no wish to acquire wealth but by honest industry; and his amusements never interfered with his hours of toil. So well was his master satisfied with his principles and conduct, that he made him foreman of the shop; and, in the general management of his business, treated him with a degree of deference, which could not fail to be highly gratifying. Indeed, his assistance in this capacity was very much needed; for his master, beside spending his evenings at the club and other meetings, had begun to manifest a dislike of business and a wandering disposition which carried him every where, but where he ought to have been. William, on the other hand, was anxious, by unremitted attention, to repay the confidence of his master. His interest now lay, not in quarrelling with the grog and conversations of the shop, but in maintaining good humour among workmen upon whom the success of his master's business depended. Among the former, therefore, every thing went merrily on; and the latter showed his satisfaction, first, by introducing William into his domestic circle, and finally, by bestowing upon him the hand of his daughter.

In this town, the daughter of a counsellor and the daughter of a master tradesman, are, in point of education, pretty much upon a level. William's wife, therefore, was a young lady of elegant appearance and showy accomplishments. At the same time, with respect to natural disposition and propriety of conduct, she was a very good young woman; and in these points of view, well qualified to adorn the house of her husband, and make him happy at home. In relation to his prospects in life also, his father in law had just spoken of giving him a share in the business; when, returning one evening from the club a little more flushed than usual, he was attacked by an inflamatory disease, which, in a few days, transferred the whole trade into his son in law's hands. It was an extensive business; and in those days, the profits of every kind of employment in Halifax were great.

Of all these fortunate events William's parents were early apprised. As a proof of his prosperity, he remitted to them a large proportion of his earnings; and at the same time, affectionately advised them to diminish their labours and add to their comforts. In declarations of filial regard, his letters were not wanting: but he spoke not of the flowery amusements of his youth and his great grandfather's ivy.

Mephibosheth Stepsure gent.

LETTER 23

To the Editors of the *Acadian Recorder*,

Gentlemen,

When Censor gave me the fearful heckling which, I dare say, some of your readers have not forgotten, a part of my last sketch was in your possession; and of course, my engagements with you left me no leisure either to feel its pain or to derive from it any improvement. Now, however, I have begun to chew the cud of disappointment and humiliation; and it is, I assure you, a bitter kind of work. When any person issuing from a cottage, has crept in among great folks, and just nestled himself comfortably, it is a mortifying thing to be told that he is no gentleman: Nor does it mend the matter one bit, when he feels a conviction that he has been told the truth. Misfortunes of this kind are a serious sort of theme: they sink deep into the mud of human feeling, and stick fast to boot. I who know from experience, can tell you that they are not to be laughed at.

Who Censor is, it would be of no use to inquire. He has concealed himself so completely, that Mr. Gosling's black wench, old Sippit's Pompey, and all their black cronies, have given up the search in despair. He has none of the *silly vanity* of old Stepsure, who signed every letter with his own hand, and then published it to the world. He is a modest man, without the least pretensions. Instead of telling who he is, he only tells his readers, that he knows every thing and can rectify every kind of disorder: he is a complete preacher and lawyer, knows all the outs and ins of high life and low life, literature and politics, commerce and

246

agriculture; and besides, can lay his hands upon the ladies, and keep the sabbath day too. With so much modesty and all those marvellous qualifications, there can surely be no danger of his landing in the dirt, as my neighbour Saunders predicts. Indeed, if all whom he criticizes, treat him with as much respect as old Mephibosheth, and receive his buffetings with as much meekness, every body will believe him to be a very great man; and when he condescends to *burst from his shell*, he will burst upon the world like one of those deeply opake stars of which he has written so sublimely.

When any of our youngsters get a sound cudgelling at Tipple's, it afterwards affords them a world of comfort to tell every body that they did not get fair play. I, on the other hand, along with a good deal of kicking and cuffing, am forced to confess that Censor has done me ample justice, when he says that my letters *may find a place on the chimney piece of the cottage, but will ever be refused admittance into the drawing room of polite life*: And farther, that *the Muses and the Graces would pronounce their ban upon them; because my fancy in no case transports me to Parnassus, to pluck a single flower which adorns and scents that delightful region.* Now all this is very true. I have been at Mount Tom and over the Cumberland mountain; but it is out of the question for the like of me to think of going to Parnassus. The Muses, I know, have not a good word to say of me; for I never sell my potatoes for flowers: and as for the Graces, I told you long ago that, when my feet first peeped into this vale of kicks and cuffettings, they made a pair of clean heels; and since that time, whenever we meet, they spring over the fence like carriboos. Now they are living with Censor; and teaching him to say *Oh heaven! who the devil*, and other graceful expressions, *which adorn and scent his delightful letters.*

It is no wonder, then, as Censor says, that my letters creep and never soar. Indeed, I have been a creeping kind of a man all the days of my life. Upon a journey, I would never have any chance with the flying on the wings of the wind sort of folk in our town: were it not that they always halt and make a long stay with the sheriff. Still, my lame feet are no reason why I may not both relish and admire the flights of other people; and I must say for Censor, that his soarings are marvellous. I shall give you a sample: "I fancied," says he in his letter to the ladies, "that I was looking at a bright unclouded hemisphere, spangled with stars that shone like living eyes. They were of all colours from the cerulean blue to the deep opake; the last of which shot forth a peculiar vividness of ray that dazzled the beholder. I rubbed my eyes hard still blurred with my late weeping." Here is a multiplicity of conceptions astonishingly sublime; the more astonishing too, as they all occurred to one man just after he had been weeping most piteously. Other puling folks get a cake or a whistle to quiet them: Censor gets a hemisphere spangled with stars, not so luminous as rush lights, nor so dull as dead eyes, but something between the two; which his own eyes, though blurred a good deal with his late weeping, enabled him to see sufficiently well for the purpose of description,—*stars that shone like living eyes*. Some writers, when they get into heroics, vie with the eagle in his flight. Censor is a wiser man: he soars downward, you see, and meets with no broken necks. Some of his stars were blue; and others, coal black, and shone like kettles. It will surprise nobody that they shot forth a peculiar vividness of ray, or that Censor was obliged to rub his eyes hard, after such dazzling sights.

It is not for the like of me, to attempt such terrible soarings with my lame supporters. It is my misfortune to be a plain man; and my mistake, to have told a plain story to plain people in plain terms. Had I been able like Censor to get upon Pegasus, and gallop to the top of Parnassus; our people might have been buried under heaps of blooming perfumes. Then, I who have recorded only the scents of Peter Pumpkin's large castle, and the flowers which our young ladies bought at Mr. Gosling's store, instead of being kicked and cuffed, would be the favourite of every body. Our girls, I am sure, would have been very proud of it. Decked with the flowers and scents of Parnassus, they would be so fine that nobody would know them. Indeed, I question if they would know themselves. But that is nothing: Censor would be my friend; and would assure his readers, that my letters describe the realities of life; and that I myself sustain most admirably the character of a plain country farmer.

But the principal source of my misfortunes I have yet to explain. Censor has told every body that I am so filthy and stink so abominably, that no genteel nose can ever come near me. "Stepsure is constantly wading in a dunghil, bespattered with dirt and all the marks of vulgarity:" and on this account, I and my letters must "ever be refused admittance into the drawing room of polite life." On the other hand, Censor is a cleanly man, as cleanly as soap suds and scrubbing can make him, and whenever he pleases, he can step softly into the drawing room, and *lay his hand upon lovely woman with a lovers softness*. To me all this is exceedingly humiliating; for it is exceedingly true. Last fall, I had a great deal of work about a large pit for catching the drippings of our cattle; and you may depend upon it, there was a good deal of wading. As for my hands, being something of the size and colour of smoked hams, I doubt if their softness would be agreeable to *lovely women;* particularly in that moulting state which Censor has so pathetically deplored. In my letters, too, I did record filthy things about the houses of our town, some on the outside and others within; and you see that Censor, who has lived all his life in a drawing room, has spurned to read them. He only got a hint of their filth by chance; and being very wroth at such doings, he resolved to shave and scrub me himself; or in other words, he undertook to teach me how I must write, if I wish to get among the ladies. Accordingly, he took me grown gentleman as I was; and did give it to me, just as other schoolmasters do; and then he put a book into my hand, and told me to read that. It was a very edifying book; particularly the chapter *Upon the dirt and filth of Mephibosheth Stepsure.* I shall give you a quotation in Censor's own words: "Steppy, my old boy, give heed to what I say; and put an end to this beastliness. There must be no talking to ladies about white stripes upon gable ends: you must speak to them only about violation; as I did in one of my letters: and then they will be able to converse with you, without either lowering their voice, or feeling a flush upon their face." With such uncommon instruction, it was easy for me to see that I was sadly to blame for recording Jack Scorem's misdeeds. I shall tell you how I got into the scrape; and I hope you will prevail upon the ladies to forgive me.

The summer before last, one of Tandem's sons, who is doing business in Halifax, came up to his father's with a number of young ladies upon a party of pleasure. The ladies had never been in the country before: of course, they were wonderfully inquisitive, and wonderfully gratified by young Tandem's information. Now, as soon as they entered our town, they began to see a spout sticking out from one house, and the boards below the windows whitened upon another. This at first passed without observation; but being repeated, it fixed their attention, and produced inquiries which made the young gentleman smile. Female curiosity was now excited; and smiles and silence at last made it intolerable. But happening to stop at Soakem's, which is exactly opposite the end of Jack Scorem's house, the young ladies applied for information to old Stot's son Hodge, who was standing before the door. Now, Hodge, like myself, had neither been at Parnassus, nor drunk the waters of Helicon. He did not, therefore, explain, as Censor would have done, that the vision which flared in beauty's eye, was caused by the

Nocturnal distillations of Jack Scorem,
Who did as all his sires had done before him.

But, I suppose he had conveyed his meaning in terms equally well understood; for the ladies, in their haste to get away, almost overturned Tandem, who was standing in the door. Considering with myself, therefore, that such paintings were peculiar to our town, I put them into the chronicles: but I must have been mistaken; for Censor assures me that we are a very cleanly sort of folks. In future, therefore, unless good and sufficient reason to the contrary appear, I shall let this point sleep; allowing every lady to feast her eye, and ask as many questions as she pleases. Only, I would just hint to you Halifax gentlemen, that, when you happen to get into Tandem's shoes, you had better tell the ladies to ask Censor. He will not bring the blush upon their cheek: He will only talk to them about violation; and then tell them, that these spouts and stripes are the evidence by which he proved, that, in our town, there are neither filthy houses nor filth.

Having never been in any of the fights of our town, Censor's belabouring, you may depend upon it, has made me feel very sore: and were it not for an event which I am now going to tell you; my writing days, I doubt, would be done. My misfortunes have been to me the source of much cogitation. Many an evening I have sitten by our fire side, brooding over calamity, and plotting how it might be avoided in future. Being altogether ignorant of the flowers of Parnassus, I have often asked myself what was to be done; and often and often, I have tried to adorn our people with cauliflowers, the flowers of brimstone, and other kinds of them with which I am acquainted. But it was altogether in vain: nobody would have known them either by the eye or by the odour; for, in our town, we have no leisure to cultivate the first; and as for the last, though Loopy and a number more fidget a good deal, they never use them.

At last, one evening, after suppering my cattle; when I had stretched out my stumps to toast them before the fire, I fell fast asleep from pure vexation; and immediately found myself and all our townsfolk at the foot of a very steep hill with a splendid edifice upon its summit. I at once perceived that it was neither Mount Tom nor the Cumberland mountain: it was a much prettier place. Upon its surface it seemed to contain a specimen of every bloom of creation; or, as Censor would say, flowery beauty feasted the eye, and odoriferous perfume floated in the breeze. When we were admiring the prospect, Jerry Gawpus perceiving a horse at a little distance, remarked that he was still in great want of a beast to supply the grey mare's place. He, therefore, requested Ehud Slush to get upon the back of the horse, and try his paces; as he might perhaps strike a bargain with the owner. Ehud was mounted in a trice: but the creature, instead of trotting along, began to raise himself upon wings, which none of us had before perceived; and his rider, after being raised a few feet from the ground, came pelt off at his tail: and it was well for him; for the animal continued his flight to the summit of the mountain. Ehud's mouth and eyes testified the amount of his terror. He declared that he had not met with the like of it since the bear catched him in the woods.

We had scarcely got over our surprise when Censor approached, with a parcel under his arm, and a large bundle of rods upon his back. *His eyes were still blurred with his late weeping.* Indeed he had rubbed them so hard, that they were as red as collops. Two of his young ladies, Folly and Arrogance, were with him. Whether it be that out of doors the order of the drawing room is inverted, or that Censor's late weeping required a little comfort, I do not know; but sure enough, instead of laying his hand upon the ladies, Folly was clapping him upon the head, which appeared to me to sound very much like one of Jerry Gawpus' empty rum puncheons. When they approached pretty near; Arrogance pointed to our people, and then to the top of the hill. I at first thought that Censor, forgetful of his promise, had been gathering sticks upon unlawful days; and that the young lady was showing him the road to the moon. But coming up to us, he pulled from his burden a good stout hoop pole; and brandishing it furiously, declared that we should drink the Castalian fountain to the mud, cull the flowers of Parnassus, and mount to the very temple of Apollo.

The thought of what was before us, and particularly the water drinking, produced among our people many a rueful countenance. Jack Scorem said, that, had it been grog, he would have swigged at it as long as he pleased: but no son of Adam that ever wore a nose on his face, should force him to drink it. But though Jack on ordinary occasions fights well, he did not know what it is to grapple with the fiend in a nightmare: one hearty stroke upon Jack's gable end, against which Censor showed a particular antipathy, reduced the man of lumber to perfect submission. To the drinking, therefore, we set; and with the persuasion of a good many blows which fell chiefly upon the sheriff's people, we did the business so completely, that not a drop remained. When we were getting up from our knees, old Driddle remarked to Miss Sippit, that it was well with us; we had got one good job over: but as for him, the worst was to come; for he never tasted any thing weaker than grog without being the worse of it.

Censor next ordered us to ascend, and to be sure to pull plenty of flowers no matter what they were: flowers, he said, were the thing: and burdocks were just as good as roses. Under his controul, accordingly, we began the mounting: but in a short time he became so engrossed with the flowers, that he forgot all about us; and then every one did as he pleased. Mrs. Grumble ordered Job to sit down with her beside a thriving patch of gall; and the rest of the old people turned down to look after the potatoes and pumpkins which grew at the bottom of the hill. Jack Scorem observing some trees at a distance, resolved to have a look at them; and Ehud in the expectation of foxes agreed to accompany him. On looking round to see what the rest of the sheriff's people were doing, I perceived them; running as fast as their feet could carry them they had kept pretty near the level ground, and unexpectedly fell in with a large plantation of cabbage. In short, none arrived at the summit of the mountain but Saunders, Miss Sippit, and myself. As we approached the temple, Apollo proceeded from the portal; and Saunders, who always kept a little before us, arriving first; he was immediately questioned what brought him there. My neighbour replied that it might well be asked, what brought him to such a heathenish high place: he was no idolater he would tell him. It was not to give his countenance to pagan abominations, that he was catched neglecting his farm and crawling over rocks and among weeds and bushes, which, for ought he could see, were of no use either to man or beast: that he had come to take care of that decent man Mephibosheth Stepsure; and he would like to see who would meddle with him. I could easily perceive that Apollo was more amused than offended by Saunders' reply. The God next questioned Miss Sippit, who told him that she had been ordered to pull flowers; but for her part, she had seen none half so pretty as those which Mr. Gawpus had just brought from Halifax: She had thought, however, of making a morning call upon his young ladies the muses; and she hoped they were at home. By a little catechising, during which Saunders was of great use, it turned out that she was the daughter of Sippit of our town, who had neglected his farm, and drowned himself in debt; and now, with a large stock of extravagance and poverty, show and starvation, is carrying on the trade of a gentleman. Apollo, therefore, directed my neighbour to duck her in a large vat of buttermilk, which stood before the temple; and then to fasten a spinning wheel upon her shoulder, and turn her down the hill. When Saunders was dismissing the young lady, he told her that now, when she had got a rock, she had better make a morning call upon his wife, and get a wee pickle tow; and then she might try the spinning o't. Thus adorned and scented, Miss Sippit began to journey homeward from that delightful region. When Apollo turned to me and asked my business there, I really did not know what to answer him: but seeing Censor approach, I begged the God to put the question to him.

Censor, on his arrival, did not need to tell us that he had not been idle. If his collection of flowers was not very valuable, their amount was abundant. After getting partly up the hill, he found that he could neither carry his blooming sweets conveniently, nor preserve them from fading: but looking accidentally behind him, he perceived at the spring a large washing tub, in which I suppose, the muses had been scouring blankets. He, therefore, ran down to it, and as the water had not collected sufficiently, a quantity of soft, summer cow dung, did very well for a substitute. Into this he stuck the stalks of his flowers: And I do declare to you, that the cow dung and the flowers together, reminded me of the blooming beauty with which our people would have shone; had I only been able to load them with the productions *"which adorn and scent that beautiful region."*

It was not necessary for the God to ask any questions. Censor remarking, that the precious contents of the tub must be handled with care, took it cautiously from his head; and then assured Apollo, that the whole merit of driving old Stepsure up the hill, belonged to himself. He said, that without the least fiction or poetic fancy about me, I had attempted to write; and strange to tell, I had chosen a subject which, above all others, requires the lofty soarings of Pegasus and the muses. I had shown that idleness is the parent of folly, filth, and wretchedness: And how had I done it? Instead of writing sublimely about folly and filth, as any ordinary farmer would have done, wherever I found dirt, I had called it plain dirt. A writer of sense, he remarked, who wished filth out of the country, instead of telling any body to take it away, would have thrown a veil over it; or put it into his pocket, and said nothing about it. In short that he had put his ban upon the chronicles; and that all the lovely women upon whom he laid his hand, would banish them from the drawing room of polite life: And then of what use would they be? He then told Apollo, that having cursed the letters of old Stepsure, he had executed a sublime conception, which could never have occurred to any body but himself. He had translated them into both prose and verse; and even the God himself, when he heard them read, would be astonished how so many sublimities and words of mellifluous sound had contrived to creep into one man's head. Both the Muses and the Graces he was sure, would be perfectly enraptured. If he might be allowed to decide upon the merit upon his own works, he would content himself with saying, that his description of the female part of parson Drone's congregation, had never been equalled by any author before him. "There," said he exultingly: "ranged before you, is an amphitheatre of beauties, *from the girl just bursting the shell* to the demure dame of wary experience." But, added he, you shall judge for yourself; and without more ado, he took from his parcel two very beautiful volumes, neatly written upon fine gilt paper; remarking, that, as he knew the taste of the God, he would begin with the poem. It had cost him he said a world of thinking what it should be called. He had thought of the *Mephiboshethiad* and also of the *Stepsuriad;* but he had at last thought to entitle it the *Mephibosheth—Stepsure's—Towniad*; and he was sure that neither Homer nor Milton could have contrived such a name. With these remarks, and clearing his pipe, of what did not belong to the subject, he thus began:

The enterprising Solomon I sing,
Who soared aloft upon a Gosling's wing:
And, also, mighty Jack with legs so limber,
Who Scored the lofty pine and made it timber:
Steer and his servant Peter a droving pair,
Old Mrs. Grumble and Jerry Gawpus' mare,
The patient Job, and the melodious Driddle,
Who swelled himself with tea, and could not fiddle:
The mighty Puff and Gypsum's nose sublime,
Worthy of fame, I'll celebrate in rhyme.
With melodies of song like any thrush,
I'll tune the pipes of fame for Ehud Slush.
I'll sing the praise of Sippit's lovely daughter,
Fanny, and Di' who every day grew fatter.
These in a lofty, tuneful strain I'll sing,
And Stepsure too who danced the Highland Fling.
Big as a pumpkin I'll swell every note;
Till ladies' hearts grow soft like squashes in a pot.
　　But what? my muse, shall I sing Loopy's dog?
Job's wasps and trap or Mrs. Whinge's frog?
Or Mrs. Drab? or Scorem's painted gable?
Or windy Hodge who overturned the table?
Such filthy melodies sing shall I never,
I'd sooner eat a pound of bullock's liver.
　　God of the silver bow assist my theme:
And then like Meph I'll ne'er be put to shame.
Tuneful Apollo, sweetest of the Gods,
With all thy flowery sweets deck Stepsure's clods:
And you, ye Muses nine of tuneful skill, ⎫
Let freshets flow in Heliconian rill: ⎬
Old Boshy's grist has come to Clio's mill: ⎭
And thou, most stately, sleek, and nimble steed,
Almost as good as our Canadian breed,
Aid me to soar aloft great Peg——

When Censor began to invoke Pegasus, I observed the
stately steed pricking up his ears: and just when the lofty

poet was pronouncing his name, great Peg, who happened to be standing behind him, applied the sole of his foot to Censor's nether works; and with good effect too, I assure you; for the poet boomed into the *bright unclouded hemisphere*, and was soon out of sight:

> No soaring flight did ever match it:
> He cut and cleaved the skies, like Scorem's hatchet.

Censor in soaring aloft, had no leisure to take his sublimities with him. I therefore picked them out of the cow dung into which they had fallen; and as Apollo could have no use for them, I put them into my pocket. "Censor," said the God, "is one of those creatures who become giants in criticism, before they have well crept into the petticoats of learning: whose arrogant pretensions are equalled only by their folly. The fellow even lacks brains to preserve consistency: he tells you in the same breath, that he is ignorant of Longinus and a judge of literature. He is one of your dealers in fine words, who conceal their want of sense under a garbage of fustian which they call the flowers of Parnassus, and with which they deck ladies and dung heaps with equal profusion. *Stars like living eyes, girls just bursting from the shell*: such are their flowers. The animal is now among flowers that better become him."

What Apollo meant by his last expression, I could not understand; nor did he give me time to inquire; for turning to Saunders, he asked him what he would have from Parnassus. My neighbour replied that he had seen nothing, either on his way up, or about the temple, of which he had any notion. He had no skill of flowers; he was no worshipper of Baal himself; and he was determined that no heathenish abomination should enter the door of his house. But he would be obliged to Apollo, and pay him beside; if he would allow him to carry away a huge pile of Peg's indigestibles, which he had seen at the foot of the mountain. The God with a smile nodded assent, and then asked me what I wished to receive. I told him I was a plain old man, already in the possession of every thing comfortable; and that my only wish was, that I might get safely home. Apollo then crowned me with laurel; and Saunders and I jogged very comfortable down the hill.

On arriving at the level ground, my neighbour proposed to take a look at his bargain. When we approached it, we found Censor peeping out of its top, weeping most piteously as he did at the play, and earnestly beseeching us to help him out of his scrapes. To his eager entreaties Saunders replied, that he would tell him another tale: that he had bought the whole from Apollo; and that neither he nor any other maggot great or small, should leave it till it left it in his carts. He added however that being in no hurry, he would sit down beside him and give him a little comfort, to keep up his spirits till the teams came. With this resolution I was very well pleased; for I felt an anxiety to have a peep at the translations in prose and verse. Accordingly, I seated myself; and learned a great deal, of which I may tell you hereafter. What happened between Censor and Saunders, I do not know. I only heard my neighbour telling him, that he would keep him where he had lighted from his soarings, till bitter repentance taught him what it was to meddle with that decent man, Mephibosheth Stepsure. Saunders, then, took a hearty parting laugh; upon which I awoke; and sure enough it was Saunders, enjoying the figure which I had cut when he entered the house. On putting up my hand to feel for my laurels, I found that my old woman, perceiving that my head, as she thought, was not very busy, had hung upon it a quantity of worsted which she was winding into balls.

From what I saw and heard upon the summit of Parnassus, I am inclined to think, that, as great Peg, is *almost as good as our Canadian breed;* so Apollo may perhaps be a critic nearly as skilful as Censor. On this account, though I have serious convictions and qualms on the score of unworthiness, I still subscribe myself.

Mephibosheth Stepsure gent.

LETTER 24

To the Editors of the *Acadian Recorder*,

Gentlemen,

Your readers will recollect that William had succeeded to his father in law's business. As it was an extensive and lucrative trade, it afforded him a cheering prospect of the object of his ambition. But the goods of life unalloyed with its ills, are the allotment of few. A view of the state of his old master's affairs was attended with the mortifying discovery, that a settlement with his creditors would leave nothing behind. For this, however, he did not, upon reflexion, find it difficult to account. His father in law's family, though, perhaps, not more extravagant than others in the same station, lived in such a stile as the profits of the business seemed to authorise. In the mean time, it was conducted in a manner, not the best calculated to secure its gains. His father in law, by attendance upon the club and other occasional meetings, had contracted a reluctance to business, which both concealed from him the real state of his affairs, and multiplied his losses. Instead of making up accounts and looking after his debtors, his mind rested upon the extent of his trade and its ostensible profits; and a final settlement showed, that, where punctuality in business is wanting, the profits cannot be secured. William, also, recollected that his old master, after spending the evening abroad, would frequently, without any apparent cause, be very much out of humour. For this he could now account, by finding among his papers a note from one of his associates, requesting the payment of thirty pounds,

261

which, the evening before, he had won from him at the club.

Still, with this disappointment, he had attained a situation in itself desireable. Of the business and its profits he could not complain; and the diminution of either he had no cause to fear. His sober habits and persevering industry had marked him out as a rising young man; and where a community repose confidence, they give credit and business.

With the state of his domestic affairs, too, he had every reason to be pleased. His wife, who was really an agreeable young woman, exerted herself to show, that, with elegant accomplishments, she possessed qualifications, more closely connected with the prosperity and comfort of her husband's house. Formerly, by her engaging manners she had gained his heart: by sustaining the character of a good wife, she now hoped to retain her conquest. In her person and house, therefore, she was all that a reasonable husband could desire: And it must be admitted, that few young people have enjoyed a brighter prospect of permanent domestic happiness.

With all these means of comfort, however, it would occasionally occur to William, that his domestic economy did not altogether accord with the pattern exemplified in the habitation of the just. In his serious moments, he felt that his happiness did not identify itself with the sanctified enjoyments of his sires. In his father's house, the morn and even were met with the songs of zion. At those times, the voice of the oracles of God was heard; and the artless effusions of the humble heart, reposing with confidence in the bosom of mercy, ascended with acceptance before the majesty on high. It was the habitation of God; and whether gladness or sorrow intervened, the peace which passeth all understanding, was the portion of its inmates. Happy, the family who are in such a case! William knew it; and, respecting his own duty and happiness as the master of a family, the example of his parents flashed conviction to his mind: but various circumstances prevented him from treading in the footsteps of his fathers. Influenced by a feeling of incapacity, the youthful mind shrinks from the direction of social devotions. It meets not the sneer of the thoughtless with the stern front of resolution. Shame shrinks from reproach. William's house, therefore, contained none of those benedictions on the bounties of God, in which he had united in the days of his youth: the morning and evening found in it no altar for domestic sacrifice. Still, his mind was by no means without the perception and feeling of moral obligation: he really felt an inclination to the path of his fathers. But the dread of reproach and ridicule was the stronger principle; and his fruits of righteousness were blighted in the bud.

It must not, however, be supposed that he was prepared to relinquish religion. A child trained up in the way that he should go, does not so easily part with the impressions of his youth. For the neglect of duty, William's mind reproached him severely. Now, a mind in this state, though averse from the duties of religion, may be very eager for its peace. Accordingly, William's turned from its painful sensations to its religious perceptions and feelings; and, making these the standard of worth, he acquired a persuasion of the goodness of his heart, which, in the mean time, restored his tranquillity. Indeed, he was what is usually termed a good hearted young man. At an act of dishonesty or meanness he would have spurned: no parents could boast of a more affectionate son; and in every case where his sympathy was invoked, the imploring suppliant met the hand of relief. It is due to him to state, that a feeling of his devotional defects excited the operation of his social principles; and if the deity had conceded to man the selection of his duties, or if attention to men could compensate for the neglect of God, his religious character would have been completely established. In mentioning the neglect of God, I do not mean to insinuate that William was noted for irreligion. On the contrary, the Lord's day found him, a regular attendant upon public worship; and the last gift of his father was preserved with a degree of care, which, though perhaps not an exact proof of its use, was a sure indication of the respect with which he preserved it. With any thing which he possessed, he would have parted rather than with his bible.

Thus, with the name of a very good young man, and in possession of a lucrative trade and domestic comfort, William entered upon public life. All this prosperity, however, was connected with a circumstance, which, though generally overlooked, has a powerful influence upon an emigrant's subsequent habits. The person who forms connexions abroad, weakens those bonds which attach him to the land of his fathers: and, in proportion to the intimacy of his new relations, there is a diminution of longing for home. William's wife was in Halifax, and his heart was there. On this account, the flowers of his youth were not now considered with equal regard; and even the green mantle of his father's habitation, though remembered with reverence, was not so closely linked with the desire and hope of revisiting it. Marriage originates in a wish for immediate happiness. In this state, therefore, the mind is not satisfied with the prospect of enjoyment in a land afar off. It has laid the foundation of its hopes; and the materials by which the structure may be reared, have no relation to remote time or place: they are collected around.

But if William had resigned his ideal happiness, he found himself amply compensated by immediate enjoyment. His growing reputation and prospects had secured to him an extensive acquaintance; and the domestic happiness of the young couple was enhanced by the additional pleasure of numerous visits and invitations.

Besides, as William and his wife possessed that frank disposition of youth, which, in receiving happiness, delights to communicate in return; they were at all times ready to display and share their domestic comforts; so that, between visitings abroad and parties at home, the time passed very pleasantly away.

But this kind of life, though agreeable and apparently harmless, produced an effect for which neither of the young people was well able to account. Formerly, their mutual happiness had flowed from themselves; but now, upon an evening when they chanced to have neither invitation nor visitors, they began to feel the time move very heavily along. They had inadvertantly rendered their neighbours essential to their happiness at home. On such occasions, therefore, to relieve their minds from domestic dulness, they would pop in upon an intimate acquaintance, and beguile the time with a simple game at cards. Neither of the young people, however, possessed a gambling disposition; for the stake never exceeded a triffle, in order to keep up the interest of the game.

In the mean time, William's attention to business secured to him general approbation; so that wealth began to flow in upon him, and with it that influence to which wealth, combined with good conduct, is justly entitled. The consequence which he had acquired in the community, exemplified itself in a variety of ways, particularly gratifying in the early stages of life. In cases of arbitration he was frequently employed, and, as a respectable inhabitant of the town, elected a member of several societies. William, on the other hand, was eager to show that all this respect was not undeserved. Every thing intrusted to him, was faithfully executed; and on this account, between arbitrations, meetings of committees, and other kinds of public business, much time and labour were abstracted from the management of his own affairs. Besides, in town, avocations of this nature are usually reserved for the evening; and no place of meeting is so convenient as a tavern. Absence from his family to a late hour, therefore, was frequently unavoidable. But this was now of less consequence than it had formerly been. Both William and his wife had discovered that they could be happy apart; and as wealth supplied the means of enjoyment to each, neither of them felt disposed to quarrel with the others arrangements. With respect to William it may be also remarked, that his frequent attendance upon meetings at the tavern produced a habit of visiting it occasionally, merely for the purpose of ascertaining what was going on. This at last introduced him to the club, where he would, of course, conduct himself pretty much like the rest of its members. I only know, that his return home did not always contribute to the peace of his family. Of his gains at the club, he would sometimes boast: his losses he never recounted.

Perhaps, at no previous period had William possessed such an accumulation of pleasures. His business was excellent, and his family enjoyed the comforts of affluence. He knew himself to be a man of character and influence; and when his mind occasionally turned to the guides of his youth; it was with this pleasing reflexion, that his filial regard had supplied them with the means of comfort. He was, also, abundantly gratified by his evening amusements, public dinners, occasional trips to the country with a few agreeable companions, and by all the other means which husbands in Halifax employ to separate their happiness and home.

Of William's religious improvement little can be said. A mind engrossed by worldly business and pleasure, can spare no time for those serious communings with God and itself, which a religious life needs. It has no inclination: And when a thought of religion does force its way into the conscience, the mind hastes to bury in forgetfulness the work of God. As yet, though William had not made his own house, a habitation for the God of his fathers; he had shown himself not willing to be without a place in his temple. Upon the public ordinances of the Church, the Lord's day had always found him a regular attendant. Now, however, the multiplicity of his avocations began to deprive his own business of a part of that attention without which it could not be retained. It, therefore, became requisite occasionally to employ the sabbath in bringing up his books, and reviewing the general state of his affairs; and, as he felt this to be a disagreeable and fatiguing task, it was usually succeeded by some cheering recreation. Such a departure from his former course was not, indeed, without serious compunctions. To practise wrong without remorse, belongs only to him who has never known right. William felt himself the abhorrence of his father; nor was his mind perfectly quieted till it acquired an assurance, that the even tenor of the life of his parent rendered him ill qualified to trace the line of distinction between irreligion and works of necessity. Various considerations, also, occurring to his mind, induced a persuasion, that, in his character, the want of religion was no distinguishing trait. Of reverence for what is holy, he was by no means devoid; for, in the course of conversation, he rarely used the sacred name or, indeed, any kind of profanity, without a feeling of self-reproach. He was sure, also, that no person could charge him with the want of benevolence: he was a dutiful son and an indulgent husband; and, in all cases of distress, his heart and hand were forward to relieve. In short, he felt himself, a good hearted man; and under all his deviations from religious practice, this consideration tranquillized his mind.

A minute detail of succeeding events it is not necessary to state. In the preceding course of life he persevered till it began to be remarked, that he was assuming a bloated and slovenly appearance. Among men of business it has been generally found, I believe, that he who dwindles into a sloven, has become something worse. With respect to

William the fact is, that, through growing inattention to his business, it had fallen into the hands of several young men who had begun trade for themselves, and, according to his early example, were making every exertion to get forward in the world. Now, where a life of dissipation meets a declining trade, it is like a stumbling block in the path of the feeble. Dissipation which blasts prospects, bereaves the mind of its fortitude. It cannot grapple with reverses· it shrinks from the task: it will rather assist misfortune to add to the accumulation of misery. William, instead of retracing his steps, resorted to the easier expedient of depositing his griefs in the lap of pleasure. To this resource, indeed, he was partly impelled by domestic calamity, which, not having foreseen, he had used no means to avert. The existing harmony of William and his wife was not now the fruit of reciprocal affection. It flowed from the gratifications which the gains of business enabled them both to enjoy. A decrease of trade, therefore, bringing along with it a diminution of comforts, terminated in dissatisfaction, mutual reproaches, and misery. A family whose want is the offspring of dissipation, is a house swept and garnished, prepared to be the haunt of every foul fiend. From domestic wretchedness, William sought relief in his pleasures abroad.

The person who relinquishes a due regard for himself, sets the community an example which is quickly followed. William's altered appearance was met by the failure of that respect with which he had been formerly treated. Indeed, by his acquaintances, though many of them were but a few paces behind him in his course, he was rather shunned than courted; and if, in their presence, his voice was at any time raised, he was treated as a person who might be allowed to speak without being heard. But a degraded mind is not always a mind prepared to meet disrespect with submission. Its own humiliating reflexions may be combined with a jealous feeling, which no common courtesy is able to soothe. It was natural for William, therefore, to seek companions who would treat him with greater deference; and ultimately, his principal haunts were a few houses in our lower street, where profligacy in its hideous forms of debasement, plentifully supplied the materials of destruction. He was now a lost man; and as he had forfeited all claim to consideration and forbearance, his few remaining articles, and among the rest the last gift of his father still as good as new, were seized and sold for his creditors' benefit. At parting with this memorial of former times, William felt a complication of fearful pangs: but a consciousness of what he had become, and a feeling of shame, prevented him from soliciting a favour which had the bible for its object.

Of William's family the state may be easily conceived. The parent who finds home the only place where there is no enjoyment, must not expect that his family will be contented with the misery from which he has fled. They too have a wish to be happy; and having no check upon the inexperience of youth, they usually seek it in the path of degradation. With respect to his parents it may be remarked, that, as long as he enjoyed prosperity, no son could outdo him in dutiful kindness. But the same infatuation which steeled his heart against domestic wretchedness, produced a total neglect of the guides of his youth. Their resources in his bounty were gradually impaired; and for a number of years, he had ceased to ask for their welfare. When an accidental recollection of them excited in his mind a pang of bitterness, he derived relief from the consoling thought, that two old people could need but little. At last, the poverty and disease of a life of dissipation, introduced him into that great receptacle of vice and misery, which you lately passed.

My own reiterated attempts to reclaim him, I have not mentioned. They were altogether unavailing. William had wandered from the way of understanding, and would not forsake the congregation of the wicked. Yet he was not always without a tormenting monitor within. The human mind, even in its most depraved state, has occasional recollections which convert the sweets of profligacy into the bitterness of death. It was William's allotment to suffer severely, as well as to enjoy. It was not unknown to him, that, when he left the habitation of his fathers, he had forsaken his God. He knew that to his vices he had sacrificed the feelings of the son, the husband, and the father; and he shared the miseries entailed by his crimes. By the loss of character and respect, his pride was wounded; and when he ventured to look beyond the last scene of his earthly debasement, a certain fearful looking for of judgment bereaved his mind of its peace. But there ensued no fleeing from the snares of death. The witching smile of pleasure had beguiled him from the paths of virtue; and her overpowering entanglements prevented his return. Where he found his misery, he sought his consolation; and when vice with her soothings tranquillised his mind; because he wished ill to none, he cherished a persuasion that he was a good hearted man.

When I overtook you upon the road, I had just been to visit him in the place of his sojourning. It was a scene of impressive instruction. He was not the William whom I had once seen, blooming in youth and animated by the inspiration of blooming prospects. He was the humiliating picture of the last stage of an ill spent life. The exhaustions of dissipation and disease had bereft him of the comliness of man, and degradation hovered around him. Though he was evidently at the very threshhold of the house appointed for all living, he was eagerly looking back with the lingerings of hope. "I certainly do feel better;" said he: "In a few days, I shall be able to stir about: And then—" Here his glazed eye turned upon the objects around, as if a proud feeling of degradation would have added, "I shall not be here." But escaping from recollections so painful, he requested me to read to him the following letter from his father, which he had just received.

My Son,

It is now a very long time since glad news from a far country have been heard in the house of your parents. Year after year we have longed, and looked, and waited in vain. We have not heard from our son: we have only learned that hope deferred maketh the soul sick. We have known the love of our son in the day of his prosperity; and we will not believe that the abundance of wealth could make him forget and forsake his parents, when age and infirmity have bowed them to the dust. Our hearts tell us that the arrows of the Almighty have wounded our child; and we mourn over sorrows which his love has concealed. My son, to hide your affliction from us, was not well nor wisely done: you could not hide us from anxiety and fear. Adversity in a strange land, needs friends to bemoan; and none can sympathize like parents. Our only hope is, that the visitations of the Lord have found you in the footsteps of your fathers. It is the good old path, where the God who afflicts, does not crush under his feet the prisoners of the earth. Blessed is he who receives the chastenings of the Lord. He doth not afflict willingly: though he cause grief, he will have compassion, according to the multitude of his mercies. My son, put it in our power to tell the God of our fathers about the afflictions of our child. Unasked, you have many a time relieved our necessities. Hear now a father's petition: relieve our minds from anxiety and fear. We can bear infirmities; we can bear want: but we cannot bear uncertainty whether our child continues in the path where it is good to hope and quietly wait for the salvation of God.

It grieves me, William, to add to your affliction by sorrowful tidings; but I dare not conceal them. They are the voice of God to our family; and my son must hear. The

Lord is feeding your parents with the bread and the water of affliction: yet they are a father's food, and we must not complain. The course of nature has brought upon us many infirmities, and our feeble steps are supported by no son: the earthly staff of our comfort is far away. Blessed be he who has said, I will not fail thee nor forsake thee: Even to old age I am he: I have made and I will bear: And blessed be the name of the Lord, who has enabled us to repose with confidence in his faithful promise. When I had strength, it was spent upon industrous labour; and the blessing of the Lord turned it into food and raiment. My strength is gone; but my hope is not perished from the Lord. Our son was once a bountiful provider of comforts: we leaned upon him, and looked for no want till we should be gathered to our fathers. The Lord has corrected us, he has broken our reed, and brought us into darkness. Yet he has said, I will make darkness light before them. He feeds the ravens: there can be no want to them that fear him.

Our little habitation, William, as well as your parents, is sadly changed. Still, our hearts cling to it: it is the only house that can give us the fond recollections of our son. It is the house of your great grandfather's fellowship with God. In the day of affliction, may my son be his follower in faith and patience! If his spirit do not rest upon our family, we shall soon have nothing which belonged to him on earth. As long as the prosperity of our son enabled him to increase the comfort of his parents, to preserve the house of our fathers and our son's flowers, was our earliest care. It was then the delight of your mother, to sit at our door in the evening, and to talk of our worthy ancestors and of the love of our son. But when old age and poverty meet, it is not in a comfortable habitation: it is not among flowers. Decay will soon make the house of our fathers as though it had not been. Nettles grow rank where our son cheered the heart of his parents by his evening amusements. There remains neither flower nor herb, but the slip of wormwood which our son planted on the day of his departure. Bitter herbs need little cultivation: it has spread every where around the habitation of our fathers.

In the days of your youth, William, the green covering of our house afforded to your mother and me, many a pleasing thought. We had planted no ivy: but we had planted you in the house of the Lord; and we hoped, that, when our son laid us in the grave, we should have one to flourish in the courts of our God. Now, the visitations of the Almighty are heavy upon us. The fire of heaven has fallen upon your great grandfather's last memorial; and in his house there is no son. We think of the sapless twigs and brown leaves of the ivy; and our hearts yearn for the soul of our son. The same stroke of heaven has closed the eyes of your worthy mother in perpetual darkness. During the day, she sits at the door, longing and listening for William who was the light of her eyes; and at even, when I lead her into the house, she says, I heard the footsteps of many; but none were the steps of my son.

My son, I tell you not these things to grieve you, but to show what a blessed portion religion is. Your mother and I are sorely tossed by the waves and billows of the Lord; but we have an anchor of hope. We learned early to know his name; and we are sure that he will never forsake us. His word tells us that he is a hiding place from the storm and a covert from the tempest; and we believe his word; for, in the multitude of thoughts within us, we feel the consolations of God: he is the shadow of a great rock in a weary land. We have arrived at old age, and we find its strength to be labour and sorrow. But we shall soon be, where the weary are at rest. We know that our redeemer liveth. Weeping may endure for a night: joy cometh in the morning. Oh that my son may meet us where the Lamb who is in the midst of the throne, wipes away tears forever: And now, William, I commend you to God and to the word of his grace. *Read your bible; obey its voice; and at the great day of account, take care*—Here, William interrupted the reading by a piercing cry. A convulsive shudder ensued. With a feeble accent he exclaimed, *My father, my bible, my Sav*—: but words failed him; and a sob transferred him into the world of spirits.

Mephibosheth Stepsure gent.

LETTER 25

To the Editors of the *Acadian Recorder*,

Gentlemen,

YOUR readers, I dare say, have not yet forgotten the great Censor's flight from Parnassus; nor how he soared feet foremost, into Peg's huge accumulation of odoriferous sweets. What became of him afterward, I may by and by tell you: it is a tale *big with fate*, and calculated to create a deep interest in all who hear it. In the mean time, I would just say to your correspondent of last week, that dating his communication from Pictou, and ascribing to me the notices contained in the Free Press, are a sort of bait which even gulls can detect. Mr. Ward, I believe, has already traced them to their source; which renders it the less necessary for me to add that my writings never extended a line beyond my letters in the Recorder. This point, therefore, I shall leave for the present; and advert to another in which your correspondent feels a deeper interest.

He is very angry, I perceive, that Censor has not been honoured with more abundant honours in the chronicles of our town; and really, I confess that I have been sadly to blame. It is true, I did praise him to the clouds; and as he delighted in perfumes, I praised him neck deep into a pile of them, which for size and scent did honour to great Peg's appetite for nectar and ambrosia. But here I left him; which I ought not to have done. I do declare to you, however, that this did not proceed from any petty jealousy upon the score of authorship; for, though I am but a plain

275

farmer, I can with half an eye discover in his works enough to convince me, that my letters will never be named on the same day with the productions of his astonishing mind. Indeed, he was a most wonderful man; and as all your readers know most marvellously gifted. Homer and Milton were of some note in their day: but neither of them could claim such powers of description as Censor; for they were never kicked from the summit of Parnassus; and so far from exploring the profundity of Pegasean sweets, I question if they even knew that great Peg was a contributor to the perfumes "which scent and adorn that delightful region."

But the fame of Censor, I assure you, does not originate in this airy flight. His translations of Stepsure's Letters have emblazoned his name; and reared for him a monument, more hard and durable than any pot metal that ever was cast. I who have dipped into both, declare to your readers, that such profundities and marvellous exhibitions of head work in the composing way, were never before presented to a wondering world. They interest every feeling of the human heart, and affect every muscle of the human frame.—When you peruse his terrific description of the battle with the pigs, it will make your hair stand on end. His piteous description, too, of the disasters which occurred at Miss Sippit's frolic, is enough to melt the very heart of a milstone. It grieves me to think that I am so ill qualified to describe the transactions, as the works of Censor ought to be described. He who is the bosom companion of those lovely women, the Muses and the Graces; and withal such a favourite of great Peg, that his prayers are uttered and answered in the same breath, in order to be seen as he really is, must be seen in his works. Our worthy old parson, to whom I had repeated a few gleanings from Censor, has pronounced him to be by far the most accomplished writer of the kind that has yet appeared. What Mr. Drone means, your readers will best understand from his own language:—"The bumbast and doggrel," says the old gentleman, "in both which Censor possesses superlative excellence, are connected with the sublime and beautiful, exactly in the same manner as the scents of Pegasus are, with the sweets of Parnassus. A sublime writer culls the productions of the mountain with fastidious care; and ascends to the temple of Apollo, with an offering worthy of the god: but writers like Censor have more capacious views; they bring to Apollo cow dung and burdocks by the tubful; and then, leaving the god and his temple to the like of Homer and Milton, they soar into Saunders' bargain."

Perhaps, some of your readers may not believe that Censor merits all the praise which our clergyman has given him. I shall, therefore, introduce them to the works of that great author, and let them judge for themselves. The chronicles of our town, as you may recollect, contained a simple account of the Battle of Scorem's corner. Mark how the lofty poet has immortalized the heroic darings of that eventful day:

> The hero great with petticoat adorned,
> To meet with less than pigs most proudly scorned;
> His sword he brandished, and the hogs gave way;
> And Shootem won the honours of the day.
> Their squeeling, grunting, snorting, as they ran,
> All proved that Hecky was a manful man.
> Had they but waited till their blood was shed,
> The mighty host had lain in heaps stone dead.

In these verses every body must perceive an astonishing degree of grandeur, which admirably befits the dignity of the subject. It was, indeed, a most terrible engagement; but the powers and pen of the poet have done it ample justice. It was the lot of the brave Captain Shootem to be exposed to such fearful perils, as no hero before him had ever experienced; and it has been his felicity, to be sung by a minstrel of unrivalled excellence: and strange to tell, by one of such marvellous modesty, that he only professes to know every thing and to do every thing better than his neighbours. You have his own word for it, that he is "a complete preacher and lawyer; knows all the outs and inns of high life and low life, literature and politics, commerce and agriculture; and besides, can lay his hand upon the ladies, and keep the sabbath day too." Without the least departure from such claims, I may also add, that as, far as his feet descended into the bowels of Mount Peg, so far in scents and sweets he has excelled every poet who has piped the praises of the ladies or sung of swine. The battle of the pigs, which is now before your readers exhibits brilliant bursts of genius. But of all the efforts of Censor's surprising mind, his description of the female congregation to which our old parson delivered his discourse upon economy, both for vastness of conception and splendour of diction, is the most complete. It has left nothing for human imagination to add, or for human heart to desire: it is beyond all praise. In extolling it to Apollo, as you recollect he did, he displayed a profundity of judgment and a Pegasean peculiarity of taste, worthy of a poet who could soar from the clouds, and embosom himself in the most affecting productions, not of your common kind of cattle, but of

Great Peg, that stately, sleek and nimble steed,
Almost as good as our Canadian breed.

I shall give it to your readers in both prose and verse; telling them at the same time, that if they can peruse it without emotion, their case is as hopeless as old Trot's, who always falls asleep when our parson preaches against idleness. It is only necessary for me farther to premise, that his prose translation, except the exordium and the substitution of the word *parson* for *play*, has been inserted in his delightful letter to the ladies, which every body has read and admired.

"Daughters of Apollo and lovely Graces, Censor permits you, along with his own muse, to describe an assemblage of female beauty from the girl just bursting the shell to the demure dame of wary experience."

"The house was uncommonly crowded; and as I arrived rather late, I had to content myself with a seat rather unfavourable. As the parson proceeded, my feeling became quite responsive to the powerful emotions he meant to excite; and such was the effect produced, that my eyes gushed; and with much difficulty, I could restrain myself from sobbing aloud. I set about to conquer this tearful mood; and after wiping my face and burnishing it with a little self assurance, I arose, wheeled round, and looked full upon the ladies. And surely, fairer or lovelier specimens of divine workmanship were never presented to the admiring eye. I was absolutely thrown into a kind of stupefaction, and my judgment reeled amid the bewilderment of my thoughts. There arranged before you is an amphitheatre of beauties, *from the girl just bursting the shell to the demure dame of wary experience.* I next fancied that I was looking on a bright unclouded hemisphere, spangled with stars *that shone like living eyes,* and shed a bland and fascinating influence. They were of all colours from the cerulean blue to the deep opake; the last of which shot forth a peculiar vividness of ray which dazzled the beholder. I rubbed my eyes hard, still blurred after my late weeping."

"Ye Muses nine and Graces three, you I have deigned to call;
And eke the muse of Censor, far greater than you all.
With scents and sweets in tubfuls, inspire and jog me on;
While I describe the female flock of worthy parson Drone:

Both girlies peeping from their shells, as snug as any
    snails:
And feather'd dames with fattened rumps, and long
    and bushy tails.
    Like herring packed the ladies were; I found myself
        too late:
But kicking old Trot on the shins, at last I got a seat.
As parson Drone proceeded on, my sympathy arose:
From my two eyes two freshets flowed, and I
    blubber'd at the nose.
That I sobb'd aloud or bellow'd out, you'd nat'rally
    conclude:
But most manfully I combatted and quell'd this tearful
    mood.
I rubb'd my eyes, and wip'd my nose, and let the
    weeping pass:
And I star'd upon the ladies with my usual face of
    brass.
Oh me! such fair and lovely sights I ne'er beheld
    before:
How I began to gape and stare! but Trot began to
    snore.
Such specimens of work divine were ne'er before
    presented:
My head turn'd round, I lost my wits, and so became
    demented.
Poetic fury seiz'd me then, and raptures most intense;
And marvellous sublimities supplied the want of
    sense.
See, reader, see with both your eyes! look straight
    before your nose!
Encircling beauties all around their lovely charms
    disclose.
See girls bursting into view, with the shell upon their
    tail;
And dames demure and wary, concealed beneath a
    vail.

A sight like this was very strange; yet not more
strange than true:
But a bright unclouded hemisphere next burst upon
my view.
With many a spangling star it blaz'd, each *like a living
eye;*
As fascinating, bland, and sweet, as e'er was mutton
pie.
Some stars were black, and some were blue, some
green, and others yellow:
And some were bright, and some were dim, and the
light of some was mellow.
But the black, in shape and size like pots, were
dazzling for certain:
With vividness of ray they glanced, as bright as Day &
Martin.
I dropp'd my tears, and then my eyes I rubb'd with
might and main;
And next I strove my scatter'd wits to muster up again.
But harder work I never tried: the labour was
immense,
To leave bombast and doggrel, and gather common
sense."

Let your readers here pause and marvel: And by and by,
when their astonishment is surmounted, I may enlarge
upon the works and untimely end of the great Censor, who
soared beyond Parnassus, and died in a dung heap.

Mephibosheth Stepsure gent.

Explanatory Notes

The explanatory notes in *The Mephibosheth Stepsure Letters* reflect a good deal about both Thomas McCulloch and the British North American province that was the chief subject of these letters. Many of the annotations identify quotations from or allusions to the Bible, particularly the Old Testament, which McCulloch knew intimately, as he did literary works such as *The Iliad* and *Pilgrim's Progress* that he also cited. McCulloch's interest in British history, especially that of the Scottish Covenanters, and his delight in Scottish words and expressions are likewise evident in these letters. The definitions of Scotticisms in these notes are taken from the *Scottish National Dictionary*. The most diverse group of notes is that which has to do with McCulloch's numerous references to people, places, events, customs, and laws relevant to early nineteenth-century Nova Scotia. These references demonstrate both the intricate texture of provincial life and McCulloch's deep understanding of its complexity. The notes are keyed to the text by page and line numbers. Items are identified the first time that they are mentioned.

10.32   *the Lines*] That is, the border with the United States. In the *Acadian Recorder* version of this letter "Passamaquoddy" is used instead of "the Lines"; Passamaquoddy Bay was in McCulloch's time the area in the Bay of Fundy between Deer Island and Campobello Island in New Brunswick and the State of Maine. The United States customs district of Passamaquoddy was established in 1790 with an office on Moose Island, and in 1803 Eastport, on the American mainland, was made a port of entry for foreign ships; both became busy centres of shipping, smuggling—and hiding. According to

George Leonard, the Superintendent of Trade
and Fisheries in New Brunswick in the early
1800s, the whole area of "the bay and islands" was
"the asylum of deserters from the British army
and navy and of criminals and absconding debtors
from New Brunswick and Nova Scotia." See
Harold A. Davis. *An International Community on the
St. Croix (1604-1930)*. Orono, Maine: University
of Maine, 1974, p. 92.

11.10-11   *the vessels, like the ark, saw many summers and win-
ters*] Compare Genesis 6:14-15; God tells Noah to
make "an ark of gopher wood. . . . The length of
the ark *shall be* three hundred cubits, the breadth
of it fifty cubits, and the height of it thirty cubits,"
or, if a cubit is measured at twenty-two inches, five
hundred and fifty feet long, ninety-two feet wide,
and fifty-five feet high. A vessel of such propor-
tions, constructed by hand by Noah and his three
sons, would obviously have taken a long time to
build. See *IB*. Vol. 1. New York and Nashville:
Abingdon Press, 1952, p. 540.

11.11-12   *In the mean time, peace came*] The Second Treaty of
Paris, which officially ended the Napoleonic
Wars, was signed on 20 November 1815.

12.17-18   *the very place where Samson turned miller*] Compare
Judges 16:21; Samson, betrayed by Delilah to the
Philistines, is blinded by them and brought to
Gaza, where "he did grind in the prison house."
See *IB*. Vol. 2. 1953, p. 796.

14.12-13   *the country of the Gadarenes*] Compare Luke
8:26-33; Jesus, visiting "the country of the
Gadarenes," cures a man possessed by "many dev-
ils," who ask Jesus to allow them to enter

> a herd of many swine feeding on the moun-
> tain. . . . And he suffered them.
>   Then went the devils out of the man, and

entered into the swine: and the herd ran violently down a steep place into the lake, and were choked.

The story is also told in Matthew 8:28-32 and Mark 5:1-13. See *IB*. Vol. 7. 1951, pp. 346-48 and 711-15, and Vol. 8. 1952, pp. 156-58.

15.12   *the Ohio*] In the early decades of the nineteenth century, particularly after the War of 1812, the territory in the United States northwest of the Ohio River became a popular place of settlement; the State of Ohio was created in 1802, Indiana in 1815, and Illinois in 1818. So infectious was "Ohio Fever" in Nova Scotia that in 1826, for example, Ohio, Yarmouth County, was named after the territory when "Nehemiah and Benjamin Churchill of Chebogue" moved "past the last settlements at the Ponds (now Lake Milo)" and called their new homes "Ohio." See *Place-Names and Places of Nova Scotia*. With an Introduction by Charles Bruce Fergusson. Halifax: The Public Archives of Nova Scotia, 1967, p. 507.

15.16   *the Cape of Good Hope . . . the Caffres*] After the Cape Colony was officially ceded to Great Britain in 1814, the area vied with North America as a desirable destination for British emigrants, and from c. 1817 on there were various schemes to assist settlement to the former Dutch colony. In July 1819, for example, the House of Commons in London "voted a sum of £50,000 for the purpose of carrying out a large emigration scheme" to the eastern region, particularly the Albany district, of the Cape; by 1821 the immigrants were being subjected to increasingly frequent raids by the Caffres (or Kaffirs), Bantu tribesmen, who stole from the settlers and sometimes murdered them and their children. See *The Cambridge History Of The*

British Empire. Vol. 8. Gen. Eds. A. P. Newton and E. A. Benians. Cambridge: At The University Press, 1936, pp. 234-40, et passim.

20.23   *a Pictou highlandman*] Many Gaelic-speaking immigrants from the Highlands of Scotland came to the Pictou area in the early decades of the nineteenth century; Earltown, for example, in Colchester County but on the Pictou County line and "both as to its origin and population closely connected with this County," was well known in Pictou as a settlement of Highlanders, mostly from Sutherlandshire (now Sutherland District), who had taken up "their abode in the woods" and encountered "many difficulties." See George Patterson. *A History of the County Of Pictou Nova Scotia.* 1877; rpt. Belleville, Ontario: Mika Studio, 1972, pp. 277-78.

31.3-4   *next year, plaster at the Lines was a mere drug*] From the time of the American Revolution gypsum, or plaster of Paris, was used as "fertilizer principally for wheat fields" in the eastern United States, and trade flourished in the mineral between Nova Scotia, which had a rich supply, and the former Thirteen Colonies. One centre of this trading, which was often illicit, was Passamaquoddy Bay. As a result of "drastic restrictions" imposed on the trade by New Brunswick, Nova Scotia, and the "American Congress" after the War of 1812, the price of gypsum "jumped from $8 to $13 per ton," and "illicit trade" increased. By the late teens and early twenties of the nineteenth century, however, too many smugglers had "forced down the price from $13 to $7.50 per ton" in the Bay area, and "the shift of grain growing to the mid-west and the discovery of calcium deposits in Ohio and Michigan" meant that Nova Scotia's gypsum was no longer needed. "By the close of the 1820's the plaster trade was almost a thing of the past" at "the Lines." See *An International Community on the St. Croix (1604-1930)*, pp. 92-94.

38.3-5   *Mrs. Soakem . . . will come upon the town*] In 1763 "*the Lieutenant-Governor, Council and Assembly*" of Nova Scotia passed An ACT to enable the Inhabitants of the several Townships within this Province, to maintain their Poor (3 & 4 George III, c. VII). This act provided that at an annual meeting held "on the first Monday in January" the "free-holders" of a township should "vote such sums of money as they shall judge necessary for the current year to support and maintain their poor" and "choose twelve inhabitants of the said township" to "assess" their fellow townsmen for the money, which was to be distributed to the needy by "overseers of the poor." See *The Statutes At Large, Passed In The Several General Assemblies Held In His Majesty's Province Of Nova-Scotia: From . . . 1758. To . . . 1804.* Halifax: John Howe and Son, 1805, p. 94.

38.8-9   *it is, as the wise man says, a sore travail and an evil disease*] Compare Ecclesiastes 4:8, in which the Preacher describes "vanity" as "a sore travail," and Ecclesiastes 6:2, in which he describes "vanity" as "an evil disease." See *IB.* Vol. 5. 1956, pp. 55 and 61.

39.26-27   It is not good for man to be alone] Compare Genesis 2:18; after God had created man and placed him in the garden of Eden, "the LORD God said, *It is* not good that the man should be alone; I will make him a help meet for him." See *IB.* Vol. 1, p. 497.

45.28-31   *But Saunders Scantocreesh used to declare that it was the language of Ashdod: that parson Drone should cast him out of the church; as Ezra did the mongrel Jews*] Com-

pare Nehemiah 13:23-30 and Ezra 10:9-44. After
the return of the people of Israel to Jerusalem in
the fifth century B.C., Nehemiah their leader
cursed the Jews who had "married wives of Ash-
dod, of Ammon, *and* of Moab," and whose "chil-
dren spake half in the speech of Ashdod, and
could not speak in the Jews' language"; Ezra the
priest insisted that all the Jews who had "taken
strange wives" should separate from them and
their children. See *IB*. Vol. 3. 1954, pp. 655-61
and 815-19.

47.12-14   *By chance he heard of Seignior Caperini, at that time
              famed for his skill in improving the paces of the human
              species*] In 1818 Mr. Geanneni, a *"Teacher of Fash-
              ionable Dancing,"* opened a school in Halifax "for
              the Instruction of Young Masters and Misses in
              the polite art of Dancing"; he also instructed "four
              days in the week" at "Mrs. HENRY and Miss
              BELLS' Schools," and he gave lessons "at private
              houses if required." His advertisement, dated 28
              March 1818, first appeared in the *Acadian Recorder*
              on 4 April 1818; the same issue contained two
              articles on Pictou Academy. See *Acadian Recorder*,
              4 April 1818, p. [4].

47.28   *the Confession of Faith*] This was "The Confession
              Of Faith; Agreed Upon By The Assembly Of
              Divines At Westminster, With The Assistance Of
              Commissioners From The Church Of Scotland,
              As A Part Of The Covenanted Uniformity In
              Religion Betwixt The Churches Of Christ In The
              Kingdoms Of Scotland, England, And Ireland,"
              and *"Approved by the General Assembly* 1647, *and
              ratified and established by Acts of Parliament* 1649 *and*
              1690, *as the publick and avowed Confession of the
              Church of Scotland, with the Proofs from the Scripture"*;
              "The Larger Catechism," also "Agreed Upon . . .
              At Westminster," approved by the Church of

Scotland in 1648, and usually published with "The Confession," included "dancings" as one of the "sins forbidden in the seventh commandment." See, for example, *The Confession Of Faith; The Larger And Shorter Catechisms, With The Scripture-Proofs at Large*. Edinburgh: Johnstone, Hunter, & Co., 1868, pp. [15], [101], and 176-77.

48.32-34   *his father's establishment consumed more butter milk and potatoes, than any of the neighbours*] In *The History And Social Influence Of The Potato*, Redcliffe Salaman argues that from the seventeenth century on "the food" of the Irish people was "the potato, and milk. As time goes on, . . . the milk grows scarcer, and the quota of the potato more voluminous. . . . one recognizes, in an ever increasing degree, that the establishment of the monophagous diet is linked in ever closer union with the social degradation of its devotees." See Redcliffe Salaman. *The History And Social Influence Of The Potato*. Cambridge: At The University Press, 1949, p. 229.

53.3-4   *they were no better than the remnant of the Hittites and Perizzites*] Compare Exodus 3:8 and I Kings 9:20-21. The Hittites and the Perizzites were among the people who lived in the "land flowing with milk and honey" that the Israelites conquered after their deliverance from Egypt; in the reign of Solomon

> all the people *that were* left of the Amorites, Hittites, Perizzites, Hivites, and Jebusites, which *were* not of the children of Israel,
>
> Their children that were left after them in the land, whom the children of Israel also were not able utterly to destroy,

were made slaves. See *IB*. Vol. 1, p. 873, and Vol. 3, p. 94.

56.11-19   *he happened to meet Deacon Sharp . . . going to sermon*
             . . . a grand juryman . . . and, when he found that he
             had nothing to pay the fine, he . . . put him into the hands
             of the sheriff] According to An ACT for the better
             observation and keeping of the Lord's Day (1
             George III, c. I), passed by the Nova Scotia General
             Assembly in July 1761, "the church wardens
             and the constables, or any one or more of them,
             shall . . . in the time of divine service, walk through
             the town . . . and apprehend all offenders what-
             soever contrary to the true intent and meaning of
             this act." If the "offender" could not pay the
             "penalty of ten shillings" for breaking the Act, he
             or she could be committed to "the common gaol of
             the county, there to remain in close confinement
             for a time not exceeding forty eight hours, nor less
             than twenty four hours." See *The Statutes At Large*
             . . . Of Nova-Scotia. 1805, pp. 64-66.

56.27-28   *Adam Smith, Ricardo, Du Say, and the French Econo-*
             mists] Adam Smith's seminal work on political
             economy, *An Inquiry Into The Nature and Causes Of*
             The Wealth Of Nations (1776), strongly influenced
             the ideas of David Ricardo (1772-1823) and Jean-
             Baptiste Say (1767-1832), two of the leading econ-
             omists of McCulloch's generation. The "French
             Economists" were the *Économistes*, or Physiocrats, a
             school founded by François Quesnay (1694-1774);
             one of their views—that land was "the sole source
             of wealth" and that therefore only "proprietors"
             and "cultivators" were productive members of
             society—would undoubtedly have appealed to
             McCulloch, especially as he analysed Nova Scotia's
             economy in the early 1820s. See *Palgrave's Diction-*
             ary Of Political Economy. Ed. Henry Higgs. Vol. 3.
             London: Macmillan, 1926, pp. 105-06.

57.15-17   *none . . . should be the means of calling his child . . .*
Ichabod] Compare I Samuel 4:19-22; when Eli's
"daughter-in-law, Phinehas' wife, . . . with child,
near to be delivered," hears that the Philistines
have defeated Israel and captured "the ark of
God" and "that her father-in-law and her husband
were dead, she bowed herself and travailed" and
gave birth to a son. Before she herself died, "she
named the child I-chabod, saying, The glory is
departed from Israel: because the ark of God was
taken, and because of her father-in-law and her
husband." See *IB*. Vol. 2, p. 902.

58.32-36   *they might have been obliged, like the Scotch Worthies, to*
wander among moors and mosses; and at last been taken
up by some of the Highland Host or of Claverhouse's
dragoons, who would have shot them or hanged
them] Originally "the Scotch Worthies" were the
leaders, martyrs, and witnesses of the Protestant
Reformation in sixteenth-century Scotland; by
the mid-seventeenth century, however, the Pres-
byterians had split into several groups, the more
extreme of which formed a Conventicler or Cove-
nanting opposition that vigorously and violently
protested aspects of the lawful authority of both
Church and State. To intimidate these Covenan-
ters, who were particularly strong in southwest
Scotland, some six thousand Highland troops,
"the Highland Host," were sent to Ayrshire and
Renfrewshire (both now in Strathclyde Region)
early in 1678. Although they stayed only a few
months, their "sojourn" was, in the words of one
historian, "a carnival of robbery. . . . They fell
upon the travellers whom they met on the country
roads. They considered themselves authorised to
enter every house. They bullied and overawed
any whom they supposed to be hiding money

from them. . . . Their pillage enriched them mar-
vellously." In the same year John Graham of
Claverhouse, later first Viscount Dundee, arrived
in southwest Scotland with his troops. Over the
next few years he and his cavalry systematically
pursued the Covenanters with the result that,
among the local people, "Bloody Clavers" and his
"dragoons" became synonymous with cruel
oppression. See J. D. Mackie. *A History of Scotland.*
Harmondsworth, Middlesex: Penguin Books,
1969, p. 239, and Alexander Smellie. *Men Of The
Covenant.* 1924; rpt. Edinburgh: The Banner Of
Truth Trust, 1975, pp. 259-60.

63.5-7   *but trust in chariots and in horses, and go down to Egypt
for help; and at last get themselves drowned in the Red
sea*] Compare Isaiah 31:1 and Exodus 15:4. In
Isaiah 31:1 the prophet warns, "Woe to them that
go down to Egypt for help; and stay on horses,
and trust in chariots." In Exodus 15:4 the song of
Moses relates, "Pharoah's chariots and his host
hath he cast into the sea: his chosen captains also
are drowned in the Red sea." See *IB.* Vol. 1,
p. 943, and Vol. 5, p. 338.

64.1-4   *the Chester folks; who once dug for money, and . . . were
glad to get away with the loss of their tools*] In 1795
three residents of Chester, Nova Scotia, explored
a man-made pit on Oak Island, four miles south-
west of Chester as the crow flies, that they thought
might contain Captain Kidd's long-undiscovered
pirate treasure. At that point they abandoned
their dig fairly quickly, but in 1804 a company,
whose shareholders included people from Pictou
County, was formed to pursue the treasure-seek-
ing operations in cooperation with the original
diggers. The men dug down ninety-eight feet, at
which point they "met with a hard, impenetrable

substance" that they supposed was the buried treasure. Before they could actually investigate their "chest," however, the pit filled with sixty feet of water, and all their efforts to remove it with bailing buckets and a pump failed. The next year the men tried to reach the mysterious object again by digging a second shaft one hundred and ten feet deep and then tunnelling towards the first, but "after tunnelling about twelve feet, water suddenly burst in, with increasing rapidity, flooding the new shaft to a depth of sixty-five feet . . . and forcing the workmen out, barely escaping with their lives." See Reginald V. Harris. *The Oak Island Mystery*. Toronto: The Ryerson Press, 1958, pp. 15-16, et passim.

70.34 *his Majesty*] Probably George IV, who succeeded his father George III on 29 January 1820.

70.34-71.3 *[a governor] who does business in a business like manner . . . and acts with an order and promptitude of decision, which gives activity to inferior offices and life to government*] Sir James Kempt. Appointed to succeed Lord Dalhousie as lieutenant governor of Nova Scotia in November 1819, under George III, he did not take his oath of office until June 1820, under George IV; he served in this position until 1828 when he left Nova Scotia to become governor-in-chief of Canada. A quiet, conciliatory administrator, in the early 1820s he worked hard to resolve in a manner just and fair to all parties the denominational disputes over education in which McCulloch himself was so much involved. See *DCB*. Vol. 8, pp. 458-65.

75.17-19 *fellows, who are ignorant of every thing but the doctrine of Balaam; and exactly like their master, constantly running unlawful roads*] Compare II Peter 2:15, in which Simon Peter warns his fellow Christians

that false prophets "Which have forsaken the
right way, and are gone astray, following the way
of Balaam *the son* of Bosor, who loved the wages of
unrighteousness," will rise among them and try to
lure them away from the teachings of Jesus. See
IB. Vol. 12. 1957, p. 194.

76.14-16   *the father of Gibeon Trick, who . . . lost both his ears
before he was of age*] According to An ACT for
punishing Criminal Offenders (32 George II, c.
XX), passed by the General Assembly of Nova
Scotia in 1758, the punishments for counterfeiters
and forgers included the loss of one ear, for per-
jurers two. The portion of the 1758 Act concern-
ing ears was clarified by the General Assembly of
Nova Scotia in 1774 by An ACT in amendment of
an Act made in the Thirty-second year of His late
Majesty's reign, entitled, an Act for punishing
Criminal Offenders (14 & 15 George III, c. X),
which enacted

> that both the ears of such offender or
> offenders as shall be convicted of perjury;
> and one of the ears of the offender or
> offenders as shall be convicted of counter-
> feiting, impairing, diminishing or imbasing,
> any foreign coin current in this Province,
> shall, for more exemplary punishment, be
> first cut off, and then nailed to the pillory.

Ear-cutting as a punishment for offenders was not
abolished in Nova Scotia until 1841 by An Act to
abolish the punishment of Pillory, Cutting the
Ears of Offenders, and Whipping, and to sub-
stitute Imprisonment in lieu thereof (4 Victoria, c.
VIII). See *The Statutes At Large . . . Of Nova-Scotia.*
1805, pp. 28-31 and 190, and *Acts Of The General
Assembly Of The Province Of Nova-Scotia. Anno
Quarto Victoriæ Reginæ. 1841*. Halifax: Printed at
the Royal Gazette Office, n.d., p. 41.

78.18   *salt hay*] The hay that grew on the salt marshes along the coast of the Bay of Fundy "was a prime source of bedding and fodder" for the early settlers. See Rosemary Eaton. *The Salt Marsh, A Meeting of Land And Sea*. Halifax: Nova Scotia Museum, 1979.

78.20   *an officer's sale in Halifax*] A British army officer frequently sold his belongings by auction when his tour of duty ended in Halifax. Two such auctions, for example, were advertised in the Halifax *Free Press* on 29 July 1823; "*Capt. DAMAS*" had for sale "A VARIETY of HOUSEHOLD FURNITURE," and "Two HORSES and a GIG," while "DR. ALDERSON, 62d *Regt.*," was selling "*all his HOUSEHOLD FURNITURE*" and "A Young HORSE, aged 5 years; harness for two horses, together with a saddle and Bridle all likewise in good order." See *Free Press*, 29 July 1823, p. 119.

81.20-21   *he who called old age a second childhood*] In *As You Like It* II.vii.139-66, Jaques, describing the "seven ages" of man, says of the "Last scene of all, / That ends this strange eventful history," that it is "second childishness, and mere oblivion, / Sans teeth, sans eyes, sans taste, sans every thing." See *The Riverside Shakespeare*. Boston: Houghton Mifflin, 1974, pp. 381-82.

82.35   *the drunkards of Ephraim*] Compare Isaiah 28:1, in which the prophet, thinking probably of the attack on Ephraim (Israel) by Assyria in the eighth century B.C., warns, "Woe to the crown of pride, to the drunkards of Ephraim, whose glorious beauty *is* a fading flower, which *are* on the head of the fat valleys of them that are overcome with wine!" See *IB*. Vol. 5, pp. 313-14.

83.5   *snooled*] That is, cowed or humiliated.

85.4-6   *I have read somewhere in an old book, that Jupiter being in a great rage . . . tossed his son Vulcan . . . out of heaven*] Compare *The Iliad*, Book 1, ll. 590-93; Hephaistos (Vulcan) reminds his mother Hera that Zeus (Jupiter), his father, is too powerful to fight:

> "There was a time once before now I was
>   minded to help you,
> and he caught me by the foot and threw me
>   from the magic threshold,
> and all day long I dropped helpless, and
>   about sunset
> I landed in Lemnos, and there was not much
>   life left in me."

See *The Iliad of Homer*. Trans. Richmond Lattimore. 1951; First Phoenix Edition. Chicago: University of Chicago Press, 1961, pp. 74-75.

85.12-13   *it rained old wives and pike staves*] A version of an old Scottish proverb that means the same as it rained cats and dogs; that is, it rained heavily.

85.20   *he was lame of both legs*] Mephibosheth attributes Hephaistos' lameness to his landing in Lemnos. In Book 18, ll. 395-97 of *The Iliad*, however, Hephaistos implies that he was born lame and, as a result, thrown out of heaven by Hera:

> "I suffered much at the time of my great
>   fall
> through the will of my own brazen-faced
>   mother, who wanted
> to hide me, for being lame."

See *The Iliad of Homer*, p. 385.

85.23-24   *nor am I . . . of royal descent like old Mephibosheth*] Compare II Samuel 4:4, "And Jonathan, Saul's son, had a son *that was* lame of *his* feet. He was five years old when the tidings came of Saul and Jonathan out of Jezreel, and his nurse took him up, and fled: and it came to pass, as she made haste to flee, that he fell, and became lame. And his name *was* Mephibosheth." See *IB*. Vol. 2, p. 1065.

86.6-9   *my cousin Harrow and I, came upon the town. . . . we were publicly advertised . . . the day of sale*] In townships where no poorhouse existed, the overseers of the poor would seek out people willing to house and feed them for usually a year in return for money collected by the townsmen for the maintenance of the poor. The paupers were thus frequently advertised and sold as Mephibosheth describes. In 1796, for example, a freeholder in Truro "proposed that on condition the Town would reimburse him the last rate he paid for the support of the Poor, and also exempt him from the present one, he would keep the Town harmless as to any expence for the victuals and attendance of old Mrs. Caldwell." At the same meeting another freeholder offered to take a young boy for one year in return for eight pounds, provided the boy could be given back to the town at any time; if the boy were taken as an apprentice, the freeholder expected to receive another twelve pounds from the overseers. See PANS, Truro Township Record Book, 1770-1837, Register of Marriages, Births and Deaths, MG4, Vol. 150, p. 53.

87.30-32   *The proposal . . . made some time ago, to adapt the state of the country to its ideas, by making all our militia men captains and colonels*] During "the First Session of the Twelfth General Assembly" of "the Province of Nova-Scotia" that met from 12 December 1820 until 3 March 1821, the Assembly passed An ACT to provide for the greater security of this Province, by a better regulation of the Militia, and to repeal the Militia Laws now in force (1 & 2

George IV, c. II). According to this act, every male resident of Nova Scotia "from sixteen to sixty years of age" had to enrol and "serve in the Militia of the County, District, Town or Place, wherein he resides." The militia itself was to be organized into regiments, divided, when the population was sufficient, into battalions. These larger units were themselves to be divided into companies consisting "of not less than thirty, nor more than eighty, men, to be commanded by one Captain and two Subalterns, and when it shall exceed sixty men, one additional Officer may be appointed." As well as the officers attached to the regiments and battalions, then, there could be as many as three officers for as few as thirty militiamen. See *The Statutes At Large, Passed In The Several General Assemblies, Held In His Majesty's Province Of Nova-Scotia: From . . . 1817, To . . . 1826.* Vol. 3. Halifax: John Howe & Son, 1827, pp. 73-74.

93.3   *my Dilworth*] Thomas Dilworth (d. 1780), an English schoolmaster, prepared several works that became standard texts for schools in Great Britain, her colonies, and the United States until well into the nineteenth century. *A New Guide to the English Tongue* and *The Schoolmaster's Assistant . . . A Compendium of Arithmetic*, both first published in the 1740s, were particularly popular. Both, along with Dilworth's other works, were imported into Nova Scotia; in 1816, for example, George Eaton, a Halifax bookseller, had for sale "Dilworth's book-keeping; [his] arithmetic; [his] spelling-book; the improved [spelling-book]," and in 1823 Robert Smith, "*Book-Seller, Prince Street, Halifax,*" advertised "Dilworth's [Spelling Book]" and his "Assistant." See *Acadian Recorder*, 29 June 1816, p. [1], and 11 January 1823, p. [3].

94.16   *Burn's Justice*] *The Justice of the Peace, And Parish Officer* by Richard Burn, an Anglican clergyman who was a justice of the peace for the English counties of Westmorland and Cumberland (both now part of the Cumbria Region), is, according to the *DNB*, "the most useful book ever published on the law relating to justices of the peace." First published in London in 1755, its "Twenty-Fourth Edition," with "Corrections, Additions, and Improvements" by Sir George Chetwynd, was issued in 1825. See *DNB*, and *The Justice of the Peace, And Parish Officer*. By Richard Burn, LL.D. Late Chancellor Of The Diocese Of Carlisle. 5 Vols. London: Printed by A. Strahan, For T. Cadell, et al., 1825.

94.17-18   *the Crook in the Lot*] Three linked sermons by Thomas Boston (d. 1732), a minister of the Church of Scotland, first published in 1737; their purpose was to illustrate "The Sovereignty and Wisdom of God in the Afflictions of Men." The first argued three propositions:

> Prop. I. Whatsoever crook there is in one's lot, it is of God's making.
> Prop. II. What God sees meet to mar, no one shall be able to mend in his lot.
> Prop. III. The considering of the crook in the lot as the work of God, or of His making, is a proper means to bring us to a Christian deportment under it.

The second and third emphasized the importance of humility and patience in bearing "the Crook in the Lot." See *The Crook In The Lot Or The Sovereignty and Wisdom of God in the Afflictions of Men Displayed*. By The Rev. Thomas Boston. With A Brief Memoir, And A Portrait Of The Author. New And Improved Edition. London: The

Religious Tract Society, [1885], pp. 3-4 and 143.

95.7-8   *a blue bonnet*] The favorite headgear of the Scottish peasant, "by the mid-seventeenth century the blue bonnet had become the symbol of a Scot." McCulloch's first parish, Stewarton, Ayrshire (now Kilmarnoch and Loudoun District, Strathclyde Region), was a centre of "the bonnet trade" and "eventually became known as the 'Bonnet Town'." See John Telfer Dunbar. *The Costume Of Scotland*. London: B. T. Batsford, 1981, pp. 154 and 157.

95.8-9   *the kittle names in the Chronicles*] In recounting the story of the Jewish people from the time of Adam to about the sixth century B.C., the writer of I and II Chronicles included long lists of "kittle," that is, intricate and difficult, names and genealogies.

96.5-7   *I was not, like Robinson Crusoe, cast upon a desolate island; and forced to try shifts which nobody had ever tried before*] The plot of Daniel Defoe's *Robinson Crusoe* (1719) would have been well known to most Nova Scotians in the 1820s. The novel was, for example, one of a number of "*BOOKS*" lately arrived "from London" that George Eaton was selling in Halifax in 1816; it was also advertised as being "on sale at the CHRONICLE PRINTING OFFICE" in Halifax in 1822. See *Acadian Recorder*, 29 June 1816, p. [1], and *Weekly Chronicle*, 22 March 1822, p. [2].

115.1-2   *Howl's hearers, called her the barren fig tree; and always affirmed that she had no life*] Compare, for example, Matthew 21:19; Jesus, returning to Jerusalem after a night in Bethany, "saw a fig tree . . . came to it, and found nothing thereon, but leaves only, and said unto it, Let no fruit grow on thee henceforward for ever. And presently the fig tree withered away." See *IB*. Vol. 7, p. 507.

115.24   *the Stuarton sickness*] In 1625 David Dickson, a non-conforming clergyman at Irvine, attracted "the whole countryside," including the people of Stewarton, Ayrshire, about six miles away, with his "Calvinistic and evangelical" preaching; "the parishioners of Stewarton, who came thither on business, were wrought up to such a pitch by his market-day sermons that many of them fell down insensible, and had to be carried out of church." The "epidemic" was called "the Stewarton sickness." See William Law Mathieson. *Politics And Religion A Study In Scottish History From The Reformation To The Revolution.* Vol. 1. Glasgow: James Maclehose And Sons, 1902, pp. 359-60.

115.25   *the Cambuslang work*] For several months in 1742 Cambuslang, Lanarkshire (now Glasgow City District, Strathclyde Region), was the scene of "a remarkable religious revival" known as "the Camb'slang Wark." Convinced by the sermons of, among others, the famous evangelical preacher George Whitefield, "many people at outdoor prayer meetings . . . experienced dramatic conversions." See Rosalind Mitchison. *Life in Scotland.* London: B. T. Batsford, 1978, p. 89, and *Ordnance Gazetteer Of Scotland.* Ed. Francis H. Groome. Vol. 1. Edinburgh: Thomas C. Jack, Grange Publishing Works, 1882, p. 225.

117.14-15   *one of Solomon's foolish women, who are clamorous and know nothing*] Compare Proverbs 9:13, "A foolish woman *is* clamorous: *she is* simple, and knoweth nothing." See *IB.* Vol. 4. 1955, p. 838.

125.32-33   *the days of Queen Ann*] Anne reigned from 1702 to 1714.

127.25-26   *his comfort was derived from the parable of the rich man and Lazarus*] In Luke 16:19-31 Jesus tells the parable about "a certain rich man" and a "beggar named Lazarus," who lay at the former's gate and waited "to be fed with the crumbs which fell from the rich man's table." After each dies, however, his situation is reversed: the rich man goes to "hell," and the beggar "into Abraham's bosom." When the rich man complains, Abraham says, "Son, remember that thou in thy lifetime receivedst thy good things, and likewise Lazarus evil things: but now he is comforted, and thou art tormented." See *IB*. Vol. 8, pp. 288-93.

133.34-134.1   *beauty . . . wherever it is combined with slovenliness . . . is, as the wise man says, like a jewel in the snout of the vilest of animals*] Compare Proverbs 11:22, in which Solomon states that "*As* a jewel of gold in a swine's snout, *so is* a fair woman which is without discretion." See *IB*. Vol. 4, p. 849.

137.34-35   I will, therefore, that the younger women marry, bear children, guide the house] I Timothy 5:14; this is one of the instructions included in the first letter of Paul to Timothy. See *IB*. Vol. 11. 1955, p. 439.

139.30-37   *This and this only, will gladden the wilderness . . . the glory of the Lord and the excellency of our God*] Compare the prophet's vision of a land restored to fertility in Isaiah 35:1-2:

> The wilderness and the solitary place shall be glad for them; and the desert shall rejoice, and blossom as the rose.
>
> It shall blossom abundantly, and rejoice even with joy and singing: the glory of Lebanon shall be given unto it, the excellency of Carmel and Sharon; they shall see the glory of the LORD, *and* the excellency of our God.

See *IB*. Vol. 5, pp. 358-59.

143.16-17   *Every man . . . knows time to be money*] The best-
known version of this saying is "Remember that
TIME is Money," the opening sentence of Ben-
jamin Franklin's "Advice To A Young Trades-
man" (1748). See *The Papers Of Benjamin Franklin*.
Vol. 3. Ed. Leonard W. Labaree. New Haven:
Yale University Press, 1961, p. 306.

151.16   *None but the brave deserve the fair*] John Dryden,
"Alexander's Feast; Or The Power Of Musique.
An Ode, In Honour of St. Cecilia's Day," 1697, l.
15. See *The Poems Of John Dryden*. Ed. James
Kinsley. Vol. 3. Oxford: At The Clarendon Press,
1958, p. 1428.

152.31-32   Blessed . . . doing] Matthew 24:46; Jesus, defining
"a faithful and wise servant" as one who feeds his
household "in due season," concludes, "Blessed *is*
that servant, whom his lord when he cometh shall
find so doing." See *IB*. Vol. 7, pp. 554-55.

153.15   Occupy till I come] Luke 19:13; in the parable
about the nobleman who travelled to a distant
country, Jesus says that before the nobleman left,
"he called his ten servants, and delivered them ten
pounds, and said unto them, Occupy till I come."
See *IB*. Vol. 8, p. 330.

153.17-18   I have been . . . finishing the work which thou
gavest me to do] John 17:4; just before his arrest
Jesus says to God, "I have glorified thee on the
earth: I have finished the work which thou gavest
me to do." See *IB*. Vol. 8, p. 744.

153.23   Well done good and faithful servant] Matthew
25:21; in the parable of the talents Jesus says that
the master, returning after a long absence, con-
gratulated his servant for doubling his five talents
with the words, "Well done, *thou* good and faithful
servant: thou hast been faithful over a few things,
I will make thee ruler over many things: enter

thou into the joy of thy lord." See *IB*. Vol. 7, p. 560.

153.27-28 them . . . lightly esteemed] I Samuel 2:30; through a man of God the Lord tells Eli the priest that he and his sons have lost His favour: "Wherefore the Lord God of Israel saith, I said indeed *that* thy house, and the house of thy father, should walk before me for ever: but now the Lord saith, Be it far from me; for them that honor me I will honor, and they that despise me shall be lightly esteemed." See *IB*. Vol. 2, p. 890.

153.29-30 seek not . . . honour . . . from God] John 5:44; Jesus asks the Jews, "How can ye believe, which receive honor one of another, and seek not the honor that *cometh* from God only?" See *IB*. Vol. 8, p. 551.

167.26-28 *our townsmen's general practice of riding in chariots and upon horses . . . the abomination of the Egyptians*] Chariots and horses, frequently associated in the Old Testament with the Egyptians, were more general symbols for the Israelites of "pagan luxury and dependence on physical power for defense." In Isaiah 31:1, for example, the prophet warns, "Woe to them that go down to Egypt for help; and stay on horses, and trust in chariots, because *they are* many; and in horsemen, because they are very strong; but they look not unto the Holy One of Israel, neither seek the Lord!" See *IB*. Vol. 5, p. 338, and *The Interpreter's Dictionary Of The Bible*. New York and Nashville: Abingdon Press, 1962, Vol. 2, p. 646.

170.16-18 *Muckle John Gib and Mrs. Buchan . . . tried to lead silly people off their feet in Scotland*] "Muckle John" Gib(b), also called "King Solomon," was a sailor who in the late seventeenth century led a group of fanatical Covenanters known as the "*Sweet Singers* of *Borrowstounness*" from Bo'ness to a spot in the Pentland Hills south of Edinburgh from where they could see the city, for them a symbol of bloodiness and sinfulness. Elspith Buchan led a small fanatical sect called the Buchanites. Given to religious fancies, literal interpretations of the Bible, and communal living, the Buchanites left Irvine in 1784 for the Dumfries area where they flourished until disillusionment with Mrs. Buchan set in. Before she died in 1791, she told her few remaining followers that she was the Virgin Mary, and, as a result, after her death they, awaiting her resurrection, refused to bury her. See Robert Chambers. *A Biographical Dictionary of Eminent Scotsmen.* New Edition, Revised. 1870; rpt. Hildesheim and New York: Georg Olms Verlag, 1971, pp. 226-27, and Gordon Donaldson and Robert S. Morpeth. *A Dictionary of Scottish History.* Edinburgh: John Donald, 1977, p. 83.

176.9-10   *what the first chapter of the Proverbs contains*] Proverbs 1 contains an exhortation to love knowledge and to fear the Lord and a warning from wisdom to those who ignore her that she will "laugh" at their "calamity" and "mock" their "fear," for they who "hated knowledge, and did not choose the fear of the LORD" shall "eat of the fruit of their own way, and be filled with their own devices." See *IB*. Vol. 4, pp. 779-92.

176.16-17   *the long speeches of Job's three comforters*] The "three friends" who come "to comfort" Job are "Eliphaz the Temanite, and Bildad the Shuhite, and Zophar the Naamathite." Eliphaz speaks in Job 4, 5, 15, and 22; Bildad in Job 8, 18, and 25; and Zophar in Job 11 and 20. See *IB*. Vol. 3, pp. 922, 932-49, 970-75, 992-96, 1015-21, 1034-39, 1058-64, 1071-77, and 1089-91.

177.28-29   *as white as the old crow imagined her brood to be*] A
             version of an old proverb; compare, for example,
             The Æneid Of Virgil Translated Into Scottish Verse,
             1553, by Gawin Douglas, "The Proloug Of The
             Nynth Buke," ll. 77-78, "Yit, by my self, I fynd this
             proverb perfyte, / The blak craw thinkis hyr awin
             byrdis quhite." See *The Æneid Of Virgil*. New York:
             AMS Press Inc. and Johnson Reprint Corp., 1971,
             Vol. 2, p. 515.

185.11-12   *The exertions of you Halifax gentlemen to promote the
             agriculture of the province*] In 1818 Lord Dalhousie,
             the lieutenant governor of Nova Scotia, was
             instrumental in establishing the Central Board or
             the Provincial Agricultural Society to act as a liai-
             son with local agricultural societies, to disseminate
             information about agriculture gleaned from
             various sources, to offer occasional incentives for
             agricultural improvements, and to import and
             distribute implements, seeds, and livestock. At the
             Board's first meeting in Halifax on 15 December
             1818, Dalhousie's gift of "a hundred guineas was
             not lost on the gentlemen of Halifax who, besides
             taking out one hundred and twenty subscriptions
             (twenty shillings each)," contributed "£350." See J.
             S. Martell. "The Achievements of Agricola and
             the Agricultural Societies 1818-25." *Bulletin Of
             The Public Archives Of Nova Scotia*, 2, No. 2 (1940),
             14.

186.22-26   *Mr. Drone is not even related to the Trulliber family. He
             does not feed pigs for sale. . . . But when our folks starve
             him, necessity has no law*] In *Joseph Andrews*, 1742, by
             Henry Fielding, Parson Adams visits Parson
             Trulliber, "just come from serving his Hogs; for
             Mr. *Trulliber* was a Parson on *Sundays*, but all the
             other six might more properly be called a
             Farmer." Trulliber, who mistakes Adams for "a
             Man come" to buy "some of his Hogs," is actually

breaking a law (21 Henry VIII, c. XIII), still in force in eighteenth-century England, that forbade Anglican clergymen from farming for profit. See Henry Fielding. *Joseph Andrews.* Ed. Martin C. Battestin. Middletown, Connecticut: Wesleyan University Press, 1967, p. 162.

187.17   *the Weekly Chronicle*] Published in Halifax, the newspaper was owned by William Minns, John Howe's brother-in-law, who issued it first in April 1786. See *DCB.* Vol. 6, p. 508.

187.18-19   *the Honorable the Attorney General*] Richard John Uniacke (1753-1830) was the attorney general of Nova Scotia during the time that the Stepsure letters were appearing in the *Acadian Recorder*; a strong believer in the Church of England, Uniacke had previously fought hard "to stop the secessionist Presbyterians led by Thomas McCulloch from turning Pictou Academy into a college, and as principal law officer he drafted the restrictive charter of the academy in 1820." See *DCB.* Vol. 6, pp. 789-92.

187.20-30   *"Turn where you will . . . a young woman's back"*] On 23 March 1822 Uniacke spoke at the "General Meeting of the Provincial Agricultural Society" in Halifax; in his speech he analysed the reasons for "the scarcity of money, the distress of the country, and the stagnation of business" and argued "that the wealth of a country did not consist in money, but in the *products of land and labour*." Because of the "high profits" and "great wages" that came so easily during the Napoleonic War,

> habits of indolence stole in amongst us, and all their attendant train of evils. Turn where you will, folly and extravagance stare you in the face. That gentleman, Mephibosheth Stepsure, had given us a picture of ourselves,

which, he was sorry to say, was too true; but he did not approve of its being hung up in the newspapers for all the world to look at. But he should be obliged to him if he would go to every door in the Province, and sound his reproofs in their ears. For his own part he was surprised to see our extravagance in dress; the East and the West, the North and the South, the whole world was ransacked to collect the rags which were to be thrown on a young woman's back.

If, Uniacke concluded, "the late war, with the wealth and extravagance it had produced, had really debauched" Nova Scotia and ruined "the present generation," he nevertheless "trusted that the next would be brought up with more industry and economy." See *Weekly Chronicle*, 29 March 1822, pp. [1]-[2].

199.25	*puddocks*] That is, paddocks, or frogs.
199.26	*kail wives*] Literally, women who sell vegetables and herbs; figuratively, scolds.
202.10	*dreich*] That is, dreary.
202.35	*grews*] That is, greyhounds.
203.16	*when the king was at Embro'*] George IV spent two weeks in Edinburgh in 1822; he thus became the first reigning monarch to visit Scotland since Charles II.
203.19	*misleered*] That is, misinformed, unmannerly, or rude.
203.22	*sloongin'*] That is, slounging, or loafing about.
203.31	*throuther*] Probably throughither; that is, in confusion, or among each other.
208.17-18	*dandy chaps . . . grasped about the middle*] In the early nineteenth century a fashionable gentleman often wore a corset, or basque belt, "to give the desired small waist and corseted look." See R. Turner

Wilcox. *The Dictionary Of Costume*. New York: Scribner's, 1969, p. 19.

211.12   *the fair of Buchlyvie*] Buchlyvie, a village on the western border of the parish of Kippen in Stirlingshire (now Stirling District, Central Region), held "fairs on 26 June and 18 Nov." See *Ordnance Gazetteer Of Scotland*. Vol. 1, p. 198.

212.30   *Kippen*] The parish of Kippen was the scene of a "famous Covenanters' conventicle, for celebration of the Lord's Supper," in 1676; the parish also mustered "between 200 and 300 men" who fought for the Covenanters "in the battle of Bothwell Bridge" in 1679. See *Ordnance Gazetteer Of Scotland*. Vol. 4. 1883, p. 412.

215.19-20   *the fair o' Kippen and the Balloch*] A "cattle fair" was held at Kippen "on the second Wednesday of December"; Balloch, a village in Dumbartonshire (now Dumbarton District, Strathclyde Region), had "a cattle fair" on 17 April and a large "horse fair" on 15 September. See *Ordnance Gazetteer Of Scotland*. Vol. 1, p. 115, and Vol. 4, p. 412.

217.3-6   *When ony body cums to this kintra to settle, by applyin' to comishoners appointit by the Governor, he gets a hunder ackers o' lan'; and if he hae a family, aiblins he'll get mair*] In Nova Scotia in the early 1820s crown lands, often in lots of one hundred acres, could be distributed by a warrant from a prominent individual like Edward Mortimer of Pictou; in 1821, for example, William MacKay, the District Surveyor, recorded that "By a warrant from the late Ewd. Mortimer Esqr. Pictou," he had "layed out unto Donald MacPherson one hundred acres, unto Owen MacPherson one hundred acres, and unto John MacPherson one hundred acres on MacLellan's Mountain." It was also possible for an individual to apply for land to the Board of Land

Commissioners in the district in which he wished
to settle; in August 1821, for instance, the *"Board
of Land Commissioners in the District of Pictou"*
granted a "Location Ticket" to Paul Fraser "to
settle upon the Land described . . . containing
Two hundred Acres . . . upon the express Condi-
tion of your building a House, and settling upon
the said Lot . . . within twelve Months." See PANS,
Crown Lands, Pictou County, 1774-1859, RG 20,
Series "C," Vol. 40, and PANS, Provincial Secre-
tary's Records, RG 7, Vol. 2, No. 109.

217.23   *mailen*] That is, mailing, or rented farm.

218.31-32   *Their fermin' is something like what we used to see about
                Fintry when we war herd callans*] Fintry, a parish in
                Stirlingshire (now Stirling District, Central
                Region), had a small population and little farm-
                ing. In 1801, for example, it had only "958" inhab-
                itants, and in the 1870s "only 1020" of its "13,881
                acres" were "in tillage and 100 under wood, the
                rest of the land being either pastoral or waste."
                See *Ordnance Gazetteer Of Scotland*. Vol. 3. 1883, p.
                29.

219.2   *gabert*] That is, a barge, or a small inland sailing
                vessel.

219.14   *plooky*] That is, plouky, or pimply.

220.36-221.1   *the scriptures say o' the locusts . . . they devoor every
                green thing*] Compare Exodus 10:15; one of the
                plagues that God sent upon the Egyptians to force
                them to let the Israelites go, the locusts "covered
                the face of the whole earth, so that the land was
                darkened; and they did eat every herb of the land,
                and all the fruit of the trees which the hail had
                left: and there remained not any green thing in
                the trees, or in the herbs of the field, through all
                the land of Egypt." See *IB*. Vol. 1, p. 909.

221.4   *Yanky cakes*] Probably fried cakes or doughnuts;

compare, for example, a nineteenth-century rec-
ipe for "Fried Cakes":

> Three eggs, two and one-half cups sweet
> milk, two cups sugar, two teaspoons of cream
> of tartar, one of soda; spices to taste; roll out
> and cut in shapes, and fry in boiling lard;
> while hot dip in fine sugar.

See *The Home Cook Book*. Compiled From Recipes
Contributed By Ladies Of Toronto And Other
Cities And Towns. St. John, N. B.: R.A.H. Mor-
row, 1878, p. 301.

221.4   *to gar a soo scunner*] Literally, to make a sow sick.

221.7   *fosy*] That is, fozy, or soft, spongy.

221.8-10   *parritch . . . drammock*] This diet of oatmeal, cab-
bage, and peas prepared in various ways, some-
times with salt, butter, and milk or water,
represents "the diet of the ordinary people, the
peasant farmers, cottars and labourers" of Scot-
land in the early nineteenth century. See
Mitchison. *Life in Scotland*, pp. 70-74.

221.13-14   *Ae family in our toon, will devoor as muckle flesh as a
hail baronry in Balfron*] Balfron, a parish in
Stirlingshire (now Stirling District, Central
Region), was divided into fourteen baronries, or
large freehold estates; in 1801 their population
was "1634," and in 1831 "2057." See *Ordnance
Gazetteer Of Scotland*. Vol. 1, pp. 110-11.

222.5-7   *The kintra's owergane wi' lazy vagabonds, wha . . . tak
up the preechin'*] The number of unorthodox sects
among dissenting Protestants and the character of
their poorly-educated preachers were subjects of
general concern in Nova Scotia in the 1820s. An
anonymous writer in the *Acadian Recorder* in 1821,
for example, explains that the "many strange and
surprising scenes . . . among dissenters . . . cannot
but excite the aversion and awaken the contempt

of well educated" clergymen in the Church of England:

> The precincts of learning are daily invaded by the intrusions of ignorance; and the sacred functions of the christian priesthood are usurped by self-appointed prophets, of the lowest intellectual form. . . . No wonder that the risible faculties of churchmen are awakened when they see a blacksmith leaving his forge and bellows to blow the flame of party zeal; a cobler leaving his stall to teach the mysteries of religion; and a knight of the thimble springing from the shop board to the pulpit, and preaching with as much popularity as if he had fallen down from Jupiter. Such preachers are often a disgrace to the cause of dissent, and even to christianity itself.

See *Acadian Recorder*, 17 March 1821, p. [2].

222.18-21   *ane o' them in the neist province, that ca'd himsel John the Babtist, endit wi' cuttin' his sister's throt, and gat himsel hang't for the deed*] In February 1805 Amos Babcock, a poor fisherman and farmer from the Shediac area of New Brunswick and a follower of the late Henry Alline's enthusiastic New Light movement, became convinced that Christ was about to return to earth and, in a fit of religious frenzy witnessed by his mesmerized family, knifed to death his sister, Mercy Hall, whom he perceived to have fallen from grace. Babcock, found guilty of murder, was hanged in June 1805. Jacob Peck, another New Light adherent who referred to himself as "John the Baptist," was one of those who had helped stir up the murderer to his destructive zeal. See *The Newlight Baptist Journals of James Manning and James Innis*. Ed. D. G. Bell. Saint John:

Acadia Divinity College and the Baptist Historical Committee of the United Baptist Convention of the Atlantic Provinces, 1984, pp. 182-86, and 331-54.

224.20-21   *some prenter body about Fa'kirk*] Falkirk, a busy market town in southeastern Stirlingshire (now Falkirk District, Central Region), had "an extensive retail trade" and was the centre of commerce for a large district that included Balfron, Fintry, and the other places mentioned by Scantocreesh. See *Ordnance Gazetteer Of Scotland*. Vol. 3, p. 3.

226.20-21   *Lord Byron and Sir Walter Scott show me how renowned lame writers may be*] George Gordon, Lord Byron, was born with "a deformed right foot"; Sir Walter Scott writes that he had a "shrunk and contracted" right leg as a result of a bout of poliomyelitis when he was eighteen months old. In the early 1820s both were very popular authors. See Leslie A. Marchand. *Byron A Biography*. Vol. 1. New York: Alfred A. Knopf, 1957, p. 25, and J. G. Lockhart. *Memoirs Of The Life Of Sir Walter Scott, Bart*. A New Edition. Edinburgh: Robert Cadell, 1842, p. 6.

228.8-9   *the Nine Mile House*] A well-known landmark in Lower Bedford, the house was opened as an inn in 1819 and became a favorite spot for Haligonians to entertain and to honeymoon. "The *old* Nine Mile House, Bedford Bason," burned down in 1860. See *Acadian Recorder*, 6 May 1860, p. [3], and Elsie Tolson. *The Captain, the Colonel and me. (Bedford, N.S., since 1503)*. Sackville, New Brunswick: Tribune Press, 1979, pp. 105-06.

229.22-23   *His . . . sure*] Isaiah 33:16; the prophet says of the righteous man, "He shall dwell on high; his place of defense *shall be* the munitions of rocks: bread shall be given him; his waters *shall be* sure." See *IB*. Vol. 5, p. 352.

230.12-13   *it contains some, who, in the great day of account, will be adjudged worthy to walk in white*] Compare Revelation 3:4; the angel of Revelation tells John to write to the church in Sardis, "Thou hast a few names even in Sardis which have not defiled their garments; and they shall walk with me in white: for they are worthy." See *IB*. Vol. 12, p. 391.

233.22-25   *William's great grandfather had been taken, to cement with his blood in the Grass Market of Edinburgh, that noble structure of civil and religious privilege which is the glory of Scotland*] In the second half of the seventeenth century, "many Covenanters went uncomplainingly to their deaths in a mood of religious exaltation at the hands of the public executioner in the Grassmarket" in Edinburgh. See Trevor Royle. *Precipitous City*. Edinburgh: Mainstream Publishing, and New York: Taplinger Publishing, 1980, p. 64.

235.17-18   *What is the man profited, who gains the world and loses his soul?*] Compare Matthew 16:26; Jesus asks his disciples, "For what is a man profited, if he shall gain the whole world, and lose his own soul? or what shall a man give in exchange for his soul?" See *IB*. Vol. 7, p. 456.

238.22-24   *he felt that he himself had fled from the presence of his father, and he thought upon Jonah*] Compare Jonah 1: 1-4; Jonah, ordered by God to go to Nineveh, flees instead by ship "unto Tarshish from the presence of the LORD." But God "sent out a great wind into the sea, and there was a mighty tempest in the sea, so that the ship was like to be broken." See *IB*. Vol. 6. 1956, pp. 875-80.

239.35-240.1 *His first thought was of Vanity Fair: but he thought not of Yielding*] Compare John Bunyan, *The Pilgrim's Progress*, 1678; Christian and Faithful, on their way to the Celestial City, have to go through a town called Vanity,

> and at the Town there is a Fair kept called
> *Vanity-Fair*: It is kept all the year long, it
> beareth the name of *Vanity-Fair*, because the
> Town where it is kept, *is lighter than Vanity*;
> and also, because all that is there sold, or that
> cometh thither, is *Vanity*.

Christian and Faithful are arrested in Vanity Fair because they will not yield to its wares; they are both beaten, caged, and put on trial; in the end, although Christian escapes, Faithful is "Scourged," "Buffeted," "Stoned," and "last of all . . . burned . . . to Ashes at the Stake." See John Bunyan. *The Pilgrim's Progress from this World to That which is to Come*. Ed. James Blanton Wharey. Oxford: At the Clarendon Press, 1928, pp. 94-104.

242.30-32   *"Herein . . . disciples"*] John 15:8; Jesus, teaching his disciples, says, "Herein is my Father glorified, that ye bear much fruit; so shall ye be my disciples." See *IB*. Vol. 8, p. 719.

247.23-24   *I have been at Mount Tom and over the Cumberland mountain*] In *The Geography And History Of Nova Scotia* (1864), "Authorized By The Council Of Public Instruction For Nova Scotia," the "COBEQUID MOUNTAINS" are described as "extending from Cape Chiegnecto, in the west of Cumberland, through Colchester to the borders of Pictou County, terminating in several isolated peaks, as Mount Thom and Roger's Hill"; "Great Cumberland Mountain," located in Cumberland County near the communities of Westchester and Westchester Station, is also part of the range. The highest peak in the chain is, according to *The Geography*, "1,100 feet." See J. B. Calkin. *The Geography And History Of Nova Scotia, With A General Outline Of Geography, And A Sketch Of The British Possessions in North America*. New And Revised Edition. Halifax: A. & W. Mackinlay, Publishers, 1864, p. 41, and PANS, Petitions, Petition regarding "damage alteration of road foot of Great Cumberland Mountain," 1840, RG 5, Series GP, Vol. 8, No. 74.

258.16-17   *he tells you in the same breath, that he is ignorant of Longinus and a judge of literature*] *On the Sublime,* a work written in Greek on the qualities of great literature, is usually attributed to Longinus; from the late seventeenth to the early nineteenth centuries, this critical treatise, probably dating from the first century A.D., was particularly influential.

262.32-34   *It was the habitation of God; and whether gladness or sorrow intervened, the peace which passeth all understanding, was the portion of its inmates*] Compare Philippians 4:6-7; Paul, urging the Philippians to "Be careful for nothing; but in every thing by prayer and supplication with thanksgiving let your requests be made known unto God," concludes, "And the peace of God, which passeth all understanding, shall keep your hearts and minds through Christ Jesus." See *IB.* Vol. 11, pp. 113-14.

263.17-19   *A child trained up in the way that he should go, does not so easily part with the impressions of his youth*] Compare Proverbs 22:6, "Train up a child in the way he should go: and when he is old, he will not depart from it." See *IB.* Vol. 4, p. 907.

272.5-7   *Blessed be he who has said, I will not fail thee nor forsake thee: Even to old age I am he: I have made and I will bear*] Compare Joshua 1:5, in which the Lord says to Joshua, "as I was with Moses, *so* I will be with thee: I will not fail thee, nor forsake thee," and Isaiah 46:4, in which God promises the house of Jacob, "And *even* to *your* old age I *am* he; and *even* to hoar hairs will I carry *you*: I have made, and I will bear." See *IB.* Vol. 2, p. 554, and *IB.* Vol. 5, p. 539.

272.16-17   *Yet he has said, I will make darkness light before them*] Isaiah 42:16; as part of God's promise to Israel, He says, "And I will bring the blind by a way *that* they knew not; I will lead them in paths *that* they have not known: I will make darkness light before them, and crooked things straight." See *IB*. Vol. 5, p. 474.

272.17   *He feeds the ravens*] Compare Luke 12:24; Jesus, teaching his disciples, says, "Consider the ravens: for they neither sow nor reap; . . . and God feedeth them: how much more are ye better than the fowls?" See *IB*. Vol. 8, p. 227.

272.18   *there can be no want to them that fear him*] Compare Psalms 34:9, in which the psalmist sings, "O fear the LORD, ye his saints: for *there is* no want to them that fear him." See *IB*. Vol. 4, p. 179.

273.31-33   *We know . . . morning*] Compare Job 19:25, in which Job, answering Bildad the Shuhite, asserts, "For I know *that* my Redeemer liveth," and Psalms 30:5, in which the psalmist, praising the Lord, sings, "weeping may endure for a night, but joy *cometh* in the morning." See *IB*. Vol. 3, p. 1051, and Vol. 4, p. 160.

275.9-13   *I would just say to your correspondent of last week, that dating his communication from Pictou, and ascribing to me the notices contained in the Free Press, are a sort of bait which even gulls can detect*] In its issues of 5 and 11 March 1823 the *Free Press* published a series of four items regarding the identity of Censor, particularly the allegation that he was a prominent legal figure. In a letter dated "Pictou, March 14, 1823," "A REAL F.———." announced that the "extract, the note, and the remark before and after" in the *Free Press* were really "a contrivance" of Mephibosheth Stepsure "to vent his wrath on somebody for the affront offered to his writings." This letter was published in the *Acadian Recorder* on 22 March 1823, one week before Stepsure's second letter on Censor appeared as the last of the second series. See *Acadian Recorder*, 22 March 1823, p. [2], and *Free Press*, 5 March 1823, p. 35, and 11 March 1823, p. 39.

275.13   *Mr. Ward*] Edmund Ward, the editor of the *Free Press*, which he had begun in 1816; Ward and the *Free Press* were continually doing battle with the more liberal *Acadian Recorder* and its contributors. See *DCB*. Vol. 8, pp. 922-23.

281.15-16   *as bright as Day & Martin*] Day & Martin's Blacking, an English product, was advertised for sale by two Halifax grocers, John Albro, "No. 128, Hollis street," and William and Edward Wallace, "33, George-Street, Market square," in the *Acadian Recorder* in 1821. See *Acadian Recorder*, 13 January 1821, p. [1].

Description of Authoritative Versions of the Work

The following provides a description of the two manuscripts that contain most of the text of *The Mephibosheth Stepsure Letters*, the twenty-five letters published in the *Acadian Recorder*, and the "William" story published in *Colonial Gleanings*. In the description of the newspaper version letters noted as being preceded by a "[rule]" begin part way down a column; the first and last words of each letter are provided.

"The Chronicles of our Town"

"The Chronicles of our Town" is McCulloch's holograph copy, written in black ink, of the eighteen Stepsure letters that he sent to Scotland in November 1822. The manuscript originally consisted of one hundred and fourteen unnumbered leaves of white wove and unlined rag paper bearing the watermark "GW 1816" and measuring 240 × 198 mm. The leaves were sewn together; now, however, the thread has loosened and one leaf is missing.

Leaf [1] has written on its recto the half-title "The Chronicles of our Town"; its verso is blank. Leaf [2], the title-page of the manuscript, has inscribed on its recto:

The Chronicles of our Town | Or | Or a Peep at America: | In a series of letters originally addressed to | the Editors of the Acadian Recorder, Hali = | fax, Nova Scotia, for the express

319

purpose of | showing our people what they never looked | at before, | By | Mephibosheth Stepsure Gent. | *Seria jocis.* Hor. | That Gentleman Mephibosheth Stepsure has given | us a picture of ourselves, which, I am sorry to say, | is too true. | Speech of the Honorable the Attorney Gene | ral at the Annual Meeting of the Central Board | of Agriculture.

Its verso is bare. Both leaves are tipped in.

Leaves [3] to [114] include the text of eighteen letters. They begin with the letter from Alexander Scantocreesh "To Willy Whooshlicat, Residenter in the Puddockdib, Parish o' Balfron" (CEECT, pp. 215-24).This letter is followed by the seventeen Stepsure letters that were published in the *Acadian Recorder* between 22 December 1821 and 11 May 1822. The text is written on the recto and verso of each leaf, except for leaf [10], which is blank, and leaf [114], which has a blank verso. Each full page of text contains twenty-seven to thirty lines. The missing leaf, which contained the last three paragraphs of Scantocreesh's letter, is leaf [9].

Leaves [3] to [114] are divided into fourteen common octavo gatherings, which are unsigned. The missing leaf and the blank leaf are the last two leaves, ([7] and [8]), at the end of the first gathering. Both this gathering and the second are unnumbered. The second, however, is number I in the sequence of thirteen gatherings that contains the seventeen letters copied from the *Acadian Recorder.* Each of Gathering II to XIII in this sequence has the relevant number recorded by McCulloch in capital Roman letters on the top left-hand corner of its first page.

Gathering [I] in this sequence begins with "Letter I." (CEECT,

p. 7) on [1ʳ] and ends with "he could have another great" (CEECT, p. 22) on [8ᵛ]. Gathering II begins with "lot of timber" (CEECT, p. 22) on [1ʳ] and ends with "in unavoidable cases." (CEECT, p. 35) on [8ᵛ]. Gathering III begins with "Mr. Soakem" (CEECT, p. 36) on [1ʳ] and ends with "And the" (CEECT, p. 48) on [8ᵛ]. Gathering IV begins with "young people" (CEECT, p. 48) on [1ʳ] and ends with "Mephibosheth Stepsure" (CEECT, p. 61) on [8ᵛ]. Gathering V begins with "Let. VI." (CEECT, p. 62) on [1ʳ] and ends with "any thing." (CEECT, p. 77) on [8ᵛ]. Gathering VI begins with "In this manner" (CEECT, p. 77) on [1ʳ] and ends with "and what = " (CEECT, p. 90) on [8ᵛ]. Gathering VII begins with "ever was wanting" (CEECT, p. 90) on [1ʳ] and ends with "But, in build = " (CEECT, p. 103) on [8ᵛ]. Gathering VIII begins with "ing the outside" (CEECT, p. 103) on [1ʳ] and ends with "believe them to be" (CEECT, p. 118) on [8ᵛ]. Gathering IX begins with "silly women" (CEECT, p. 118) on [1ʳ] and ends with "shame." (CEECT, p. 133) on [8ᵛ]. Gathering X begins with "Still it must be admitted," (CEECT, p. 133) on [1ʳ] and ends with "his genius soared" (CEECT, p. 147) on [8ᵛ]. Gathering XI begins with "far above chopping and rolling." (CEECT, p. 147) on [1ʳ] and ends with "a farmer can" (CEECT, p. 161) on [8ᵛ]. Gathering XII begins with "no more work" (CEECT, p. 161) on [1ʳ] and ends with "contains a" (CEECT, p. 176) on [8ᵛ]. And Gathering XIII begins with "large fund" (CEECT, p. 176) on [1ʳ] and ends with "Mephibosheth Stepsure Gent." (CEECT, p. 190) on [8ʳ].

Some time after "The Chronicles of our Town" was sent by McCulloch to Scotland, it was gone through by at least one person who occasionally pencilled in corrections and revisions of a word or passage and at various places added, again in pencil, either an "#" or an "X." Neither the source or sources of these marks nor the reason for their being made can now be ascertained.

"The Chronicles of our Town" was given to the Public Archives of Nova Scotia in 1936 by McCulloch's granddaughter, Miss Isabella McCulloch. It is now held in the McCulloch Papers, MG1, Vol. 555, No. 82.

"William"

"William" is McCulloch's holograph copy, written in black ink, of the story that had originally appeared as part of the second book of Stepsure letters published in the *Acadian Recorder* from 28 December 1822 to 29 March 1823. The manuscript, prepared initially for submission to the *Edinburgh Christian Instructor*, was most likely taken by McCulloch himself to Scotland in 1825 where it was accepted for publication, along with McCulloch's story "Melville," by William Oliphant of Edinburgh. The manuscript was used as printer's copy when Oliphant prepared *Colonial Gleanings. William, And Melville* for publication in January 1826.

The manuscript originally consisted of twenty loose leaves of the same size and quality of paper as used in "The Chronicles of our Town," that is, white wove and unlined rag paper bearing the watermark "GW 1816" and measuring 240 × 198 mm. The text of the story was inscribed on the recto and verso of each leaf, except for the verso of each of leaves [6] and [12], which were blank. There are approximately twenty-seven to thirty lines of text per page. Each page is numbered in the top left-hand corner. Leaves [5], [7], and [10], that is, pages 9-10, 13-14, and 19-20, are missing from the manuscript.

The first page begins with the address "To the Editor of the

Christian Instructor" and continues with a note to the editor commencing "Sir," and reading:

> By inserting the following little narative in your valuable paper, you will afford useful information to parents who feel inclined to send their children abroad. It is part of a series of sketches originally published in this province, and generally admitted to be an exact representation of North American manners. They that will be rich, fall into temptation and a snare, and into many foolish and hurtful lusts, which drown men in destruction and perdition.

"I Tim 6 9" has been added below "destruction and perdition." The note is signed "Pictou, Nova Scotia." The address, the note, and the signature are crossed out.

The story begins in the middle of the first page after the title "William" (CEECT, p. 228). The text is then continuous until the end of p. 8, which ends "who had returned" (CEECT, p. 234). The text in the manuscript recommences on the top of p. 11, which begins "Here is the rule" (CEECT, p. 235). The last words, half-way down on p. 11, are "*of Christ*" (CEECT, p. 236). The text in the manuscript then recommences at the top of p. 15 with "upon Jonah" (CEECT, p. 238) and ends at the bottom of p. 18 with "But this" (CEECT, p. 241). The text then runs continuously from the top of p. 21, which begins "temptation is" (CEECT, p. 243), to the bottom of p. 23, which ends "grandfather's ivy" (CEECT, p. 245). After the blank and unnumbered p. [24] the top of p. 25 begins with "To the Editor of the Christian Instructor," "Sir," and the sentence "Your readers will recollect that William had succeeded to his father in law's business." These are all crossed out, and the text recommences "As William had succeeded" (CEECT, p. 261). It then runs continuously to the bottom of p. 40, which ends "spirits" (CEECT, p. 274).

"William" was given to the Public Archives of Nova Scotia in 1936 by McCulloch's granddaughter, Miss Isabella McCulloch. It is now held in the McCulloch Papers, MG1, Vol. 555, Nos. 53-68.

Acadian Recorder

First Series

Letter 1

Vol. 9, No. 51 (22 December 1821)

Text: p. [2] cols. 2-5

> [rule] | *To the Editors of the Recorder.* | [rule] | Gentlemen,— | Happening some time ago . . . my neighbour's trading career. | [signed] MEPHIBOSHETH STEPSURE.

Letter 2

Vol. 10, No. 1 (5 January 1822)

Text: p. [2] col. 6 - p. [3] col. 3

> [rule] | Number 2. | *To the Editors of the Recorder.* | Gentlemen— | Soon after . . . the rest of the company. | [signed] Mephibosheth Stepsure.

Letter 3

Vol. 10, No. 2 (12 January 1822)

Text: p. [2] col. 4 - p. [3] col. 1

> [rule] | Number 3. | *To the Editors of the Recorder.* | Gentlemen— | I formerly observed . . . and the grog before him. | [signed] Mephibosheth Stepsure.

Letter 4

Vol. 10, No. 3 (19 January 1822)

Text: p. [2] cols. 1-3

> Number 4. | *To the Editors of the Recorder.* | Gentlemen— | Though your paper affords . . . from going at large. | [signed] Mephibosheth Stepsure.

Letter 5

Vol. 10, No. 4 (26 January 1822)

Text: p. [2] cols. 1-3

> Number 5. | *To the Editors of the Recorder.* | [rule] | Since my last letter . . . driven out of the land. [signed] M. S.

Letter 6

Vol. 10, No. 5 (2 February 1822)

Text: p. [2] cols. 1-2

> Number 6. | *To the Editors of the Recorder.* | Gentlemen, | According to promise . . . tell them about the last. | [signed] Mephibosheth Stepsure.

Letter 7

Stranger's Letter

Vol. 10, No. 5 (2 February 1822)

Text: p. [2] cols. 2-3

> [rule] | *To the Editors of the Recorder,* | Gentlemen, | The province has now arrived . . . farther investigation. | [unsigned]

Letter 8

Vol. 10, No. 6 (9 February 1822)

Text: p. [2] cols. 2-5

> [rule] | Number 7. | *To the Editors of the Recorder.* | Gentlemen, | Calling upon our parson . . . as Bill Scamp did old William. | [signed] Mephibosheth Stepsure.

Letter 9

Vol. 10, No. 8 (23 February 1822)

Text: p. [2] cols. 3-6

> [rule] | Number 8. | *To the Editors of the Recorder.* | Gentlemen, | I have somewhere read . . . I began the world. | [signed] Mephibosheth Stepsure.

Letter 10

Vol. 10, No. 10 (9 March 1822)

Text: p. [2] cols. 2-5

> [rule] | Number 9. | *To the Editors of the Recorder.* | Gentlemen, | I formerly stated . . . which a farmer ought to desire. | [signed] Mephibosheth Stepsure.

Letter 11

Vol. 10, No. 11 (16 March 1822)

Text: p. [2] cols. 1-3

> Number 10. | *To the Editors of the Recorder.* | Gentlemen, | During the first year . . . and what are its fruits. | [signed] Mephibosheth Stepsure.

Letter 12

Vol. 10, No. 12 (23 March 1822)

Text: p. [2] cols. 1-3

> Number 11. | *To the Editors of the Recorder,* | Gentlemen, | I formerly told you . . . glad to see one another. | [signed] Mephibosheth Stepsure.

Letter 13

Vol. 10, No. 13 (30 March 1822)

Text: p. [2] cols. 1-4

> Number 12. | *To the Editors of the Recorder*, | Gentlemen, | At
> our marriage, as I stated . . . and I wear them. | [signed]
> Mephibosheth Stepsure.

Letter 14

Vol. 10, No. 15 (13 April 1822)

Text: p. [2] cols. 1-4

> Number 13. | *To the Editors of the Recorder*. | Gentlemen, | At
> our marriage, as you may recollect . . . now very willing to
> cultivate, am | [signed] Mephibosheth Stepsure.

Letter 15

Vol. 10, No. 16 (20 April 1822)

Text: p. [2] cols. 1-3

> Number 14. | *To the Editors of the Recorder*. | Gentlemen, | I
> formerly stated . . . I have been all along telling you, I am |
> [signed] Mephibosheth Stepsure.

Letter 16

Vol. 10, No. 17 (27 April 1822)

Text: p. [2] cols. 1-3

> Number 15. | *To the Editors of the Recorder.* | Gentlemen, | Since I wrote you last . . . the chronicles of our town. | [signed] Mephibosheth Stepsure.

Letter 17

Vol. 10, No. 19 (11 May 1822)

Text: p. [2] cols. 3-6

> [rule] | Number 16. | *To the Editors of the Recorder.* | Gentlemen, | Since I began to write . . . they wish to be like | [signed] Mephibosheth Stepsure, Gent.

Second Series

Letter 18

Scantocreesh (1)

Vol. 10, No. 52 (28 December 1822)

Text: p. [2] cols. 2-4

> [rule] | *To the Editors of the Accaudian Re-* | *corder,* | SIRS— | This cums to let you kno . . . remains your humle servent, | [signed] ALEXANDER SCANTOCREESH.

Letter 19

Vol. 11, No. 1 (4 January 1823)

Text: p. [2] cols. 3-5

> [rule] | Number 1. | *To the Editors of the Acadian Re-* | *corder,* | Gentlemen, | The importunity of my neighbour Scantocreesh . . . will put other thoughts in his head. | [signed] Mephibosheth Stepsure, gent.

Letter 20

Scantocreesh (2)

Vol. 11, No. 2 (11 January 1823)

Text: p. [2] cols. 2-5

> [rule] | Copy of a letter from Alexander | Scantocreesh, farmer in our | town, to Willy Whooshlicat, Re- | sidenter in the Puddockdib par- | ish of Balfron. | *Auld and respeckit frien'* | This cums to let you kno . . . humle servant to command till death, | [signed] Alexander Scantocreesh.

Letter 21

Vol. 11, No. 3 (18 January 1823)

Text: p. [2] cols. 2-5

> [rule] | Number 2. | *To the Editors of the Acadian Re-* | *corder,* | Gentlemen— | Through the importunities of my old lady . . . *me at the right hand of Christ.* | [unsigned]

Letter 22

Vol. 11, No. 4 (25 January 1823)

Text: p. [2] cols. 2-5

> [rule] | Number 3. | *To the Editors of the Acadian Re-* | *corder,* | Gentlemen— | Your readers will recollect . . . his great grandfather's ivy. | [signed] Mephibosheth Stepsure gent.

Letter 23

Vol. 11, No. 6 (8 February 1823)

Text: p. [2] cols. 1-4

> Number 4. | *To the Editors of the Acadian Re-* | *corder,* | Gentlemen, | When Censor gave me . . . I still subscribe myself. | [signed] Mephibosheth Stepsure gent.

Letter 24

Vol. 11, No. 7 (15 February 1823)

Text: p. [2] cols. 1-4

> Number 5. | *To the Editors of the Acadian Re-* | *corder,* | Gentlemen, | Your readers will recollect that William . . . the world of spirits. | [signed] Mephibosheth Stepsure gent.

Letter 25

Vol. 11, No. 13 (29 March 1823)

Text: p. [2] cols. 1-2

Number 6. | *To the Editors of the Acadian Re-* | *corder,* | Gentlemen, | YOUR readers, I dare say . . . and died in a dung heap. | [signed] Mephibosheth Stepsure gent.

Colonial Gleanings

Title-page: COLONIAL GLEANINGS. | [rule] | WILLIAM, | AND | MELVILLE. | [rule] | Their inward thought is, that their house | And dwelling-places shall | Stand through all ages—— | *Psalms.* | [rule] | EDINBURGH: | PUBLISHED BY WILLIAM OLIPHANT, 22, | SOUTH BRIDGE STREET; AND SOLD BY M. OGLE, | AND CHALMERS & COLLINS, GLASGOW; J. FIN- | LAY, NEWCASTLE; BEILBY AND KNOTTS, BIR- | MINGHAM; J. HATCHARD & SON, HAMILTON | ADAMS & CO. J. NISBET, AND J. DUNCAN, LON- | DON; AND R. M. TIMS, AND W. CURRY, JUN. & CO. | DUBLIN. | [rule] | M.DCCC.XXVI.

Size of leaf: 138 × 85 mm.

Collation: 12°, π³ A-L⁶ M⁶(− 3) [$1 and 3 signed (− M3)], 72 leaves, pp. *1-7* 8-61 *62-65* 66-144

Contents: p. [1] blank, p. [2] frontispiece, p. [3] title-page, p. [4] blank, p. [5] preface, p. [6] blank, pp. [7]-61 text of "William", p. [62] blank, p. [63] half-title for "Melville", p. [64] blank, pp. [65]-144 text of "Melville", p. 144 colophon, "EDINBURGH: | PRINTED BY J. COLLIE."

Head-titles: "WILLIAM." appears on p. [7].
              "MELVILLE." appears on p. [64].

Running-   From pp. 8-61 "WILLIAM." appears on each
titles: page. From pp. 65-144 "MELVILLE." appears on
              each page.

Notes: The NSHD copy, the only copy available for exam-
              ination, is not in the original binding. It is bound
              with the following:

              WORDS OF PEACE. | BEING AN |
              ADDRESS, | DELIVERED TO THE
              CONGREGATION OF HALIFAX IN |
              C O N N E X I O N   W I T H   T H E
              PRESBYTERIAN CHURCH OF | NOVA-
              SCOTIA, IN CONSEQUENCE OF SOME
              CON- | GREGATIONAL DISPUTES
              W H I C H   R E Q U I R E D | T H E
              INTERFERENCE OF PRESBYTERY. | *By*
              THOMAS M'CULLOCH, | PICTOU. |
              [rule] | Scripture | here | PUBLISHED BY
              A MEMBER OF THE CONGREGATION.
              | [rule] | HALIFAX: Printed by EDMUND
              WARD, at his Office, No. 15 | Barrington
              Street, | 1817.

              The NSHD copy is signed "Isabella M'Culloch" on
              the title-page on the rule just below "COLONIAL
              GLEANINGS."

Copy: NSHD PR 9298 M13 W56 J. J. Stewart Collection

Other Published Versions of the Work

The following list records the two editions and one periodical appearance of versions of the Stepsure letters published since McCulloch's death. At least one location is given for each entry.

First Canadian Edition

1862

Letters Of Mephibosheth Stepsure. Reprinted from the *Acadian Recorder* Of the years 1821 and 1822. Halifax: H. W. Blackadar, Buckingham Street, 1860.
  Copies: NBSAM Macleod Collection (no call number); NSWA A 819.7 M131 23148 John D. Logan Collection; NSWA A 819.7 M131 32569
  Note: The title on the cover correctly gives 1862 as the date of publication. These copies have been microfilmed for CEECT.

Eastern Chronicle
(Book One, Letters 1-4)

1882

"Letters Of Mephibosheth Stepsure." *Eastern Chronicle* (New

Glasgow, Nova Scotia). Reprinted from the *Acadian Recorder* of
the year 1821 and 1822. Letter I, 20 April-27 April 1882;
Letter II, 27 April-4 May 1882; Letter III, 11 May-25 May
1882; Letter IV, 22 June-6 July 1882.

Copy: PANS

Note: The letters appear on the first page of the *Eastern
        Chronicle* under the heading "Miscellany" and the title
        "Letters Of Mephibosheth Stepsure." On 20 April
        1882 the introduction to the letters acknowledges the
        author as "the late Rev. Dr. Thomas McCulloch, Min-
        ister of Prince St. Church, Pictou, a gentleman of
        whose versatile talents Nova Scotia, as the country of
        his adoption, is justly proud."

Second Canadian Edition

1960

The Stepsure Letters. Thomas McCulloch. Originally published
under the title *Letters Of Mephibosheth Stepsure.* Introduction:
H. Northrop Frye. Note on Thomas McCulloch: John A.
Irving. Bibliographical Note: Douglas G. Lochhead. General
Editor: Malcolm Ross. New Canadian Library, No. 16.
[Toronto]: McClelland and Stewart Limited, [1960].

Copy: OOCC

Note: The date of publication appears on the verso of the
        title-leaf. No place of publication is indicated. There
        have been several later printings of this edition.

Variants in the Manuscript Copy-texts

This table records McCulloch's revisions that affect meaning in "The Chronicles of our Town" and in "William." Each entry in this list is keyed to the CEECT edition by page and line number and to either "The Chronicles of our Town" or "William." The entries are keyed to "The Chronicles of our Town" by gathering, leaf, and either the recto (ʳ) or the verso (ᵛ) of each leaf. They are keyed to "William" by page number. In each entry the reading of the CEECT edition is given to the left of the square bracket; the rejected reading in the manuscript to the right. A wavy dash indicates that the same word as in the CEECT edition appears in the rejected reading.

"The Chronicles of our Town"

7.2	*I* [1ʳ]	Acadian] Halifax
10.35	*I* [2ᵛ]	converting] selling
15.3	*I* [5ʳ]	his] *omitted*
23.36	II [1ᵛ]	clergyman] parson
23.36	II [1ᵛ]	parson] old gentleman
30.7	II [5ʳ]	that of] *omitted*
35.2	II [8ʳ]	much] fast
37.16	III [2ʳ]	it] *omitted*
49.22	IV [1ᵛ]	other] *omitted*
50.14	IV [2ʳ]	as he said,] *omitted*
54.9	IV [4ʳ]	had] *omitted*
56.11	IV [5ᵛ]	meet] ~ with
73.14	V [6ᵛ]	hard work] a great deal to do
82.29	VI [4ᵛ]	say] therefore ~
83.24	VI [5ʳ]	too,] *omitted*
84.1	VI [5ʳ]	shall] will
88.21	VI [7ᵛ]	saved] spared
88.29	VI [8ʳ]	shall] will
93.35	VII [2ᵛ]	recollect,] ~, that

96.4	VII [4ʳ]	In] I formerly stated, that, with a lot of land, a few acres chopped, and a pair of lame legs, I began the world. ~
104.20	VIII [1ʳ]	projecting] standing
110.28	VIII [4ᵛ]	and rain] rain
122.18	IX [3ʳ]	you] *omitted*
123.15	IX [3ᵛ]	complaining of her husband;] *omitted*
126.4	IX [5ʳ]	each of the latter] the latter of each
128.31	IX [6ᵛ]	that came] which came
132.28	IX [8ᵛ]	young] *omitted*
140.4	X [4ᵛ]	running] *omitted*
149.30	XI [2ʳ]	all] *omitted*
152.2	XI [3ʳ]	his] their
179.4	XIII [2ʳ]	my own life] our town
182.30	XIII [4ʳ]	is] are
217.5	A [2ʳ]	and] *omitted*
221.35	A [5ᵛ]	his] *omitted*

"William"

231.6	4	plantations] estates
233.12	7	and gold] or gold
234.9	8	long been] been long
238.34	15	pictured] depictured
240.9	16	him] them
240.9	16	his] their
261.5	25	it was] William had succeeded to[1]
262.29	27	heard] ~ there
263.14	28	was the stronger principle] were the stronger principles
263.28	28	or meanness] *omitted*
264.8	29	possessed] owned
264.12	29	public] a ~
264.17	29	attach] attached
264.29	29	collected] concentrated
265.10	30	had] *omitted*
265.23	30	it] *omitted*

267.21	33	distinguishing trait] ingredient
267.26	33	an] *omitted*
268.3	33	trade] business
268.8	33	reverses] the ~
269.5	35	plentifully supplied] is ~ ~ with
271.12	37	have] has

[1] "William had succeeded to" is the final reading in the "William" manuscript.

Emendations in Copy-texts

This list records all the emendations made in this edition of *The Mephibosheth Stepsure Letters* to its copy-texts. The copy-text for Letters 1 to 17 is "The Chronicles of our Town" manuscript. For Letters 18 to 25 the copy-text is one of the *Acadian Recorder*, "The Chronicles of our Town," the "William" manuscript, or *Colonial Gleanings*. In this list A stands for the *Acadian Recorder*; B for "The Chronicles of our Town"; C for "William"; and D for *Colonial Gleanings*. O denotes the emendations that have their source with the Oliphant editors and that are recorded on the manuscript of "William," and M the emendations made in this manuscript by McCulloch in response to the revisions suggested by the Oliphant editors. Ed indicates corrections or adjustments made in the copy-texts by the editor solely on her authority. Each entry in this list is keyed to the page and line number of the CEECT edition. In each entry the reading of the CEECT edition is given before the square bracket; to the right of the semi-colon that immediately follows the symbol denoting the source of the emendation, the original reading as found in the copy-text and the letter symbol for the copy-text are recorded. In the entries the wavy dash indicates that the same word (and nothing else) as in the CEECT edition appears in the copy-text, and the inferior carat signifies that a mark of punctuation or other accidental in the CEECT edition is omitted in the copy-text.

7.1	LETTER 1] Ed; Letter I. > B
8.11	of] A; ~ of > B
10.3	saving.] A; ~∧ > B
11.6	which] A; ~ which > B
17.1	LETTER 2] Ed; Let. II. > B
17.2	To the Editors of the *Acadian Recorder*,] Ed; *omitted* > B

17.3	Gentlemen,] Ed; *omitted* > B
23.33	was] A; ~ was > B
24.4	the] A; ~ the > B
26.15	by] A; ~ by > B
26.22	family] A; fami/ ly > B
28.1	LETTER 3] Ed; Let. III. > B
28.2	To the Editors of the *Acadian Recorder*,] Ed; *omitted* > B
28.3	Gentlemen,] Ed; *omitted* > B
31.19	the] A; ~ the > B
33.15	disease.] A; ~∧ > B
33.32	called] A; caled > B
36.22	attendants] A; attend/ ants > B
39.1	LETTER 4] Ed; Let. IV. > B
39.2	To the Editors of the *Acadian Recorder*,] Ed; *omitted* > B
39.3	Gentlemen,] Ed; *omitted* > B
42.26	therefore] A; there/ fore > B
43.6	destruction.] A; ~∧ > B
44.27	can.] A; ~∧ > B
49.19	and] A; & > B
51.1	LETTER 5] Ed; Let. V. > B
51.2	To the Editors of the *Acadian Recorder*,] Ed; *omitted* > B
51.3	Gentlemen,] Ed; *omitted* > B
56.24	talk] A; take > B
62.1	LETTER 6] Ed; Let. VI. > B
62.2	To the Editors of the *Acadian Recorder*,] Ed; *omitted* > B
62.3	Gentlemen,] Ed; *omitted* > B
64.17	according] A; accor/ ding > B
68.1	LETTER 7] Ed; *omitted* > B
68.2	STRANGER'S LETTERS] Ed; Stranger's Letters > B
68.3	LETTER 1] Ed; Let. I > B
68.4	To the Editors of the *Acadian Recorder*,] Ed; *omitted* > B

68.5	Gentlemen,] Ed; *omitted* > B
69.30	without] A; with > B
70.4	cultivation] A; cultvation > B
71.5	country] A; county > B
73.1	LETTER 8] Ed; Let. VII. > B
73.2	To the Editors of the *Acadian Recorder*,] Ed; *omitted* > B
73.3	Gentlemen,] Ed; *omitted* > B
81.37	Scantocreesh] A; Santocreesh > B
83.28	judgment] A; judment > B
85.1	LETTER 9] Ed; Let. VIII. > B
85.2	To the Editors of the *Acadian Recorder*,] Ed; *omitted* > B
85.3	Gentlemen,] Ed; *omitted* > B
85.5	tossed his] A; toss his > B
91.19	master's sons,] A; ~, ~∧ > B
91.24	of] A; ~ of > B
95.17	the] A; ~ the > B
96.1	LETTER 10] Ed; Let. IX. > B
96.2	To the Editors of the *Acadian Recorder*,] Ed; *omitted* > B
96.3	Gentlemen,] Ed; *omitted* > B
101.33	my seed] A; my ~ ~ > B
106.17-18	assure you,] A; ~, ~∧ > B
107.9	Mephibosheth] A; M. > B
108.1	LETTER 11] Ed; Let. X. > B
108.2	To the Editors of the *Acadian Recorder*,] Ed; *omitted* > B
108.3	Gentlemen,] Ed; *omitted* > B
110.8	his house] A; his ~ ~ > B
111.12	as well as] A; as well > B
111.13	good] A; ~ good > B
111.35	a hurry] A; hurry > B
114.12	off] A; of > B
118.9	Saunders'] Ed; Saunder's > B
119.1	LETTER 12] Ed; Let XI. > B

119.2	To the Editors of the *Acadian Recorder*,] Ed; *omitted* > B
119.3	Gentlemen,] Ed; *omitted* > B
121.22	additional] A; addional > B
123.10	spry.] A; ~∧ > B
126.16	times.] A; ~, > B
126.25	kind] A; ~ kind > B
131.1	LETTER 13] Ed; Let. XII. > B
131.2	To the Editors of the *Acadian Recorder*,] Ed; *omitted* > B
131.3	Gentlemen,] Ed; *omitted* > B
134.6	Scant's.] A; ~∧ > B
136.7	altogether] A; alto/ gether > B
136.13	grievous sin] A; grievous > B
137.21	transgressors] A; trans/ gressors > B
143.1	LETTER 14] Ed; Let. XIII. > B
143.2	To the Editors of the *Acadian Recorder*,] Ed; *omitted* > B
143.3	Gentlemen,] Ed; *omitted* > B
149.13	occasions] A; occasion > B
151.28	communings] A; com/ munings > B
152.3	annoy] A; an/ noy > B
155.1	LETTER 15] Ed; Let. XIV. > B
155.2	To the Editors of the *Acadian Recorder*,] Ed; *omitted* > B
155.3	Gentlemen,] Ed; *omitted* > B
161.19	tradesman.] A; ~∧ > B
163.18	neighbours.] A; ~∧ > B
164.7	recollect] A; reccollect > B
167.1	LETTER 16] Ed; Let. XV. > B
167.2	To the Editors of the *Acadian Recorder*,] Ed; *omitted* > B
167.3	Gentlemen,] Ed; *omitted* > B
172.35	displeased.] A; ~∧ > B
173.10	indulgence] A; indul/ gence > B
179.1	LETTER 17] Ed; Let. XVI. > B

179.2	To the Editors of the *Acadian Recorder*,] Ed; *omitted* > B
179.3	Gentlemen,] Ed; *omitted* > B
180.33	here] A; her > B
186.9	surely] A; sure/ ly > B
189.17	Saunders'] Ed; Saunder's > B
189.24	town,] A; ~. > B
189.26	humoured] A; humour/ ed > B
189.36	are very] Ed; ry *manuscript torn* > B
191.1	BOOK TWO] Ed; *omitted* > A
197.1	LETTER 18] Ed; *omitted* > A
197.8	toon] Ed; loon > A
198.6	Pate] Ed; Pale > A
198.22	and semple] Ed; and ~ ~ > A
198.32	them.] Ed; ~∧ > A
199.26	tongs] Ed; longs > A
200.8	to] Ed; ~ to > A
200.19	drinkin'.] Ed; ~∧ > A
202.6	Tipple's] Ed; Tip-/ le's > A
203.5	minister] Ed; minist[e]r *The e is upside down.* > A
203.13	the] Ed; she > A
203.15	him.] Ed; ~∧ > A
203.16	Scotland] Ed; Scot/ land > A
203.26	whipper-in] Ed; whip/ per-in > A
204.10	telling] Ed; ~' > A
204.11	riffraff] Ed; rlffraff > A
204.25	gude,] Ed; ~. > A
205.1	LETTER 19] Ed; Number 1. > A
205.13	acquired] Ed; ac/ quired > A
205.28	body] Ed; bo/ dy > A
207.4	ne'er do wells] Ed; ne'erdowells > A
207.8	cannot] Ed; caunot > A
207.12	connexion] Ed; connection > A
207.24	other.] Ed; ~∧ > A
208.10	expence] Ed; expense > A
208.28	writing] Ed; wri/ ting > A
209.22	complete] Ed; com/ plete > A

209.34	business] Ed; busi/ ness > A
209.35	occurred] Ed; occur/ red > A
210.28	our] Ed; onr > A
211.1	gentleman.] Ed; ~∧ > A
211.4	pocket.] Ed; ~∧ > A
211.28	Saunders] Ed; Saun/ ders > A
211.31	produced] Ed; produc/ ed > A
211.32	neighbour] Ed; neigh/ bour > A
211.35	before] Ed; be/ fore > A
212.7	existed] Ed; exist/ ed > A
212.31	enabled] Ed; ena/ bled > A
213.13	account] Ed; ac/ count > A
213.28	accompanied] Ed; ac/ companied > A
214.9-10	ne'er do wells] Ed; ne'erdowells > A
215.1	LETTER 20] Ed; *omitted* > B
215.2	Copy of a letter from Alexander Scantocreesh, farmer in our town, to] A; To > B
216.2	gat himsel stickit in some drucken quarrel] A; was stickit by the papist eedolaters > B
216.23	this] A; the > B
216.24	ony] A; an > B
216.26-27	Twa or] A; Twa > B
216.30	about] A; ~ the kintra > B
217.17	over] A; across > B
217.18	filled] A; then ~ > B
217.20-21	to this kintra a penny siller] A; a penny siller to this kintra > B
217.22-23	at ony time get] A; get at ony time > B
217.24	wha] A; that > B
218.5	and our] A; and > B
218.22	him. I] A; ~. Wi' gude helth and moderat labour, he is sure in time to hae every thing comfortable. ~ > B
218.25	on sae weel] A; sae weel on > B
218.30	and] A; ~ then > B
218.32	we used to see] A; used to be > B

218.34	syne] A; then > B
219.10	rich] A; walthy > B
219.14	the] A; ~ the > B
219.32	kind] A; sort > B
220.6-7	young fok] A; youth > B
220.7	anes] A; fok > B
220.12	aye] A; *omitted* > B
220.25	bravery] A; wastery > B
220.30	borro' or buy] A; buy or borro' > B
220.33	they're] A; they are > B
221.15	aye] A; *omitted* > B
221.34	villain] A; neerdoweel > B
221.36	neerdoweel] A; villain > B
222.5	kintra's] A; province is > B
222.6	revelashons. Then they] A; revelashons; and then > B
222.11	three nichts] A; nichts > B
222.25	ither] A; idle > B
223.8	fashed] A; ~ wi' a host and spittin' > B
223.9	maks] A; mak > B
223.10-11	does get his observes out; they're] A; gets ower wi' the croichlin', his observes are > B
223.16	hostin'] A; either ~ > B
223.23	the minister] A; Mr. Drone > B
223.23	as] A; ~ as > B
224.16	kintra's] Ed; kintta's > A
225.1	LETTER 21] Ed; Number 2. > A
225.23	expences] Ed; expenses > A
226.10	ne'er do well] Ed; ne'erdowell > A
227.21	were] Ed; wera > A
228.6	anticipated] Ed; anticipat/ ed > A
228.16	expence] Ed; expense > A
229.2	looking] Ed; look/ ing > A
230.30	this] O; the preceding > C
231.2	zealous] D; jealous > C

232.11	destruction] D; destruc-/ > C
233.6	a wealthy and a] O; the wealthy and > C
233.9	gentleman] D; gentlemen > C
233.19	remarkable] O; noted > C
233.31	road] O; street > C
234.32	mean time] Ed; meantime > D
234.34	great grandfather] Ed; ~-~ > D
235.15	reflexion] Ed; reflection > D
235.26	bible] Ed; Bible > D
237.1	LETTER 22] Ed; Number 3. > A
238.21	great grandfather] Ed; ~-~ > D
238.25	reanimated] O; reassured > C
239.19	appearance] D; general appeance > C
240.5	consisted in] O; were > C
240.5	art] O; trade > C
240.12	the masters] D; their masters > C
240.20	grasping] O; griping > C
241.6	stings] O; bites > C
241.8-9	bitters . . . re-visited.] D; bitters. During the course of the day, also, many devices to raise the wind, as it is usually termed, were employed; so that the bottle stood constantly beside them, and received the treatment of an intimate acquaintance. > C
241.13	freely] O; *omitted* > C
241.14-15	in contributing to their comfort] D; if times were low with the bottle > C
241.21	his] O; a > C
241.24	abhorrence] M; view > C
242.3	sunday] Ed; Sunday > D
242.9	sabbath] Ed; Sabbath > D
242.16	sabbath] Ed; Sabbath > D
242.36	great grandfather's] Ed; ~-~ > D
243.16	a pattern] D; the pattern > C
244.6	manifest] O; exemplify > C
244.34	fortunate] O; joyful > C
244.35	apprised] O; advertised > C
245.1-2	diminish their labours and add to their] O; combine less toil with additional > C
245.1-2	and add] Ed; & add > O

245.3	letters were] D; letter was > C
245.5	Mephibosheth Stepsure gent.] A; *omitted* > C
246.1	LETTER 23] Ed; Number 4. > A
246.4	heckling] Ed; heekling > A
246.16	theme] Ed; them > A
246.27	complete] Ed; com/ plete > A
247.2	sabbath] Ed; Sabbath > A
247.22	*region.*] Ed; ~/\ > A
248.13	conceptions] Ed; con/ ceptions > A
249.2	kicked] Ed; kick/ ed > A
249.6	themselves] Ed; them/ selves > A
249.9	character] Ed; cha/ racter > A
249.13	abominably] Ed; abomina/ bly > A
249.17	admittance] Ed; admit/ tance > A
249.22	exceedingly] Ed; ex/ ceedingly > A
249.25	wading.] Ed; ~/\ > A
249.28	particularly] Ed; par/ ticularly > A
250.22	information] Ed; informafion > A
250.27	produced] Ed; produc/ ed > A
251.8	chronicles] Ed; Chronicles > A
251.13	gentlemen] Ed; gentle/ men > A
251.23	going] Ed; go/ ing > A
252.8	creation;] Ed; ~; > A
253.9	Apollo.] Ed; ~, > A
255.8	from that] Ed; fromthat > A
255.10	answer] Ed; an/ swer > A
255.11	begged] Ed; beg/ ged > A
255.24	reminded] Ed; re/ minded > A
255.26	productions] Ed; produc/ tions > A
255.27	*region*] Ed; *regi/ on* > A
255.30	cautiously] Ed; cautionsly > A
256.6	have] Ed; *omitted* > A
256.8	chronicles] Ed; Chronicles > A
256.22	parson] Ed; Parson > A
257.10	rhyme] Ed; ryhme > A
258.17	literature] Ed; litera/ ture > A
259.7	neighbour] Ed; neigh/ bour > A

259.8	bargain.] Ed; ~∧ > A
259.10	beseeching] Ed; beseech/ ing > A
259.23	neighbour] Ed; neighbonr > A
261.1	LETTER 24] Ed; Number 5. > A
261.21	looking after] O; dunning > C
261.24	profits cannot be secured] M; gain is gone > C
262.12	woman] D; women > C
262.14	the] O; *omitted* > C
263.6	resolution] O; religion > C
263.7	shrinks] O; hastens its retreat > C
263.14	ridicule] O; shame > C
264.6-7	the respect with which he preserved it] O; its safety > C
264.11	possession] D; the ~ > C
264.24	revisiting it] O; personal visitation > C
264.34	an] O; *omitted* > C
265.3	communicate] O; give > C
265.32	executed] O; done > C
266.2	a tavern] D; the tavern > C
266.10	visiting it] O; stepping over > C
266.13	conduct] D; con-/ conduct > C
267.15	himself] D; him/ self > C
267.24	self-reproach] O; reproof > C
268.27	altered] O; bloated and slovenly > C
269.32	receptacle] O; emporium > C
270.1	wicked] O; dead > C
270.14	bereaved] D; bereav-/ > C
271.22	chastenings] D; chastening > C
272.20	hearts cling] D; heart clings > C
274.6	Mephibosheth Stepsure gent.] A; *omitted* > C
275.1	LETTER 25] Ed; Number 6. > A
275.2	To the] Ed; the > A
275.21	chronicles] Ed; Chronicles > A
276.18	profundities] Ed; pro/ fundities > A
276.22	terrific] Ed; terific > A
276.32	works.] Ed; ~∧ > A

277.16   chronicles] Ed; Chronicles > A
278.14   genius.] Ed; ~∧ > A
278.21   displayed] Ed; dis/ played > A
278.21   judgment] Ed; judgement > A
279.21   an] Ed; ~ an > A
280.11   you'd] Ed; yon'd > A

Line-end Hyphenated Compounds in Copy-texts

The compound or possible compound words that appear in this list were hyphenated at the end of a line in the copy-text used for the relevant section of this edition of *The Mephibosheth Stepsure Letters*. The copy-text for the first twenty-one entries is "The Chronicles of our Town" manuscript. After that, for the rest of the entries, a note indicating the copy-text for the next section of entries appears each time the copy-text changes. In these notes A stands for the *Acadian Recorder*; B for "The Chronicles of our Town"; C for the "William" manuscript; and D for *Colonial Gleanings*. The compound or possible compound words have been resolved in the CEECT edition in the manner indicated below. In order to decide how to resolve these words, examples of their use within the lines of the copy-text itself were sought. When, however, these compounds or possible compounds were not used other than at the end of a line in the copy-text, the *Oxford English Dictionary* was consulted for examples of how they were transcribed in the eighteenth and nineteenth centuries, and their resolution was based on this information. The words in this list are keyed to the CEECT edition by page and line number; a word appears each time it has been resolved.

IN THE FOLLOWING SECTION, THE COPY-TEXT IS B.

8.29	Goose-Hill
9.20	gumflowers
21.1	nowhere
25.22	greybeard
26.1	clapboards
26.3	weather-beaten

48.29	schoolmaster
65.8	overlooked
76.4	hard-working
91.21	blacksmith's
94.15	hymn-books
103.33	forehanded
104.14	clapboards
111.8	axe-handles
111.10	handspikes
112.18	chuffy-cheeked
121.25	clever-spoken
122.5	townsfolk
136.22	townsfolk
169.1	castle-building
174.4	priest-ridden

IN THE FOLLOWING SECTION, THE COPY-TEXT IS A.

197.11	neerdoweel
210.12	workhouse

IN THE FOLLOWING SECTION, THE COPY-TEXT IS B.

217.32	neerdoweel
220.10	clishmaclaver's
220.26	ta'booth
223.3	naebody
223.8	whenever

IN THE FOLLOWING SECTION, THE COPY-TEXT IS A.

224.8	naething
224.11	naething
229.8	overturned

IN THE FOLLOWING SECTION, THE COPY-TEXT IS D.

235.13	footsteps

IN THE FOLLOWING SECTION, THE COPY-TEXT IS C.

240.8	workmen
243.36	foreman

IN THE FOLLOWING SECTION, THE COPY-TEXT IS A.

251.5	overturned

Line-end Hyphenated Compounds
in CEECT Edition

This list records compounds hyphenated at the end of a line in this edition of *The Mephibosheth Stepsure Letters* that should be hyphenated in quotations from it. The words in this list are keyed to the CEECT edition by page and line number.

76.4	hard-working
94.15	hymn-books

Historical Collation

This list records variant readings that affect meaning between the CEECT edition of *The Mephibosheth Stepsure Letters* and each of the authoritative versions of the Stepsure letters. In this list A stands for the *Acadian Recorder*; B for "The Chronicles of our Town" manuscript; C for the "William" manuscript; and D for *Colonial Gleanings.* O indicates the changes suggested by the Oliphant editors in the manuscript of "William," and M the further revisions made in this manuscript by McCulloch as a response to the Oliphant editors. Each entry in this list is keyed to the page and line number of the CEECT edition. In each entry the reading of the CEECT edition is given to the left of the square bracket. Immediately to the right of the square bracket and before the semi-colon the letter symbol or symbols indicate the version or versions that have the same reading as the CEECT edition. Further to the right of the square bracket the variant reading or readings and the source or sources of each are recorded. Thus the entry "x.y our townsmen] C; my townsmen all > A" indicates that at page x, line y the CEECT edition and the "William" manuscript read "our townsmen" but that the *Acadian Recorder* contains the variant reading "my townsmen all." When there is more than one comparison version, a second reading appears to the right of the square bracket if each comparison text has a variant reading; the different readings are divided by a semi-colon. An identical substantive reading in each of the comparison texts is indicated by the appearance after the carat of the letter symbol for each version. When appropriate, in passages of more than ten words ellipsis dots have been used to shorten the entry. In recording the variant readings, dropped letters have been supplied, upside-down letters have been corrected, and line-end hyphens have been resolved. All these changes have been made silently. In the entries the wavy dash indicates that the same word (and nothing else) as in the CEECT edition appears in the variant reading. A note in the list indicates each time the copy-text changes.

IN THE FOLLOWING SECTION, THE COPY-TEXT IS B.

7.1	LETTER 1] *omitted* > A; Letter I. > B
7.2	*Acadian Recorder*] B; *Recorder* > A
7.7-8	we . . . still] B; is a very good sort of man; but > A
7.9	our townsmen] B; my townsmen all > A
7.12	they] B; *omitted* > A
7.18	preaching and starving] B; starving and preaching > A
7.18	as he has] B; having > A
7.20	other persons] B; others > A
7.23	at any time be found] B; be found at any time > A
7.26-27	that, by means of] B; by using > A
7.27	he would live] B; of living > A
7.29	to Polly; and a more likely couple are seldom] B; and a likelier couple were not often > A
8.2	with his produce] B; *omitted* > A
8.2	with him] B; along ~ ~ > A
8.5	not very] B; never very > A
8.6	good] B; very ~ > A
8.7	and barn] B; or barn > A
8.7	Solomon Gosling] B; Solomon > A
8.8-10	Indeed . . . needed.] B; *omitted* > A
8.11	a] B; the > A
8.18-19	originate in the want of industry] B; arise out of idleness > A
8.19	labour] B; industry > A
8.21	inclination] B; stomach > A
8.23	slow but sure] B; sure but slow > A
8.25	Gosling family] B; family of the Goslings > A
8.32	returns more prompt and lucrative] B; more prompt and lucrative returns > A

8.34	he went down to Halifax] B; my neighbour went to town > A
8.36	home] B; *omitted* > A
8.36	adapted] B; suited > A
9.3	used] B; employed > A
9.10	the riding disposition of Americans] B; America > A
9.12	town] B; township > A
9.12	the shoes] B; horse shoes > A
9.15	Accordingly, my neighbour's] B; Solomon's, accordingly, > A
9.18	provided] B; had ~ > A
9.22	viewed] B; considered > A
9.25-26	in appearance little inferior] B; little inferior in appearance > A
9.29-30	for Solomon, by becoming a merchant, had become Mr. Gosling] B; for such he had now become by becoming a merchant > A
9.31	our townsmen and their families] B; my neighbours > A
10.3-4	upon sundays, appeared so neat and genteel] B; appeared so neat and genteel upon Sundays > A
10.5	his flock had not enabled] B; I did not see that his flock had enabled > A
10.6	own] B; *omitted* > A
10.7	complacent] B; his ~ > A
10.8	improved] B; considerably ~ > A
10.9-10	most ... money] B; greater part of my neighbours being already in debt > A
10.10-11	the other traders to whom they were already in debt] B; other traders about; and considering that if they took their money to these > A
10.12	be placed] B; go > A
10.12	took] B; carried > A
10.13	very] B; *omitted* > A
10.14	also] B; *omitted* > A
10.18	succeeded] B; followed > A

10.21	cash] B; money > A
10.22	had] B; *omitted* > A
10.23	money, now] B; cash > A
10.24	cordiality] B; present ~ > A
10.26	little] B; nothing > A
10.26	books] B; his ~ > A
10.28	he] B; my neighbour > A
10.28	these] B; they > A
10.29	beside paying them] B; he would be able to pay them all > A
10.29	he would] B; and > A
10.32	the Lines] B; Passamaquoddy > A
10.32	that] B; who > A
10.34	they] B; *omitted* > A
10.35-36	by converting his farm into goods, had just commenced trader] B; had just commenced trader by selling his farm > A
11.2	the latter] B; these last > A
11.4	that time] B; this time > A
11.21	standard] B; ordinary, clerical > A
11.25	very] B; *omitted* > A
12.2	or] B; and > A
12.8	Mr. Holdfast] B; *omitted* > A
12.11	hardships] B; hardship > A
12.26	work] B; ~ in a day > A
12.29-30	generally . . . praise] B; wishes to receive credit for it among his neighbours > A
12.31	take] B; happen, that it would ~ > A
13.5	recollect] B; remember > A
13.5	some] B; one or two > A
13.6-7	excellent . . . farm] B; Mr. Gosling's best marsh > A
13.14-16	admits . . . teacher] B; allows that Mrs. M'Cackle has done justice to their education > A
13.22	bid] B; bidden > A
13.23-24	and nobody . . . kitchen] B; *omitted* > A
13.28	townsfolk] B; townsfolks > A

13.29	dressing] B; dressings > A
13.30	often] B; frequently > A
13.35	attend to the business] B; look after the butter making > A
13.36	wedding] B; marriage > A
14.7	going past] B; passing > A
14.9	which] B; who > A
14.18	explore] B; examine > A
14.22-23	escaped from punishment] B; passed from observation > A
14.23-24	of driving . . . pulling] B; has yet been invented to drive a pig straight forward, but to pull > A
14.26	it] B; the unclean beast > A
14.28	about] B; round > A
14.29	the complete dispersion] B; complete discomfiture > A
14.29-32	Our . . . butter and] B; From such trials as these, you townsfolks, who have nothing else to do but to > A
14.33	separation from his family] B; unfortunate confinement > A
14.34	them] B; his family > A
14.34-35	a neighbour] B; an acquaintance > A
15.1	when I was visiting them, came] B; was come > A
15.3	the fruits of his study] B; his labour, made his visit short, and > A
15.10-11	Respecting their destination, however] B; *omitted* > A
15.11-12	a considerable diversity of opinion] B; however, a diversity of opinion about where this should be > A
15.20	Gosling family] B; Goslings > A
15.25	to supply] B; for the supply of > A
15.26-28	For . . . paper] B; As your warriors for the winter have not yet opened their campaign, I hope you will find room in your paper for the preceding accounts of my neighbour and his family > A

15.28-29   To . . . interesting] B; It will not, I know, be very
              interesting to your readers in general > A
15.31   it will be impossible for them] B; they will not be
              able > A
15.33   gratify a considerable number] B; oblige a great
              many of your readers > A
15.34   perceive] B; see > A
16.1   learn] B; hear > A
16.2   since he quitted the farming] B; *omitted* > A
16.2-6   I . . . company] B; Should you oblige them and
              myself thus far, I may be induced to send you, at
              some future period, the sequel of my neighbour's
              trading career > A
17.1   LETTER 2] Number 2. > A; Let. II. > B
17.2   To the Editors of the *Acadian Recorder*] *To the*
              Editors of the Recorder > A; *omitted* > B
17.3   Gentlemen] A; *omitted* > B
17.4   After] B; Soon after > A
17.17   Tipple's] B; Mr. ~ > A
17.23   *anither*] B; anither, after a gude deal o' fleechin'
              an frazin' to get it > A
17.25   *The foul thief*] B; Deil > A
18.10   had never been] B; never were > A
18.12   Holdfast] B; ~ the sheriff frequently > A
18.15   call in their acquaintances] B; invite theirs > A
18.20   the sheriff's] B; Mr. Holdfast's > A
18.29-30   so . . . passage] B; well secured > A
18.32-33   the hazy atmosphere of the] B; a dark > A
18.33   had made] B; makes > A
18.33   my] B; the > A
18.35   townsmen] B; townsfolk > A
18.35-36   Mr. Holdfast] B; the sheriff > A
19.6   respectable] B; very ~ > A
19.10-11   I shall, for their information,] B; for their infor-
              mation, I shall > A
19.17   the profits of] B; *omitted* > A

19.18-19	grasped . . . requires] B; tried to better their circumstances by trade > A
19.23-33	Mr. Gosling . . . town] B; my account of Mr. Gosling and himself. Far be it from Mephibosheth Stepsure, either by dry wipes or wet wipes, to attempt a reformation which worthy parson Drone has long ago given up in despair. Some of your readers, I doubt, like our clergyman's hearers, apply every thing to their neighbours. Every reasonable man must now be satisfied respecting the truth of both what I have already said, and what I have yet to say; and, therefore, I shall proceed to my account of Mr. Gosling's fellow lodgers > A
19.34	formerly] B; have already > A
19.36	arrived at] B; reached > A
20.2	that] B; this > A
20.3	running] B; ~ up > A
20.21	commenced] B; begun it > A
20.25	he] B; *omitted* > A
20.34	finish] B; have finished > A
21.2	showed their kindness by] B; were very kind in > A
21.3	people] B; folks > A
21.3	passed] B; slipt > A
21.14	folk] B; folks > A
21.15	spring] B; the ~ > A
21.20-21	both . . . humour] B; do something for him in the fall > A
21.23	knew] B; ~ well > A
21.26-27	In the morning he might jump into the woods] B; He might jump into the woods in the morning > A
21.29	who, besides] B; besides > A
21.31-32	the vessels came out to Mr. Ledger] B; Mr. Ledger's vessels came out > A

22.3   hard] B; very ~ > A
22.16   another] B; a > A
22.21   town] B; settlement > A
22.28-29   as every youngster knows,] B; *omitted* > A
23.1   in order] B; *omitted* > A
23.5   people] B; folks > A
23.7   Thus, Jack] B; Jack, thus > A
23.13   for] B; *omitted* > A
23.14   provisions] B; ~; for all which Mr. Ledger was
            bound > A
23.16-17   right there. His present number of *dittos*] B; fair
            and square. The number of dittos in his present
            account > A
23.18   for these he now found] B; he now found for
            these > A
23.22   disappointed] B; ill pleased > A
23.23   refrain from] B; avoid > A
23.24   Now, in] B; In > A
23.26   Scorem] B; ~, therefore, > A
23.27   number] B; amount > A
23.29   was] B; were > A
23.31   to get] B; get > A
23.32-33   by farming, however] B; however, by farming >
            A
23.36   clergyman] B; parson > A
23.36   parson] B; old gentleman > A
24.1   gentleman] B; man > A
24.4   almost] B; *omitted* > A
24.6   lend] B; ~ out > A
24.11   folks] B; people > A
24.12-13   to be] B; be > A
24.18   say] B; declare > A
24.24-25   the occurrence of] B; *omitted* > A
24.30   hearty] B; good > A
25.9   own] B; *omitted* > A
25.10   to] B; *omitted* > A
25.20   other hand] B; contrary > A

25.24	be frequently] B; frequently be > A
26.2	the paint] B; all ~ ~ > A
26.3	stripe] B; strip > A
26.10	other articles] B; the like > A
26.15	had] B; were > A
26.18	credit] B; credits > A
26.19	returned] B; ~ home > A
26.26	would] B; used to > A
26.28	generally] B; commonly > A
26.29	Tipple's] B; Mr. ~ > A
26.34	Tipple's] B; Mr. ~ > A
26.36	prepare him for encountering domestic storm] B; fortify him against the reception of Mrs. Scorem > A
27.3	As] B; Accordingly, as > A
27.5	that he] B; which he > A
27.17	grog.] B; ~. By publishing this, you may encourage me to introduce you to the rest of the company. > A
28.1	LETTER 3] Number 3. > A; Let. III. > B
28.2	To the Editors of the *Acadian Recorder*] *To the Editors of the Recorder* > A; *omitted* > B
28.3	Gentlemen] A; *omitted* > B
28.4	in our town it has been] B; it has been, in our town, > A
28.6	the most of] B; *omitted* > A
28.7	eager] B; in general ~ > A
28.13-15	When . . . remember] B; I remember, when parson Drone came among us, he tried to persuade us > A
28.18-19	to the most of us it appeared very plain] B; it appeared very plain to the most of us > A
28.19	of us] B; *omitted* > A
28.21	you may depend upon it] B; *omitted* > A
28.21	rich] B; wealthy > A
28.24	Reverend] B; ~ Mr. > A
28.24	being last year] B; last year being > A

28.26	declares] B; affirms > A
29.7	the most] B; most > A
29.11	town] B; township > A
29.12	also] B; *omitted* > A
29.14	comfortably] B; snugly > A
29.16-17	about them very snug and thriving] B; thriving about them > A
29.23-24	shall not presume to decide] B; cannot tell > A
29.25-28	The only . . . truck] B; and says that the only objections to his opinion are, that, though our folks are great traders in watches, horses, and other things > A
30.1	town. Much] B; ~. Like most of our young folks, he began the world early. ~. > A
30.7	that of] B; *omitted* > A
30.9	good] B; great > A
30.9	soon] B; both > A
30.12	industrious activity] B; labouring > A
30.15	considerable] B; a good deal of > A
30.22	brought] B; was giving > A
30.25	his plaster concern] B; trading > A
30.27	of no use] B; mere lumber > A
30.27	was] B; ~ now > A
30.30-31	many . . . raise] B; in our town > A
30.32	possessing] B; owning > A
30.35	excites the envy of neighbours] B; has excited envy > A
31.1	so fast rich] B; rich so fast > A
31.2	were, therefore] B; therefore, were > A
31.5	a trade] B; trade > A
31.9	our] B; my > A
31.11	frequently a merchant] B; it frequently happened that merchants > A
31.13	price] B; profit > A
31.15-16	Were . . . offended] B; There is not one of my neighbours who would not kick mightily at the name of rogue > A

31.16	one] B; any > A
31.22	them all] B; the whole > A
31.25	apt] B; very ~ > A
31.26-27	plaster . . . Lines] B; plaster was now a drug at the Lines, on account of the multitude of carriers > A
31.31	purchasers] B; buyers > A
31.32	buying] B; purchasing > A
31.36	merchants] B; traders > A
32.3	to do] B; do > A
32.13	stood] B; ~ it > A
32.15	by] B; in > A
32.17	credit] B; trust > A
32.23	long] B; for a long time > A
32.25	of] B; hard with > A
32.29	you] B; *omitted* > A
32.31	she said] B; *omitted* > A
32.34	Gypsum's] B; ~ house > A
33.3	persons deprived] B; people who are from home, from the want > A
33.9	of the] B; in his > A
33.10	in] B; up > A
33.12	observe to] B; warn all > A
33.16	swelled and inflamed, and then] B; became worse and worse till it > A
33.17-19	when . . . surface] B; *omitted* > A
33.22	discovered] B; found out by mere accident > A
33.24	does not produce] B; has not > A
33.24-25	I am sure] B; *omitted* > A
33.27	Boniface] B; *omitted* > A
33.31	eager] B; very ~ > A
33.31	would] B; he ~ > A
33.33	going past] B; passing > A
33.33	Tipple's] B; Mr. ~ > A
33.35-36	town very frequently passed] B; township passed by > A
34.3	a] B; *omitted* > A
34.11	then] B; *omitted* > A

34.15	thundered in his ears] B; denounced > A
34.22	ineffectual] B; fruitless > A
34.28	told them] B; said > A
34.30	might choose] B; chose > A
34.32	temptation] B; temptations > A
34.34	wormwood and the gall] B; gall and wormwood > A
34.37	granting a licence to every person who asks for it] B; giving licenses to all who request them > A
35.1	taverns] B; the ~ > A
35.14-15	generally known in the town] B; known > A
35.20	the whole] B; whole > A
35.24-25	to take . . . hour] B; to chat an hour with them and take a glass of grog > A
35.28	corresponding exertions] B; a corresponding exertion > A
35.32-34	Besides . . . avoided] B; From the hurry of travellers, also > A
35.35-36	neglected. But this, at first, happened only] B; omitted; but, at first, this only happened > A
36.9	arrived at great] B; acquired much > A
36.11-12	When a traveller arrived, instead of bustling about as formerly] B; Instead of bustling about, as formerly, when a traveller arrived > A
36.13	growing] B; now ~ > A
36.14-15	the cooking . . . girls] B; the girls had the cooking and other in-door affairs > A
36.19	very well] B; always > A
36.20	looked] B; they ~ > A
36.31	For the sake of character, such a person] B; Such a person, for the sake of character > A
36.35	upon] B; on > A
37.4	also, learned] B; learned, also > A
37.4-5	this is a kind of knowledge, which] B; this kind of knowledge > A
37.5-6	very powerfully] B; strongly > A

37.12	perceiving how affairs] B; understanding how things > A
37.16	At] B; when, at > A
37.18	therefore, he] B; *omitted* > A
37.21	When] B; I remember, when > A
37.25	the sensible gentleman] B; he > A
37.29-30	conduct and character] B; character and conduct > A
38.2	become] B; be > A
38.10-11	those who . . . need] B; he who, instead of minding his farm, is always running about, needs > A
38.12	they halt] B; he stops > A
38.13	lazy] B; mere ~ > A
38.14-15	and fine looking girls they are] B; who are really fine looking girls > A
38.15	or] B; and > A
38.16	miseries] B; misfortunes > A
38.17	and] B; for > A
38.20	over] B; upon > A
39.1	LETTER 4] Number 4. > A; Let. IV. > B
39.2	To the Editors of the *Acadian Recorder*] *To the Editors of the Recorder* > A; *omitted* > B
39.3	Gentlemen] A; *omitted* > B
39.4	instructions] B; instruction > A
39.8	have been] B; was in former times > A
39.15	have] B; am > A
39.15	merely] B; only > A
39.24-25	in the town a great many young people] B; a great many young people in the township > A
39.25-26	took for his text these words] B; for his text, gave out this portion > A
39.28	imagined] B; thought > A
39.29	myself] B; ~ a little > A
40.1	Peter] B; old ~ > A
40.8	satisfaction] B; approbation > A
40.14	said] B; would say > A

40.14	be] B; is > A
40.17	by] B; *omitted* > A
40.20	says he, "to *home*] B; to *home*, says he > A
41.6	faces] B; countenances > A
41.10	a couple of] B; two > A
41.18	also] B; too > A
41.22	lots] B; farms > A
41.24	permit] B; admit > A
41.28	it] B; his weight > A
41.31-32	During . . . boys] B; From the hurry of the affairs, the boys were left to manage the farm > A
41.33	the] B; *omitted* > A
41.35	night] B; nights > A
41.36-42.1	done wrong; and another, neglected] B; neglected; and another thing, done wrong > A
42.5	she plainly told him] B; plainly she said to him > A
42.10	Caleb, by electioneering] B; By electioneering Caleb > A
42.12	House of Assembly] B; house > A
42.14	appointed] B; made > A
42.15	the spring] B; spring > A
42.21	upon the whole his gain] B; the prospect of profit > A
42.22	the work] B; it > A
42.33	get into] B; destroy > A
43.1	crop] B; crops > A
43.2	his] B; the > A
43.16	was] B; were > A
43.16	During] B; In the course of > A
43.20	with] B; along ~ > A
43.20-21	the prospect of bickering, and a corresponding] B; a sort of > A
43.23	disputes] B; bickerings > A
43.26	corresponding] B; proportionable > A
43.29	By these means, the] B; The > A
43.29	became] B; was now > A

43.30   was] B; *omitted* > A
43.32-33   upon either side viewed as any great hardship] B;
             considered as any great hardship upon either side
             > A
43.36   about] B; of > A
43.36   But] B; ~, I believe > A
44.2   body] B; person > A
44.4   too] B; *omitted* > A
44.7   people] B; folks > A
44.9   take] B; took > A
44.9-12   When . . . taste] B; In the course of the day, also,
             when they were quenching their own thirst; from
             respect they would ask Mr. Castup the commis-
             sioner to taste > A
44.12   much] B; a great deal > A
44.13   was not willing] B; did not wish > A
44.14   induced] B; forced > A
44.15   As] B; Being > A
44.16   then] B; *omitted* > A
44.17   set] B; would ~ > A
44.17   a good] B; an > A
44.17-18   Besides, sustaining the character of] B; As > A
44.18   he] B; also, ~ > A
44.19   and, on this account, though] B; Though > A
44.19   boys] B; own ~ therefore > A
44.21   him] B; himself > A
44.22   were] B; would be > A
44.28   little] B; no > A
44.28   late] B; *omitted* > A
44.29   profits] B; profit > A
44.30   and at last] B; when > A
44.32-35   for . . . charms] B; for home had no charms > A
44.36   occasionally returned] B; would come home > A
45.1-2   circumstance unavoidable in the life of a gen-
             tleman] B; state in which all gentlemen occasion-
             ally are, and it gave her no uneasiness > A

45.2   recurrence] B; repetitions > A
45.8   than] B; but > A
45.16   and exposed to a great variety] B; exposed to all
              kinds > A
45.22   do not know] B; cannot tell > A
45.34   seemed] B; still ~ > A
45.35   became] B; become > A
46.2-3   for a . . . home] B; nobody should see him from
              home for a long time to come > A
46.7   listeners on the outside heard strange noises] B;
              strange noises were heard by listeners in the out-
              side > A
46.9   had really become a lodger with Steer] B; really
              haunted the house > A
46.10-14   but . . . necessary] B; *omitted* > A
46.14-16   In . . . dark] B; Mr. Gawpus the new merchant, it
              is true, got himself terribly frightened by some-
              thing, in passing it one dark night afterward > A
46.20   on hand a large lot of cattle] B; a large lot of cattle
              on hand > A
46.24   cattle] B; ~ on hand > A
46.24   and, as] B; ~ had not even been allowed to go
              once out of doors; and ~ > A
46.26   give him] B; give Steer > A
46.26-27   that he might] B; to > A
46.29   early] B; younger > A
46.34   and] B; ~ from the youngsters > A
47.1-2   little business himself] B; himself little business >
              A
47.4   droves] B; drovers > A
47.9   considerably] B; a little > A
47.9-10   his evenings] B; the evening > A
47.12   chance] B; accident > A
47.14-15   from the quality of his limbs] B; *omitted* > A
47.15   concluded that] B; thought > A
47.20   parson Drone's congregation] B; the township >
              A

47.27	declared] B; said > A
47.29	will ever] B; consent > A
47.30	farther] B; further > A
48.2	for these thirty] B; these twenty > A
48.2	now fit for nothing] B; fit for nothing else > A
48.3	commencement] B; the ~ > A
48.4	of all] B; *omitted* > A
48.4	our] B; the > A
48.5	great] B; good > A
48.8-9	after waiting] B; having waited > A
48.12	on this account, had] B; therefore > A
48.15-22	frosted feet . . . labours?] B; his feet frosted is a real object of sympathy. > A
48.23-24	Peter's were beginning to mend] B; Mr Longshanks, were getting well > A
48.29-30	our schoolmaster, Mr. Pat O'rafferty] B; Mr. Pat O'Rafferty our schoolmaster > A
48.30	comrade] B; companion > A
48.32	come] B; came > A
48.35-36	with . . . day] B; which so pleased his father, that the old gentleman told him one day that > A
48.36-49.1	declared himself] B; was > A
49.1	that] B; *omitted* > A
49.4	was very willing] B; had no objection > A
49.12	done long] B; long done > A
49.12-13	the knowledge of his master] B; his master getting notice of it > A
49.15	Now, the] B; The > A
49.23	accustomed to cure] B; in the practice of curing > A
49.29	gave orders] B; ordered > A
49.33	soon learned] B; heard > A
49.34-35	been very glad to oblige] B; very gladly obliged > A
49.35-36	a little unwilling to expose himself to] B; not willing to run > A

50.1-3	during . . . But] B; he amused himself all summer with codfishing. Here > A
50.5	agreeable] B; comfortable > A
50.7	and, as] B; As > A
50.10-11	of course, he became a lodger with Tipple] B; he naturally lodged with Mr. Tipple > A
50.11	very] B; *omitted* > A
50.12-13	was for some time] B; for some time was > A
50.13	his landlord] B; Mr. Tipple > A
50.14	as he said] B; *omitted* > A
50.15	also] B; *omitted* > A
50.16	requested] B; begged > A
50.16	Pat] B; him > A
51.1	LETTER 5] Number 5. > A; Let. V. > B
51.2	To the Editors of the *Acadian Recorder*] *To the Editors of the Recorder* > A; *omitted* > B
51.3	Gentlemen] *omitted* > A, B
51.9-10	boldly girded himself with his armour] B; went out > A
51.10-11	at that season of the year] B; in a time of snow; merely because he was known to have been a man of war in his youth > A
51.13-14	in . . . described] B; any such characters, as I have described, in the province > A
51.15	as my old woman says] B; though I say it > A
51.17	neighbours'] B; neighbour's > A
51.20-21	that gentleman's kind] B; Mr. Holdfast's kindly > A
51.21-22	grateful for his] B; sensible of this gentleman's > A
51.24	too] B; *omitted* > A
51.24-25	a censorious old] B; an old censorious > A
51.28	For my own part] B; *omitted* > A
51.29	But to] B; I feel a little, however, that I should > A
51.29-52.1	is a little trying] B; *omitted* > A

52.3	spouse] B; ~ Dorothy > A
52.8	business] B; affair > A
52.13	which] B; that > A
52.20	shut out] B; secluded > A
52.21	become almost] B; I may say, become > A
52.23	derived from] B; *omitted* > A
52.26	ought to] B; should > A
52.31	axe] B; spade > A
52.33	furnish] B; supply > A
53.3	harrows] B; barrows > A
53.8	the villains] B; them > A
53.12	Beersheba] B; Bethsheba > A
53.16	I] B; ~, on the other hand > A
53.20	very] B; *omitted* > A
53.27	some] B; a little > A
53.32	his] B; ~ own > A
53.36	south] B; southward > A
54.1	cousin's] B; *omitted* > A
54.3	and they had] B; who > A
54.7	the rest] B; them since > A
54.8	signature] B; name > A
54.11	put my name to] B; sign > A
54.12	My neighbour, it would appear] B; I found that my neighbour > A
54.14	made] B; had ~ > A
54.16	positive] B; flat > A
54.18	to us] B; us > A
54.19-21	but, among . . . disappeared] B; but it produced a sad bustling among the rest of the company. The cards disappeared in a moment > A
54.24	on] B; upon > A
54.26-27	believe . . . breath] B; believe, he was received with real respect by them all; for religion forces an assent to its excellence, and the breath > A
54.32	or] B; and > A
54.35	guard] B; warn > A

54.35	and neutrality] B; *omitted* > A
54.36	beginnings] B; beginning > A
55.2	the] B; a > A
55.3	and, I] B; ~ for myself, ~ > A
55.5	our] B; the > A
55.12	else] B; or > A
55.21	Mr. Drone] B; the parson > A
55.26	throat] B; throats > A
55.30	pockets] B; pocket > A
55.35-36	leisure to moralize] B; time for moralizing > A
56.4	Here] B; When by ourselves > A
56.5	he had got into the possession of] B; the stranger had become acquainted with > A
56.6	us] B; *omitted* > A
56.8	lodged] B; had ~ > A
56.8	Tipple's] B; Mr. ~ > A
56.18	he conscientiously] B; conscientiously > A
56.24	talk] A; take > B
56.25-26	I only remember] B; All that I remember, is > A
56.27	had] B; *omitted* > A
56.27	Ricardo] B; ~, Major Torrens > A
56.28	left him] B; parted > A
56.29	to give him] B; that he would give the stranger > A
56.30	to keep] B; keep > A
56.30-31	Afterward, as] B; and afterward, when > A
56.33	speaking] B; talking > A
57.5	to] B; how ~ > A
57.10	business minutely] B; matter completely > A
57.21	completely] B; perfectly > A
57.21	Accordingly, the poor man was] B; The poor man was, accordingly > A
57.25-26	the parson] B; Mr. Drone > A
57.27	Tipple] B; Mr. ~ > A
57.30	proceeded] B; prepared > A
58.5	very much] B; generally > A

58.22	have lent] B; lend > A
58.28	that] B; *omitted* > A
58.35	shot] B; either ~ > A
59.3	that] B; *omitted* > A
59.5	feet] B; legs > A
59.5	excellent] B; fine > A
59.7	that] B; *omitted* > A
59.10	he said, were] B; was > A
59.22	guineas] B; ~; and twenty guineas in these days, were not easily got > A
59.30	on] B; upon > A
59.36	variety] B; great ~ > A
60.4	I] B; with the consent of the sheriff, ~ > A
60.6	that] B; *omitted* > A
60.6	letters] B; ~ in short hand > A
60.7-8	but . . . them] B; but it was of no use to send them, unless they were transcribed > A
60.9	but when you may receive them] B; and you may depend upon receiving them. But when this may be > A
60.12	do.] B; ~. Mephibosheth Stepsure. > A
60.13	has] B; have > A
60.15	great] B; good > A
60.16	evening] B; evenings > A
60.18	Accordingly, in his usual way] B; In his usual way, accordingly > A
61.17	events] B; ~ and departures > A
61.19	Respecting the sheriff's lodgers he] B; He > A
61.20	the vagabonds] B; them > A
61.25	Mephibosheth Stepsure] B; M. S. > A
62.1	LETTER 6] Number 6. > A; Let. VI. > B
62.2	To the Editors of the *Acadian Recorder*] *To the Editors of the Recorder* > A; *omitted* > B
62.3	Gentlemen] A; *omitted* > B
62.19	the] B; *omitted* > A
62.20	after those] B; *omitted* > A

63.3	neighbour] B; ~ Fairface > A
63.4	Saunders] B; ~ Scantocreesh > A
63.8-9	that gentleman] B; he > A
63.13	Jock] B; Jack > A
63.15	sleighs] B; chaises and ~ > A
63.16	our] B; my > A
63.17	intended to buy] B; had any design of buying > A
63.25	Saunders] B; my neighbour Scantocreesh > A
63.26	townsmen] B; townsfolk > A
63.26	joke him] B; joke Saunders > A
63.30	cash] B; money > A
63.30	hard] B; bad > A
64.2	and at last got so deep] B; but got so deep at last > A
64.4	their] B; all ~ > A
64.6	great] B; good > A
64.18	neighbours] B; near ~ > A
64.18	other] B; others > A
64.20	configurated] B; fashioned > A
64.21-22	keep a sharp look out] B; look sharp > A
64.32	he had now] B; now, he had > A
65.2	tracks] B; tracts > A
65.4	Accordingly, the trap] B; The trap, accordingly > A
65.10	foxes] B; ~; and, as a commencement of the business, he carried home with him traps to the amount of sixteen dollars > A
65.11	managed with care] B; carefully managed > A
65.19	In . . . all] B; Good farming or indeed farming at all, in such a case > A
65.23	not in] B; out of > A
65.29	gains] B; gain > A
65.30	family] B; house and ~ > A
65.30-31	rags and wretchedness] B; wretchedness and rags.—Still they contrive to keep life in > A
65.31	the town] B; for bait > A

65.34-35	in her own way too, is a very industrious woman] B; too, is a very industrious woman in her own way > A
66.8	with] B; *omitted* > A
66.16	of it] B; *omitted* > A
66.16	got off] B; lighted from > A
66.21	Ehud] B; Slush > A
66.24-25	a destructive animal] B; destructive animals > A
66.26	black] B; plenty of ~ > A
66.28	were to] B; should > A
66.33	I] B; *omitted* > A
68.1	LETTER 7] *omitted* > A, B
68.2	STRANGER'S LETTERS] B; *omitted* > A
68.3	LETTER 1] *omitted* > A; Let. I > B
68.4	To the Editors of the *Acadian Recorder*] *To the Editors of the Recorder* > A; *omitted* > B
68.5	Gentlemen] A; *omitted* > B
68.15	ruin] B; a ~ > A
68.24-25	we need] B; the province needs > A
68.25	withhold his exertions] B; be a niggard of his knowledge > A
69.15	these] B; those > A
69.16-17	I believe, is just as often] B; is just as often, I believe > A
69.17	permit] B; ~ them > A
69.18	tidings] B; the ~ > A
69.19	the labour of industry] B; hard work > A
69.21	country] B; county > A
69.24-25	of . . . his] B; a good farmer blame the country, or complain of bad > A
69.27	but] B; ~, still > A
69.29	usually] B; *omitted* > A
69.30	without] A; with > B
69.33	which are] B; *omitted* > A
69.34	of Nova Scotia] B; *omitted* > A
69.36	luxuriance] B; luxuriances > A

70.4   that] B; this > A
70.4   to] B; *omitted* > A
70.17   often] B; *omitted* > A
70.18   if] B; ~ it were > A
70.23   exists] B; is, in existence > A
70.26   or] B; nor > A
70.34   individuals] B; ~ who may lie in wait to deceive > A
71.2   gives] B; give > A
71.2   offices] B; officers > A
71.8   great] B; good > A
71.10   said chiefly] B; chiefly said > A
71.11   know] B; knew > A
71.22   there] B; these > A
71.25   depression] B; depressions > A
71.35   enjoys] B; enjoy > A
72.16   question] B; quest > A
72.17   reply] B; answer > A
72.22   embarrassment] B; embarrassments > A
72.25   xxx xxxx] B; *omitted* > A
73.1   LETTER 8] Number 7. > A; Let. VII. > B
73.2   To the Editors of the *Acadian Recorder*] *To the Editors of the Recorder* > A; *omitted* > B
73.3   Gentlemen] A; *omitted* > B
73.10   scrapes them] B; scrapes > A
73.11-13   But . . . presence] B; But work about a farm goes ill on without a master's eye > A
73.14   our . . . meet] B; he has a great deal to do to make the two ends to meet > A
73.15   if he] B; if our parson > A
73.21   the most] B; a great many > A
73.22   their] B; our > A
73.22-23   greater part of the town] B; most of us > A
73.26   he] B; the parson > A
74.1   decently] B; respectably > A
74.6   Mr. Drone says that he] B; He > A

74.7	so much] B; such > A
74.9	the parson] B; Mr. Drone > A
74.11	have escaped] B; escape > A
74.12-13	idleness, extravagance] B; extravagance, idleness > A
74.13	community] B; ~. Even our worthy clergy have not escaped his reproaches > A
74.21	services] B; labours > A
74.27	ought to subject himself to] B; is called to bear > A
74.30	to say farther] B; farther to say > A
74.32	transmit to] B; send > A
74.34	person proposes] B; man offers > A
75.6	vows] B; declares > A
75.8	on] B; *omitted* > A
75.15-17	those . . . fellows] B; villains > A
75.18	constantly] B; are ~ > A
75.19	by] B; *omitted* > A
75.20	men's] B; folk's > A
75.26	could] B; can > A
75.28-29	chronicles of our town] B; book of chronicles > A
75.30	townsmen] B; town > A
75.30	at present] B; *omitted* > A
75.32-33	they are in the fair way of improvement] B; our townsfolk are in a fair way of getting better > A
75.34	affirms] B; says > A
75.35	large stock] B; great deal > A
76.7	him] B; William > A
76.14-15	the father . . . man's] B; Gibeon Trick; whose son ran through his father's > A
76.17	boy] B; *omitted* > A
76.19	indeed] B; it is true > A
76.20	smart] B; sharp > A
76.24	do] B; to ~ > A
76.35	as it both] B; both, as it > A
77.1	toil] B; useless ~ > A

77.2	remark] B; frequently say > A
77.11-12	skin of the black fox] B; black fox skin > A
77.28	interruption] B; any ~ > A
78.1	he] B; *omitted* > A
78.8-9	for the . . . himself] B; he would have almost paid for them himself, for the sake of seeing him so fine > A
78.18	and] B; with > A
78.22	ought to] B; should > A
78.23	old] B; infirm > A
78.25	William] B; he > A
78.29	be sometimes] B; sometimes be > A
78.31	Soon after] B; Much about the same time that > A
78.34	other] B; *omitted* > A
79.2-3	at some] B; some > A
79.5	uncle the deacon's] B; uncle's the deacon > A
79.9	was at times] B; at times, was > A
79.11	badly] B; bad > A
79.13-14	very healthy and stout] B; healthy and stout, and people of this description are not the most sympathising > A
79.24	length] B; last > A
79.25	in the morning had done himself] B; had sometimes done himself in the morning > A
79.34	have scarcely] B; scarcely have > A
79.35	astonishes] B; ~ the mind > A
80.2	called] B; ~ in > A
80.3	purchasing] B; buying > A
80.18	fighting man] B; man of war > A
80.24	began to throw out] B; threw out a great many > A
80.26	was proceeding] B; began > A
80.30	for being off without delay to a lawyer] B; was for being off to a lawyer directly > A
80.35	seemed] B; appeared > A
81.3	are] B; were > A

81.12	Mr.] B; old > A
81.34	genteel] B; very ~ > A
81.37	Jock Scantocreesh] B; Jack Scantocreesh, my cousin Harrow's family > A
82.6	woman] B; ~ Dorothy > A
82.16	chaise] B; ~; and a fine chaise > A
82.26	cheated] B; ~ him > A
82.27-28	the character] B; a name > A
82.28-29	will not] B; cannot > A
82.29	true] B; exactly ~ > A
82.30	William] B; old ~ > A
82.33	happen the villain: that he] B; happen: that the villain > A
83.12	Scotch] B; the ~ > A
83.14	set] B; put > A
83.23	will soon become able] B; soon become able both > A
83.24-25	Fathers, too, who are getting old, should] B; Fathers who have become old, should also > A
84.1	shall] B; will > A
85.1	LETTER 9] Number 8. > A; Let. VIII. > B
85.2	To the Editors of the *Acadian Recorder*] *To the Editors of the Recorder* > A; *omitted* > B
85.3	Gentlemen] A; *omitted* > B
85.4	read somewhere] B; somewhere read > A
85.4	that] B; ~, at one time > A
85.13	had, in the course of his descent] B; in the course of his descent, had > A
85.20	was] B; found himself > A
85.25	only know] B; know nothing; but > A
85.27-28	about . . . poor] B; into the town very poor, about the time that I was born > A
86.12	were] B; was > A
86.15	into] B; to > A
86.17	disformed] B; deformed > A
86.18	the poor] B; poor > A

86.20	to his] B; home ~ ~ > A
87.1	had] B; *omitted* > A
87.5	about him comfortable] B; comfortable about him > A
87.13	many] B; a great ~ > A
87.18	do but] B; but do > A
87.21	before] B; ever > A
87.27	could] B; will > A
87.33	few] B; a ~ > A
87.34	could] B; can > A
87.37	lad] B; ~; and being occasionally not so well dressed as the rest of the family > A
88.2	jobs] B; things > A
88.2	work upon] B; job about > A
88.11	and] B; nor > A
88.21-22	Here your readers must not] B; Your readers must not here > A
88.29	shall] B; will > A
88.31	house] B; will ~ > A
88.32	put] B; will ~ > A
89.1	As for] B; For the > A
89.12	for] B; *omitted* > A
89.16	travel] B; travail > A
89.34	job] B; ~ of any kind > A
90.5	any of] B; *omitted* > A
90.10	boy] B; lad > A
90.15	but] B; and > A
90.19	hurry] B; ~ according to the old farming > A
90.21	both] B; not only > A
90.22	and] B; but > A
90.32	without] B; if he wanted > A
90.34	my] B; *omitted* > A
91.11	upon this subject, learn a lesson] B; learn a lesson upon this subject > A
91.13	affirms] B; often ~ > A
91.14	very] B; *omitted* > A

91.29	part] B; thing > A
91.31	woman] B; Dorothy > A
91.34	so] B; *omitted* > A
91.35	folks] B; ~ in this way > A
92.14	daughter] B; daughters > A
92.20	Indeed, the whole family] B; The whole family, indeed > A
92.25	evening] B; evenings > A
92.29	cyphering] B; ~ a little > A
93.2	legible] B; tolerably ~ > A
93.3	with] B; *omitted* > A
93.5	thus] B; so > A
93.21	stopping] B; staying > A
93.28	is] B; was > A
94.23	had] B; *omitted* > A
94.25	make] B; ~ it > A
94.26	sunday] B; the Sunday > A
94.34	ever bought] B; even brought > A
95.4	almost] B; *omitted* > A
95.12-13	passed ... evening] B; passed many an hour in the evening with pleasure and profit > A
95.22	out well] B; well out > A
95.28-29	a pair of] B; my > A
96.1	LETTER 10] Number 9. > A; Let. IX. > B
96.2	To the Editors of the *Acadian Recorder*] *To the Editors of the Recorder* > A; *omitted* > B
96.3	Gentlemen] A; *omitted* > B
96.4	In] B; I formerly stated, that, with a lot of land, a few acres chopped, and a pair of lame legs, I began the world. ~ > A
96.12	not of] B; of not > A
96.20	at] B; in > A
96.21	remarked] B; said > A
97.3	little leisure] B; not much spare time > A
97.3	and] B; so that > A
97.4	one] B; some > A

97.14	to me] B; *omitted* > A
97.24	but] B; and > A
97.29-30	my neighbour Saunders expresses it] B; Saunders Scantocreesh says > A
97.33	learn] B; see > A
98.10	propensities] B; wants > A
98.11	debt] B; debts > A
98.11	leaves] B; leave > A
98.19	by the labour] B; altogether by the labours > A
98.21-22	in order that a merchant may live, he must] B; hence, a merchant cannot live, unless he > A
98.24-25	this . . . other] B; the country, a merchant could not live, unless the one half of us could afford to pay the debts of the whole > A
98.25	a farmer, therefore] B; therefore, a farmer > A
98.36	upon] B; on > A
99.7	in the way of] B; by > A
99.9	often] B; very > A
99.10	it] B; *omitted* > A
99.11-12	were always very ungrateful when their suits were decided] B; when their suits were decided, were always very ungrateful > A
99.18	within a little brush something very inviting] B; something very inviting within a little brush > A
99.19-20	Quirk's little patch of] B; his > A
99.20	When he] B; When Quirk > A
99.25	abundance of law] B; law in abundance > A
99.26-27	on . . . said] B; as the lawyers said, on account of the intricacy of the business > A
99.32	very] B; *omitted* > A
99.34	uniformly] B; always > A
100.2	a number] B; those > A
100.5	on] B; in > A
100.6	any who proceed] B; a farmer who proceeds > A
100.7-8	their . . . farms] B; his neighbours about trespasses, or protect himself against them by selling his farm > A

100.12	The satisfaction of viewing it, I recollect] B; At that time, I recollect, the satisfaction of viewing it > A
100.19	Scruple] B; Sharp > A
100.22	the] B; away > A
100.23-24	out of curiosity, had come] B; had come out of curiosity > A
101.2	Scruple declared that Deacon Sharp] B; Sharp declared that Deacon Scruple > A
101.6	creature] B; ~; and, that when Meph was so careful to fence out other people's cattle, he had better take care not to send his own about his farm > A
101.18-20	though . . . people] B; they are in general very good people > A
101.21	assist] B; help > A
101.26	minds] B; ~, condoling > A
101.28-29	during the first year, a great deal to do] B; a good deal to do the first year > A
102.1	assist] B; help > A
102.10	folks] B; people > A
102.24	very frequently contained] B; had usually > A
102.29	the standing] B; a standing > A
103.1	some] B; many > A
103.4	considering] B; thinking > A
103.8	"Meph," says he, "I'll tell you] B; I'll tell you, says he, Meph > A
103.10	got] B; *omitted* > A
103.15-16	to buy] B; *omitted* > A
103.22	unite] B; display > A
104.11	thankful] B; ~ to Providence > A
104.17-18	a violent . . . clapboards of] B; sad havoc among the clapboards in > A
104.20	projecting] B; standing > A
104.24	our] B; the > A
104.26	parts of improvement] B; things > A
104.30	roof, or corners of his house] B; or roof, or the corners > A

104.31   of farming] B; *omitted* > A
105.1   at once] B; *omitted* > A
105.5-6   during winter, were shivering over huge fires] B;
                were shivering before huge fires in winter > A
105.24   are] B; I have found to be > A
105.31   into] B; in > A
105.33   around my little hut] B; about my house > A
105.34   master] B; ~, I remember > A
106.2   These] B; Those > A
106.7-8   ill cultivated fields and miserable fences] B; fields
                ill cultivated and as wretchedly fenced > A
106.11   shall] B; will > A
106.12   a few] B; ~ very ~ > A
106.14-15   lame Meph] B; Mephibosheth Stepsure > A
106.19   Meph] B; Mephibosheth > A
106.34   or axe handles] B; axe handles, or for any other
                use > A
107.7   by] B; with > A
107.9   Mephibosheth] A; M. > B
108.1   LETTER 11] Number 10. > A; Let X. > B
108.2   To the Editors of the *Acadian Recorder*] *To the*
                Editors of the Recorder > A; *omitted* > B
108.3   Gentlemen] A; *omitted* > B
108.6   exertion] B; labour > A
108.23   together] B; to each other > A
109.4   About that] B; About this > A
109.6   remarks] B; observes > A
109.19   this] B; that > A
109.21   not] B; neither > A
109.27   couple of chests] B; chest or two > A
110.2   I assure you, are requisite] B; are requisite, I
                assure you > A
110.14-15   my own part] B; myself > A
110.18   comfortable] B; very ~ > A
110.20-21   neither . . . day] B; give me none of their jaw > A
110.26   prospect] B; prospects > A

110.28-29	perfected the desolation of nature] B; descended in succession > A
110.29	these] B; the > A
110.30-33	These . . . life] B; I have always considered these, as the preparations of nature for a returning crop > A
110.34	amid] B; in the midst of > A
111.1	they] B; *omitted* > A
111.4	on] B; *omitted* > A
111.7	spring] B; the ~ > A
111.12	as well as] A; as well > B
111.24	felt] B; ~ at times > A
111.26	To relieve myself, therefore, from solitude] B; In such a case > A
111.27	often] B; usually > A
111.35	being in a] A; being in > B
112.18	good natured] B; *omitted* > A
112.19	could] B; would > A
112.21	for] B; to > A
112.31	exactly say] B; tell > A
113.9	upon] B; on > A
113.14	is] B; was > A
113.14	ever] B; *omitted* > A
113.19	a] B; the > A
114.10	but] B; ~ the parson and > A
114.14	comfortably] B; comfortable > A
114.14	number of] B; great many > A
114.22	not one] B; none > A
114.30	could] B; would > A
114.36	are] B; were > A
115.2	affirmed] B; assumed > A
115.12	into] B; in > A
115.25	work,] B; ~, (both businesses of the same sort,) > A
115.26	slowly on] B; on slowly > A
115.28-29	must, of course, be] B; was > A

115.29	in] B; *omitted* > A
115.33	he] B; *omitted* > A
115.36	were] B; was > A
116.12	countenances] B; grim ~ > A
116.13	ran] B; run > A
116.18-19	before proceeding to it, we had better] B; we had better first > A
116.22	ladies] B; two ~ had > A
116.23	had] B; *omitted* > A
116.27-28	his house was small and the evening very fine] B; the evening was very fine and his house small > A
117.13	on this account] B; therefore > A
117.18	preying] B; living > A
117.19	the year] B; their time > A
118.7-8	by the ministration of Mrs. Sham and Miss Clippit] B; *omitted* > A
118.8	For my own part] B; With respect to myself > A
118.9	that] B; ~ that > A
118.10	both] B; is ~ > A
119.1	LETTER 12] Number 11. > A; Let XI. > B
119.2	To the Editors of the *Acadian Recorder*] *To the Editors of the Recorder* > A; *omitted* > B
119.3	Gentlemen] A; *omitted* > B
119.12	good] B; large > A
119.13	are] B; go > A
119.16	part] B; parts > A
119.24	would] B; could > A
120.1	explained] B; ~ all > A
120.5	keep] B; strive to ~ > A
120.14	to] B; of > A
120.34-35	and sensible] B; *omitted* > A
120.35-36	To me this was] B; This was very > A
121.4	longtailed] B; *omitted* > A
121.5	yet] B; *omitted* > A
121.27	comfortable] B; very ~ > A
121.35	in quest of] B; after > A

122.2	loves] B; likes > A
123.12-13	This . . . relief.] B; *omitted* > A
123.14-15	the other day, with black eyes, to the parson] B; with black eyes to the parson, the other day > A
123.17	her husband should] B; he should > A
124.1	my spouse] B; Dorothy > A
124.12	that] B; *omitted* > A
124.15	my spouse] B; Dorothy > A
124.18-19	in Widow Scant's little hut, more gratitude] B; more gratitude in Widow Scant's > A
124.20	mansion] B; house > A
124.22	my spouse] B; Dorothy > A
124.30-31	contentment and cheerfulness] B; cheerfulness and contentment > A
125.4	but] B; ~ every body knows that > A
125.5	out of] B; from > A
125.7	in the mean time frees the mind] B; frees the mind in the mean time > A
125.14	impedes the progress] B; prevents the increase > A
125.24	still he] B; he still > A
125.25	among] B; amidst > A
125.26-27	whence he came, and where he learned his religion] B; whether he came from Scotland originally or from New England > A
125.30	apparel is] B; clothes are > A
125.31	some] B; *omitted* > A
126.1	part] B; ~ of it > A
126.4	in each of the latter] B; *omitted* > A
126.5	snug and comfortable] B; snugly in each of them > A
126.21	and that] B; that > A
126.23	comfort] B; comforts > A
126.30	may] B; *omitted* > A
127.9-10	as . . . duty] B; is an indispensable duty, as it affords the means of doing good to others > A

127.11	professes] B; possesses > A
127.17	where] B; when > A
127.24	people] B; folks > A
127.30	wanted neither] B; neither wanted > A
127.35	about] B; of > A
127.36	to] B; for > A
128.11	visitation] B; dispensation > A
128.13	Job, judging] B; judging > A
128.14	woman] B; ~, who knew so well how to sympathise with affliction > A
128.14	made] B; he ~ > A
128.20	in her own way, exerted herself] B; exerted herself, in her own way > A
128.31	that came in] B; which came into > A
128.34	load] B; burden > A
128.34	feels] B; has > A
129.1	these] B; this > A
129.2	the] B; a > A
129.6	our townsmen] B; my neighbours > A
129.25	submitting] B; allowing himself > A
129.28	her] B; his > A
129.33	in the taking] B; *omitted* > A
130.1	pace] B; step > A
130.2	meet] B; see one another > A
131.1	LETTER 13] Number 12. > A; Let. XII. > B
131.2	To the Editors of the *Acadian Recorder*] *To the Editors of the Recorder* > A; *omitted* > B
131.3	Gentlemen] A; *omitted* > B
131.11	own] B; *omitted* > A
131.12	had, before our marriage] B; before our marriage, had > A
131.19	Loopy's or old Stot's] B; old Stots or Loopy's > A
131.21	afterward] B; afterwards > A
131.25	people] B; townsfolk > A
131.26-27	upon subjects of this kind] B; *omitted* > A
131.29	pocket] B; ~ in these times > A

132.18	examples] B; instances > A
132.20	poverty] B; ~, as you know > A
132.31	upon the circuit] B; *omitted* > A
132.33	stripes] B; strips > A
133.3	to do] B; *omitted* > A
133.6	humour] B; humours > A
133.17	misconduct] B; mismanagement > A
133.22	the] B; a > A
133.22	when] B; than > A
133.26	he seen it] B; it been seen > A
133.27	gained] B; obtained > A
133.34	Mere beauty] B; Beauty by itself > A
134.9	lame old] B; old lame > A
134.10	even] B; *omitted* > A
134.17	woman] B; kind of ~ > A
134.17-18	folks who think themselves uncommonly religious] B; religious folks > A
134.20	dissatisfaction] B; discontent > A
134.22	who] B; *omitted* > A
134.34	did] B; should > A
134.36	would] B; will > A
135.2	the way] B; their way > A
135.6	were neither] B; never were > A
135.8	town] B; township > A
135.17	particularly which did not] B; above all, to > A
135.18	make] B; to ~ > A
135.23	grafted] B; ingrafted > A
135.27	an] B; *omitted* > A
135.29	found] B; ~, I believe > A
136.7	they are] B; he is > A
136.24	recollect] B; ~, that > A
136.25	sit] B; set > A
136.29-32	only . . . themselves] B; consider that it is so written in the chronicles of our town, and written too by Mephibosheth Stepsure > A
136.36	with] B; along ~ > A

137.8	economy] B; domestic ~ > A
137.8	time] B; ~, I remember > A
137.18	in] B; *omitted* > A
137.21	worthy] B; old > A
137.26-27	needed encouragement or reproof] B; conveyed reproof or encouragement > A
137.27	stated] B; observed > A
137.29	flock] B; congregation > A
137.30	blame] B; to ~ > A
138.7	is] B; was > A
138.15	countenance] B; countenances > A
138.16-17	The . . . but] B; for, though the oldest had acquired a good deal of brass, > A
138.21	At present, therefore, I shall] B; I shall, therefore at present, > A
138.29	helped] B; soon ~ > A
138.31-32	now observe its result] B; next view its results > A
139.1	gives] B; give > A
139.8	the young] B; young > A
139.16	merciful] B; beneficent > A
139.17	protect him from misery] B; thus protect him from innumerable miseries > A
139.26	now] B; and, ~ > A
139.32	excellency] B; excellences > A
140.4	running] B; *omitted* > A
140.15	in which] B; where > A
140.18-19	man: hers . . . sorrow] B; man. To the female, therefore, it belongs, to be the sweetner of his toil and the soother of his sorrow > A
140.23	her abode] B; the place of ~ ~ > A
140.28	and] B; who > A
141.6	family] B; house > A
141.7	connected with domestic management] B; about it > A
141.12	care is] B; cares are > A
141.18	with your work] B; in your labour > A

141.21	dressing] B; clothing > A
141.24	frolicking] B; frolickings > A
141.25	involve your husbands in] B; get your husbands into > A
142.15	the trousers] B; trowsers > A
142.16	their wives] B; some of ~ ~ > A
142.16	perhaps] B; *omitted* > A
142.18	shall] B; will > A
142.20	ponder] B; consider > A
143.1	LETTER 14] Number 13. > A; Let. XIII. > B
143.2	To the Editors of the *Acadian Recorder*] *To the Editors of the Recorder* > A; *omitted* > B
143.3	Gentlemen] A; *omitted* > B
143.21	farm] B; property > A
143.22	very] B; *omitted* > A
144.2	of] B; about > A
144.3	necessity] B; hard ~ > A
144.4	exertion] B; exertions > A
144.4	duly] B; daily > A
144.6	he would have become] B; it would have rendered him > A
144.8	occurrences] B; trifling ~ > A
144.8	however] B; *omitted* > A
144.26	his liking] B; liking > A
144.29	news] B; ~; and will continue to wander till his legs fail him > A
145.6	would] B; *omitted* > A
145.13	juryman. I] B; ~. In our town, I assure you, the business of the courts is well looked to: it is never intrusted to either blind or lame. ~ > A
145.15	maintains] B; supports > A
145.22	all] B; well > A
145.28	With respect to] B; As for > A
145.29	Boshy] B; Mephy > A
145.29	regarded] B; listened to > A
145.32	this] B; ~ I must say > A

145.34	his] B; ~ own > A
145.35-36	work; because his mind is elsewhere, labour goes on slowly] B; farm, labour goes on slowly, because his mind is elsewhere > A
146.1	moved on] B; went to work > A
146.15	mend] B; mends > A
146.30	was excluded from dignities: it] B; *omitted* > A
146.35	honour] B; high honours > A
147.8	or] B; and > A
147.15	are] B; ~ among us > A
147.18	Hecky] B; Hec > A
147.21	and got] B; got > A
147.26	as] B; like > A
147.27	for] B; *omitted* > A
147.28	genius] B; ~ gave him an elevation of thought which > A
148.3	young] B; going > A
148.27	skewered] B; skivered > A
150.14	night] B; evening > A
150.31	Captain's lower habiliments] B; trowsers > A
150.32-34	by . . . But] B; *omitted* > A
151.5	offspring] B; family > A
151.14	militia] B; a ~ > A
151.30	very] B; pretty > A
151.32	he] B; *omitted* > A
152.18	these] B; others > A
152.29	could] B; would > A
152.33	surprise] B; some ~ > A
152.35	better] B; a ~ > A
153.4	the discharge of these duties] B; these exercises > A
153.6	are] B; is > A
153.9	active principles] B; activity > A
153.18	*work*] B; *works* > A
153.22	prostrate at the altar of God] B; praying > A
153.30-32	look . . . respectability] B; seek honour in a path where want of respectability awaits them > A

153.32   justices] B; only ~ > A
154.6   empty parade] B; show > A
154.9-11   course . . . domestic] B; life in which you are
           employed, is a course which the deity honours
           with the means of > A
154.16   Old] B; Justice > A
154.18   sometimes] B; *omitted* > A
154.20   magistrates] B; justices > A
155.1   LETTER 15] Number 14. > A; Let. XIV. > B
155.2   To the Editors of the *Acadian Recorder*] *To the*
           Editors of the Recorder > A; *omitted* > B
155.3   Gentlemen] A; *omitted* > B
155.6-8   being . . . first] B; from a number of the first, I was
           relieved, by being neither a constable nor jury-
           man, justice of the peace nor captain of militia > A
155.22   return] B; ~ again > A
156.8   other] B; in ~ > A
156.11   the] B; a > A
156.17-18 to acquire by a perusal of books] B; by a perusal of
           books, to acquire > A
156.23   merely] B; *omitted* > A
156.27   this] B; that > A
156.33   their] B; this > A
156.35-37 in the . . . abroad] B; now forces them abroad, in
           the face of reason and religion, and at the expense
           of true enjoyment in time and happiness forever
           > A
157.3   both. Whoever] B; both: and whoever > A
157.3-4   will reduce] B; reduces > A
157.9   he will, by the perusal of books,] B; by the perusal
           of books, he will > A
157.25   occasions to go] B; causes to be > A
158.3   One of our townsmen] B; A man in our town > A
158.4   his longest sermon] B; one of his longest sermons
           > A
158.5   purchasing] B; buying > A
158.6   six] B; three, ~ > A

158.8	bought] B; purchased > A
158.10	find] B; finds > A
158.11	travel] B; running about > A
158.13	as I formerly stated, are pretty long] B; are pretty long; as I stated to you before > A
158.19	collect] B; collected > A
158.24	folk] B; folks > A
158.28	considerable] B; ~ of > A
158.32	very] B; *omitted* > A
159.7	principle] B; plan > A
159.9	among] B; amongst > A
159.11	remain] B; continue > A
159.14	merely] B; just > A
159.19-20	have been always] B; was > A
159.21	expectation] B; hope > A
159.24	payments] B; payment > A
159.26-27	my management] B; how I managed > A
160.6	has been] B; was > A
160.8-9	These remarks I hope will satisfy your readers] B; All your readers will now be satisfied, I hope > A
160.16	give] B; gave > A
160.19	that] B; *omitted* > A
160.34	more, they adjourn to his house, and perhaps] B; any more, they find it most convenient to adjourn to his house and > A
161.7	haste] B; hurry > A
161.9	our townsmen] B; the neighbours > A
161.16	causes] B; the cause > A
161.21	implement; and these] B; article; which > A
161.23	travelling] B; running > A
161.24	usually] B; generally > A
161.26	But my] B; And my own > A
161.28	my] B; the > A
161.33	being] B; *omitted* > A
161.35	ever thinks of returning] B; except Saunders and a few others, carries home > A

162.16	Slack] B; him > A
162.18	then] B; *omitted* > A
162.24	as sharp] B; sharp > A
162.28	I was married, Mosey also] B; my spouse and I were married, Mosey > A
163.2	of young people] B; young folks > A
163.2	were inclined] B; liked > A
163.5	greater part] B; most > A
163.6-7	On this account, his own crop] B; His own crop, therefore > A
163.18	must] B; was to > A
163.19	a collar] B; the collar > A
163.20	were lost] B; or the dog was lost > A
164.1	Halifax] B; *omitted* > A
164.5	lands] B; land > A
164.20	did not sow] B; never sowed > A
164.22	employed] B; followed > A
164.23	that] B; *omitted* > A
164.32	that he rarely gave] B; as rarely to give > A
164.35	grounds] B; ground > A
165.8	abundant nor more frequent] B; frequent nor more abundant > A
165.18-19	more ground than] B; so much ground as > A
165.28	good] B; snug > A
165.29	snug] B; good > A
167.1	LETTER 16] Number 15. > A; Let. XV. > B
167.2	To the Editors of the *Acadian Recorder*] *To the Editors of the Recorder* > A; *omitted* > B
167.3	Gentlemen] A; *omitted* > B
167.6	perceive] B; see > A
167.12	sorts] B; sort > A
167.13	very] B; as > A
167.13	heart] B; ~ as any body > A
167.16	people] B; township > A
167.21	they returned] B; returning > A
167.27	upon] B; on > A

168.3	when] B; that, ~ > A
168.4	of] B; for > A
168.9	among] B; amongst > A
168.11	are] B; were > A
168.13	they] B; *omitted* > A
168.14	their parents] B; the parents > A
168.16	vagabonds] B; vagabond > A
168.24	also] B; *omitted* > A
168.27	all at once become] B; are all at once converted into > A
168.34	Indeed, our people] B; Our people, indeed > A
169.6	saddle] B; get upon > A
169.7	under the tuition of] B; by > A
169.14	to sit] B; sit > A
169.14	to walk] B; walk > A
169.22	occasionally] B; now, often > A
169.28	tub] B; washing ~ > A
169.31	longtailed] B; long tail > A
170.2	said] B; told you > A
170.5	who] B; ~ was > A
170.9	word; and] B; word. > A
170.11	that labourers might be sent] B; for labourers to come > A
170.17-18	with . . . Scotland] B; tried in Scotland to lead silly people off their feet with their ravings and nonsense > A
170.19	doctrine] B; doctrines > A
171.3-4	our youth] B; the youth among us > A
171.6	knowledge] B; instruction > A
171.26	this] B; the > A
171.27	admit] B; receive > A
171.33	as a] B; for > A
172.8	declaring] B; sometimes ~ > A
172.11-12	you know, a cardplayer] B; a card player you know > A
172.15	discovers] B; mistakes > A

172.16	to be] B; for > A
172.18	for] B; at > A
172.21-22	at times exposed] B; exposed at times > A
172.32	their cards] B; the cards > A
173.1	amusement] B; amusements > A
173.15	in any other way] B; otherwise > A
173.24	misery] B; wretchedness > A
173.28	him] B; home > A
174.2	not] B; never > A
174.2	men] B; youth > A
174.9	perhaps] B; probably > A
174.15	farther] B; further > A
174.18	with] B; for > A
174.20	their] B; *omitted* > A
174.30	time] B; period > A
174.32	endeavours also] B; also endeavours > A
174.34	the recollection] B; a recollection > A
174.35	remembrance] B; recollection > A
175.4	Gladly she would have] B; She would have gladly > A
175.11	world] B; ~ comfortably > A
175.28	when a boy, he had experienced] B; he had experienced, when a boy > A
175.31	exactly see] B; see exactly > A
176.4	contains] B; contain > A
176.7	accordingly] B; according > A
176.21	Mr.] B; Dr. > A
176.23	matters] B; things > A
176.23	do] B; did > A
176.27	means of] B; *omitted* > A
177.5	last] B; length > A
177.11	*terminate in*] B; *improve into* > A
177.18	townsmen consider me as rather an] B; townfolk account me a rather > A
177.24	always been] B; been always > A
177.34-178.1	upon the subject of] B; respecting > A

179.1	LETTER 17] Number 16. > A; Let. XVI. > B
179.2	To the Editors of the *Acadian Recorder*] *To the Editors of the Recorder* > A; *omitted* > B
179.3	Gentlemen] A; *omitted* > B
179.4-5	the history . . . events] B; my own life, a variety of events has occurred in our town > A
179.11	notices] B; ~, to show you how we are getting on > A
179.21	assisting] B; visiting > A
179.27-28	they suffer no damage at home] B; at home, they suffer no loss > A
180.1	must] B; may > A
180.3	both] B; not only > A
180.4	and] B; but also > A
180.11	requisite] B; necessary > A
180.16	anticipated] B; expected > A
180.16	people] B; folks > A
180.18-19	In particular, old Stot's son Hodge] B; Old Stot's son Hodge, in particular > A
181.5	gowns] B; gown > A
181.9	the] B; *omitted* > A
181.10-11	for conducting the business in genteel stile, a better choice] B; a better choice for conducting the business in genteel stile > A
181.19	young] B; *omitted* > A
181.26	how] B; indeed, ~ > A
182.10	Hodge] B; the poor fellow > A
182.30	is] B; are > A
183.1-2	with perfect equanimity, bear] B; bear with perfect equanimity > A
183.13	very badly with the belly ache] B; with the belly ache very badly > A
183.21	lady] B; old ~ > A
183.21	upon opening] B; that he should open > A
183.36	a scientific] B; an > A
184.1	dancing] B; ~ myself > A

184.6	its] B; his > A
184.19	music] B; the ~ > A
184.21	such a specimen of] B; a specimen of such > A
185.16	their] B; the > A
186.2	how careful he is] B; his care > A
186.4	The] B; But the > A
186.5	resolved] B; and resolving > A
186.11	is] B; ~, in many respects > A
186.21	the other part of his] B; his public > A
186.22	Trulliber] B; Tulliber > A
186.27	restricted] B; limited > A
186.29	now] B; *omitted* > A
186.32	has] B; is > A
187.1	going] B; a ~ > A
187.8	and] B; ~ also > A
187.13	said] B; had ~ > A
187.14	had learned] B; should learn > A
187.17	Weekly] B; *omitted* > A
187.31	could] B; would > A
187.35-36	getting into the company of] B; meeting with > A
188.6	that I possess] B; myself possessed of > A
188.12	have] B; am > A
188.24	Scantocreesh] B; Saunders > A
188.29-30	into the newspapers] B; in the papers > A
188.36	would] B; will > A
189.11	wishes] B; wished > A
189.19	might] B; would > A
189.21	militia] B; a ~ > A
189.27	first] B; former > A
189.31	consider] B; remember > A
189.36-190.1	keep it up till they are very angry] B; make themselves more angry still > A
190.1	be] B; do > A
190.2	complaints] B; ~ and receiving the consolation which their case deserves > A

190.3-4   they might transfer their rage against the exposure of folly] B; instead of continuing their displeasure against the exposure of folly, they might transfer their rage > A

190.5   I] B; For my own part, ~ > A

190.7-10   if . . . them] B; would be a very decent sort of folks, if they had only good management > A

IN THE FOLLOWING SECTION, THE COPY-TEXT IS A.

197.1   LETTER 18] *omitted* > A

205.1   LETTER 19] Number 1. > A

IN THE FOLLOWING SECTION, THE COPY-TEXT IS B.

215.1   LETTER 20] *omitted* > A, B

215.1-2   Copy . . . to] A; To > B

215.25   be] B; *omitted* > A

216.2   gat himsel stickit in some drucken quarrel] A; was stickit by the papist eedolaters > B

216.23   this] A; the > B

216.24   ony] A; an > B

216.27   or] A; *omitted* > B

216.30   weemen] B; weeman > A

216.30   about] A; ~ the kintra > B

216.36   the grun'] B; grun' > A

217.17   over] A; across > B

217.18   filled] A; then ~ > B

217.20-21   to this kintra a penny siller] A; a penny siller to this kintra > B

217.22-23   at ony time get] A; get at ony time > B

217.24   wha] A; that > B

218.5   and our] A; and > B

218.22   him. I] A; ~. Wi' gude helth and moderat labour,
            he is sure in time to hae every thing comfortable.
            ~ > B
218.25   on sae weel] A; sae weel on > B
218.30   and] A; ~ then > B
218.32   we used to see] A; used to be > B
218.34   syne] A; then > B
219.10   rich] A; walthy > B
219.32   kind] A; sort > B
220.6-7   young fok] A; youth > B
220.7   anes] A; fok > B
220.12   aye] A; *omitted* > B
220.25   bravery] A; wastery > B
220.30   pocks] B; frocks > A
220.30   borro' or buy] A; buy or borro' > B
220.33   they're] A; they are > B
221.15   aye] A; *omitted* > B
221.34   villain] A; neerdoweel > B
221.36   neerdoweel] A; villain > B
222.5   kintra's] A; province is > B
222.6   revelashons. Then] A; revelashons; and then > B
222.11   three nichts] A; nichts > B
222.25   ither] A; idle > B
223.8   fashed] A; ~ wi' a host and spittin' > B
223.9   maks] A; mak > B
223.10-11   does get his observes out; they're] A; gets ower wi'
            the croichlin', his observes are > B
223.16   without] A; ~ either > B
223.23   the minister] A; Mr. Drone > B

IN THE FOLLOWING SECTION, THE
COPY-TEXT IS A.

225.1   LETTER 21] Number 2. > A; William > C, D
225.2   To the Editors of the *Acadian Recorder*] A; *omitted*
            > C, D

225.3   Gentlemen] A; *omitted* > C, D
225.4-229.13 Through the importunities . . . mentioned build-
                 ings.] A; Some time ago, a little business called me
                 to our metropolis. As I had never been in Halifax
                 before, curiosity induced me to devote a few
                 hours to the inspection of its various parts. After a
                 great deal of strolling, I found myself in the street
                 which contains the poors' house and jail. Accident
                 has placed them together, as if for the purpose of
                 showing at one glance, the different results of a
                 life of thoughtlessness and folly; for such in gen-
                 eral are the characteristics of those who, in
                 Halifax, become inhabitants of the poors' house
                 or [and > D] jail. As I was proceeding slowly
                 along, engrossed by those musings which the first
                 view of a town naturally produces, I was joined by
                 an old man of respectable appearance from the
                 first of these buildings. > C, D

            IN THE FOLLOWING SECTION, THE
            COPY-TEXT IS C.

229.13   Proceeding] C, D; As we were going > A
229.14-15   travelled over the ordinary topics, as far as] C, D;
                 just arrived at that part of the common topics,
                 which > A
229.18   said he] C, D; he added > A
229.21   content.] C, D; content with little; and > A
229.22   the best] C, D; this > A
229.28   when convinced] C, D; with a conviction > A
230.3-4   Among . . . relief] C, D; Much, as you know, is
                 done among themselves to relieve the wants > A
230.4-6   impostors . . . and tells] C, D; they are often
                 deceived by impostors from the country, no
                 unfortunate settler in our town ever told his dis-
                 tresses in Halifax, and told > A

230.7	collectively] C, D; in the gross > A
230.7-8	a violation of justice] C, D; unjust and unreasonable > A
230.8	much] C, D; ~, which ought > A
230.9	industry] C, D; ~ judiciously applied > A
230.10-11	life; nor is it without] C, D; life. In every department there are > A
230.11	deportment] C, D; conduct > A
230.13	account] C, D; retribution > A
230.13	adjudged] C, D; found > A
230.14-15	enough . . . abode] C, D; that which make the heart of every parent tremble > A
230.15	Its] C, D; The > A
230.16	surprising] C, D; strange > A
230.17	strange] C, D; wonderful > A
230.18	by] C, D; from > A
230.19-22	having . . . narrative] C, D; we seated ourselves upon the brink of a rivulet which flows behind the town; and as nearly as I can recollect, the following is the amount of his relation > A
230.30	this] O, D; the preceding estate was advertised > A, C
230.31	for sale] C, D; *omitted* > A
230.33	shattered] C, D; broken down > A
231.2	zealous] D; jealous > A, C
231.3	increased] C, D; added to > A
231.4	power] C, D; influence > A
231.4	have very gladly] C, D; very gladly have > A
231.5	village.] C, D; ~: and > A
231.5-6	upon any of his American plantations, a] C, D; in the States; one > A
231.7	its last vestige] C, D; every vestige of it > A
231.11	defence] C, D; protection > A
231.15	he] C, D; his mind > A
231.16-17	honeysuckle and the rose] C, D; rose and the honey suckle > A
231.21	possessed] C, D; owned > A

231.23	consequence] C, D; effect > A
231.25	youthful villagers] C, D; youth > A
231.26	families] C, D; ~ in the village > A
231.26-28	In . . . people] C, D; The religious sentiments which are cherished by the mass of the common people in Scotland > A
231.29	in] C, D; with > A
231.30	dread] C, D; a ~ > A
231.31	often] C, D; *omitted* > A
231.32	less acute] C, D; much less > A
231.33	a] C, D; *omitted* > A
231.34	emigration] C, D; going abroad > A
232.2	them] C, D; *omitted* > A
232.5	in a few years, had] C, D; had in a few years > A
232.6	destroyed] C, D; broken > A
232.8	were amassing a fortune] C, D; must be fast making their fortunes > A
232.14	voice] C, D; consent > A
232.16	parish] C, D; kirk > A
232.16-17	it was never filled by a worthier man] C, D; a worthier man had never filled the office > A
232.19	make his fortune abroad] C, D; push his fortune in foreign parts > A
232.20	of William] C, D; *omitted* > A
232.23	his] C, D; William's > A
232.27	grief] C, D; pain > A
232.29	snares] C, D; temptation > A
232.31	valuable] C, D; precious > A
232.34-36	To those . . . stranger] C, D; Of filial affection William was by no means devoid > A
233.2	bewildered] C, D; had ~ > A
233.5	their declining] C, D; them in the evening of their > A
233.6	a wealthy and a] O, D; the wealthy and > A, C
233.7	his father] C, D; the father > A
233.9	gentleman] A, D; gentlemen > C

233.12	and] C, D; or > A
233.12-13	His . . . afflictions he] C, D; He was one, who, in the afflictions of his people > A
233.14	walked] C, D; stepped > A
233.17	tranquillizes] C, D; calms > A
233.19	remarkable] O, D; noted > A, C
233.19	the splendour of its] C, D; splendour of > A
233.23-24	to cement . . . Edinburgh] C, D; to the Grass Market of Edinburgh, to cement with his blood > A
233.25	privilege] C, D; liberty > A
233.25-26	This worthy martyr, at the end of his little habitation] C, D; At the end of his little habitation, this worthy martyr > A
233.28	supplied it with an unfading mantle of green] C, D; had supplied it with a verdant covering > A
233.30	guided with care] C, D; carefully guided > A
233.31	road] O, D; street > A, C
233.34-234.1	in front . . . and his] C, D; which led to the house, William was at his evening's occupation in the midst of his flowers. His > A
234.7-9	to sit . . . amusements] C, D; on such an evening as this, to sit at their door; and contemplate their son, making even his hours of amusement, subservient to their comfort > A
234.9	long been] C, D; been long > A
234.10	is] C, D; ~ now > A
234.17	he thought upon] C, D; His thoughts turned to > A
234.17-18	lawns and groves] C, D; groves and lawns > A

IN THE FOLLOWING SECTION, THE COPY-TEXT IS D.

234.19	resolved] D; ~ with himself > A

234.20-22   groves . . . demesne] D; the laburnum and lilac, and recline upon the primrose and violet > A

234.24   habitation] D; habitations > A

234.25   their] D; ~ own > A

234.26   who will] D; must they grapple with the king of terrors when there is no son to > A

234.31-32   a few years hence he would] D; he would in a few years > A

234.36-235.2 you . . . proclaimed] D; and ambition, William, is dragging you to parts where, perhaps, the testimony of Jesus is not known > A

235.3   by] D; with > A

235.5   inflamed] D; aroused > A

235.6   productions of the] D; the commodities of those > A

235.7-9   When . . . hopes] D; and when you, in the same circumstances, grasp at wealth, you must grapple with temptations which have bereaved his mind of religious sentiment and well grounded hope > A

235.11-12   But . . . cure] D; and in the mean time, skill cannot relieve him from a shattered frame, which makes him turn with distaste from the richest luxuries of nature and art > A

235.15   with it you may get] D; you may get along with it > A

235.17   the man] D; a man > A

235.24-25   had arrived: William's] D; was come: his > A

235.26   grasped] D; was met by > A

235.27   father] D; parent > A

235.28   inspire you with] D; instil into your mind > A

235.28   witness] D; see > A

235.30   you would at last mingle with] D; along with your parents, you would at last join > A

235.31-32   putting yourself in the way of evil] D; now putting yourself in temptation's way > A

IN THE FOLLOWING SECTION, THE
COPY-TEXT IS C.

235.35   long] C, D; ~ even unto this day > A

235.36   I desire not your greatness] C, D; It is not your
greatness that I desire to see > A

236.3   *on*] C, D; in > A

IN THE FOLLOWING SECTION, THE
COPY-TEXT IS A.

237.1   LETTER 22] Number 3. > A; *omitted* > D

237.2   To the Editors of the *Acadian Recorder*] A; *omitted*
> D

237.3   Gentlemen] A; *omitted* > D

237.4-5   Your . . . father.] A; *omitted* > D

IN THE FOLLOWING SECTION, THE
COPY-TEXT IS D.

237.5-8   In . . . heart] D; It was not of a kind calculated to
produce lightness of heart in a religiously edu-
cated young man, who was forsaking his parents
and might see them no more > A

237.9   moralisings] D; moralising > A

237.11   last words] D; charges > A

237.17   of Scotland] D; in Scotland > A

237.18   terms nearly synonymous] D; so closely con-
nected, that, where the one is, the other follows of
course > A

237.18-21   The . . . considered] D; Neither the qualifications
necessary in order to the acquisition of wealth, nor
the influence of the human character, is usually
taken into the account > A

237.22	disappointment] D; and ~ > A
237.27	affection] D; the heart > A
237.29	towering] D; lowering > A
238.1-2	in every direction, the eye met only] D; from the vessel nothing was apparent but > A
238.3	Of such a scene, the first effect] D; The first effect of such a scene > A
238.4	next] D; second > A
238.4-5	the want] D; a passenger's want > A
238.9	seldom] D; rarely > A
238.13	a] D; the protection of ~ > A
238.14	preserved] D; separated > A
238.16	fears] D; alarm > A
238.20	enjoyments] D; comforts > A
238.21	paternal] D; parental > A

IN THE FOLLOWING SECTION, THE COPY-TEXT IS C.

238.24	He had his bible, it is true] C, D; It is true he had his bible > A
238.24	its] C, D; he had placed himself in a situation in which ~ > A
238.25	more] C, D; the return of > A
238.25	reanimated] O, D; and fair wind reassured > A; reassured > C
238.26	mind] A, C, O, D; hopes > O
238.28	unusual] C, D; uncommon > A
238.30	Britain be aware] C, D; the mother country knows > A
238.30	will] C, D; must > A
238.32	rarely] C, D; seldom > A
238.33	his mind an unexpected shock] C, D; a shock to his mind > A
238.34	pictured] C, D; depictured > A

239.1   habitations of men] C, D; habitation of man > A
239.3   He] C, D; The mind > A
239.5   his mind] C, D; it > A
239.7   the] C, D; our > A
239.8   appears] C, D; is seen > A
239.9-11   where . . . old] C, D; surmounted by the hemlock
               and spruce; to which the occasional visitations of
               the spray have given the appearance of a stunted
               old > A
239.12   the very] C, D; rather a > A
239.13   despair] C, D; ~, than the abode of affluence and
               hope > A
239.13-14   kindred feelings] C, D; these impressions > A
239.18   mingled] C, D; mixed > A
239.19   appearance] D; general aspect > A; general
               appeance > C
239.20   brooding over] C, D; pondering on > A
239.30   our] C, D; the > A
239.36   but he thought] C, D; his second was > A
240.1   Yielding] A, C, D; yielding > O
240.5   consisted in] O, D; were comprised in > A; were
               > C
240.5   art] O, D; trade > A, C
240.5-6   he had learned from his father] C, D; his father
               had taught him > A
240.7   a master tradesman] C, D; master tradesmen > A
240.9   him] C, D; them > A
240.9   his] C, D; their > A
240.12-13   so that to the masters a supply of new hands was
               always a relief] D; so that to their masters a supply
               of new hands was always a relief > C; which always
               rendered a supply of new hands, a desirable relief
               to their masters > A
240.13-14   was immediately] C, D; found himself imme-
               diately > A
240.19   was] C, D; *omitted* > A

240.20   grasping] O, D; griping > A, C
240.23   cherished] C, D; fanned > A
240.27-28   and at the same time] C, D; with > A
240.32   which nestled] C, D; that built their nests > A
240.35   revisit] C, D; visit > A
240.36   abode] C, D; habitation > A
241.2   was] C, D; felt > A
241.3   review] C, D; observation > A
241.4   which fascinate] C, D; that fascinate > A
241.6   stings] O, D; bites > A, C
241.8-9   bitters; and, during the course of the day, the
                bottle was often re-visited] D; bitters. During the
                course of the day, also, many devices to raise the
                wind, as it is termed, were employed; so that the
                bottle stood constantly beside them, and received
                the treatment of an intimate acquaintance. > A;
                bitters. During the course of the day, also, many
                devices to raise the wind, as it is usually termed,
                were employed; so that the bottle stood constantly
                beside them, and received the treatment of an
                intimate acquaintance. > C
241.10-11   his servants] C, D; the workmen > A
241.13   happened] C, D; chanced > A
241.13   freely] O, D; *omitted* > A, C
241.14-15   in contributing to their comfort] D; if times were
                low with the bottle > A, C
241.17-18   less allied to wit than to obscenity and profana-
                tion] C, D; more allied to obscenity and profana-
                tion than to wit > A
241.21   deportment] C, D; impressions > A
241.21   his] O, D; a > A, C
241.23   made himself] C, D; become > A
241.24   abhorrence of] M, D; view > A, C; horror at > O
241.26   might] C, D; would > A

IN THE FOLLOWING SECTION, THE
COPY-TEXT IS D.

241.28   formed without a] D; made without a just > A
241.30   bold and obtrusive] D; obtrusive and daring > A
241.31   the neglect of] D; disregarding > A
241.33   odious epithets and jeers] D; jeers and odious
              epithets > A
242.3   character of a] D; nature of > A
242.6   toil] D; labour > A
242.8   enjoyments] D; enjoyment > A
242.9   house] D; ~, as in other religious families > A
242.10   was] D; is > A
242.11   was entertained] D; is charmed > A
242.12   a relation] D; relations > A
242.13   sires] D; ancestors > A
242.15   ascended] D; ascend > A
242.24   on the shelving projection] D; upon the projec-
              tion > A
242.26   decay] D; the doom of dissolution > A
242.28   room] D; place > A
242.31   shall ye] D; *ye shall* > A
242.34   and] D; *omitted* > A
243.1   proper] D; natural > A
243.4   sentiments] D; sentiment > A
243.4   feelings] D; feeling > A

IN THE FOLLOWING SECTION, THE
COPY-TEXT IS C.

243.5   rare] C, D; accidental > A
243.5-6   there is against religion an overwhelming
              odds] C, D; the odds against religion are over-
              whelming > A

243.6   season] C, D; period > A
243.7-8   glided past; nature resigned her sway to the
               fell] C, D; was succeeded by the chilling > A
243.9   spring] C, D; the ~ > A
243.9   the] C, D; *omitted* > A
243.10   in which] C, D; where > A
243.15   his shopmates' vices] C, D; the vices of his shop-
               mates > A
243.16   recognised] C, D; viewed > A
243.16   a pattern] A, D; the pattern > C
243.16   a correct] C, D; correct > A
243.18   a] C, D; the > A
243.18   exertion] C, D; his exertions > A
243.19   evening] C, D; the ~ > A
243.22   gratifications] C, D; debasing ~ > A
243.23   These] C, D; Those > A
243.26   were] C, D; ~ used > A
243.31   groundless] C, D; *omitted* > A
243.33   wish to acquire wealth] C, D; conception of
               acquiring money > A
243.35-36   his principles] C, D; both ~ ~ > A
244.2   deference] C, D; confidence > A
244.6   manifest] O, D; exemplify > A, C
244.6   of] C, D; to > A
244.14-15   latter showed his satisfaction] C, D; satisfaction of
               the latter exemplified itself > A
244.29   attacked by] C, D; seized with > A
244.32-33   the profits of every kind of employment in
               Halifax] C, D; of every kind of employment in
               Halifax the profits > A
244.34   fortunate] O, D; joyous > A; joyful > C
244.34-35   early apprised] O, D; of course, advertised > A;
               early advertised > C
245.1-3   affectionately . . . not of] O, D; wrote to them in a
               very affectionate strain; insisting, that, in the
               assurance of his filial regard, they should now
               combine less toil with additional comforts. But he

thought it unnecessary to trouble them with further directions about > A; affectionately advised them to combine less toil with additional comforts. In declarations of filial regard, his letter was not wanting: but he spoke not of > C

245.5   Mephibosheth Stepsure gent.] A; *omitted* > C, D

IN THE FOLLOWING SECTION, THE COPY-TEXT IS A.

246.1   LETTER 23] Number 4. > A

261.1   LETTER 24] Number 5. > A; *omitted* > C, D

261.2   To the Editors of the *Acadian Recorder*] A; *omitted* > C, D

261.3   Gentlemen] A; *omitted* > C, D

261.4-5   Your . . . business.] A; *omitted* > C, D

IN THE FOLLOWING SECTION, THE COPY-TEXT IS C.

261.5   As it was] It was > A; As William had succeeded to > C, D

261.6-7   it afforded . . . ambition] C, D; he was therefore, cheered with flattering prospects and hopes > A

261.7   the] C, D; to possess ~ > A

261.8   are] C, D; is > A

261.8   A view of] C, D; Sanguine expectation and disappointment in some form, are frequently combined. On looking into > A

261.9-10   was . . . creditors] C, D; it mortified him to learn, that a fair settlement of his debts > A

261.11-12   he did not, upon reflexion, find it difficult] C, D; several circumstances which now occurred to his mind, enabled him > A

261.17-18	His . . . meetings] C, D; By attendance upon the club, and other occasiocal meetings, his father in law > A
261.21	looking after] O, D; dunning > A, C
261.23	showed] C, D; proved > A
261.24	profits cannot be secured] M, D; gain is gone > A, C; profits cannot be expected > O
261.26	frequently] C, D; sometimes > A
261.27	cause] C, D; reason > A
261.27-28	For . . . papers] C, D; Among his papers he found > A
262.1	won from him] C, D; promised > A
262.3	had attained] C, D; arrived at > A
262.4	desireable] C, D; highly ~ > A
262.5	he could not complain] C, D; calculation showed him a gratifying result > A
262.5	the] C, D; a > A
262.6	cause] C, D; reason > A
262.6	His sober] C, D; Sober > A
262.12	woman] A, D; women > C
262.14	the] A, O, D; *omitted* > C
262.14	and comfort] C, D; *omitted* > A
262.15	Formerly, by her engaging] C, D; By her attracting > A
262.17	retain] C, D; secure > A
262.17	In] C, D; ~ attention to > A
262.19	admitted] C, D; confessed > A
262.20	have] C, D; in a similar station > A
262.20	brighter] C, D; more encouraging > A
262.20	permanent] C, D; the permanence of > A
262.22-23	With . . . William] C, D; To William, however, with all these means of comfort, it would frequently occur > A
262.27-28	In his father's house, the morn and even] C, D; In the house of his fathers, the morning and evening > A

262.28	with] C, D; by > A
262.29	voice] C, D; instructing and consoling ~ > A
262.30	in] C, D; upon > A
262.32	majesty on high] C, D; throne of God and of the Lamb > A
262.32	habitation] A, C, D; spiritual peace > O
262.33	gladness] C, D; joy > A
263.2	prevented] C, D; withheld > A
263.3	footsteps] C, D; path > A
263.4	youthful] C, D; young > A
263.5-6	the thoughtless] C, D; profligacy > A
263.6	resolution] O, D; religion > A, C
263.7	shrinks] O, D; hastens its retreat > A, C
263.8	on] C, D; upon > A
263.9	in which he had united] C, D; to which he had been accustomed > A
263.9-11	the morning . . . sacrifice] C, D; it possessed no altar for the domestic sacrafice of the morn and even > A
263.11	the] C, D; a > A
263.12	moral] C, D; religious > A
263.12-13	an inclination to the path of his fathers] C, D; a leaning toward the part of the just > A
263.14	ridicule] O, D; shame > A, C
263.14	was the stronger principle] C, D; were the stronger principles > A
263.17	relinquish] C, D; resign his > A
263.19	neglect of duty] C, D; want of devotional gratitude > A
263.20-22	though . . . peace] C, D; may, with a reluctance to duty, combine an eager desire for the peace of religion > A
263.22	Accordingly] C, D; *omitted* > A
263.24	making these the standard of worth] C, D; by these means > A
263.25-26	in the mean time] C, D; *omitted* > A
263.30-31	imploring suppliant] C, D; voice of misery > A

263.34   attention] C, D; redoubled ~ > A
264.2   insinuate that William was noted for irreligion] C,
                D; say that William had relinquished religious
                duty > A
264.5-6   perhaps not] C, D; not perhaps > A
264.6-7   the respect with which he preserved it] O, D; its
                safety > A, C
264.8   rather] C, D; sooner > A
264.10-11   in possession] D; with the prospect > A; in the
                possession > C
264.11   a lucrative trade and domestic comfort] C, D;
                domestic comfort and of a lucrative trade > A
264.12   public life] C, D; a ~ ~: And thus far, with the
                success of his exertions he had unquestionably
                reason to be pleased > A
264.15   an emigrant's subsequent] C, D; subsequent > A
264.16   weakens] C, D; loosens > A
264.17   attach] C, D; attached > A
264.19   longing] C, D; his ~ > A
264.24   revisiting it] O, D; personal visitation > A, C
264.25-26   In this state, therefore, the mind] C, D; A mind in
                this state, therefore, > A
264.26   enjoyment] C, D; future ~ > A
264.28-29   have . . . collected] C, D; are concentrated > A
264.31   William had resigned his] C, D; William's mind
                had partly lost its > A
264.32   found himself] C, D; conceived himself to be > A
264.33-35   growing . . . was] O, D; character as a rising young
                man, had secured to him extensive approbation
                and acquaintance; and the young couple found
                their happiness > A; growing reputation and
                prospects had secured to him extensive acquain-
                tance; and the domestic happiness of the young
                couple was > C
265.1   that] C, D; the > A
265.3   delights to communicate] O, D; is eager to give >
                A; delights to give > C

265.5   visitings abroad and parties] C, D; evening parties abroad and > A

265.8   effect] C, D; unforeseen ~ > A

265.10   had] C, D; *omitted* > A

265.11   chanced] C, D; happened > A

265.12-13   the time move very] C, D; that the time moved > A

265.17-18   Neither of the young people, however,] C, D; It must not, however, be supposed that either of the young people > A

265.19   in order] C, D; *omitted* > A; just sufficient > O

265.22   general approbation] C, D; the approbation of all with whom he had occasion to deal > A

265.25   acquired] C, D; now ~ > A

265.29   elected] C, D; admitted > A

265.32   executed] O, D; done > A, C

265.33   meetings] C, D; meeting > A

265.34-35   business . . . affairs] C, D; employments, a great deal of extraneous business was added to his own > A

265.36   Besides, in town, avocations] C, D; Now, in Halifax affairs > A

266.1   reserved for] C, D; managed in > A

266.2   a tavern] D; the tavern > A, C

266.2-3   Absence from his family to a late hour, therefore] C, D; By these means, absence from his family to a late hour > A

266.7-8   felt disposed to quarrel with the others arrangements] C, D; was disposed to quarrel > A

266.9   also] C, D; *omitted* > A

266.10   at] C, D; in > A

266.10-11   visiting it occasionally] O, D; stepping over occasionally when he had no appointment > A; stepping over occasionally > C

266.11   for the purpose of ascertaining] C, D; to learn > A

266.12	at last introduced him] C, D; introduced him ultimately > A
266.13	he would, of course, conduct] C, D; it may be presumed he conducted > A
266.16	at the club] C, D; *omitted* > A
266.18	period] C, D; ~ of life > A
266.20	excellent] C, D; good > A
266.21-29	He . . . home] C, D; He knew also that his parents, though not so often in his thoughts as formerly, were comfortably at home. In the mean time, he was himself farther gratified by the pleasure resulting from his evening amusements, public dinners, occasional trips to the country, and a variety of other relaxations from business > A
266.30	William's] C, D; his > A
266.30	little] C, D; not a great deal, I doubt > A
266.31-32	pleasure, can spare no time] C, D; pleasures, has little leisure > A
266.33	It] C, D; Indeed, it > A
266.36	own] C, D; *omitted* > A
267.1	for] C, D; of > A
267.2	not willing] C, D; unwilling > A
267.4	had always] C, D; *omitted* > A
267.6	attention] C, D; ~ which it really needed, and > A
267.8	bringing] A, C, D; writing > O
267.10	felt] C, D; experienced > A
267.10	task] C, D; employment > A
267.12	departure] C, D; deviation > A
267.13	serious] C, D; secret > A
267.13-14	To . . . right.] C, D; *omitted* > A
267.14-15	William felt himself] C, D; He felt himself at times > A
267.16	it acquired an assurance] C, D; he felt assured > A
267.17-18	the life . . . trace] C, D; his father's life rendered him not a fit judge of > A

267.20-22   in . . . was no distinguishing trait . . . devoid; for, in] C, D; he himself could not be characterized from his want of religion. In > A; in . . . made no part . . . devoid; for, in > O

267.23-24   sacred name or, indeed, any kind of profanity] C, D; name of the Deity, or any other kind of profane language > A

267.24   self-reproach] O, D; reproof > A, C

267.25   the] C, D; *omitted* > A

267.26-27   and an indulgent husband] C, D; an indulgent husband and father > A

267.29   all his] C, D; his various > A

267.31   A] C, D; With a > A

267.31-32   it is not necessary to state] C, D; I shall not detain you > A

267.34   Among men of business it] C, D; It > A

268.1-2   through growing inattention to his business, it had fallen] C, D; his growing inattention to business had allowed it to fall > A

268.3   and] C, D; ~ who > A

268.4   early] C, D; *omitted* > A

268.5   where] C, D; when > A

268.7   feeble] C, D; faint > A

268.9   assist] C, D; aid > A

268.11-12   depositing his griefs in the lap of pleasure] A, C, D; forgetting his business in a succession of enjoyments > O

268.13-14   not having foreseen, he had used no means to avert] C, D; as it had not been foreseen, could not be averted > A

268.15   now] C, D; as formerly > A

268.18   A] C, D; The > A

268.18-20   bringing . . . mutual] C, D; combining with itself a diminution of comforts, ultimately produced mutual dissatisfaction > A

268.22-23   foul fiend] A, C, D; evil spirit > O

268.26   sets] C, D; gives > A
268.27   William's altered] O, D; Accordingly, William's
                  bloated and slovenly > A; William's bloated and
                  slovenly > C
268.28   with which he had been formerly treated] C, D;
                  which he had once enjoyed > A
268.28-29   Indeed, by his] C, D; By his former > A
268.36-269.1   common courtesy is able to soothe] C, D; ordinary
                  attentions are sufficient to appease > A
269.5   hideous forms of debasement, plentifully sup-
                  plied] C, D; most debased forms, is plentifully
                  supplied with > A
269.15-21   Of . . . degradation] C, D; Of the state of his family
                  I shall say nothing > A
269.22   remarked] C, D; observed > A
269.23   dutiful kindness] C, D; filial affection > A
269.25   wretchedness] C, D; misery > A
269.27   impaired] C, D; diminished > A
269.29   excited] C, D; planted > A
269.29   mind] C, D; heart > A
269.29   derived] C, D; found > A
269.30   from] C, D; in > A
269.31-32   the poverty and disease of a life of dissipation] C,
                  D; poverty and disease > A
269.32   receptacle] O, D; emporium > A, C
269.33   misery] C, D; wretchedness > A
270.1   wicked] O, D; dead > A, C
270.2   tormenting] C, D; powerful and ~ > A
270.4   recollections] C, D; ~ and anticipations > A
270.5-6   It . . . enjoy] C, D; Where vice rests upon the ruins
                  of a religious education, one serious thought may
                  overturn with appalling terrors, the whole fabric
                  of its happiness. To suffer as well as to enjoy, was
                  the allotment of William > A
270.7   his fathers] C, D; the just > A
270.8   knew] C, D; was aware > A

270.10-11   he shared the miseries entailed by his crimes. By
             the] C, D; at times, the feelings of the miseries
             which his crimes had entailed, bereft him of
             peace. The > A
270.11-12   his pride was wounded] C, D; wounded his pride
             > A
270.12   when] C, D; whenever > A
270.13-14   certain . . . peace] C, D; fearful looking for of
             judgement proved to him a foretaste of the ter-
             rors of the Lord > A
270.16   paths] C, D; path > A
270.17   her] C, D; *omitted* > A
270.18   he sought] C, D; therefore, ~ ~ > A
270.21   was a] C, D; ~ still ~ > A
270.26   inspiration] C, D; inspirations > A
270.27   the last stage of an ill spent life] C, D; an ill spent
             life in the last stage of its existence > A
270.27   exhaustions] C, D; exhaustion > A
270.28   bereft] C, D; bereaved > A
270.29   hovered around] A, C, D; surrounded > O
270.31   eagerly looking back] C, D; still looking eagerly
             behind him > A
270.36   escaping] C, D; turning > A
271.6-7   longed, and looked, and waited in vain. We] C, D;
             looked and waited; but we > A
271.7   son] C, D; child > A
271.8-9   We . . . prosperity] C, D; In the day of our son's
             prosperity, we have known his love > A
271.10-12   the abundance . . . them] C, D; he would willingly
             forsake us, when the course of nature has bowed
             us > A
271.14   sorrows] C, D; affections > A
271.15   son] C, D; dear William > A
271.15   affliction] C, D; trials and sorrows > A
271.17   Adversity] C, D; Affliction > A

271.19-20   the visitations . . . your] C, D; adversity has found
              our son in the path of his > A
271.20   path] C, D; way > A
271.21   his] C, D; *omitted* > A
271.22   chastenings] D; chastening > A, C
271.25   in] C, D; into > A
271.26-28   Unasked . . . fear] C, D; Many a time you have
              relieved our necessities: we now need relief which
              no wealth can purchase > A
271.29   We can bear infirmities] C, D; *omitted* > A
271.29   want] A, C, D; to ~ > O
271.30   child continues] C, D; son is walking > A
271.32   God] C, D; ~. Parents, William, sinking with age
              and sorrow into the grave, are become your peti-
              tioners: relieve our minds from anxiety and fear
              > A
271.33-34   It . . . tidings] C, D; I have sad news to tell my son.
              I know that they will grieve > A
272.1-2   and the . . . must not] C, D; of sorrow: yet it is the
              provisions of a father, and we ought not to > A
272.3   The course of nature has brought upon us] C, D;
              Hard fate is no proof of little affection: his well
              beloved son was a man of sorrows. We are now
              feeling that grey hairs bring with them > A
272.9-10   in . . . labour] C, D; on his fatherly care. In looking
              back to days that are past, it is a comfort to us both,
              that our strength was spent in industrious labour
              > A
272.11   My] C, D; Our > A
272.12   my] C, D; our > A
272.12-16   Our . . . and] C, D; About our daily food he has >
              A
272.20   hearts cling] A, D; heart clings > C
272.20   it is] C, D; we have found it a Bethel. It is > A
272.21   that] C, D; which > A
272.23   In the day of affliction, may my son] C, D; May my
              son, in the day of affliction > A

272.25	which] C, D; that > A
272.25	on] C, D; upon > A
272.26	the prosperity of our son] C, D; our son's prosperity > A
272.27	to preserve the house] C, D; the dwelling place > A
272.28	was our earliest care] C, D; were first regarded > A
272.29	the delight of your mother] C, D; your mother's delight > A
272.31	our] C, D; her > A
272.31	old age] C, D; grey hairs > A
272.34	our] C, D; my > A
272.34-35	cheered the heart of his parents by his evening amusements] C, D; bestowed his evening labours > A
273.1	our son] C, D; my William > A
273.2-3	has spread every where around the habitation of our fathers] C, D; is now a plant large and spreading > A
273.4	days of your youth, William] C, D; youthful days of our son > A
273.5	our house afforded to your mother and me] C, D; the habitation of our fathers afforded us > A
273.7	you] C, D; our child > A
273.7-8	we hoped . . . should] C, D; hope said, that, when we should be laid in the dust, our dwelling place would > A
273.9-10	Now, the visitations of the Almighty are] C, D; The visitations of the Almighty are now > A
273.10	heaven] C, D; ~, William > A
273.14	son] C, D; child > A
273.14-16	closed . . . day] C, D; shut out your good old mother from the light of day. As often as possible > A
273.17	at even] C, D; in the evening > A
273.18	into the house] C, D; in > A

273.18   heard] C, D; have ~ > A
273.20-21   My . . . show] C, D; I have been telling my William
              many sorrowful things: but I can also tell him > A
273.21-23   Your . . . hope] C, D; When the Lord has brought
              upon your parents many heavy afflictions, he has
              given us the valley of Aehor for a door of hope >
              A
273.24-30   are . . . But we] C, D; believe his word, that he
              cannot forsake us. We > A
273.33   my] C, D; our > A
273.35   William] C, D; my son > A
273.36   *Read*] C, D; Remember the last charge of a father,
              read > A
274.2   by] C, D; with > A
274.3   exclaimed] C, D; uttered > A
274.6   Mephibosheth Stepsure gent.] A; *omitted* > C, D

              IN THE FOLLOWING SECTION, THE
              COPY-TEXT IS A.

275.1   LETTER 25] Number 6. > A

Appendices

Censor's letter *"On Mephibosheth Stepsure"* was first published in the *Acadian Recorder* on 28 December 1822. The letter from "A REAL F.——." appeared in the same newspaper on 22 March 1823. In the transcription of the text of each letter the corrections incorporated by CEECT are indicated in square brackets.

On Mephibosheth Stepsure.

Halifax, December 24, 1822.

MESSRS. EDITORS—

My last letter was short, and I do not mean that this should be a long one. The public of late have been so much cloyed with epistles lengthened out to three or four columns of close printing, that their fatigued appetite now prefers a neat little high-seasoned dish to a luxurious entertainment of three courses— And moreover, this wordiness of diction connected, as it was, with a paucity of incidents and characters was a leading fault of the letters which are to be the objects of my present criticism. Longinus in his discourse on the Sublime, (I quote from a translation, for I am ignorant of the original,—a piece of information perhaps, which it would have been prudent to conceal;) states it as a great beauty in a critic, to write his remarks and animadversions in a strain which will fitly exemplify the manner of composition that he is to praise or [b]lame. As I disapproved much of the length of Stepsure's letters, especially as the author obviously laboured to draw them out into unconscionable prolixity, and seemed to have tasked himself, not to stop when his materials were spent, but to fill up his complement of verbose chit-chat among his characters; it would be hightly censurable in me to run into this error, and tire him and my readers with a like repetition of dulness. On this account I shall confine myself at

431

present to less than two columns of your weekly paper. But I have begun at the wrong end; as in justice I ought first to point out the merits of these letters on our domestic manners.

It is confessed by all ranks, that the province stood much in need of the severe chastisement which was so timeously applied by this corrector of morals. Our country people unquestionably set a false estimate on their TIME, which to the lower and middling classes, is equal in value to money. They spent it without thought; and in place of employing it in the improvement of their farms, squandered it shamefully in riding about on horseback or in gigs and sleighs, in frolics, in lounging about the smith's shop, in tippling, and too often in attending preachings on the days appointed to man for labour. Had they been prompted to these conventicles from feelings of piety and holy zeal, there would be little cause for reproach; but it is much feared, that they gave a bodily attenda[n]ce merely to get rid of the hours which hung heavy on their hands.

They were no less lavish of what MONEY came into their possession, than of their time. A taste for show, finery and expense swallowed up, like Aaron's rod, the virtues of prudence and economy. Our farmers seem incapable of keeping one farthing beside them.—Avarice is none of the vices of this generation; for no sooner is a dollar got than it is gone. We have many characters among us who drive their gigs with plated harness every day, that six months in the year rise of a morning without twenty shillings of paper, silver or gold at their command. This is a disgraceful state of society, and shows that extravagance is too predominant among us. We dress, eat and drink above our circumstances, and are engaged in a constant race with poverty and the sheriff. The whole price obtained for the farm produce brought to Halifax is by most people laid out on goods of one kind or another before they quit the town, and they return home as pennyless as they came. The circulating medium is therefore centred about the capital; and the country is devoid of all specie for the purposes of exchange. Common transactions are done in barter, and debts of whatever standing are nearly irrecoverable.

Few people pay any thing, till they are quickened by the compulsion of the laws. Nothing can account for this, but the wasteful habits of the people. They live on the very verge of their incomes; and any credit they may have is employed in procuring additional gratifications, which otherwise could not be reached. If you meet our farmers at church or market, attending courts of justice or travelling on a journey whether of pleasure or business, you would fancy them to be gentlemen of moderate fortunes, so imposing are their dress, equipage and appearance; but if you have any dealings with them, the delusion ceases, and you behold the nakedness of the land. The common beggars in the streets of London have more ready cash than they: for on their backs and bellies the last shilling is expended. Saunders Scantocreesh's stocking of doubloons has no parallel out of the township of our author, and everywhere else would be a fiction. To correct these faults in our manners was a laudable design, and the execution of the papers was such as in a great measure to attain the end in view. Regular industry directed to the cultivation of the earth was well delineated in the characters of Scantocreesh, of 'Squire Worthy and of Stepsure himself; while less profitable methods of employment were cried down by the fate of Jack Scorem, by ridiculing fox catching, dealing in watches and such like trafficking invented by idleness as a excuse for business. Ample and unqualified praise is justly due to our author both for the conception and developement of these characters. They were copied so exactly from nature, that in every county of the province their prototypes were found; and men every where discovered among their neighbours and acquaintance the very individuals who were so admirably hit off. The letters were genuine copies taken from originals, and the likeness struck easily every beholder. But with this I have finished my panegyrics; and a more painful but no less essential duty remains to be performed. The merits of these essays were obscured with several defects which I shall mention; that Stepsure, should he again address the public, may step a little surer on the delicate ground on which he has trodden.

Nothing, I think, should find a place among moral strictures, that is offensive to decency. A lady of the finest feelings should be able to read aloud in any company these letters from beginning to end. There should be no allusions that would call the colour to her cheek, or force her to lower & interrupt her voice. A filthy image however true, a reference to those actions of the body over which modesty in all ages has drawn a veil, a line on the shingles below a garret window are unworthy of a grave moralist. They deform, without adding to the truth of his pictures, and always weaken the general effect. He should purify his own imagination from every thing unholy and unchaste before he attempts to reform the age. A violation of decency is less pardonable than a deviation from the unities.

I have more to say in way of blame. Although our country people are a time and money spending race, they are far from being dirty in their houses or persons. Exceptions may be pitched on to the general rule, but on the whole their habits lean to cleanliness and comfort. Much therefore which has been said by Mephibosheth on this head is not a candid portrait of our province, and is wide of the truth as a distinguishing characteristic. If a frog has ever found its way into the broth pot, the contents would not be palatable to ninty-nine out of a hundred; neither would the house dog be an acceptable bedfellow.

But the chief fault of our author, as a moral painter, is the sameness of his characters. They have neither colouring nor relief. They appear on the canvass in the same lifeless and uniform group. The language is never varied, nor rendered applicable to their parts. We are not let into the diversities of their tempers or views by appropriate diction; for Parson Drone preaches in the very same style in which Stepsure courts his wife, and the vagabonds converse in the jail. Even the several characters themselves are not distinct. After one or two of them are read and studied, you become acquainted with the rest. There is no novelty to keep the attention from falling asleep, no discrimination to attest the hand of the master. They are a set of dull prosing fellows brought together with little art, and cast in a common mould.

Lastly, the language of the letters is throughout tame and inelegant. Perspicuous it is and sometimes terse, but never graceful nor dignified. The fancy of the writer in no case transports him to Parnassus to pluck a single flower which adorns and scents that delightful mountain. It creeps but never soars; and after all its workings are read and surveyed, the most stupid poet could not cull an image fit for the humblest versification. Both the Muses and the Graces would pronounce their ban on the letters; the first for the insipidity and coldness of the composition, the last for the offences against delicacy with which they are interspersed.

On the whole these letters are praiseworthy in the design, and are calculated to do good by applying a wholesome corrective to our manners: but the execution betrays neither a chaste imagination, nor much power of language. As moral portraits they may find a place on the chimney piece of the cottage, but they will ever be refused admittance into the drawing-room of polite life.

CENSOR.

Letter from "A REAL F.——."

For the Acadian Recorder.

Pictou, March 14, 1823.

Mr. Holland, Sir,

This post has brought us published, the extract of the letter which was mentioned last week in the Free Press about accusing a legal character of being Censor. I have read the extract and the note signed S——; and as I know a little about this business, I shall, with your permission and with a good end in view, give an account of it. You must know that the affairs of our town are as much talked of among ourselves as in the province, by reason of the chronicles of our lame Mephibosheth; and every thing connected with them has much interest here. And for which we were all last week very busy in guessing what could be the meaning of the extract; and this post has set us all comparing, doubting, reasoning and coming at some sort of a conclusion about the matter. Let me first tell you, sir, that the letters of Censor made a great noise here, & some of us were as keen in condemning them, as others were in defending & praising them. When the first came out, it was very generally thought here to be Mephibosheth himself, & such was the current opinion a week; but on the arrival of the second, in which his writings and himself were so roughly handled, it was supposed to be Agricola; as there is always envy and spite among writers like other men, whose interests and views clash and jar. We afterwards heard that they were written by a young student at law, a gentleman in the army, a parson at Newport, another at Halifax, and also a lawyer who shall be nameless. All these reports were in circulation here, but Mephibosheth from first to last laid them at Agricola's door, and made no secret of his mind. He told me with his own mouth that he knew well who had mixed the pickle, and though he laughed it over, I could see that he felt grievously sore. His reply to Censor, which appeared soon after, showed his suspicions and his resentment; and although it was admired by some of his friends here as very witty, the most of us considered it as too gross and rather unworthy of the old gentleman. We could have wished for his own sake that he had never written it, or at least never owned it with his name. But this answer fell far short of the whacking threatened and intended, and therefore, before he set out for Halifax the end of last month, we understood that he sent his club shoes to his friend and crony, the shoemaker here, to get steel pieces fixed not on the heels as others wear them, but on the points of the toes; for he has a vile trick, when he is angry and crabbed, of kicking desperately on the shins, and his club feet are well made for this purpose[.] This, as we often regret, is the blindside of our neighbour, and the more is the pity, because otherwise he is a quiet harmless, painstaking, industrious body, minding his own business, repairing his fences, scraping the dirt from about the doors, else hauling and chopping his firewood. The next thing I shall mention to you, sir, is, that since Mephibosheth has signed himself Stepsure Gent., and got forward in the world, he has turned lazier, and instead of doing every thing with his own hands as formerly, and writing out roundly and fairly his chronicles, he has employed a chubby burly headed young man for this purpose, who is in this respect very serviceable to him and to our township. Take as a proof, that we always know the contents of each succeeding chapter of the chronicles, before it appears in the Recorder; because this under-strapper acquaints us, and especially when he is a little mellow, of all particulars, and points out the passages which he has helped either in making or mending. Our curiosity is thus partly satisfied beforehand, as we know what is to happen or to be said.

It was, by this way and means, we learned that Censor was to be severely punished for meddling with his betters. Something awful was to happen at Halifax, and it was openly talked of before he began the journey. The secret as I take it, and as it is believed here, is neither more or less than this. The extract, the note, and the remarks before and after is a contrivance of our misguarded townsman, I fear, to vent his wrath on somebody for the affront offered to his writings, but we are wondering much what new information he has got to make him change his man. He seems on a new scent and resolved to take penny worths on more than one and thus show that he has not steel capped his club shoes for nothing. Some of his well wishers are very anxious that he should return home as fast as convenient, despi[t]e the sneers and witticisms of Censor who certainly wrote with no good will, and I think envies his merit as an historian, and betake himself to his usual employments again about his farm. By publishing this, sir, it may do good by preventing further mischief, for when one follows his passions, he forgets his duties and often himself; and it may both induce Censor to write, if he ever writes again, with more sense and moderation, and Stepsure to bear with more meekness the ill natured and ill advised observations of some rival scribbler. "Blessed are the meek, for they shall inherit the earth. Blessed are ye, when men shall revile you and persecute you, and say all manner of evil against you falsely. Rejoice and be exceeding glad for great is your reward in heaven."

A REAL F.———.